THE TALISMAN - MOLLY'S STORY

ELIZA J SCOTT

For my family, thank you for believing in me.

CHAPTER 1

Exhilaration danced in Molly's large brown eyes as she free-wheeled her old Raleigh bike down the steep track from her home at Withrin Hill Farm. She gripped the handlebars for dear life as she bumped and bounced her way over the potholes, her skinny legs sticking out at right angles, a cloud of dust trailing in her wake. She shook the rebellious mass of chocolate-brown curls that flew out behind her as the balmy summer wind slipped across her face, stealing away her peals of laughter as soon as they left her mouth, scattering them everywhere.

It was the first day of the summer holidays and the sun was beaming down from a bright blue sky, its golden rays pouring like molten gold over the pretty moorland village of Lytell Stangdale. 'Woohoo!' Molly cried with sheer joy just as a pheasant darted out in front of her, heckling as it went. 'Mind where you're going!' she shouted, swerving to avoid it.

'Woah!' In the next minute, she dodged a huddle of her Uncle John's hefted ewes that had parked themselves in the middle of the track. 'S'cuse me, ladies,' she called as she whizzed by. They continued their ruminating, unfazed and uninterested.

She was almost at the bottom of the hill when raised voices, carried on the wind, caught her attention, muffled words laced with anger. As she cocked her ear an ice-cold prickle ran up her spine; instinct alerting her that things weren't right.

With her heart pounding, Molly put her head down and pedalled for all she was worth. Gritting her teeth, she careered around the corner and was confronted by a sight that made her sick to her stomach. Two youths were looming over a crumpled heap in the middle of the road, their faces distorted with hate, as they took thudding, angry kicks at it. 'Please stop,' the crumpled heap pleaded, but to no avail.

'Oy, get off him! Leave him alone!' Molly bellowed, anger flooding her body as her bike skidded to a halt. She leapt off, threw the bike to the ground, and raced towards them as fast as she could, her body suddenly propelled by a gargantuan surge of adrenalin. 'Stop it! Stop it! Stop it!' She gave a blood-curdling scream, her heart pounding wildly in her chest.

The youths stopped and, with mouths agape, turned to watch the wild-looking girl who was charging at them with eyes full of fury.

'Waaarrrggghhh!' Molly gave a war-like cry as she got within striking distance, tackling the nearest thug with a well-aimed, newly-learnt taekwondo kick. He staggered back into the gutter, winded, where he landed with a thud while his friend looked on in stunned silence.

'Shit, she's a psycho. Come on, let's get out of here!' the ape gasped, and pulling himself up, he hobbled off down the road towards Danskelfe.

'Coward! And there's plenty more where that came from,' Molly yelled after him.

Things were moving fast, but in Molly's mind — as she would tell people when she recounted the tale — everything felt like it was happening in slow motion. She gulped down a fortifying breath and turned to the remaining thug. A good foot taller than her, he was now looming over her, hands on hips and an arrogant smirk across his face that she wanted to wipe right off. 'Come on then, when you're big enough, short arse,' he sneered and went to grab her shoulders. With lightning-quick reflexes, she dodged him and grabbed a fallen branch she'd spied earlier — even in her state of heightened anxiety, she saw that it was good and solid.

'And what the bloody hell do you think you're gonna do with that stick, you stupid cow?' He smirked, jutting his jaw arrogantly.

Gripping the branch tightly in both hands and using every ounce of strength she could muster, Molly took a swing at him, knocking him right off his feet and into a freshly dolloped pile of horse muck. 'That's what the bloody hell I'm going to do with it, you pathetic, spineless bully!'

Stunned, the boy, who she thought looked about seventeen — a couple of years older than her — scrambled to his feet rubbing his arm. 'What the hell d'ya think you're doing defending that piece of scum?' He stood upright, his top lip curled in a snarl.

'Well, from where I'm standing there's only one piece of scum I can see, and I'm looking right at it.' Molly held his gaze, tightening her grip onto the oak branch. She cast a quick glance over at the injured boy who lay groaning in the middle of the road.

'That right?' The boy snatched the branch out of her

hands, yanking her towards him as he did so. With a sneer, he threw it onto the ground. 'You know, you're going to be very sorry you said that.' He gave her a hard shove before clenching his fists.

Molly's heart was pounding in her ears, but anger was doing an efficient job of over-riding any fear she may have felt. She swallowed hard and braced herself.

'Come on, Mart, it's not worth it,' the boy's friend shouted from a safe distance.

'Oh, I'm gonna make it worth it,' he said, pounding a fist into the palm of his hand. 'You're nothing more than a scrawny country bumpkin with a big gob.'

'Hit a girl would you? What a big man you are,' Molly snarled at him. And, as he lunged for her, she once more garnered her strength. 'Waaarrgghhhh!' she yelled as she clenched her fist and delivered a lightning-quick blow to his chin, its force catching even her by surprise. It sent him flying backwards and, once more, into the steaming pile of horse muck. Acting quickly, she followed it up with a sound kick to the balls for good measure.

'Aaargghh!'

'I think it's time you and your scabby mate buggered off, don't you?' she said through gritted teeth, wiping her hands down the front of her denim dungarees as he gingerly pulled himself to his feet.

Nursing his bruised jaw with one hand and his throbbing nuts with the other, the thug turned to Molly, 'You're all flaming mental out here. Nowt but crazy, inbred sheep-shaggers.'

Molly went to grab her branch, but he hastily turned towards the direction of the village and limped gingerly back to his accomplice.

'And you both bloody stink!' Her nose wrinkled as it

finally registered his acrid body odour that hung in the air. 'Try having a bath, you smelly gits!'

Satisfied that the thugs weren't going to give them any more trouble, Molly ran over to the boy who was still lying in the road. A trickle of blood was making its way from his nose, and he had a cut to his head where more blood was already congealing, making his raven curls sticky. 'Are you okay? Can you move? Do you need an ambulance? Do you need your mum and dad?'

'I...er...I...Do you always ask so many questions?' A shaky voice came back at her.

'Oh, er, sorry. Ouch, that looks really painful.' She scrunched her nose up and frowned at the colourful bruise that was already blooming at his left eye.

'I'm not sure exactly which part of me hurts the most, to be honest but, yes, I think I can move.' He rolled over and tried to sit up. 'Ow,' the boy gasped. 'My ribs have taken a bit of a battering, my head's pounding but,' he ran his tongue around the inside of his mouth, 'thankfully, I've still got all my teeth. So you don't need to call an ambulance. In fact, I don't want any fuss at all. I just want to go home.'

Molly pursed her lips. 'Okay, but we need to get those injuries cleaned up and get some dressings on them – no fuss, I promise. I'm really good at that sort of thing, I'm going to be a nurse when I leave school. Come on, you don't look fit to walk, I'll give you a croggy back to my grandma's house — there'll be no one in. I was actually on my way there to take her Labrador, Henry, for a walk while she's out for the day.' Molly sat back on her haunches and brushed a handful of wayward curls out of her face.

'I, er, I don't want to put you to any trouble; I'm sure I'll be fine.' He winced as Molly helped him up.

'No arguments, you're obviously not fine.'

'Are you always this bossy? And, out of interest, what's a *croggy* when it's at home?'

'In answer to your first question, yes, I'm always getting told I'm bossy, especially by Mark — he's my older brother — and my cousin Jimby. Oh, and my teachers, come to think of it. And in answer to your second, I can't believe you've never heard of a croggy before.'

'Sorry, I haven't.'

'Well, it's when two people ride one bike at the same time. You can sit on the seat, and I'll stand on the pedals and...well...pedal. You'll have to hold onto my waist so you don't fall off, but it'll be the quickest way to get us to my grandma's, and it's pretty much on the flat from here so it shouldn't be too hard. I'm stronger than I look.' Molly put her hands on her hips and beamed at him.

'You don't say.' The boy mustered a small smile.

'So, what was that all about?' Molly's brow furrowed as she placed a mug of tea on the kitchen table in front of the boy. 'There, drink that, it's got four sugars in; it'll be good for the shock.'

'Thanks.' His voice still shaky, he watched as Molly filled a white enamel dish with warm water, added a splash of antiseptic solution and brought it across to where he was sitting. She snapped on a pair of surgical gloves from her grandma's first aid box, dipped a clump of cotton wool into the liquid and dabbed gingerly at the cut on the boy's head. 'Sorry if this hurts.'

'Ouch!' He winced, shrinking away from her a little. 'It does sting a bit, but not as much as the kicking that caused it.'

'Sorry, I'll try to get it done quickly.' She pulled a sympathetic face. 'Like I said, I'm going to train to be a nurse when I leave school. My mum says I'll be good at it. I'm not squeamish or anything. And I saved my brother's finger when he nearly chopped it off, by telling him to wrap a bag of frozen peas round it. The hospital said if it wasn't for that he probably would've lost it.'

'Sounds like I'm in good hands then.'

'Yep, you are,' she said, dabbing carefully at his bruised and bloodied cheekbone. 'How old are you, by the way?'

'Sixteen.'

'A year older than me.' Molly paused. 'So, are you going to tell me why those horrible thugs were kicking ten sorts of shit out of you?'

He gave a heavy sigh as a shadow fell over his face. 'Can't you guess?'

'Er, no. If I could, I wouldn't be asking you. You seem like a canny enough lad to me and the fact that Henry hasn't left your side says a lot — he's very fussy about people.' Molly looked down at the Labrador who was enjoying having his head stroked on the boy's lap. She pursed her lips as she turned her attention to the congealed blood on his hair.

'Well, for the last couple of weeks I've been staying with my family in Middleton-le-Moors.' He hesitated and took a deep breath. 'We're part of the...'

'The fair,' Molly finished his sentence for him as the penny dropped.

The boy hung his head and nodded. 'Yes.'

'So does that mean you're a...'

'Yeah, I'm a...I'm a gipsy.' He swallowed and paused for a few seconds, glancing up at her. 'Told me they couldn't stand "Gippos."'

'Oh.' Molly stopped what she was doing and looked at him, reading fear and sadness in his eyes.

'It's okay, I'll understand if you want me to leave.' He went to stand, but she gently pushed him back into his seat.

'What? They thought it was okay to beat you to a pulp because you're a gipsy?' She could feel her anger boiling up again. 'Oh my God, that's absolutely disgusting. The cowardly bloody bas…'

'It's okay, I'm used to it, though it's usually just name calling and not so much of the beating, thankfully.' He gave a small smile which was brought to an abrupt halt thanks to the split in his top lip.

'Actually, it's not okay. They need teaching a lesson.'

'Er, from what I saw earlier, I think you gave them one. You were pretty awesome, Boudicca.' The boy looked up at her, a twinkle of amusement in his inky black eyes.

'Thanks,' she said with a giggle.

'Weren't you scared?'

'Didn't have time to be. When I get mad, I get absolutely, totally fearless. You should ask my brother, he's seen me like that loads of times, the annoying toad that he is. Calls me a hellcat.'

'Poor brother.'

'Hey, you.' Molly gave him a gentle nudge before taking off the surgical gloves. 'There, all done.'

Gingerly, the boy got to his feet and held out his hand. 'Thank you. I'm Camm, by the way, Camm Ackleton.'

'Molly Harrison.' She smiled and shook his hand, being careful to avoid the cuts and bruises that speckled it.

'Pleased to meet you, Molly Harrison.' He gave a lopsided grin that Molly thought was rather nice.

'Camm? I like that, it's unusual. Is it short for anything? Cameron? Camembert? Er, no, that's cheese isn't it?'

He tried to laugh but winced at the pain it caused. 'Nope, it's just Camm. I'm named after my granddaddy. It's a Romany Gipsy name. It means beloved. Or crooked nose, which judging by the way mine's feeling at the moment, I reckon my parents must've had a premonition when they named me.'

Molly giggled and looked closer at Camm's nose, taking in the freckles that were scattered across it and spread across to the apples of his cheeks. 'You've got nothing to worry about on that score, your snitch looks fine to me.' She glanced up at the coal black eyes that glittered back at her and felt an unexpected flutter in her stomach. It wasn't just his nose that looked fine now she thought about it. Those big dark eyes edged with thick, black lashes, that told of a different life, those full lips that curled up at the corners as if constantly smiling at something secret.

'Snitch? That a Yorkshire word?' He cut through her thoughts.

'Er, probably, not sure.' Molly shrugged. His array of cuts and bruises didn't disguise the fact that Camm was tall, dark and handsome — a real dish.

'Right.' He nodded, his eyes roving over her face for a moment. 'Here, take this.' He rummaged around in an inside pocket of his jacket before pulling out a small silver object. 'Oh, no. It's broken in two.'

'What is it?' Molly peered into the palm of his hand and saw what looked like a finely worked silver charm-like object, the size of a ten-pence piece. It appeared to be broken right down the middle, splitting two initials: "C" and "M".

'It's a talisman. For luck. It was my grandaddy's and they're his and my grandma's initials; she was called Mahala. See, they're the same as ours.' He paused, and

Molly felt his gaze heavy on her face. 'He passed it on to me a few years ago. Here, you take this half and I'll keep this one.' Camm's fingers brushed hers as he handed Molly the piece with the C, sending a jolt of something powerful but unfamiliar right to her core. She glanced up at him and, judging by the smile that played around those full lips, she knew he felt it too.

Molly cleared her throat, feeling uncharacteristically shy, and tried to ignore the butterflies that were suddenly tumbling around her insides. 'Not sure it brought you much luck after what happened today,' she said with a frown.

'Oh, but it did, Molly Harrison. It brought me to you.' Camm stepped closer, cupping her face in his hands, his thumbs caressing her cheeks as he gazed into her eyes. She gulped, wondering if he could hear her heart that had started thudding in her chest. 'All of this was meant to be. I believe the talisman was broken for a reason. And one day, when you need me, it will bring me back to you, you'll see.'

Molly's thoughts were running riot around her head and, before she had chance to form a single word, she felt Camm's lips brush tenderly against hers.

'Oh!' she gasped when he released her. 'Wow.' She pressed her fingertips to her mouth.

Camm laughed, his eyes dancing before his expression turned serious. 'I have to go now beautiful Molly, my saviour. The fair is leaving Middleton-le-Moors tomorrow and my family are moving on, so I've got to help get things ready with the vardos and the ponies,' he explained.

'Vardos?'

'Caravans, you know, the traditional, green painted ones?'

'Oh, right, yeah.'

'But, until we meet again,' he kissed her once more, his

lips lingering, reluctant to leave, 'goodbye sweet Molly Harrison. And thank you for coming to my rescue, I hope I can repay the debt someday.'

And, while Molly was still reeling from being kissed by this handsome stranger, he turned and left the cottage.

CHAPTER 2

It had been just over five months since Molly Pennock, husband Pip, eighteen-year-old identical twins Ben and Tom and one-year-old Emmie had moved out of their barn conversion halfway down Withrin Hill, and into the rambling Georgian farmhouse that had been Molly's childhood home. To say it felt like their feet hadn't touched the ground was an understatement. Moving house while setting up a campsite with a baby in tow was definitely not for the faint-hearted.

It was always the intention that, when her parents — Annie and Jack — were ready to retire from farming, Molly and Pip would swap homes with them and pick up the reins of the farm, together with the help of the twins. Molly's older brother, Mark, was never part of the equation, having moved to New Zealand a good ten years earlier.

However, the unexpected advancement of her father's Parkinson's disease and advice from the doctor that he should think about retiring, had pushed their plans forward, with little regard for timing, which couldn't have been worse. Within days of Jack's prognosis, and at the age of thirty-five, Molly discovered she was pregnant, almost eighteen years after she'd given birth to the twins. She was never one to shy away from a challenge and had been unhappy in her job as a district nurse for years. With this in mind, she and Pip decided they might as well take the bull by the horns and bring their plans forward. In their usual style, the couple agreed they'd cope with whatever life threw at them, no matter what. 'Bring it on,' Molly had said as they'd set the wheels in motion.

Though she'd kept it to herself, Annie had been concerned that her husband would have to give up farming well before his doctor had advised. Acutely aware that the move would be an extra pressure on Molly and Pip, she'd been keen to make it as smooth as possible for them. She'd had the farmhouse redecorated in Farrow and Ball's finest egg-shell hues and the old carpets replaced with Molly's favourite sisal. The broad elm floorboards in the living room had been newly sanded, re-varnished and covered with a scattering of Persian rugs, while the original flagstones in the kitchen were scrubbed clean and re-sealed. The bright and airy kitchen was Annie's favourite room with its thick, primrose yellow walls. It had been fitted with solid oak units a couple of years earlier, courtesy of local joiner, Ollie Cartwright — her niece Kitty's new husband — though the stalwart four-oven cream Aga was the very same one that had been belching out heat since Molly was a child. Homely and warm, it was the room where the family had always gathered. Annie would miss it when she left.

EVEN THOUGH THEY'D taken over the farm, there was no way Pip could give up his dream job of head gamekeeper on the Danskelfe Estate — owned by local landed gentry, the Hammondely family (pronounced Hamley). He'd worked his way up over the years and was reluctant to throw it away. But it didn't mean it would hinder his enthusiasm for their new venture: the campsite. Quite the contrary. Like every other farm in the area, Withrin Hill Farm needed to diversify to survive, and he and Molly had been able to bring their earlier plan to fruition. While they were happy to continue sheep farming, they'd busily set-to and were converting a couple of the flatter fields into a campsite — and a campsite with a difference. Glamping was what they had in mind, and they were going to make it the best in North Yorkshire.

Being able to turn his hand to anything, and in possession of a creative imagination, Pip could visualise almost any object with sufficient headroom as a camping opportunity. And his piece de resistance was the "Withrin Express". He and the twins had converted an old train carriage into luxurious sleeping accommodation, complete with an ensuite bathroom, heating and electric lights. Kitty and Ollie had spent their wedding night in it the previous weekend and had completely fallen in love with it. It had given Pip all the incentive he needed to push on with their project.

'I THINK we'll be happy here, love,' said Pip wrapping his arm around Molly and taking a sip from his bottle of beer. The pair were standing by one of the large windows in the kitchen, looking out across the moor, taking a moment to relax after a busy day. Molly felt they'd finally got everything settled in and where it needed to be. Feeling grubby and tired, she rested her head on his shoulder and sighed.

'I'll drink to that,' she said with a smile, clinking her glass of wine against his beer.

CHAPTER 3

The July sunshine streamed in through the tall Georgian windows of the kitchen at Withrin Hill farmhouse, adding an extra dash of warmth to the yellow walls. Molly had been joined by Kitty and their childhood friend, Violet — a fifties inspired glamour-puss who was dating Kitty's brother, Jimby. They'd called in for a catch-up and a cuddle with their god-daughter, Emmie, and were sitting around the scrubbed pine table, sharing a pot of tea and putting the world to rights. They'd been best friends since forever and, despite Kitty's disastrous hiatus of a marriage to the monster that was Dan Bennett, they'd stuck together through thick and thin. Even when Vi had moved away to go to university in York, and when she'd decided to stay there and set up her PR company — regular visits back to the village and her parents meant she always kept in touch. The longest they'd gone without seeing each other was a six-month stretch when Violet had made a sudden decision to go travelling on her own after she'd graduated.

'So, how's it going, Moll?' asked Vi, her trademark floral perfume wafting around the kitchen.

'Surprisingly well, though my days are so busy, by the end of them I'm absolutely knackered and fall asleep as soon as my head hits the pillow. And I snore like a great big pig apparently.' She feigned offence as she popped a spoonful of mashed banana into Emmie's open mouth. Kitty and Violet exchanged glances and giggled.

'Sounds about right,' said Vi, arching a sculpted eyebrow that was tinted the same shade as the glossy waves of her aubergine hair.

'Well, it's hardly surprising you're shattered when you think about everything that's been going on in your life for the last year. New baby, new home, new livelihood. You've had the lifestyle change to beat all lifestyle changes.' Kitty's elfin features took on an earnest expression as she looked across at her cousin.

'Yeah, but she thrives on it. Look at that sparkle in her eyes.' Vi sat back in her seat and folded her arms, taking in the rich chestnut curls of Molly's chin-length bob, and big brown eyes that were so like her cousin's. 'Always loved a challenge has our Moll, haven't you, chuck?'

'Hmmm. These bloody great bags under my eyes say otherwise. But, having said that, I wouldn't swap any of it, especially this delicious little pudding.' Molly smiled adoringly at her rosy-cheeked cherub who responded by slapping her podgy little hands against the table of her high chair and grinning broadly. 'And getting away from district nursing was definitely the right thing to do; I don't have a single day's regret about that. Not one. All that paperwork, urghh. And don't get me on to the amount of scraggy testicles I had to...'

'Stop right there, Moll.' Vi held her hands up. 'I thought you'd promised us there'd be no more body parts or testicle talk when you finished nursing.'

Molly scrunched up her nose and gave a snort. 'Soz, Vi. Old habits and all that.'

'Forgiven.' Vi rolled her eyes at Kitty. 'But you look a lot less stressed I have to say. I reckon little Emmie here has got you all chilled out. And if these delicious ginger cookies are anything to go by, you're becoming a right little domestic goddess, too,' she said, giving her biscuit a thorough dunking.

'Yep, and not a cream-filled biscuit in sight.' Kitty chuckled at the memory of the ferocious craving Molly had during her pregnancy with Emmie.

Molly pretended to gag. 'Oh, don't. Anyway, enough about me, missus, don't you think it's time you spilt the beans? You've been looking like the cat that got the cream ever since you got here.' Molly scraped around the bowl before spooning the last of the mashed banana into Emmie's mouth and turned to Kitty, eyebrows raised.

'Yep, I was thinking the very same thing, Moll. Come on, Kitts, spill,' agreed Vi. 'There's something more than the "just married" look about you.'

'Er, well...oh, er!' Kitty, fiddling with one of her dark, cropped curls, was interrupted by a loud belch from Emmie who beamed around at them all proudly, showing four pearly white teeth.

'Hmmm. Just like her mother,' said Vi.

'Yeah, Pip calls her my mini-me, isn't that right, bubba?' Molly wiped banana drool from Emmie's chin and plopped a kiss on top of her daughter's bird's nest of chocolate brown curls.

'Bababagagagababa,' replied Emmie.

'He's not wrong. Anyway,' Vi pulled her gaze away from her god-daughter, 'don't keep us in suspense, Mrs Cartwright.'

'Oh, yes. Well, Ollie and I have some news — but we're keeping it quiet for the moment so you can't say anything to anyone, and please don't mention it to the kids, because they don't know yet.' Kitty glanced from one set of expectant eyes to the other. 'We're having a baby.' She beamed, laying her hands across the gentle round of her stomach, her eyes sparkling and her face flushed with happiness.

'Oh, that's fantastic news, Kitts. I bet Oll's over the moon.' Molly rushed over to hug her cousin. 'I'm so pleased everything's worked out for you, you deserve to be happy.' She pressed a kiss to Kitty's cheek.

'Congrats, Kitty. That's just the best news. When's baby Cartwright due then?' Vi beamed, reaching across and squeezing her friend's hand.

'Ollie's thrilled; we both are, and it's due around February time, but I need to have a scan to confirm the date. We just want to get to the three-month stage before we share it with everyone, you know with me losing baby William when I was married to Dan. I know this is different, but... just in case there's a problem.' Molly noticed the shadow that passed over Kitty's face.

'Well, at least you're not going to have a bonkers age gap between yours, unlike me. I can tell you, if any planning had been involved in the timing of our sprogs Pip and me would definitely not have gone for a massive gap of eighteen years!' Molly shook her head. 'Not that we'd swap you for the world, would we little gorgeous?'

'Babababababababa,' Emmie replied and promptly hurled her beaker across the kitchen, missing Vi's nose by millimetres.

'Your mother says pretty much the same thing on a Friday night after a couple of glasses of wine, Em,' said Vi as she bent to pick up the beaker.

'Anyway, enough about me. We came up to see how you're doing and to hear all about your exciting plans for the campsite,' said Kitty.

'We already know you've got no regrets about leaving nursing with all those varicose veins and the testicles you used to love wittering on about,' Vi said with a grin.

'Have I bugger. But as far as the campsite's going everything's taking shape nicely. There's only one problem: Reg,' she said, turning to look at Vi. 'That bloody cockerel of Jimby's has decided his territory includes our farm and has started turning up at the crack of dawn and letting rip with his crowing; cocky little sh...you know what! Struts about like he owns the place.'

'Sorry,' Vi grimaced. 'I'll have a word with Jimby, see if he can sort him out. I have no idea why he insists on keeping him, all he does is cause trouble.'

'Thanks, Vi. Pip's threatened to neck the little bugger if he comes back.'

'Him and half the village,' added Kitty.

The latch of the Victorian pine door clattered and Pip bowled in, straight from the moors, filling the kitchen with the scent of heather and fresh air. Phoebe, the black Labrador, hurtled towards him, her tail wagging furiously.

'Thought you were trying not to curse in front of the little one, Moll? That'll be another pound in the swear box.' He smiled good-naturedly. Days of exposure to all kinds of weather had left his skin weather-beaten and tanned and the tips of his dark-blonde hair bleached golden. He was wearing his usual game-keeping garb of khaki cargo pants and khaki t-shirt.

'Years of living with you means it's a hard habit to break I'm afraid, Pip.' Molly smiled at him.

'Now then, lasses, how are you both diddlin'?' Ignoring

Molly's comment, he grinned at Kitty and Vi as he strode towards Emmie, who squealed in delight at seeing her daddy.

'Dadadada,' she beamed up at him, reaching her arms out to be picked up.

'And how's my little princess?' he asked, a smile warming his broad moorland accent as he scooped her up and covered her face in kisses. She responded by wrapping her chubby arms around his neck and cooing in delight.

'Hiya, Pip, how's work going?' asked Vi.

'Champion thanks, Vi. Keeping busy, you know how it is. There's always something needs doing.'

'Now then, Pip.' Kitty returned the Yorkshire greeting. 'Looks like you've got a proper little daddy's girl there. Moll's just been telling us about the delights of an eighteen-year age-gap between kids.'

'Don't go there.' He shook his head as he jigged Emmie up and down, his broad smile and the look of pure adoration in his slate-grey eyes betraying his true feelings. 'Any chance of a cuppa, Moll?'

'I'm sure I can squeeze one out of the teapot for you,' she replied. A moment later, she emptied the stewed looking contents into a mug, added a dash of milk and slid it across the table to him. 'There you go, that'll fettle you.'

'Thanks, love. By heck, you could stand a spoon up in that.'

'Well, you'll need something strong before you go and see that wayward old grandmother of yours,' Molly said.

'Oh, no. What's Granny Aggie done now?' Pip groaned. 'Don't tell me she's been sending mucky texts to the vicar again?'

'I'm afraid so. And it's your turn to sort her out.'

'Aye, it would be. What's she been saying this time?'

'Hang on, I'll just get my phone, make sure I get the wording right.' Molly picked her phone up from the dresser. 'Ah, here we go.' She giggled and cleared her throat. 'She says she wants us to know she licked Rev Nev's sausage...'

'She what?' said Pip, horrified while Vi and Kitty snorted with laughter.

'You heard. She said she licked it and she wants some more — and we've got to tell him that, by the way. She then goes on to say that she's got a drippy tap...'

'I'll give her a drippy bloomin' tap.' Pip shook his head.

'And she wants you to go and look at it, but not this afternoon, because she's going dogging with Little Mary and Pete.' The last few words came out in a splutter. She looked across at Kitty and Violet who were giggling uncontrollably. It was obviously infectious as Emmie joined in, too.

'Little Mary? Can you imagine, bless her?' laughed Kitty. The tiny, gentle-natured old spinster with her rows of neatly set curls had recently adopted her nephew's equally elderly longhaired and very cheeky dachshund, Pete, and was hardly a candidate for dogging.

'Have you any idea what she really means?' asked Vi.

'Well, I do know that Rev Nev was given a load of sausages by Harry Cornforth over at Oakleyside Farm — it's their new venture, rearing free-range pigs and selling their pork and products locally. Anyway, being the kindly old soul he is, Rev Nev shared them out amongst some of the old folk — Granny Aggie being one of them, and she clearly *liked* them,' Molly explained.

'Bet he regrets that now,' chipped in Pip.

'Too right,' agreed Molly.

'And the dogging part?' Vi cocked an eyebrow.

'That'll be taking Pete for a walk with Little Mary — she calls "dog-walking", "dogging", unfortunately. The old minx reckons it's the predictive text on her phone that puts all the wrong words in, but with the track record she's got, I doubt that very much.'

'Well, at least we know she didn't *lick* the vicar's sausage,' chuckled Kitty.

Pip shook his head. 'On that note, I'm off. I'd just come to let you know that Jason's lending me his mini-digger so I can get started on the road up to the camping fields. Reckon I should get it done in a couple of days, with help from the twins of course.'

'That's great, we need to get cracking before the weather changes and the track ends up like a quagmire. Hugh Heifer reckons rain's forecast in a couple of weeks,' said Molly.

'Well, he's never wrong, so I'd best get on sharpish. And once I get that done, I'll be able to level off part of that field next to the one with the shepherd's hut ready for my next plan.'

'Ooh, sounds like things are steaming ahead,' said Kitty.

'They need to, Pip keeps having more bright ideas and keeps coming home with things to convert into camping accommodation,' said Molly with a sigh.

'Aye well, I'd hate to miss out on an opportunity to make our campsite that little bit special.' He smiled patiently at his wife. He was as laid back as she was feisty, though it hadn't gone unnoticed with her family and friends how much recent motherhood had taken the edge off her quick temper.

LATER THAT DAY, Molly was feeding the hens with Emmie when Pip appeared. 'You need to come and have a look at the bathroom, Moll.'

She turned to him, noting the sparkle in his eyes. 'Is it finished?'

'Yep. Come on, climb aboard Derek and I'll take you down there.' The three of them jumped into Pip's beloved Landie and headed along the track to the stone barn he and the twins had been working on for the last couple of weeks.

'Tada,' he said, opening the new oak door. With Emmie on her hip, Molly stepped inside, the smell of "new" tickling her nostrils.

'Dat,' said Emmie, pointing a chubby finger and grinning.

'Pip!' she gasped. 'It's fantastic.' Molly ran her hand along the huge, free-standing roll-top bath that took pride of place in the centre of the room, sitting below a statement crystal chandelier that hung from age-darkened beams. She wriggled her toes as she felt the heat rising from the old flags, which had been painstakingly lifted while underfloor heating was laid, then carefully re-set and sealed. 'Oh, wow, look at this,' she said, admiring the walk-in shower with its huge chrome rose above.

'The lighting's all wired up, too. Look.' Beaming, Pip pulled the light flex, and the shower cubicle was immediately bathed in a soft blue glow while the chandelier glittered in understated elegance.

Molly looked all around her. 'Oh, Pip, it's stunning. You and the lads have done an amazing job.'

'You like it then, missus?' He grinned at her.

'I love it! I'm going to have to have a try in here myself.' She glanced around at the column-radiator towel rail that was set against, white-painted stone walls.

'The open fire's more for effect,' Pip said, nodding towards the large inglenook fireplace which housed a dog-grate. It'll look cosy and romantic and that bath's big enough for two.' He waggled his eyebrows at her, making her giggle.

'Give over, you can never pull yourself away from your country pursuits magazines long enough for any romance.' She smiled and nudged him with her shoulder.

'Don't know what you mean,' he said, nudging her back.

'We'll have to keep this locked, keep it exclusive and make sure people know that it has to be booked and paid for in advance. They'll have to come to the house and get the key. It'll have to be for adults only, too,' Molly said, thinking aloud.

The only way to reach the campsite was along the track that led to the farm house and out at the other side, thus ensuring privacy and exclusivity. It was set out in clearly defined areas, with one field for traditional tent camping, while the glamping field had a section with a dozen wooden camping pods. Each had its own sectioned-off area complete with fire pit, barbecue and a set of solid wood table and chairs.

In a separate side of the glamping field was "The Withrin Express". Next to that was a shepherd's hut Pip had salvaged from his childhood home, Wychwood Farm, on the road out of the quaint Georgian market town that was Middleton-le-Moors. He'd found it at the bottom of a field, tatty and forgotten about, but still good and solid. His dad was glad to get rid of it and it had been a labour of love for Pip to restore it and paint it a subtle sage green.

Next along from this was a large, old chicken coop which Pip had found being used for storage of a fleet of old lawnmowers that Jack had hung on to but didn't work. That had been scrubbed with Jeye's Fluid to within an inch of its life and allowed to dry out before being given several coats of cream eggshell paint.

Molly and Pip had enlisted Ollie, and the three had planned the interiors down to the minutest of details. Every inch of space was utilised and, thanks to Ollie's carpentry skills, nowhere felt cluttered or claustrophobic.

'He's a man on a mission,' said Molly's mum, when she told her that Pip's next project was to get hold of an original gipsy caravan.

'Well, I hope he finds one soon, he's been wittering on so much about it, he's beginning to drive me mad.' Molly smiled and raised her eyes heavenwards. 'He's also mentioned getting a decent play area for the kids, and an onsite shop. Honestly, his ideas and enthusiasm is exhausting. I'm struggling to keep up. He's even joked about having a small area with beach huts, deck chairs and sand, would you believe?'

'Yes, I would believe.' Annie laughed. 'And it's lovely to see your dreams coming true, and with ready-made jobs for the twins, too. It couldn't be better. Your dad and me were getting so worried about you, you seemed so unhappy in your job, but now...'

'Yep, it couldn't be better — except for wishing that Dad didn't have Parkinson's.'

'Ah, well, he does, lovie,' Annie said with a sigh, 'and there's nothing we can do about it.'

'Well, apart from that, everything's worked out. Ben's loving his course at college, especially since it allows him a day's placement at the farm every week. And Tom seems happy enough working full-time for us.' Molly smiled; if anyone had told her two years ago that her life would have turned out as perfectly as this, she would have laughed in their face.

CHAPTER 4

It had been a crazy busy day for Molly and Pip, with wall-to-wall multi-tasking, job-juggling and the need to be in more than one place at the same time. Finally, with Emmie fast asleep in her cot, and the twins doing whatever they did of an evening, the couple found themselves with a rare moment of peace and quiet and slumped on one of the large squishy sofas in front of the telly in the living room. Pip was enjoying a chilled bottle of beer and Molly a glass of white wine, while outside, the sun was disappearing over Great Stangdale Rigg, and the sky had taken on a soothing, mellow hue. Molly had flicked on a couple of table lamps, and their soft lighting cast a warm glow up the walls. This was her favourite room — their "best" room — and painted a deep ox-blood red, while the original Georgian panelling was painted a cream eggshell. A battered antique leather chair sat alongside the sofas, with a throw in muted moorland shades draped over its back, a cushion propped against its sturdy arms.

'Mmmm, this is nice,' Molly sighed. She swung her legs round, resting her feet on Pip's lap as she plumped a cushion behind her back. 'Just listen to that peace and quiet. Bliss.'

'Aye, lass, it is.' Pip smiled, giving her leg an affectionate rub.

'Doesn't seem to happen very often these days, a bit of you and me time. There's always at least one of the kids around making a racket or people calling in — not that I mind it — I love having a house full, but sometimes it's just nice to...' Her words were swallowed by a wide yawn. 'Ooh, that fire's making me sleepy.' Despite it being the middle of summer, the farmhouse was perched in an exposed spot on Withrin Hill and could get chilly of an evening; consequently, there was always a fire blazing in the large inglenook fireplace with, more often than not, Phoebe stretched out in front of it, snoring gently.

'Don't suppose you know what day it is next Friday, do you?' Pip took a sip of his beer and turned to look at Molly, an eyebrow cocked quizzically.

'Erm,' Molly frowned as she wracked her brains. 'Erm, today's the twenty-fifth?'

'Nope, today's the twenty-seventh.'

'The twenty-seventh, so tomorrow's the...there's thirty-one days in July, which means,' she counted on her fingers, 'Oh my God, of course! It's the sixth of August. Our anniversary! With everything that's been going on, I'd completely lost track of time. I don't even know what I've had for breakfast at the minute, never mind what day of the week it is.'

'Good job one of us is on the ball enough to remember in time to book a romantic table for two at the Sunne on Friday the sixth of August at seven-thirty prompt, isn't it?'

'A romantic meal, just you and me?' Molly smiled as the thought sank in; she couldn't remember the last time they'd gone out just the two of them.

'Aye, lass, just thee and me. And I'm giving you plenty of notice because I know you'll say you have nowt to wear, but you've got a good ten days to find summat. And you don't need to worry about shopping with little bubba upstairs, my mum says you can drop Emmie off at hers and tootle off to York, shopping to your heart's content.'

Molly tried to suppress a groan at the mention of her sour-faced mother-in-law.

'But, the twins are out at an eighteenth over in Danskelfe next Friday, so they won't be able to...'

'Before you say it, the babysitter's taken care of. I've spoken to your mum and dad, and they're more than happy to do it. And good old Jimby's offered to do the taxi service back so we can both have a drink. See, I've thought of everything.'

Molly eyed Pip suspiciously. It was always a battle to get him dressed up and out for a meal, never mind a romantic one, and this latest news was somewhat out of character. 'You're up to something, aren't you?' She narrowed her eyes at him. 'I can tell. That's what all this wining and dining's about. Come on, you might as well spill the beans because I'm going to find out sooner or later.' She pursed her lips as she swirled the wine around her glass.

'I don't know what you mean! Can't a bloke take his wife out for a slap-up meal on their anniversary without being accused of being up to summat?' You've got a suspicious mind, you have, Molly Pennock.' He wagged a finger at her.

She wagged one back at him. 'That, Pip Pennock, is because I know you too well. This is the man who buys his wife a hoover as a gift. Or, worse, a couple of bloody pigs for Valentine's day. This is not the man who arranges romantic evenings and a day's clothes shopping.'

'Don't try telling me you don't think the world of them

pigs.' Pip folded his arms across his chest and stretched his legs out onto the coffee table in front of him.

'That's beside the point, you're trying to butter me up before telling me that you've spent a sodding fortune on some hare-brained object to turn into camping accommodation. I just know it. Either that or you've gone and bought another vehicle that we don't need, to add to your collection.'

Molly could feel her temper beginning to rise. Pip had a weak-spot for Landies (especially the old, series variety), motorbikes, Polarises and quad-bikes, and he didn't need much of an excuse to dip into their savings pot for one. In fact, they were about the only things he'd dip into his pocket for, and Molly knew he owned more than he fessed up to.

Pip shook his head in disbelief. 'Well, I'm disappointed that you think so little of me. And I'm hurt a bit too, if I'm honest. I've put a lot of effort into organising everything so you wouldn't have owt to fret about.' He looked genuinely hurt and Molly was beginning to think she'd misjudged him. Her eyes roamed his face, trying to read his expression. Guilt suddenly crept over her; she knew she was quick to judge, quick to fly off the handle.

'I'm sorry, Pip. It's a lovely gesture, and I can't wait. Just ignore me, I'm being a cow.'

Pip held his arm out, and Molly leaned in for a cuddle. 'Apology accepted.' He gave her shoulder a squeeze. 'And you aren't a cow.'

'I am, but I'll make it up to you.' She snuggled into him.

'Sounds interesting, how're you going to do that then?' Pip waggled his eyebrows at her, making her laugh.

'Hah! Not what you're thinking! More like, I promise not to nag the next time you want to read any of your gamekeeper crap in bed. Or when you wear that daft tiger-print onesie the lads bought you.'

'I doubt that very much. Anyroad, wouldn't be the same without you giving me earache, love,' he said, which earned him a gentle prod in the stomach.

Molly rested her head on Pip's shoulder, and the couple sat together in contented silence, Molly watching the flames dance in the fire, Pip half-watching a wildlife programme on the television while he fiddled with her hair, wrapping her dark curls around his fingers. Her eyes felt heavy with sleep, but she was loath to tear herself away from her husband and their rare moment of peace together. Life had been so hectic recently and she'd be quite happy to stay on the sofa and cuddle with him all night.

'So, how many years of wedded bliss will it be next Friday, then?' Pip's voice broke into Molly's thoughts.

'Hmm, let's see. I fell pregnant with the twins when I was sixteen, had them when I was seventeen. They're eighteen now, and we got married two years after they were born. So that'll make it...?'

'A complicated way of working it out?'

'Sixteen years,' said Molly, ignoring Pip's sarcasm.

'Sixteen years, and never a cross word.'

'Funny bugger.' Molly gave him another prod in the ribs, making him chuckle.

'And I still love you as much as I did when I married you.' He gave her shoulder a squeeze. 'Seriously, I do, Moll.'

'And I still fancy the pants off you as much as I did when I first set eyes on you. Even though you're a pain in the arse sometimes, I knew I had to get my claws into you somehow, and I knew it'd be a right battle getting you to notice me. Thought I'd always be your mate's pesky kid sister.'

'Well, nowt's changed there, to be honest.'

'Cheek,' she giggled. 'Anyway, have we got time to go out on a date? Haven't you got too much on, what with those poachers and everything, never mind the work we have to do here?'

Pip looked at her, the flames from the fire dancing in his eyes. 'I've always got time for you, Molly love.' Stroking her cheek, he leaned across and kissed her.

'Pip.' Molly pulled away from him.

'Yeah.'

'I'm really knackered.' Molly didn't want him to get his hopes up for romance.

He paused, his eyes roving her face as he processed the meaning behind her words, disappointment fleetingly swept across his face as it dawned. 'Aye, me too, lass. Me too.'

His disappointment lasted all of two minutes, by which time he'd fallen asleep and was snoring soundly.

CHAPTER 5

Molly first set eyes on Pip when she moved up to the secondary school in Middleton-le-Moors. He was two years above her, in the same form as her brother, Mark, and didn't know she existed. With his trendy boy-band haircut and Scandinavian slate-blue eyes, she was smitten from the word go. She'd find any excuse to be around him, dragging her friends along to watch him play football or rugby, cheering him on like a groupie at a rock concert. Molly couldn't believe her luck when Mark started to hang around with him and let slip that Pip was a member of the local Young Farmers. She'd shown no interest in the society beforehand, but on hearing this news, she'd talked Kitty and Violet into joining with her. And, religiously every Tuesday evening, with Molly wearing her best clothes, off they'd head to whichever farm the meeting was being held at. But Pip didn't notice Molly, not even when his granny, Aggie, moved to a small cottage in Lytell Stangdale, and Molly found any excuse to "accidentally" bump into him, which she tried to do as much as possible. And he looked so hunky in the gamekeeper garb he wore as an apprentice to the head-keeper on the Danskelfe Estate, it made butterflies go crazy in her stomach.

For five long years, Molly carried around an ache in her heart as her love was well and truly unrequited, until the Young Farmers' Christmas party, hosted by the Welford family at Tinkel Bottom Farm, when a dance with Pip changed everything.

The theme for the party was cocktail dresses and dinner jackets, and the young farmers jumped at the chance to get dressed up for a change — living out in the sticks usually meant that wellies, waxed jackets and wheelbarrows were the order of the day. Molly had spent an age over her hair and makeup and was wearing a newly purchased metallic, black slip-dress that flattered her newly emerging curves. The look was finished off with a pair of silver strappy heels. For the first time in her young life, she felt glamorous.

She was in a huddle with Kitty and Vi, chatting about how handsome the boys looked, their conversation bubbling over when Molly spotted Pip. 'Oh, bugger, there's Pip, there's Pip.' She was practically jumping up and down on the spot. 'Ohmigod, he looks so hunky in his tuxedo. I could snog his face off. Ohmigod, ohmigod, ohmigod, he's looking this way. Look! No, don't look, I don't want him to know we're talking about him!' she squealed.

'He's more than looking this way, Moll, he's walking this way. And he's carrying two cans of pop.' Kitty's eyes were wide as Pip sauntered over to them, trying just that little bit too hard to look cool and casual.

'Shit. Do I look alright?' She smoothed her hair, then her dress.

'You look drop-dead gorgeous, Moll,' grinned Vi.

'But don't keep swearing, Moll. It isn't ladylike,' whispered Kitty.

'Since when has Molly been ladylike? Oh, heck, he's here.'

'Now then,' he said, flicking his floppy fringe and holding out one of the cans. Molly's heart skipped a beat, and her face flushed scarlet; she would recount many times later how thankful she was for the dim lighting.

'Thanks,' she said, taking the can and doing her best not to sound flustered.

'Wanna dance to the next song?' he shouted above the music. He was shuffling from one foot to the other and not quite making eye contact with her.

Molly could feel the weight of her two friends' eyes upon her. 'Yeah, if you like.' She shrugged, affecting an air of couldn't-care-less, but secretly wondering how the hell she was going to be able to dance when her legs were in the process of turning to jelly.

'Cool.' Pip took a swig from his can, belched loudly and loped off.

'Stylish,' said Vi, eyebrows arched, her top lip curled in disgust. Kitty sniggered.

'He's just so totally hunky.' Molly gazed after him, lovestruck.

'Yeah, belching all over the girl you've just asked to dance is very hunky. And close your mouth, hun, you look like you're catching flies.' Vi gave her friend a nudge. 'Don't you know you're meant to play it cool with boys, specially the older ones.'

'Well, I'd like to see you try to play it cool when the man of your dreams finally – after bloody yonks of never even noticing you were born — asks you to dance. And, taking all that into consideration, I think I'm doing a bloody good job.'

'You think?' said Vi, blushing as Kitty's big brother Jimby walked by and gave her a wink.

A YEAR LATER, Molly and Pip were still dating when disaster struck, and Molly discovered she was pregnant.

She'd ignored the signs at first, hoping they'd go away. But after two missed periods and horrendous sickness that she'd tried to hide, she confided in Kitty and Violet.

'Are you okay, Moll? You don't look very well,' said Kitty. They were sitting in Violet's bedroom, listening to music, when Molly had rushed to the loo to be sick. Seeing the concerned expressions on her friends' faces when she returned, Molly promptly flopped down onto the bed and burst into tears.

'I'm pregnant,' she sobbed into her hands.

Kitty and Violet sat stunned, as her words sank in. 'Oh, Moll, are you sure?' Kitty rushed to her side, wrapping an arm around her.

'Yes.' Molly sniffed through her fingers.

'Have you told your mum?' Vi moved to the other side of her, rubbing her arm.

'No.' Her sobbing increased.

After some gentle coaxing, Kitty and Vi managed to persuade her to speak to her mum; there was no way she could ignore it any longer. So, when they had the farmhouse to themselves, Molly had approached Annie, who took the information on board calmly and quietly. 'Does Pip know?' she asked.

'No.' Molly shook her head, her voice no more than a whisper.

'Oh, lovie. Come here.' Annie wrapped her arms around her daughter, kissing the glossy curls on her head. 'Why didn't you come to me sooner? You must've been absolutely terrified.'

'I was. I am, Mum. And I don't know what to do.' With that, the tears flowed.

Annie didn't know whether to be relieved or annoyed at what she'd just learned. Relieved because she'd been watching Molly fading away to nothing as her appetite had dwindled and dark circles had hung beneath her eyes giving them a hollow appearance. Annoyed because, at just sixteen, her daughter was pregnant. Pregnant! And in a position where she had to face some difficult decisions. It's not like she hadn't sat her down and told her about the birds and the bees. She was a farmer's daughter, for God's sake, she knew how babies were made. And she also knew how to prevent it. Annie took a deep breath; she'd hide her feelings, the last thing Molly needed at this moment was a lecture.

'Right then, this is what we're going to do.' Annie passed Molly a mug of sweet tea. 'Can you drink this without it making you feel queasy?' Molly nodded, it was about the only thing she'd been able to keep down for the last few weeks. 'First of all, we're going to have to tell your dad.' Molly shrank at the thought.

'He's going to hate me. And then go after Pip with his shotgun.'

'Don't be daft, he'll do neither. You know what your dad's like; he's a soft as washing, but he needs to be told.' Annie sipped her tea. 'Then you're going to have to tell Pip.'

Molly scrunched up her eyes and swallowed the lump that had suddenly lodged in her throat. 'I know, but I daren't. He's going to hate me, too.'

'Well, if I know Pip like I think I do, I doubt very much that he'll hate you. He'll be shocked right enough, but he's a good lad, and I've seen the way he looks at you, chick; the pair of you may be young, but he thinks the world of you.'

Her mum's words made Molly's tears flow once more. 'D'you really think so?' she asked between sobs.

'I know so.' Annie gave her daughter's hand a squeeze.

MOLLY'S DAD had been shocked to hear that his little girl was "in the family way" as he'd put it. But her mum had been right, he didn't hate her and, after the initial bomb-shell moment had worn off, his words had been of support and reassurance; they'd do whatever they could to help.

Molly didn't have her mum with her when she told Pip. She'd asked him to meet her in the village so they could go for a walk. She had something to tell him she said — thinking neutral ground would be better for both of them. When she saw him, her mind was in turmoil, suddenly crowded with the words she'd planned to use. But they stuck in her mouth, reluctant to leave. *How on earth do you throw that into the conversation? 'Hey, did you enjoy the Young Farmers meeting the other night? Oh, and, by the way, I'm up the duff.'*

She sensed Pip looking at her, confused; he could tell she was distracted, that she wasn't really listening to what he was saying, wondering why she was so quiet. Molly was never quiet. If she had something on her mind, or if you'd annoyed her, you knew about it. Big time. She was feisty and couldn't keep her feelings hidden. He'd told her that was what he liked about her. 'You can bite someone's head off, but as soon as you've got whatever it is off your chest, you're fine, back to normal. Everyone knows where they stand with you,' he'd said. But with this quiet Molly, he was treading on unfamiliar territory.

They were walking along Great Stangdale Rigg, past the

ancient carved boundary marker, Aud Bob, when Pip had put his arm around her. She'd shrugged it off, before stopping and turning to face him, the gentle breeze ruffling her curls. Gnawing at her bottom lip and fiddling with a long thread of her cardigan, she struggled to make eye contact with him.

Just as she took a fortifying breath, Pip spoke. 'Look, if there's somebody else, just say it, Moll.'

'What?' She brushed a handful of stray hair out of her eyes, scrunched her face up and looked at him, confused.

'You're breaking up with me, right?'

'Breaking up with you?'

'Well, this is what we're doing here, isn't it? You're gonna dump me?' He swallowed hard, and the sadness in his eyes cut Molly to the quick.

'Pip, the last thing I want is to break up with you.' Her heart was racing, and her pulse began to thrum loudly in her ears as a wave of nausea washed over her. She didn't know what she was more desperate to do, throw up or throw her arms around him.

'Thank God for that. I thought that's what you were going to say.' He looked relieved. 'I love you, Moll, I really do.' He placed his hands on her shoulders, and she began to cry.

Molly's mind was a battleground of emotions. He'd never told her he loved her before. She'd never told him, either. 'Well, you won't love me when you find out what I've got to tell you. That'll definitely make you not love me.'

'What's the matter? What d'you mean?' His eyes scanned her face as fat tears streamed down it. 'Molly?'

'Oh, bloody hell, there's no easy way to say it. I'm pregnant, Pip. I'm bloody pregnant.' She watched his expression change as he stood in silence, absorbing the bombshell she'd just dropped.

'Shit,' he said quietly. 'You're sure?'

She nodded.

'Right, well. I think we need to sit down while I take this on board and think a minute.' He headed over to a mossy wooden seat that overlooked the dale. She followed, sitting down beside him, aware of the cold dampness of the wooden slats seeping through the fabric of her jeans. She shivered — a combination of cold and anxiety.

With his head in his hands and his elbows resting on his knees, Pip listened quietly as she told him how she'd bought a pregnancy test in a chemist in Middleton-le-Moors, brought it home and waited for the results in her bedroom. 'I was absolutely terrified,' she said. 'But Mum and Dad have been great and said they'd support me whatever my decision.'

'And have you made a decision?' He turned to her, his expression inscrutable.

She took a deep breath. 'I know I'm young, and if any planning had gone into this, I wouldn't have chosen to get pregnant at the age of sixteen, but I am pregnant, and I can't change that now.'

'Well, you could but...'

'Trust me, Pip, I've thought of every option, and the only one that feels right is to keep the baby. But I'll understand if you don't want to go out with me anymore. I'm not doing it to tie you down,' she said, her voice wavering.

'What about your plans to go travelling with Kitty and Violet? And your plans to train as a nurse, Moll? How will you do all of that with a baby?'

'I can't. I'll have to give up on the idea of travelling and the nurse training will have to wait.'

He nodded, his eyes fixed to the floor.

'Look, Pip, I've had time to think about all of this, but you haven't; you're still in shock. Why don't you go home and let it all sink in? Though, you could come back to mine for a bit if you want. My mum and dad'll be fine with you.' She had a sudden vision of his mother's face, hard and cold; the polar opposite of her own mum. She shuddered at the thought of how she'd take the news.

Pip rubbed his chin; she wondered if he was thinking the same as her. 'Aye, that might not be a bad idea, lass. Get the bollocking I deserve out of the way. And after that, I wouldn't mind hearing what they think we should do. I respect their opinion, though I doubt very much that they'll respect me now.'

Molly rested her head on Pip's shoulder, and he wrapped his arm around her. 'They don't think anything less of you, Pip. I only just found out that they had to get married quick because Mum fell pregnant with Mark – I hadn't clicked. They understand, they've been there, and they've been lovely.'

The following day, Pip arranged to meet Molly to talk about what they should do. 'How did it go?' she asked, her stomach gurgling with anxiety. They were sitting at the kitchen table at Withrin Hill.

Pip puffed out his cheeks. 'Well, they were shocked – as you can imagine — and my dad took it better than my mum.'

'Oh, shit.' Molly winced. 'I bet she hates me even more now.'

'She doesn't hate you, Moll,' he fibbed. Telling his parents hadn't been easy. His dad, once he'd recovered from the shock, had been supportive, but his mother had been apoplectic. Pip had listened in silence, his head cowed, as she'd ranted and raged.

'Don't you realise if *she* keeps the baby, you'll be throwing your life away on a girl you hardly know?' she'd screamed at him. 'She's always been obsessed with you, and now she's trapped you! Stupid, stupid girl! You're both just children yourselves. You know nothing about life, never mind being responsible for another one. And how do you think you're going to support *that girl* and a baby on your wage as an apprentice gamekeeper? I'll tell you how; you're not, you're going to bloody-well struggle.'

'Calm down, Ros,' his dad had said, putting his hand on her arm. 'Getting all het-up like this isn't going to help anyone.'

'Get off, Allan!' She'd shrugged his hand off angrily. 'Well, it helps me. And I'll tell you this, Philip, I hate that girl for doing this to you. I absolutely bloody hate her!'

Molly listened quietly as Pip relayed a heavily edited version of what had happened. 'So what are you going to do?' Her heart was hammering in her chest, and a tear spilt onto her cheek as she prepared herself for the inevitable.

Pip took her hand. 'Look at me, Moll.' He tipped her chin towards him. 'I meant what I said yesterday, about loving you. And nothing's happened to change that.'

She looked at him, wiping the tear away with the back of her hand. 'I love you too, Pip,' she sniffed.

'I love you too much to let you go. Whenever I think of myself in the future it's always with you there, Moll.' He paused for a moment. 'What I'm saying is, that I want to stand by you — if you'll let me? And, I know we're too young to get married, but I'd like us to get, sort of, engaged.' He produced a small box from the pocket of his waxed jacket that was hanging on the back of his chair, while Molly looked on. 'I know it's not the fanciest, but it was all I could afford. You can have a better one when we've got a bit of money behind us.' He opened the lid and passed it to Molly. 'Will you get engaged to me, Molly?'

'Oh, Pip!' She flung her arms around him and sobbed wracking great tears into his shirt.

'Is everything alright?' Annie asked. She'd been waiting anxiously in the living room, giving the pair some space while they chatted, but hearing Molly get upset, she felt she had to intrude.

'Oh, Mum. Look what Pip's given me.' She held her hand up to her mum, showing the ring with its tiny little diamond that shone shyly back at her.

'Oh, congratulations the pair of you.' She smiled, enveloping her daughter in a hug. She kissed Molly's cheek and said, 'I'll just see if your dad's free, we've got some ideas to put to you.'

Over lunch, Molly's parents explained that they'd been thinking and, if the pair liked the idea, Pip could move in and stay at the farm – it meant he'd be nearer to work on the Danskelfe Estate. They'd already submitted plans to the local council to convert the old barn, halfway down the hill, into a house. Their original intention had been to let it out, but Molly and Pip were welcome to move into it if they wanted to.

'You must've been up half the night thinking of this, Mrs Harrison,' said Pip.

'Oh, and the rest,' Annie replied with a laugh. 'Obviously, Molly's nurse training will have to go on hold until the baby's old enough, by which time she'll be able to go to college part-time and study for it, while I look after the little one.'

'You'd do all of this for us?' Pip was flabbergasted. The

kindness shown by Molly's parents stood in stark contrast to his own parents' reaction.

'Of course,' said Jack. 'Why wouldn't we? Molly's our daughter. Granted, we're not over the moon about the timing of things, but the pair of you are made for each other, so...' He shrugged his shoulders.

'It's what we'd do anyway, just a little earlier than expected.' Annie smiled.

'Thanks, Mum and Dad. You're the best.' Molly flung her arms around Jack.

Two weeks later, Molly and Pip attended their first antenatal appointment at the hospital in York. Molly's heart was beating like the clappers as she lay on the bed awaiting her ultrasound scan. 'Right, Molly, this might feel a little chilly,' said the sonographer, squeezing a blob of gel onto the small round of Molly's abdomen.

'Ooh!' Molly gasped, and Pip took her hand in his.

After scrutinising the screen for a few moments, the sonographer smiled. 'Well, it looks like we've got two babies in there, Molly.'

'Two?'

'Yes, twins.' The sonographer nodded, smiling, as she continued to roll the transducer over Molly's stomach.

'Twins,' echoed Pip.

Molly was too stunned to say anything further.

'You never did do things by halves, did you, Moll?'

Six months later, at the age of seventeen, Molly was delivered of identical twin boys, Ben and Tom. They had their mother's large brown eyes and their father's easy-going temperament.

Two years after this, Molly and Pip were married in St. Thomas's, the local church, with Violet and Kitty as bridesmaids. Molly's dreams had been in a hurry to come true.

CHAPTER 6

'Right then, Emmie, let's get you to Grandma and Grampy's house. Auntie Kitty's dropped Lucas and Lily off there, and they're waiting to play with you. They'll be wondering where we've got to, won't they?' Molly popped a soft denim sunhat trimmed with daisies onto her daughter's dark curls. 'Gorgeous!' she bent down and pressed a smattering of nibbly kisses on Emmie's chubby cheek which was met with squeals of delight.

'Mamamama.' Emmie held out her arms for Molly to pick her up. 'Dat! Dat!' she pointed to a tiny basket with a scattering of multicoloured flowers stitched on it.

'You want your basket?' Are you going to help Grandma and Grampy collect eggs from the hens?' Emmie nodded, and Molly reached across for it, handing it to her daughter's outstretched hand.

'Backit.' Emmie beamed.

'Yes, basket. Good girl.' Molly smiled. It was true what Vi had said about her being more laid back since she'd had Emmie. Well, that and the fact that she'd given up nursing. If she'd carried on with that she would be heading for a break-down by now she was sure of it. She'd lost track of the number of staff who'd been signed off work through stress since she'd left. Their dedicated team had been so short-staffed and over-stretched; it was only a matter of time before something went horribly wrong with a patient and Molly had felt anxious about being a part of that. So, unexpectedly falling pregnant and having to take over the running of the farm last year had forced her hand and given her the perfect excuse to leave without having a guilty conscience that she was leaving her colleagues in the lurch.

Her plan today was to make a start on painting the vintage horsebox Pip had picked up and restored for the glamping field — her mum had offered to have Emmie so she could crack on with this. But before she could set to work, Molly needed to pop into the village to pick up a couple of things. She quickly scribbled a note to Pip and the twins, telling them what she was up to — she didn't need to add that she'd be calling in on Kitty and Violet at Romantique, the workshop situated behind Vi's home at Sunshine Cottage, where they made and designed vintage-inspired underwear, burlesque costumes and, more recently, wedding dresses — they'd assume she'd do that anyway.

Molly stepped out of the porch and into the dry warmth of the day. 'Phew!' She blew a straggle of stray hairs off her face as she sent a handful of hens scattering, feathers flapping, clucking and complaining vociferously as they went. The neat farmyard was a sun-trap, and they'd been sitting in the shade, hiding away from the unforgiving heat of the sun. 'Oops! Sorry ladies, didn't know you were there.' The leader of the pack, Delores, scuttled off with her tales of woe to the cockerel, Bernard, joining the rest of his harem who were jostling for position close behind. He fluffed up his feathers, stretched out his neck and gave a feeble cock-a-doodle-do in

support. The early August heat was obviously getting to
him, too, thought Molly, though at least there was no sign
of Reg.

The smell of warm vinyl hit her as she opened the door
to her four-wheel drive, ready to pop Emmie in her car seat.
'I think we need the windows open before we set off, don't
you, Em?' She put her key in the ignition and pressed the
button for the electric windows then set the air vents on to
full before heading over to lock the door of the farmhouse.
As she did so, the sound of a dog barking nearby was carried
on a light wisp of a breeze that sneaked by the farm build-
ings and circled round the yard. Their sheepdog, Meg,
who'd been dozing in the shade of a wooden bench pricked
up her ears. The bark was unfamiliar, it didn't sound like it
belonged to Pip's working dogs, Labrador, Teal, or Sprocker,
Bert. And Molly doubted it would belong to her parents'
black Lab, Sally; she was old and deaf and rarely barked.

As she made her way back to the car the sound of sheep
bleating noisily made Molly's heart sink; she instinctively
knew something wasn't right. There'd been an increasing
number of sheep worrying incidents, and the local farmers
were keen to find out whose dog was responsible. One name
kept cropping up whenever it was mentioned: the Mellisons.

The family had moved into the village a few years
earlier, believing themselves to have brought a much-
needed injection of intellect and quality. The rest of the
village thought otherwise.

When it was put to the local bobby, PC Snaith, that the
Mellison's lurcher, Rufus, was responsible, he told them that
having suspicions was one thing, but they would have to
provide him with proof if he was to do something about it.
In the meantime, more sheep had been worried, and the
culprit ran around scot-free.

With this rankling in her mind, Molly hurriedly snatched up her mobile phone from the dashboard of the car and set it in camera mode before heading towards the field. She didn't have far to go before the sound of the barking got louder and appeared to be coming from the field with her dad's prize-winning flock of Cheviots, or Chevvies as he called them. He'd been breeding them for the last ten years, and there were several champions among them. Thanks to the help of Pip and the twins, he hadn't had to give them up, despite his Parkinson's getting worse.

Shielding her eyes from the sun with her hand, she studied the field carefully. The sheep were darting around frantically, obviously distressed. And in the middle of them, tearing around, out of control, was a large, lurcher-type dog wearing a Hi-Vis reflective collar. There was only one dog who wore such bright accessories all year round, and that was, Rufus. The Mellison's dog.

With her hands shaking with anger, Molly filmed the scene for several seconds. It went against the grain for her not to try and stop the dog, but PC Snaith's words rang loud in her ears, and she wanted to make sure she had sufficient clear footage that could serve as evidence. 'Gotcha,' she muttered, before trying to call Pip, who was out working on the moor. 'Bollocks!' There was no signal. With her pulse racing, she ran back to the car, wiping the prickle of sweat from her brow, and reversed up the drive to a higher vantage point. Jumping out of the vehicle she sighed with relief. 'Five bars, thank God.' Only to be disappointed when her call went straight to voicemail; Pip was obviously out of range. Undeterred, she called her cousin. 'Jimby, I need your help. That daft sodding dog of the Mellisons is running loose in amongst Dad's sheep. There's blood on at least two of them. I've tried shouting, but it's too wound up to take any notice. Please get here as quick as you can.'

'Shit! That bloody family. You call PC Snaith, I'm on my way.' Jimby, who was working in his forge, dropped everything and ran across the yard to his Landie, calling out to Ollie, whose workshop was just across from Jimby's, to join him.

'Rufus! Rufus!' A woman's voice screeched from further down the field. Molly squinted, trying to get a better view. A tall woman appeared. She was wearing brightly coloured running gear, and a Hi-Vis tabard with a luminous yellow cap stretched over her head. There was only one person who would wear such ridiculous clothing in this heat: Aoife Mellison. And she was charging about after her stupid dog.

Molly had set her camera filming again and tried to get the woman into focus. 'Bugger!' she spat as the battery discharged.

'Rufie! Come to Mamma! Treats! Come to Mamma, Rufie!' Molly's lip curled at the ridiculous way Aoife was calling for her out-of-control dog. Apparently bored of worrying sheep, the dog turned and ran to his owner who hurriedly fixed a lead to his collar and ran off down a public bridleway towards the village.

In the next second, Molly heard the rumble of a Landie and turned to see Jimby and Ollie pull up and leap out.

'Where is the bloody thing?' asked Jimby running a hand through his closely cropped, dark curls.

'Gone,' replied Molly shaking her head, feeling full of hell.

'I'm sure I just saw a woman wearing the same type of bright clothes that Aoife Mellison wears when she's running. She had a dog lead in her hand and was charging up here, screaming her head off about something,' said Ollie, placing his hands on his hips.

'Yep, I saw her too; it was definitely Aoife Mellison and definitely her dog. I managed to film it running around like a lunatic on my mobile before the battery died, but I don't think I managed to get any with her on it.'

'Well, hopefully that'll be enough to get her prosecuted and her dog brought under control,' said Jimby.

'I wonder how many of your dad's sheep have been hurt? We'd best think about calling the vet before we go and check.' Ollie checked his mobile for signal.

'Oh, God, Dad's going to be devastated,' said Molly dragging a hand down her face. 'Those Chevvies are his pride and joy, especially since he gave up the farm. I don't know how I'm going to tell him.'

The three agreed that Molly should head back up the track with Jimby's phone and try to get a signal and call Chris the vet. Jimby and Ollie would go and check on the sheep. They also agreed not to say anything to Molly's dad until they knew exactly what the score was with the sheep.

'Emmie!' Molly suddenly remembered her little daughter. 'Bless her, she's been as quiet as a mouse while I was distracted by that bloody dog.' She hurried over to the car to find her daughter blissfully asleep.

AFTER DROPPING Emmie off at her parents, Molly headed to the village shop, where she shared what had happened that morning with the owners, Freddie and Lucy Dowson.

'You can guarantee they'll deny it, though,' Freddie observed. 'They won't ever accept that anything to do with them is capable of doing anything wrong. Even that gorm-less dog.'

'It's true I'm afraid, Moll.' Lucy nodded. 'Little Mary was in yesterday saying how she'd had to have a word with Aoife about Rufus doing his business in her garden and she was basically called a liar. Apparently, Aoife looked right down her nose at her, and behaved all superior, before storming off.'

'That I can well believe. But I managed to film her dog worrying Dad's sheep on my phone camera. Not sure how she's going to wriggle her perfect family out of that one. I'm just hoping it's clear enough to get something done about it. PC Snaith said...'

Their chat was interrupted by the tinkling of the bell on the shop door followed by a forty-a-day voice. 'Well, hello, Molly. Haven't seen you for a while. How's that gorgeous husband of yours?' Molly cringed and turned to see that Anita Matheson, or Maneater Matheson, as she was known locally, had slinked into the shop in a cloud of stale ciga-rettes and acrid perfume. She was wearing a low cut, cling-ing-in-all-the-wrong-places leopard-print mini-dress while a clutter of brassy creole earrings dangled from her ears.

'Now then Ma...er, Anita. He was fine the last time I asked, why?' Molly bristled at Lytell Stangdale's ageing vamp. She was in her mid-sixties but looked a good ten years older, thanks to over-use of sunbeds, which had left her skin parchment dry and riven with deep lines, the worst of which were gathered like pleats around her thin lips. She put Molly in mind of an over-cooked scrawny chicken.

'Oh, nothing.' Anita smirked and pushed a handful of brightly painted talons into her frazzled yellow hair. 'Just, I've recently taken a course on Indian head massage, and I'm looking to build up my clientele. I know how Pip works long hours and might be in need of a little, er, relaxation. Thought he might like to give it a try. You, too, Freddie, you'd be more than welcome.'

'Your usual is it, Anita?' Unsmiling, Lucy reached up for two packets of cigarettes and placed them on the counter. 'What about us women, don't we need a bit of relaxation?' she asked curtly.

'Ooh, that's not what I was saying. It's just I've got more of a rapport with men, me. I find it easier to communicate with them. Been told I can work wonders with my hands.' Anita licked her lips suggestively at Freddie who was doing his best to hide behind the counter. 'In my experience, women tend to see me as a threat. Present company excepted, of course.'

'Oh, of course.' Molly gave Lucy a knowing look.

Anita paid for her cigarettes and turned to leave, winking at Freddie as she went. 'You know where I am if you need me, handsome. Or your twins, Molly, I'd happily do them.' She smirked as she closed the door behind her.

'Count to ten, Molly,' said Lucy between clenched teeth.

'That woman has no shame,' Molly snarled as the three of them watched Anita prowl her way across the road. 'And her perfume absolutely stinks.' As she wafted a hand in front of her face, she noticed Dave Mellison cycle by. She felt her emotions morph from repulsion to seething anger as adrenalin kicked in and her pulse rate surged. She'd bide her time with that family, get things done the right way round. She couldn't wait to hear what PC Snaith had to say.

'And have you heard the latest with that lot?' Freddie nodded towards her.

'What, apart from the sheep-worrying?'

'Oh, there's more. Dave was in here the other day saying how he was taking the kids camping, reckons he's been on some sort of extreme endurance training course and is going to show them how to start a campfire.'

'Please tell me you're kidding.' Only this morning Pip had been telling her how he and the other local game-keepers had put out more fire warnings after the county had enjoyed several long weeks of warm, dry weather and no rain.

'Trust me, I wish I was. He said he's taking them up on the moor, where there's no creature comforts, so they'll have to rough it – he's taking a tent, though, so it won't be that rough, and he's going to teach them how to cook on an open fire.'

'Pip'll have a fit. Did he say whereabouts on the moor he was thinking of doing this madness? If it's on the Danskelfe Estate, Lord Hammondely will string him up by the knackers.'

'No, he didn't get that far, but next time he comes in, I'll try and find out for you.'

'Thanks, Freddie. Something needs to be done. I don't know how I'm going to break it to my dad that we've just had to have three of his sheep put down because of that out-of-control bloody dog of theirs. He's going to be gutted.'

'Don't tell me you're talking about the dreaded Mellisons?' Rosie Webster had just hurried into the shop and grabbed a couple of packets of biscuits off the shelf. Her usually groomed appearance had been replaced by dusty work clothes and her chin-length auburn hair had been fastened back with a rolled-up paisley scarf.

'Hi, Rosie, how did you guess?' asked Molly.

'It's not difficult. It's always one of their names that seem to crop up whenever anyone's having a problem. And my family can't seem to shake Aoife off at the moment.'

'Still got the hots for your Robbie, has she?' Lucy asked with a giggle.

'Oh, don't.' Rosie looked exasperated. 'She keeps saying she's going to be my first appointment when my beauty rooms are open, and I know it's only so she can come and see him.'

Rosie and Robbie Webster had bought Kitty's ex-in-laws' house and were currently converting one of the large downstairs rooms into a couple of treatment rooms for her to work from.

'Oh, she's turned her attentions to Robbie has she?' Molly laughed. 'From what I remember when she had the hots for Kitty's ex, Dan, she's pretty persistent and has skin as thick as a rhino. He won't shake her off easily.'

'Oh, poor Robbie,' Rosie said with a sigh. 'Anyway, I'd best dash, the builders are waiting for their tea.' She paid for her goods and left the shop.

'Those Mellisons are a bloody liability. They've come into this village with no intention of blending in or understanding the country code. Instead, they strut around like they're better than everyone else, as if we should be learning from them. They're absolutely clueless. The other day, Freddie even overheard Aoife telling someone on her mobile phone that by moving into the village, they'd made the gene pool more superior.' Lucy's tone was scornful, her face flushed with anger.

'Cheeky cow!' snarled Molly. 'I can't bloody stand the woman after the way she treated Kitty and how her horrible daughter bullied Lily.'

Aoife had developed an unrequited crush on Kitty Cartwright's ex-husband, Dan. He was a barrister, and Aoife had declared that they were on the same intellectual level. She'd taken an intense dislike to his wife, the easy-going and mild-mannered Kitty, telling her that she wasn't good enough for Dan. It had led to several unpleasant interactions between the pair.

Just as Molly was about to leave, armed with a box full of Lucy's famous dipped chocolate flapjack for herself, Kitty and Violet, Lycra Len bowled in wearing his trademark bright yellow Lycra cycling gear. He looked windswept and hassled.

'Hiya, Len, everything alright?' asked Freddie.

'No, it bloody well isn't. That effing layabout, Dave Mellison, has just nearly taken me out on my bike as I was cycling back on the road from Arkleby. Headed straight for me on my side of the road, he did. Thinks he bloody owns the place, the tosser!'

'That bloody family again.' Molly groaned.

'He's probably off to prop up the bar at the Fox and Hounds in Danskelfe and gone the long way round, so Aoife doesn't get suspicious,' said Freddie. 'I've heard that's where he spends a lot of his time, boasting about this and that, instead of working or bumming around the village.'

'Oh, aye. It's a bloody hard job being a landscape gardener. Or it would be if he actually ever did any work.' Len shook his head.

'*Executive* landscape gardener, you mean Len,' said Lucy sarcastically. 'Don't forget that's what he calls himself.'

'Executive gobshite, more like,' said Molly.

'Executive layabout, gobshite,' added Freddie.

'Executive, arrogant, layabout, gobshite,' put in Lycra Len.

Their laughter had gone some way to lighten Molly's mood. 'Ah well, thanks for making me smile. I'd best head off with these now. See you later, folks,' Molly called over her shoulder her as she left the shop.

As she crossed the road towards Sunshine Cottage, the ear-splitting sound of a cockerel crowing sliced through the peace of the village. It was followed by a voice, shouting loudly and if Molly wasn't mistaken, it sounded like it belonged to retired farmer, Hugh Heifer, and it appeared to be getting closer.

'Get off my Daisy, you menace!' the voice yelled.

Molly turned to see Hugh, who despite the heat, was wearing his usual garb of thick, tweed jacket tied around the middle with a length of twine, ill-fitting wellies and a grubby-looking flat cap. He was walking his latest prize heifer, Daisy, with Jimby's obnoxious cockerel, Reg, riding majestically on her back. Judging by Hugh's expression, he was furious and was waving his walking stick at the bird, trying to knock him off. But Reg was having none of it and flapped his wings angrily while Daisy bayed in consternation.

Laughing to herself, Molly opened the gate and followed the path round to oak-framed building that housed Romantique. 'Only me, ladies, and I bring tasty gifts,' she trilled, her eyes instantly drawn to the mood-boards and sketches that adorned the walls, the fabric samples and jars of beads and crystals that sparkled from their wooden shelves.

'Now that's what I call perfect timing, Moll. We've just been saying how peckish we are, haven't we, Kitts?' Vi grinned at Molly.

'Hiya, Moll. Yep, we're starving. My body's definitely telling me I'm eating for two. I'm always famished.' Kitty smiled, patting her baby-bump.

'Well, hopefully a fat slice of Lucy's chocolate flapjack spesh should take the edge off your appetite.'

'Ooh, sounds fab. I'll stick the kettle on.' Vi jumped up and headed over to the tiny kitchen area, clickety-clacking in her four-inch heels, her curvaceous bottom wiggling in her figure-hugging ankle grazers as she went.

'Oh, ladies, that dress is just gorgeous. Who's it for?' Molly's jaw dropped in admiration as she headed towards a tailor's dummy fitted with an exquisite ivory silk gown trimmed with delicate antique lace and hundreds of crystals. It shimmered iridescently under the workshop lights.

'Lady Carolyn Hammondely,' said Kitty. 'And we're all getting an invite to the wedding, apparently.'

'Wow! It's stunning. She's going to look amazing.'

'Mind, don't let on you've seen it, Moll. We should've had it covered over really,' said Kitty making her way over to the small table in the kitchen area.

Molly made a gesture of zipping her mouth. 'Not a word will escape my lips. But seriously ladies, this dress is absolutely gorgeous. Makes me almost wish I could marry Pip all over again.'

'Well, you should! You know, you could renew your vows and we could make you a wedding dress as a present, couldn't we, Vi?' Kitty looked across at her friend.

'Course we could. I'd love that. We did a good job of yours didn't we, Kitts?' Violet walked towards the table with three mugs of tea on a tray.

'Ooh, yes. Mine was gorgeous. Perfect. In fact, I wish I could wear it again.' Kitty smiled dreamily.

'Now don't go putting hare-brained ideas into my head. We've got enough on what with the farm, the campsite, babies, teenage twins and the bloody Mellison dog worrying Dad's sheep again.'

'You're joking? About the Mellison's dog, I mean.' Kitty looked outraged; she'd had a gut full of that family.

'Seriously, something needs to be done about them,'

added Vi as Molly explained what had happened earlier that morning. 'Where's it all going to end?'

'Wowzers,' said Molly as she checked her watch. 'I don't know where the time goes when us three start nattering. Would you believe I've been here nearly an hour and a half?'

'Time flies when you're having fun, babes.' Vi scooped up the mugs and popped them into the small sink.

Conversation had moved on from the Mellisons, and Molly had shared her news of how Pip had booked them a table at the Sunne for a romantic anniversary meal. 'I can't shake the feeling he's got an ulterior motive, though. Do either of you two know anything about it?' she asked. Both denied all knowledge, but Molly had clocked the look that passed between them.

'Right, well if you're not going to spill the beans, I'd best be off and rescue Emmie from my mother's cooking. She was threatening to make Yorkshire puddings and the last time she did that, we had to use a spoon to eat them they were that runny.'

'Eugh.' Vi grimaced.

Kitty chuckled. 'And didn't you say they were like cinders the time before that?'

'Yep, pure carbon. Hard to say which were worse. If she could just aim for something in between, we'd be laughing.' Molly rolled her eyes good-naturedly as she picked up her bag from the back of the chair and slung it over her shoulder.

'Actually, before you go, don't forget my Burlesque class

tomorrow night, village hall, seven-thirty. Be there or be square.' Vi waved a finger at her.

'Wild horses wouldn't keep me away. Watching Big Mary and Pat Allison shake their tassels is the highlight of my week,' Molly said with a grin. 'See you, lasses.'

'Bye,' called Kitty and Vi.

CHAPTER 7

'PC Snaith says he needs to see your mobile phone footage of that daft dog chasing your dad's sheep, so you'll have to let him have your phone, Moll.' Pip shovelled a forkful of pork chop into his mouth and chewed vigorously. Being outdoors, walking all over his patch of the moor for the bulk of his day, gave him a hearty appetite and he didn't have an ounce of fat on him.

Molly stood looking puzzled for a few seconds. 'He needs to take my phone?'

'Aye.' Pip nodded, chewing. 'So he can see if the video is good enough for the Mellisons to be prosecuted for having an out of control dog.' He took another generous portion of food, eyeing Molly warily; he knew she wouldn't be happy about giving up her phone.

'Well, he can't have it. There must be some way, in this day and age, that he can have what I've filmed without actually taking my phone.' She had her hands on her hips and a challenging look in her eye that spelt trouble.

'Aye, I s'pose so.' Pip looked thoughtful. He'd be the first to admit that technology wasn't his thing.

'So, we're just going to have to work out a way how to do it. I'm just not handing over my phone, never to see it again or for all of the local police force to look at my photos or read my messages. That stuff's private.'

Pip sighed and put his knife and fork down on his plate. 'Look, Moll, I'm just telling you what he said. And it's not like you've got owt you shouldn't have on there...or have you?'

'What d'you mean "owt I shouldn't have"?' The penny dropped, and Molly grimaced. 'Oh, don't be so bloody ridiculous.'

Hearing Ben and Tom snort with laughter they turned. 'Yes?' said Molly. 'Is there a problem?' She raised an eyebrow at her boys who bore a strong resemblance to Pip, with his fair complexion and dark blonde hair. Molly's contribution came through in the large brown eyes and curls.

'Aw, man, you should hear yourselves, you two. You're like a right couple of old farts.' Ben sniggered, shaking his head.

'That's just what I was thinking. Talk about being behind the times,' added Tom through a mouthful of carrots. He swallowed and rolled his eyes. 'Look, I'll say this very slowly so you can understand. But you know how when you've taken loads of photos of Emmie or the campsite or, God forbid, mine and Ben's ugly mugs?' Amusement dancing in his eyes, he looked expectantly from one parent to the other.

'Yes, what about it? And while we're on, less of your bloody cheek, me laddo.' Molly went to give her son a swipe with the tea-towel she was holding, and he ducked, laughing.

'Well,' Ben took over explaining, waving his fork around in the air as he did so, 'just like you do with those photos, you simply upload them to your laptop and then send the ones Snaithy needs as email attachments. Or, if that's too tricky, you could save them to a memory stick.'

'And hand the said memory stick over to Snaithy. Thus, hanging on to your phone. Simples.' Tom smiled.

'That's exactly what I was going to say,' nodded Pip, shooting Molly a lopsided grin which she returned with an "Oh really?" look. 'And while we're talking techno stuff, I was actually thinking about getting myself on that Tweeter thing.' He glanced across at the twins, who couldn't eat for laughing.

'Oh, man, that's just brilliant, "Tweeter",' snorted Ben, making Emmie giggle.

'It's wicked.' Tom struggled to swallow his mouthful. 'You're such dinosaur, Dad. It's "Twitter", and please promise me you won't go anywhere near it.'

'You've got no worries there, son, he won't have a clue how to,' said Molly. 'And, while we're on the subject of mobile phones,' she said, spooning some mashed potato into Emmie's mouth.

Pip picked up on her expression and groaned. 'Oh, don't tell me, flaming Granny Aggie's been texting the vicar about licking his sausage?'

Molly pressed her lips together and nodded. 'Yep, 'fraid so. He collared me in the village this morning and showed me the text. I had a right job on trying not to laugh.'

'Aww, man. That's rank.' Ben shoved his plate away. 'S'put me right off me pork chops, that has.'

'Mother, d'you have to, that's minging? We can't unhear that now, we're scarred for life.' Tom curled his top lip in disgust. 'But if you don't want them chops, Ben, I'll eat 'em for you.'

'You're alright, ta. I've suddenly re-discovered my appetite,' he said, pulling his plate back.

'Aye, and you're going to have to start being careful what you say around Emmie soon, Moll. Little ears and all. Isn't that right little gorgeous?' Pip leaned across to Emmie in her highchair.

'Dadadada.' Emmie beamed broadly at him, showing a gloopy mouthful of half-chewed food.

'That's me, my little angel.' Pip beamed back at her. 'Here, Moll, I've finished so I'll take over here, and you can get stuck into yours in peace.'

Molly slid out of her chair and into the one vacated by Pip. A cloud suddenly crossed her face. 'Thanks, Pip. You know, we're going to have to break it to Dad about his sheep before he hears it from someone else. Poor old sod.'

'Aye, we'll head down there after we've got this little one to bed. Tell him then. Fancy popping to the pub for a drink after? Jimby and Ollie said they were going to pop in with the lasses.' He looked across at Molly, taking in her troubled features; she gave a worried smile as she nodded.

LIANNE AND JEFF CONLEY were heading down the path from Daisy Cottage, on their way to the Sunne Inne, just as Molly and Pip pulled up outside. The couple and their two daughters hadn't lived in the village for long and were considered brash by some, but they were kind-hearted and would do anything for anyone.

'Hiya, you two.' Lianne's voice, as subtle as a corncrake, rattled around the village. She gave them a toothy grin as she chewed vigorously on a piece of gum, deftly moving it to one side with her tongue so she could speak. 'Poppin' in for a pint are you?'

'Aye, just a quick one.' Pip held open the door for them. 'After you.'

'Ta very much, babes,' she said, popping a bubble between her teeth.

'Ta, mate.' Jeff smiled at him, flashing a gold tooth.

The Sunne Inne was a typical North Yorkshire moorland longhouse dating back to at least the 15th century, its heavily thatched roof slumped on top of three-feet-wide uneven walls that had been lime-washed in the traditional way. Low Yorkshire sliding-sash windows glazed with wobbly Georgian glass blinked lazily in the still-bright sunshine. Once in a state of pitiful neglect under the ownership of Hacky Harold, it had been bought by Bea and Jonty Latimer who'd lovingly restored it until it once more took its rightful place as the hub and heart of the village.

Molly loved the atmosphere of the pub, with its distinctive aroma of wood-smoke from the fire that constantly burned in the large inglenook fireplace and mingled with the sumptuous smell of Bea's wholesome cooking. It was a place to relax and forget the troubles of the day. And as she stepped through the door, it felt as if the room wrapped its arms around her and pulled her in. She sighed as the tension lifted from her shoulders, her eyes falling on the tasteful tweed fabric of the soft furnishings as they headed towards the bar where all the usual suspects were lined-up.

Bill Campion from Camplin Hall Farm was in deep conversation with Hugh Heifer's son, John. From the sound of it, they were complaining bitterly about the price they were getting for milk. *Things were no better there then*, she thought.

Further along, Ella Welford, the part-time barmaid —
and relative of hers — was making a shandy for Tom Storr.

'That your tractor parked out front, Tom?' Pip asked.

'Aye, 'tis, lad.' Tom nodded; he collected and restored
vintage tractors, regularly using them to get him to and from
the pub.

'She's a little beauty.'

'She is that. And she saves me aud legs from having to
struggle with that pull up the bank-side.' Tom lived at
Oakley Garth, a small-holding situated half-way up a steep
track on Oakley Bank. He was a regular at the pub and
enjoyed a game or two of dominoes with Ella's dad, Pete,
Hugh Heifer and Violet's dad, Ken.

'Good evening, folks.' Jonty, who was standing behind
the long oak bar, greeted them with a warm smile. 'Usual is
it?' he asked, peering down his long aquiline nose and above
a pair of glasses that were perched precariously on the end
of it.

'Aye, a pint of your good stuff and a glass of wine for our
lass, please, Jonty.' Pip's broad North Yorkshire accent was
poles apart from Jonty's plummy tones.

'Heard about what happened earlier today with your
father's sheep, Molly. I'm terribly sorry.' Jonty leaned in,
speaking quietly. 'Though, the village grapevine informs me
that you may have proof of whose dog is responsible for all
this shocking sheep worrying.' Steadily, he pulled a pint of
local beer for Pip. 'If it's any help, Bea and I saw Aoife racing
back to her house this morning with a face like thunder and
her dog covered in blood. We wondered what on earth had
happened, but she was in no mood to talk. Just ignored us
when we asked if she was okay.'

'Really?' Molly absorbed the information. 'Actually,
we've just left my parents' after having to tell my dad. It was

bloody awful seeing him so upset. But you're right, I managed to film something on my phone. I just hope the police think it's good enough quality to use. Pip's dropping it off with PC Snaith tomorrow, so we should find out soon enough. But I'll tell him to mention what you saw.'

At that moment Bea breezed in from the garden at the rear of the pub. 'Hi there, folks, good to see you.' She smiled warmly, her glossy blonde bob held back by the pair of tortoiseshell glasses perched on her head. 'Your chums are all sitting outside waiting for you, enjoying the last of the day's sun.' She nodded in the direction of the back door. 'I've just deposited some snacks, so I'd be quick if you want to try some. And, as ever, I'd be grateful to hear what you think.'

'Ooh, sounds tempting.' Molly picked up her glass of wine. 'Come on, Pip, let's get some while we can.'

Pip didn't need telling twice. Bea regularly tested out new food ideas on their group of friends, and they were always well-received.

The rear garden was a sun trap, and the warm, golden rays that reached down were being lazily soaked up by the wonky whitewashed walls. An eclectic variety of planters and pots filled to busting with blooming annuals in soothing shades of purples, pinks and whites were artfully dotted around the place. A pink rose rambled up a trellis, disappearing over the wall where it clambered up the branches of a large rowan tree, it's sweet, soapy fragrance, perfuming the air as the light summer breeze brushed over it.

Nomad and Scruff, the Latimer's rescue dogs, who were flaked out between the barbecue and a table of people enjoying a meal, raised their heads half-heartedly as Molly and Pip walked by them.

'Ey up, look who's arrived,' said Jimby, grinning broadly

at them as they headed over to the table where he sat with his arm casually draped around Vi. 'Got a pass out for the evening, did we?'

'Aye, summat like that.' Pip grinned back.

'Yep, we made the most of the twins being at home to babysit Emmie and sneaked out before they had time to argue about it,' added Molly.

'Good for you, Moll. Luckily, Noushka's not got any dance classes tonight, so she was free to look after Lucas and Lils,' Kitty said, referring to Ollie's teenage daughter from an earlier relationship and her two children from her ill-fated marriage to Dan.

Ollie jumped up from his seat next to Kitty and pulled over two weather-proof rattan chairs. 'There you go, you can park yourselves on these. He smiled, his gentle aquamarine eyes twinkling.

'Cheers, Oll,' said Molly. 'Ooh, that looks delicious.'

'Aye, Bea's letting us test some new ideas for the menu. Wait till you try the prawns, they're absolutely bloody mwah!' Jimby kissed his fingers.

'Mmmhmmm. And whatever she's done with the halloumi is just amazing,' Vi enthused, licking the flavour off her lips and, with it, her trademark purple lipstick. 'Here, try some.' She passed the bowl of deep-fried cheese pieces towards Molly and Pip.

'Thanks, Vi. Ooh, they do look good,' said Molly as she picked up a slice and popped it into her mouth. 'Oh, wow!'

'That good, eh, missus?' Pip smiled as he tried one for himself. 'Mmm. I see what you mean.'

Molly leaned back in her chair, stretching her legs out in front of her as she felt herself beginning to relax, the earlier tensions of the day slipping away along with the sun that disappeared over the willow fencing at the far end of the garden. She took a slow sip of her wine, savouring the crisp apple flavours and enjoying the cool feeling as it slipped down her throat. She pressed her glass against her cheek and looked around her at the wonderful group of people she felt lucky to call family and friends, feeling her heart squeeze with happiness.

Violet, glamorous as ever in a figure-hugging fifties-style dress splashed in blowsy lilac coloured roses, was showing Molly and Kitty her latest tattoo – an intricate flower arrangement on the inside of her wrist that Molly didn't quite get. She was explaining the meaning of it when Molly's attention was caught by the harsh tones of an affected accent: Teesside distorted by fake Queen's English, it was being swirled awkwardly around the owner's mouth and jarred with Molly's ears. She cringed as the relaxed atmosphere in the garden leached away. There was only one owner of a voice like that: Aoife Bloody Mellison. A snarl tugged at her top lip, and it hadn't escaped her attention that Kitty flinched, which was hardly surprising after the hard time she'd had with that woman.

They watched as Aoife strutted by, looking down her nose, her lantern jaw jutting defiantly. She was closely followed by husband Dave, who was a good few inches shorter than her.

'Small man syndrome is the reason for that ridiculous ape-swagger of his,' whispered Vi.

'Not sure why he thinks that's such a good idea when it only serves to draw attention to what a short-arse he is,' said Kitty scornfully, her eyes flashing. 'Same could be said of that sleazy little pony tail, too. That only draws attention to the fact that he's almost totally bald. He'd be better off giving it the chop.'

'It's not like you to pass comment like that, Kitts. That sort of harsh stuff is usually down to Vi and me.'

'Hmm. After the experience I had with that family last year, trust me, I could say far worse. He's a prat!' She took a sip of her fizzy water, peering at her friends over the top of the glass. 'What?'

'Go, Kitty, Queen of Sass,' said Violet.

'I'll drink to that,' said Molly as she clinked her glass against Violet's gin and tonic.

Pip leaned across to his wife, nodding in the direction of the Mellisons. 'That's all we bloody need when we're supposed to be having a nice time.'

'I know,' groaned Molly. It was nigh on impossible to escape Aoife's loud voice which was jabbing its way into her brain.

Molly was doing her best to ignore her, but the woman appeared determined to be heard, talking about Rufus, making it difficult for Molly to concentrate on the conversation her friends were having. Aoife was repeating how she hadn't had time to take him on any walks today, and how he hadn't been out of their garden. He was under the weather, she said. Her sister, Trish, had called in and had a coffee with them. She seemed overly keen for Molly and Pip to hear this information.

'That woman is so transparent, Molly,' Vi said, sotto voce.

'Don't worry, I'm onto her.' Molly pressed her lips together; if Aoife wanted to play games, then bring it on. 'Dad had to have three of his sheep put down today thanks to some irresponsible owner allowing their dog to rampage around the moor. It got into the field with his prize-winning flock of Chevvies and worried some of them so viciously, we had to get the vet out to put them out of their misery,' said

Molly, her volume matching Aoife's. Two could play at that game.

Aoife's voiced silenced for a moment, her ear cocked towards Molly's table. 'I, er, Trish was, er, just saying how well-behaved Rufus is and I told her that, just as I do my children, I expect my dog to behave impeccably, too. Which, er, of course, they do.'

Molly snorted and was rewarded with a scowl from Aoife.

'Any idea whose dog was responsible?' asked Ollie, he knew what Molly was up to.

'Oh, we know exactly whose dog was responsible. And I've got mobile phone footage to prove it. It'll be in the hot sweaty hands of the police by tomorrow morning. They asked us to let them have it as proof of who needs to be prosecuted.' Molly glared at Aoife, whose eyes bulged back at her.

Less than an hour later the Mellisons had gone, leaving a much lighter atmosphere in their wake. The friends were able to relax once more. Gerald Ramsbottom and Big Mary — the local ageing artist and his Amazonian wife and muse who hailed from County Durham — had arrived in a riot of colour. Gerald's foot-long beard had been freshly dyed fuchsia pink to match the shoulder length hair on his head and his voluminous cotton trousers. Big Mary appeared to be draped in slouchy toga-like cloth covered in vivid splashes of colour. 'Hiya, peepsh. All okay?' Gerald asked in his sing-song Geordie accent. Molly stifled a giggle; he was still struggling with the set of second-hand false teeth he'd supposedly bought from eBay.

'Hello, folks, lovely evening for it.' Big Mary gave them a cheery gap-toothed smile.

'Hi,' the friends chorused and watched the pair settle

into the chairs at the other side of the garden, Scruff and Nomad following close behind thanks to the packets of crisps the couple were armed with.

Molly swirled her wine around her glass and glanced at the faces around the table. 'So, can anyone shed any light on why Pip here as booked us a table in the pub for a romantic — his words, not mine — anniversary meal? Not that I'm suspicious, or anything, it's just that it's not the sort of thing he normally does.'

Pip went to protest, and Molly took a sip of wine, raising her eyebrows questioningly as she did so.

'Pigs is all I've got to say to you!' she said when she'd swallowed her mouthful.

'Washing lines,' added Kitty.

'Steam-cleaners,' chipped in Violet.

'I'd say you were on pretty shaky ground there, Pip, me aud mucker.' Jimby grinned, triggering his dimples.

'Aye, you do have a bit of a track record, mate,' added Ollie.

'Thanks, you two. What happened to blokes sticking together?'

The pair shrugged their shoulders, still smiling.

'What can I say, I'm a changed man.' He gave Ollie and Jimby a look that Molly couldn't quite discern, though it didn't escape her attention that the pair started to shuffle uncomfortably. And she could have sworn she saw Kitty and Vi exchanging a furtive glance.

'Hmm. So, it's just my wicked mind that thinks he's trying to compensate for something he's done that he shouldn't have or to soften the blow of a new piece of machinery he hasn't 'fessed up to yet, is it? Can I take your silence as a guarantee that I'm not going to suddenly hear about a new quad bike, or an off-roader or vintage motor bike or another lump of metal, when we should be spending money on the campsite, hmm?' She took another swig of her wine, noticing Ollie wince as she finished her sentence.

'Come on, lass. Don't go dragging other folk into stuff like that. Nobody knows owt — not that there's owt to know. I just booked the table because I thought it'd be nice for you to have a break away from the kitchen and for us to spend some quality time together without worrying about the farm or the campsite for a few hours.'

Molly still wasn't convinced that it wasn't guilt that appeared to be making their friends squirm ever so slightly, or struggle to make eye contact with her. But her teasing was only gentle, and she didn't want the conversation to take on a serious tone. Pip was Pip; he'd always secretly bought stuff and he always would. She didn't really mind. Well, not that much anyway.

'Oh, well. If no one's going to tell me otherwise, I suppose I'll have to believe you. But in the meantime, Pip, love, I do believe it's your round.' She grinned, waving her empty wine glass at him.

Jimby slapped him on the back when he went to protest. 'Hah! She's got you there, mate. Good and proper.' Not known for his generosity, Pip was regularly teased for having short arms and deep pockets — apart from when it came to his vehicular hobby.

'Too right. I've been stitched up like a proper bloody kipper.' Pip rubbed a hand across the stubble of his chin. 'Same again, is it?' he asked reluctantly, turning to Ollie and Jimby. 'Didn't know I'd have to pay you two for your silence.'

Jimby threw his head back and laughed heartily, tipping his chair off balance. 'Warrghhh!' he yelled, the humour in his eyes replaced by horror, his arms and legs flailing wildly as he struggled but failed to save his chair from toppling backwards and hurling the remnants of his beer into his face.

'What the...?' said Molly, as she and the others turned to see Jimby, flat on his back with his feet sticking up in the air, while he fended off Nomad and Scruff who were enthusiastically licking beer off his face.

'Wah! Get off, Nomad! Off Scruff! Bugger off you little twa...bleargh! Jesus, Nomad, get your tongue out of my mouth, you little bloody minger!' The garden was filled with the sound of laughter as everyone watched Jimby try to wrestle the dogs off him.

'Jimby, you are such a daft arse.' Vi was bent double, giggling.

'Don't all rush to help at once,' he said as he struggled to his feet, rubbing his hands across his face. 'Yak! Those two bloody hounds have got a bad case of dog breath.'

'Nice one, Jimbo,' said Ollie, wiping tears of laughter from his eyes.

'That's what I call karma, Jim,' chuckled Pip.

WITH PEACE RESTORED, the evening melted away into a gentle dusk. Pip yawned. 'Right, Moll, I think it's time we were heading back. I'm up early in the morning, and there's only so much fizzy orange I can take while I'm watching you knock the wine back.'

'Yep, and little Emmie will be on the dawn patrol too,' Molly agreed, draining the last of her wine.

CHAPTER 8

Molly had just finished bathing Emmie and was settling her down for bed in crisp pink and white striped cotton pyjamas. She was smiling down at her daughter, smoothing her cheek while Emmie's eyes succumbed to sleep. *She looks good enough to eat*, Molly thought as she inhaled her clean, soapy smell. She turned away and tiptoed to the door, pulling it to when Tom's voice burst into the calm as he came hurtling into the house.

'Dad! Dad! Mum, where's Dad?' The panic in his voice set her senses on high alert.

She shot along the landing and down the stairs, her heart racing and her pulse thrumming in her ears. 'Tom, what on earth's the matter? What's happened?'

'Where is he?' Tom raked his fingers impatiently through his dark blonde curls, his eyes wide with shock.

'He's just popped into the village to speak to Jimby. Why?' She felt panic rise in her as she took in Tom's ashen face.

'Shit! Oh, Christ. I need to call the fire brigade. You call Dad. Quick, Mum!'

'Okay, but why?' The urgency in her son's voice made Molly's stomach lurch.

'The moor's on fire up yon side of Tinkel Top Farm. Looks like it's taking hold fast and the breeze is blowing it our way. Tell Dad to come quick and bring Uncle Jimby with him. Ollie, too. Anyone. We need as many people as we can get to beat out the flames.'

Molly's hand flew to her mouth as fear clenched its fingers around her heart. 'Oh, shit. Where's Ben?'

'In the barn, grabbing as many fire beaters as he can.' Tom snatched up the phone from the hall table and punched in the emergency numbers. 'Yes. Yes, fire brigade. Quick! There's a fire up on Great Stangdale moor near Tinkel Top Farm, and it's getting out of control quickly. Moving towards Withrin Hill. Please, send someone out quick!'

As her son provided more details to the operator, Molly raced to the kitchen in search of her mobile. Spotting it on the table she grabbed it, checking for signal. Two bars. *Thank God,* she thought as with a shaking hand she called Pip's number. It rang but, as usual, went to voicemail. 'Shit! Shit! Shit! Don't you ever pick up, Pip?' She sent a text, all fingers and thumbs, and watched intently to see that it had been delivered. Within seconds Pip called her, and she shared the details Tom had given her.

'Your dad's on his way, and he's bringing Jimby and Ollie,' Molly called to Tom. 'They're trying to get others to help, too.'

The siren of the fire engine based at Danskelfe could be heard setting off from the other side of the dale, its whine pulled along on the breeze, together with the smell of burning heather. Molly ran upstairs to look out of the landing window.

'That's the fire engine on its way, Tom. Should get there any minute.' A huge plume of smoke was now visible accompanied by vivid, angry flames leaping high into the air, inching ever closer. 'I'd best warn Grandma and Grampy. They'll be wondering what's going on.'

A niggling doubt began to scratch away at the back of Molly's mind. She couldn't help but think that the Mellisons had something to do with this; Dave and his so-called extreme endurance training. His boasting about a camping trip, him bragging how he was going to teach his obnoxious little brats how to make a campfire.

'Mamma, mamama, mamama.' The raised voices had woken Emmie. Molly hurried back into her bedroom to see the little tot standing up in her cot, her chubby hands holding onto the side, while tears poured down her cheeks.

'It's alright, bubba. Mummy's here,' she soothed, scooping the little girl up and delivering kisses to her warm curls as she patted her back. 'Let's go downstairs and have a cuddle. Sensing the panic that filled the air in the house, Emmie clung onto Molly tightly.

The sound of Pip's Landie arriving in the yard alerted them to his arrival. Molly hurried to the back door to see him, Jimby and Ollie tumble out and race to the barn where Ben and Tom were scrabbling together the spare fire-beaters. The smell of burning was much stronger outside, the plume of smoke more intense.

'You get yourself back inside with Emmie,' Pip called out. 'The fire-engine should be up there anytime. We'll go and beat out what we can.'

'Be careful. All of you. Boys, you listen to your dad, okay? Do as he tells you and stay safe,' she shouted across the yard.

By now the breeze had picked up, and the smoke had

become thicker and darker. From the elevated position of Withrin Hill Farm, Molly could see that it had begun to drift down the valley side and into the village of Lytell Stangdale, blocking out the remains of the evening sun. Feeling helpless and with her stomach churning, she hoped the firefighters would get the blaze under control soon.

Once inside the farmhouse, Emmie stopped crying and her eyes became heavy with sleep. Molly popped a soother into her mouth, and the baby sucked on it vigorously, tiny sobs escaping intermittently. She began playing with her ear, a sure sign that slumber was calling. It wouldn't take long for her to drift off.

Pacing from room to room, absent-mindedly humming a lullaby and patting Emmie's back, Molly was soon aware that her daughter was sound asleep and headed upstairs where she lay her gently in her cot and backed quietly out of the room.

As Molly headed to the landing window for a better view of the moor, she heard the wail of another siren making its way up to Tinkel Top Farm. Middleton-le-Moors fire station must have sent an engine out, too. Things must be bad. In the distance, she could see that the flames had encroached onto Withrin Hill Farm land and were getting worryingly close to their freshly-baled silage. Panic twisted the knot of nerves in her chest and made her heart beat faster. The land was tinder dry, had been for weeks, and she knew how quickly fire could get out of control in such conditions, how dangerous it was; it took no prisoners.

AFTER PACING BACK AND FORTH, checking to see that the fire was still a safe enough distance from their home, Molly had sat down in the armchair by the Aga and been dozing fitfully when she heard Pip's Landie rumble into the farm yard, the doors slamming, heralding the return of her husband and her boys. She squinted at the clock on the wall; they'd been gone for over four hours. She jumped up and ran to the kitchen just as they walked in, heat-scorched faces and the acrid smell of burning clinging to their clothes.

Pip wiped his forehead with the back of his hand; he looked exhausted, as did the twins.

'Oh, thank God you're all alright!' Feeling tears begin to prickle her eyes, she ran over to them, pulling them all into a hug. 'Bugger, you don't half stink, though.'

Pip stood back and ran a hand wearily over his face. 'Aye, I think the three of us could do with a shower. And a beer. I'm absolutely bloody parched.'

'How bad was it?' Molly hurried to the fridge and pulled out three beers. She removed the lid from the first one and handed it to Pip. 'I could see the flames getting closer and higher.'

Pip puffed out his cheeks and released a noisy sigh. 'Ta, love.' He took the bottle. 'Pretty bad. One of the Danks's fields that was just about ready to be silaged has gone, half of that one of ours at the top's gone, and the fire spread to the Danskelfe Estate moorland.' He headed over to the table and pulled out a chair, flopping down onto it before taking a long swig of his beer. He wiped his mouth with the back of his hand. 'And I'm afraid all of those bales of ours have gone as well. No human casualties, though. Thank God.'

'Human casualties doesn't bear thinking about.' Molly nodded, handing the other two beers to her sons. Ben coughed, pulling a face at the bitter taste of smoke. He quickly sluiced it away with a mouthful of beer.

'You should've seen it, Mum, I've never seen flames leap so high,' said Tom, his voice dry and croaky.

'We've all got massive blisters on our hands with bashing the flames out for so long. And the heat was unbelievable. I think Dad's lost his eyebrows,' added Ben.

Molly peered closely at her husband's blackened face. 'Oh, God, I think you're right. And his fringe looks a bit frazzled, too. You obviously got too close, Pip. You should be careful.'

'I was careful, it's just the breeze picked up unexpectedly, and the fire jumped a bit close. I think Jimby and Ollie will be the same, as well as quite a few others. All the local farmers came out to help. And some from Danskelfe and Arkleby. These two did brilliantly, though. I'm proud of you both, lads.'

'Cheers, Dad.'

'Yeah, cheers.' Both boys pulled out chairs from the kitchen table and collapsed onto them.

'I'm proud of all three of you. And so glad you're all back unscathed. I'll let you have your beers, then I'll take a look at those blisters.' She smiled, relief writ large across her face. 'Any idea what started it?' Molly reached inside the fridge and grabbed the bottle of wine that she'd been chilling for tonight — though she thought she'd be enjoying it in more relaxed circumstances.

'Well, we're not a hundred per cent certain, but John Danks thought he saw smoke from a barbecue or some small camp fire at the far end of one of his fields. The next thing he knew, there was smoke billowing everywhere and massive flames leaping up to the sky.' Pip coughed, clearing his throat from the taste of burning heather. 'By heck my throat's dry. I might need another one of these.' He took a long swig from his bottle.

'You know what I'm thinking, don't you?' Molly filled a glass with the wine, glancing across at Pip.

'Oh, aye, I do. And you're not the only one. PC Snaith was up there, too, and I filled him in on what we'd heard that knob-head Mellison saying.'

'He said they'd need proof, though,' added Ben. 'And we know how slippery that "perfect" family can be.'

IN BED THAT NIGHT, Molly snuggled up close to Pip, her mind troubled by "what ifs". What if the flames had leapt out and caught him or the boys? What if one of them had to be rushed to hospital with severe burns? What if one of them had been killed? She shuddered at that.

The thoughts clenched an icy grip around her heart, and she cuddled in closer to Pip. His hair was still damp from the shower, and the citrus aroma of shower gel combined with a faint whiff of burnt heather lingered on his skin. She still had to pinch herself that she was married to this easy-going, affable man. And tonight, she felt especially lucky to have him. 'Night, Pip. Love you,' she whispered.

'You feeling alright, Moll?' He joked, it was out of character for her to be soppy. 'Love you, too, lass.'

CHAPTER 9

By the following morning, the smoke had cleared from the valley, and the thatched rooftops of Lytell Stangdale were once again visible, but the air was still heavy with the smell of scorched moorland. Taking the off-roader, Pip and Molly headed over to the site of the blaze. Acres of charred, still-smoking ground lay out in front of them. It was a forlorn sight.

'What a bloody shame.' Pip pressed his lips together. 'Could've been worse, though. If it had taken hold late at night when it was dark it could so easily have spread further. Could've got as far as our farm as well as the Danks's'. Then livestock would've been involved, or worse.' Molly could see how upset her husband was. He loved his job and the land he looked after, took pride in it.

'Doesn't bear thinking about, Pip.' She rubbed his arm.

'It doesn't. Lord Hammondely is full of hell about it. Wants to make sure the culprits have their arses prosecuted off them. I think if he could have them put in the stocks on the village green he would.'

'And if it's who I think it is, I'd be more than happy to pelt them with heaps of dog muck.'

'I think there'd be a queue behind you as well.' He gave a smile that didn't reach his eyes. 'But, in the grand scheme of things, at least no one was injured.'

Molly folded her arms across her chest and turned to look at Withrin Hill Farm, the breeze blowing her hair loosely around her face. She tucked the wayward strands behind her ears. 'True, but it's a real shame about all our silage. I dread to think how much money's gone up in flames there.'

'Aye. And when I think of all those hours wasted gathering it all and stacking it...we'll have to source some from outside for winter now.'

'I suppose the insurance will cover the loss.'

'Hopefully. But just seeing it like this, well, you know?' He shrugged his shoulders and exhaled noisily. 'And with the shooting season just around the corner.' His voice tailed away.

'I know.' Molly rubbed his arm. 'Oh, and by the way, while we're on the subject of bad news, Mum's invited us for tea tonight.'

'Oh, bugger. I'd best fill up on something edible before we go then. Get a good lining on my stomach. That bean dish she did last week meant I couldn't stray too far from the toilet for a good five days.' Pip frowned and rubbed his stomach at the memory.

'Mmm. I'm not sure what it was supposed to be, but it was bloody lethal. I've told her I'll make pudding, though. So I'm going to take some of our home-grown raspberries and rustle up a quick cranachan.'

'Cranachan. Now you're talking. My favourite.' He grinned.

MOLLY WAS out of fresh cream for the cranachan so, with Emmie in tow, she headed down to the village shop. She parked up her car in a space on the opposite side of the road, next to the pond and in the shade of the long arms of a weeping willow tree. As she unfastened her daughter from her car seat, old Freda Easton waddled by. Despite it being a good twenty-eight degrees, she was still swaddled in her old checked mac which was pulled taut around her generous middle and secured by a length of frayed Charley band. Her usual grimy deerstalker hat was perched on her equally grimy, grey hair and her feet were encased in a pair of cow-muck-encrusted wellies that squelched when she walked.

'Morning, Freda.' Molly smiled at her.

'Morning.' Freda nodded.

'Poo-poo!' shouted Emmie, clasping both chubby hands to her nose. 'Poo-poo!' Emmie had a point, Freda was ripe.

'Ssshhhh!' said Molly, mortified that the old lady might hear her. Even though it was evident that the woman didn't trouble soap and water, the last thing Molly wanted was for her feelings to be hurt; she was a kindly old soul. Though, if rumours were true, her family was absolutely loaded, but being the black-sheep of the family, Freda had shunned their way of life in favour of being self-sufficient and living back-to-basics. She was obviously doing something right, as she never ailed anything and was as hardy as the sheep that grazed the moors.

Molly hitched Emmie up onto her hip and hooked her bag over her free shoulder. 'Come on, little miss, let's go and see Freddie and Lucy in the shop.'

'Bakkit.' Emmie pointed into the car for the basket that went everywhere with her.

'Oops. Silly Mummy, I nearly forgot it, didn't I?'

The bell tinkled as Molly opened to door to the shop-cum-deli. She felt her hackles bristle as she saw Aoife Mellison standing at the counter. Aoife turned, visibly blanching when she saw Molly. 'Right, I'd better get this lot back,' she said, her usual affected accent suddenly slipping into her native Teesside. She grabbed her shopping and hurried out of the shop blanking Molly as she went.

'Was it something I said?' Molly looked at Lucy and Freddie.

'That was odd, wasn't it?' agreed Lucy. 'She was just going on about how her, Dave and the kids had spent a cosy night in, in front of the telly. She must've mentioned it half a dozen times.'

'Yeah, it was like she was trying to drill it in to us,' added Freddie. 'Anyone would think she was trying to set up an alibi.'

'Well, I'm not buying it,' said Molly.

'And neither am I. When we mentioned hearing the fire brigade and all that smoke that filled the village, she suddenly got very shifty, didn't she, Fred?'

'Aye, she did.' He nodded. 'And I don't believe that it's a coincidence that Dave was in here yesterday, buying sausages and burgers and shooting his mouth off about his extreme endurance skills, and right after he was bragging about it, there's a blazing fire on the moor.'

'Well, thanks to him being an irresponsible di...' Molly looked at Emmie and stopped herself. 'Thanks to him being irresponsible on the moor, Pip, my boys and a load of other blokes, including Jimby and Ollie were risking their lives with the fire brigade, trying to put the fire out. We lost all our silage, as did the Danks's. And poor old Pip lost his eyebrows. Could've been a lot worse though.'

'D'you think it was them that called the fire brigade?
Asked Lucy.

'Nope, that was Tom.'

'That family are a disgrace.' Freddie shook his head.

'But we've got no proof it was them at the moment.
We've just got a bloody good idea that it was.'

'Weeties!' Emmie pointed to the sweets lined up on the
counter.

Lucy smiled. 'Ahh, you've been a patient girl while we've
been chatting to your mummy, haven't you? You can have
these from Freddie and me – as long as it's okay with
Mummy?' She picked up a bag of chocolate buttons, ready
to give to Emmie.

'Ooh, they're your favourites, bubba. Yes, that's fine with
me. Thank you, Lucy. Say thank you, Emmie.'

'Tanka,' said Emmie, giving a toothy smile.

'Right, I'd best be off,' said Molly as she paid for her
shopping. 'Snaithy's coming round this afternoon, and I've
got to make some cranachan to take to Mum and Dad's —
were going there for tea. God help us. If you never see me
again, you know why.' She laughed as she gathered up her
bag and left the shop.

WHEN MOLLY RETURNED HOME, PC Snaith's car was parked
in the yard alongside Pip's Landie. Delores and co were
busily scratting about in the ground around them, clucking
noisily as Molly's car pulled up.

She walked into the kitchen, glancing at the police officer's hat which was set on the table in front of him. He and
Pip were chatting and sipping tea. Phoebe gave a cursory

bark and trotted over to her, tail wagging and bashing against the furniture.

Pip looked up and smiled; she noted he still looked tired from his evening battling the fire. 'Ey up, Moll. I've just been talking to Snaithy here about last night. The police think there might be the remains of a tent and campfire in amongst it all. Kettle and pans, as well. Looks like that's what started the fire.'

'Is that what you think? It was caused by a campfire?' She put her bag of shopping on the worktop by the sink and set Emmie into her high-chair. 'Any more tea in that pot?'

'Aye, there's plenty, love. And how's my little princess?' Pip ruffled Emmie's hair and was rewarded with a wide smile. 'If you pass us that mug, Moll, I'll fill it for you.'

PC Snaith folded his arms across his chest, the rolled-up sleeves of his shirt revealing sunburnt arms. He looked a good ten years younger than his thirty-two years, the smattering of freckles across his nose and his short, auburn hair cut lending him a boyish look. He inhaled deeply. 'In answer to your question, Molly, aye, it would suggest that's what started the fire, but it's early stages, and I've still got a few more people to question. And some of my colleagues are still up there, gathering evidence.'

Molly filled a beaker with milk and handed it to Emmie then joined the men at the table. Turning to PC Snaith, she said, 'You might want to go and have a chat with Lucy and Freddie from the village shop. Apparently, Dave Mellison was there recently boasting about his "extreme endurance" skills.'

'Oh, really?'

'Yes, really.' She continued to share what she'd heard earlier, while the police officer made notes in his neat black book, listening intently and nodding as she spoke.

'I hear you've got some footage of a dog worrying your dad's Chevvies as well. Wouldn't mind a look, if that's okay?'

'Yep, of course. But I haven't had time to transfer it to a storage thingy yet. Well, the twins were going to do it for me, but what with the fire and everything, they haven't got round to it,' Molly explained as she scrolled through her phone and showed him the video.

'Hmmm. While it's obvious there's a dog worrying sheep, it's a bit too grainy to see exactly what type of dog it is from here.' PC Snaith rubbed his hand across his chin.

Molly felt her heart sink to her boots. 'But what about the collar? There's only one dog around here who has to wear a collar as bloody stupid as that one.' Frustration was creeping up her, making her bristle. Why did Snaithy have to be so sodding reasonable?

'Aye, no one else would deck themselves or their dog out the way that lot do. You'd think they were going on some mountain-climbing expedition in extreme conditions the way they dress just to go for a walk along the dale. It's like they're trying to prove that they're mega-outdoorsy and have all the gear or summat,' said Pip.

PC Snaith smiled sympathetically. 'Don't fret, we'll do all we can to find the person, or people, responsible and bring them to justice. We just have to go about it the right way and gather as much evidence as possible, or the CPS will just bin the case before it gets to court. And we don't want that.'

'Too bloody true. Sorry, officer, it's just so frustrating... the things that family have done to mine since they moved here it's...' Molly's words were cut off by a loud burp from Emmie, the sound filling the kitchen. Phoebe's eyes shot open, and her ears twitched.

PC Snaith's eyebrows nudged his auburn hair-line as he

looked across at Emmie. 'Did that massive sound come from that angelic-looking little thing?'

'Well, it wasn't me,' said Pip 'Can't vouch for Moll, though.'

'Nope, it was Daddy's little princess,' Molly said with a chuckle.

'It was bigger than her,' said PC Snaith.

'Aye, she's just like her mother,' Pip laughed.

'So we keep getting told,' sighed Molly.

PC Snaith smiled. 'Right, well, I think that's my cue to head off down into the village, do a bit of digging and see what I can find out.' He tucked his notepad into his shirt pocket. 'But if you could let me have that footage as soon as possible that'd be great.' He put his hat back on and headed towards the door. 'Thanks for the tea, folks.'

CHAPTER 10

The following afternoon, Molly was folding washing on the kitchen table, catching up with jobs while Emmie was flat out having her nap. For such a simple task it seemed to be taking a lot of effort. The room was stiflingly warm, and the sunlight bouncing off the yellow walls seemed to add to the general stuffiness. Molly felt swamped by lethargy. She'd thrown all the windows wide open, trying to tempt a breeze into the house, but to no avail. And the loose-fitting cotton shift dress she was wearing didn't seem to be helping. She'd scooped her thick curls up into a ponytail to keep her neck cool. *That was a waste of time*, she thought as a trickle of sweat ran down it.

She looked across at Phoebe who was comatose under the table; it wasn't great to be a black Labrador when the weather was this hot, but she had the right idea. A snooze would be perfect right now...

Just as Molly was contemplating sitting down and giving in to temptation, Pip burst through the door. *How could he be so bloody enthusiastic in this heat*, Molly wondered, feeling a prickle of annoyance. She noted the broad smile plastered across his face, the sort that said he'd been up to something.

'I'll just finish this then I'll stick the kettle on, make you a cuppa.' She eyed him suspiciously and picked up one of Emmie's dresses to add to the ironing pile.

'Oh, don't go worrying about that at the minute. I've got something to show you. But first, you have to close your eyes and hold out your hand.'

Molly folded the dress in two, smoothing it as she gave him a sideways look. 'The last time you said that to me I ended up pregnant with Emmie,' she said, giving in to the reluctant smile that played around her lips.

'You've got a dirty mind, you have, Molly Pennock!' He took the dress out of her hands and set it down in the washing basket. 'Now, are you going to do as I say, or what?'

'As long as you promise not to put anything yucky in my hands.' She blew a stray curl off her face and giggled.

'Can't promise anything like that. But enough chat. Just shut your eyes — and your gob — and give me your hand.' Pip took her hand and led her towards the door. 'Keep them eyes shut, Moll,' he warned.

'Okay, okay, keep your knickers on. Ouch!' She tripped over a hen who clucked and squawked irritably, giving her a nasty little peck on her exposed toes in return.

'Mind out the way, Delores.' Pip guided Molly into the yard. 'There, you can open your eyes now,' he said. 'Tadah!'

Dazzled by the bright rays of the afternoon sun, Molly blinked, shielding her eyes with her hand; it took several seconds for them to regain the ability to focus. 'Oh, wow!' Her mouth hung open as her eyes took in the sight. Stood before her was an original gipsy vardo. Admittedly, it had seen better days, and its paint was peeling — quite badly in some places — but they'd been after one of these for ages.

'She's a beauty isn't she?' Pip stood with his hands on his hips admiring the campsite's latest acquisition.

'She's gorgeous.' Molly nodded, excitement bubbling away inside. 'Where did you find her?' She started circling the caravan, taking in its proportions, her imagination already racing ahead with ideas of how to decorate and furnish it. The door let out a groan as she opened it and she took a furtive peek inside. Her eyes alighted on the bed, the shelves, the wood carving on the wall; her nose twitched at the faint smell of wood smoke from the tiny stove, mingling with damp. 'To think that this was somebody's actual home. It's incredible,' she said.

'It had been left in one of dad's fields. He says it was after the fair at Middleton-le-Moors. Just abandoned with nowt inside it. He asked around, but no one seemed to know owt about it so he said we could have it. I was fair capt,' he said. 'Looks genuine, like a proper gipsy one. And it would fit in with the timing of the fair and the gypsies who run it,' he said.

'Mmm. It'll be perfect in the glamping field, wont it? I've got some bits and bobs that I've been gathering from charity shops and car boot sales that'll look perfect inside it. And I managed to pick up some vintage fabric that's spot-on for the curtains. I've been saving it for one of these.' Molly felt her mood lift.

'I knew you'd be chuffed. There's a fair old bit of work to do on it, but nowt that I can't manage myself, apart from one of the wheels is a bit dodgy, but I'll ask Ollie to make us another one, and it'll be right as rain.' He grinned across at Molly, his teeth gleaming white in his tanned face.

It was hard for either of them to believe that the dream they'd first talked about years ago was finally becoming a reality. Their thinking had been ahead of its time, before glamping was even a thing. Owing to the capricious nature of the weather on the North Yorkshire Moors they'd knocked an idea about for some kind of soft camping, so people wouldn't have to cancel their plans if the weather was unkind and made sleeping in a tent more like a hardship than a break from the daily grind.

Everything suddenly felt like it was slotting into place — though the pair wished it wasn't at the expense of Molly's father's health. Pip was still able to do a job he loved, Molly had given up nursing, and running the campsite was shaping up to being something even better than they'd planned. She'd even thought about putting an advert in one of the glossy magazines. She'd definitely do it when the vardo was finished. Would they get it done before the end of this summer? She hoped so, maybe with the twins' help.

The twins...thought of them momentarily sent Molly off on a different train of thought, Tom in particular. Mothers' intuition told her he had something on his mind but she couldn't quite put her finger on it; she'd mention it to Pip later.

'Right, lass. Time for that cuppa you promised me.' Pip rubbed his hands together, his smile in no hurry to be budged.

'Yep, let's get out of this heat, it's stifling.'

'You're absolutely right there, Mrs Pennock.' He moved across to her and wrapped his arm around her shoulders, giving her a squeeze and a peck on the cheek.

INSIDE, Molly sat the kettle on the Aga and turned to look at Pip. 'I'm thinking of inviting our lot over for a meal on Saturday evening, unless you have any objections?'

'Nope, no objections. I think it sounds like a champion idea. Though, after what happened the other night, I think we'd best leave off the barbecue till this scorching weather's over and done with.' Pip had headed over to the sink and began washing his hands, splashing a couple of handfuls of cold water over his face as an afterthought. 'Fwahh! That feels better.'

Molly threw him a towel from the Aga rail. 'No, I wasn't thinking of a barbecue, more like a big ham joint, with cold buffet type stuff. And it would be nice to eat outside in the walled garden. I can get some fairy lights strung about the place, make it look pretty.' She nodded in the general direction of the garden just off the farm yard, edged with deep beds that brimmed with a riot of English country cottage blooms. Espalier apples and pears in old Yorkshire varieties were trained over parts of the walls with rambling roses running in between.

'I'm liking the sound of that, missus. Shall I mention it to Jimby?'

'You can do, but I'll be texting Kitty and Vi anyway; I know what you men are like for details — or lack of them — and I want to let everyone know that kids and dogs are invited, too.' She knew if she left it to Pip, only half the message would get across.

CHAPTER 11

'Right then, I can't squash anymore ice in there.' Pip rubbed his wet hands down the front of his jeans. He was in the pantry and had been filling a large galvanised trough with bottles of wine and a mountain of ice-cubes.

Molly went over to have a look, the cool of the pantry a welcome relief after the warmth of the kitchen. She rested her hands on his shoulders and peered round him, laughing out loud when she saw what he'd been working on. 'Bloody hell, Pip, there's no way any of that booze is going to be anything other than icy cold.'

'That's precisely the idea,' he said, making a final adjustment.

'I'm not sure how you're going to get the bottles out though.'

'Leave that to me, Moll. Don't you go worrying your pretty little head about that.' The pair wandered back into the kitchen to see Ben looking very pleased with himself.

'Me and Kristy have just finished making the sangria,' he beamed at them, proudly holding up a large glass carafe full of it. 'Taste's dead good.'

'Mmm. It's delicious,' agreed Kristy, her ice-blue eyes shining as she tucked a strand of long, glossy black hair behind her ear before taking a sip through a straw.

Molly smiled at Ben's new girlfriend, today was the first time Pip and Molly had met her, and they'd liked her instantly. 'Just take it easy with that, if you've put vodka in it, it'll be potent stuff,' she cautioned, wiping her hands on her pinny before turning to her husband. 'Right, Pip, now you've done with chilling the wine, can you carve this ham for me, into slices of about so thick?' She pinched her fore-finger and thumb together to demonstrate, before moving the gammon joint towards him.

'Aye, no problem. By heck, it looks bloody good, Moll.' It was a huge piece of meat that Molly had boiled in a mixture of fruit juices before piercing it with cloves, slathering it with a tangy, thick cut marmalade, giving it a generous sprinkling of rich, dark sugar and a final roasting in the Aga. 'Mmm. And it tastes good, too,' said Pip sampling a small slice. 'Just so you know, I've appointed myself head of quality control on all things food and booze related.'

'And, I'll be your assistant.' Ben nipped over to the table and pinched a sliver. 'Aww, man. That's bloody good, Mother!' He passed a chunk to Kristy who nodded her approval.

'Hey, no more, you lot, or there'll be none left for anyone else.' She smiled, flicking at Ben with the tea-towel, missing him as he jumped deftly out of the way.

The low thrum of a Landie engine caught their attention, carried through the open kitchen window as it climbed up the track to the farm. 'They're here,' called Tom as he came inside, wiping his feet on the doormat. He'd been putting out more chairs in the walled garden and generally making sure everything was set out as Molly had instructed.

'Ey up, that ham looks good.' His eyes fell upon it appreciatively.

'Go on then, you might as well have a try; everyone else has.' Molly rolled her eyes good-naturedly, passing him a chunk.

'Mmm. Ta.' Tom popped the ham into his mouth. 'Mmmhmmm. S'good.' He nodded enthusiastically as he chewed.

Just then, Jimby pulled up in the yard, yanking on the handbrake and jumping down from his vehicle. He went round to the rear, opening the door so the occupants could spill out. Ethel— Kitty and Ollie's black Labrador — landed first, nose in the air sniffing in the myriad notes of food. She was quickly followed by their cocker spaniel, Mabel, and his own spaniels, Jarvis and Jerry, who shot out after and raced into the kitchen, on a mission to seek out the source of the delicious aromas. 'Don't mind me,' he chuckled.

'Now then, mate.' Pip walked over to him and shook his hand.

'Now then.' James returned the greeting, patting Pip on the shoulder with his free hand. 'By, you've picked a grand day for it.'

'Aye, couldn't ask for better weather, could we? Pip looked up at the broad expanse of cornflower blue sky that spread out above the farm, golden rays of sunshine reaching down from it.

'Well, maybe for it to be a little bit cooler. That would be nice.' Vi slipped out of the passenger seat, rocking a fifties vibe in a pair of mint green pedal-pushers, a crisp white short-sleeved blouse with Peter Pan collar and black ballerina flats.

'You'll be grumbling it's too cold before you know it.' Pip

loved Vi, but when she moved to York, he'd always thought she'd gone soft and turned into a bit of a princess.

'By, there's some lovely foodie smells coming from the kitchen, Pip.' Ollie patted his friend on the back.

'Now then, Oll. Aye, your hounds seem to think so; they headed straight in there. Our Moll's been busy in the kitchen all day, churning out some good stuff. Wait till you see the size of the profiteroles. Bloody enormous they are.' He shook Ollie's hand, laughing.

'Thank goodness she's a better cook than Auntie Annie,' said Kitty, looking relaxed in a short-sleeved ethnic cotton dress in shades of red that complemented her dark hair. Her cheeks flushed, and she put a hand to her mouth. 'Oops, she's not here yet, is she? I'd hate to hurt her feelings.'

'No, don't worry about that. She'll be arriving a bit later on with Jack, they've been to York, shopping. Poor bloke.' Pip grinned. 'But you're absolutely right, her cooking's chronic. We had tea there the other night, and my guts were rumbling that much, I felt like I was going to start with the shi...'

'Thanks, Pip, I don't think we need to hear about that.' Molly interrupted, making Anoushka and Lucas giggle. 'Hiya, folks. Come on in, don't let Pip keep you gabbing out here.'

'Too right, man desperately in need of a beer here.' Jimby mimed being a goldfish and tipped an imaginary glass to his mouth. 'And we definitely don't need to know the workings of your ar...'

'Jimby,' Vi warned.

'Sorry.' He waggled his eyebrows at her before she turned him round and pushed him through the door.

'Where's Emmie, Auntie Molly?' Lily lisped, as she ran up to her, grinning a gappy smile; she'd obviously lost another tooth, which Molly thought made her look very sweet.

'She's waiting for you in the kitchen, Lil. And can I just say how gorgeous you look in that summer dress and pretty hairband?'

'Thanks, Auntie Molly. Noushka got me the hairband for my birthday, didn't you, Noushka?' Lily beamed.

'I did, Lils. I knew you'd love it as soon as I saw it.' Anoushka, all tall and blonde and beautiful, took her step-sister's hand and led her to the kitchen.

'Ah, bless, Kitty. How lovely is that?' Molly pressed a hand to her chest.

Kitty beamed. 'I know, Ollie and I are over the moon that they all get on so well. Lucas absolutely adores her, too. She makes a fuss of him about his football, always comes to watch him with us. And tells him she needs tips from him now she plays in the girls' football team. It's really boosted his confidence, especially since, well, you know.'

'It just goes to show how things work out, Kitts.' Molly smiled, it warmed her heart to see her cousin glowing with happiness. 'And you've got yourself a lovely man there and a little bubba on the way,' Molly whispered the last part.

'I know. Honestly, Moll, I never imagined I could be this happy after everything...' Kitty smiled at her cousin, her eyes shining.

Molly patted her arm. 'I couldn't be happier for you, hun, you deserve it.' She looked towards the Landie. 'No Bryn?'

'No, he's on holiday with his mum in Spain. We Skyped him, and he says he's really sorry to miss it, but I told him there'd be other times,' said Kitty, referring to her ex-husband's sixteen-year-old love-child. Since Kitty had found out about him, he'd become a welcome and much-loved

member of her new family unit, and the reality was
nowhere near as odd as it sounded.

'True, there will be. Anyway, come on into the kitchen
and meet Ben's new girlfriend, Kristy. She's absolutely stunning, lovely with it, too. Farmer's daughter from Skeltwick
over by York, he met her at college. And she's staying over, if
you know what I mean? First time we've let this happen,
feels a bit weird, but, well, he's eighteen.' Molly pressed her
lips together and gave a shrug.

Kitty followed her cousin into the kitchen which was
filled with the delicious aroma of food, mingling with
laughter and banter. Her brother, Jimby, was in his usual
place as life and soul of the party, cracking corny jokes and
telling of his latest mishap chasing after Reg.

'Any road, Jimbo, it's about time you got that flaming
wayward bird of yours under control,' said Pip.

'Steady on there, mate. I really don't think there's any
need to talk about Violet like that,' chuckled Jimby, earning
himself a sharp dig in the ribs from his girlfriend.

'Don't be a ratbag, Jimby,' said Kitty, joining in with
everyone else's laughter.

'Don't worry, Kitts, I'll make him suffer later.' Vi gave
him a pointed look.

'Sounds interesting.' Jimby grinned, rubbing his hands
together.

Under Molly's instruction, everyone grabbed a plate of
something and headed to the walled garden, setting things
down on the trestle table that was covered with a sage green
and white polka dot tablecloth. Bunches of cut flowers had
been placed in jam jars at intervals along its length,
mismatched cutlery was gathered in a mini galvanised
bucket, and paper napkins were stacked in a wicker basket
on one of the corners. A gazebo was set up at the far end for

those who were keen to escape the glare of the afternoon sun.

'Make sure you keep the door shut, or the hens'll be in helping themselves to everything,' Molly called out, shooing Delores away.

'Oh, this looks gorgeous, Moll.' Vi gazed around at the rambling roses in full bloom that scrambled across the golden sandstone walls, the pastel coloured bunting strung across from one side to the other.

'Tom's to thank for the bunting and fairy light distribution.' Molly set down a stack of plates as the son in question pinched another piece of the ham. He gave a thumbs-up, chomping on his mouthful.

'And me and Kristy made this,' said Ben, handing Violet a generous measure of sangria.

She took a sip, and her eyebrows shot up. 'Wowzers!' She handed the glass to Jimby. 'Have a mouthful of that.'

'Sure you mean a mouthful, Vi? asked Molly. 'The size of Jimby's cakehole, there'll be none left.'

'Funny bugger,' retorted James, taking the glass, all eyes upon him. 'Christ! That's bloody rocket fuel! It'll put hairs on your chest, Vi.' He flashed her one of his trademark cheeky grins.

'Ahh, just what I've always wanted,' she said, smiling back at him.

WITH STOMACHS FULL OF FOOD, the friends settled back in their seats, the hum of easy-going chat floating on the air as they soaked up the warmth of the day. Ben spent much of the afternoon red-faced as he was teased about Kristy, with Pip and Jimby adding a plentiful supply of stories to embarrass him which he batted away good-naturedly.

'What about you, Tom? When are you going to bring a girlfriend home, so we can pull your leg?' Jimby teased, flicking a bee away from his face.

'After seeing what you've done to Ben, that'll be never,' he replied making everyone laugh.

'Leave him alone, Jimbo.' Molly glanced across at the more sensitive one of her twins, wondering if it was matters of the heart that were responsible for the troubled expression he wore when he thought no one was looking.

'Right, time for a bit of fun, me thinks,' announced Jimby, taking heed of the subtle warning tone in his cousin's voice. He stood up, reached into the back pocket of his jeans and pulled out a handful of balloons. 'Come on lads and lasses, time for a game of water-bombs with the master.' Striding towards the door of the walled garden, with more than a glint of mischief in his eyes, he gave a whistle. 'Come on hounds, that includes you.' The dogs jumped to attention and trotted after him, tails wagging excitedly.

'How old are you exactly, Jimby?' Violet rolled her eyes and was rewarded with a cheeky grin.

'I think he's stuck circa age nine,' added Kitty.

'It'll end in disaster,' said Molly, watching as most of the group followed him, leaving her to chat with Kitty, Violet and her mum, who had arrived with her dad as they were half-way through eating. Jack was currently dozing in the shade of the gazebo alongside Emmie who was sleeping soundly in her pushchair.

She leaned across to her little daughter, gently pressing the back of her hand against the delicate skin of the baby's flushed, plump cheek. Emmie's eyelashes fluttered for a moment. She felt warm — but not uncomfortably so.

Sitting back in her seat, Molly swirled the golden Pinot Grigio around her glass before taking a slow sip, its cool, crispness setting her taste buds tingling. She sighed as a wave of happiness washed over, so strong it brought a lump to her throat. She swallowed it down quickly — it wasn't like her to do sentiment. But Molly had to acknowledge to herself that she'd never felt so content with her lot in life and, not a day went by when she didn't find it hard to believe that she could be this lucky. Granted, they'd had a bumpy start to their life together, her and Pip — falling pregnant at sixteen wasn't her finest hour, she was the first to admit — and she knew she could be a grouchy, moody cow at times. But despite everything — including her mother-in-law being a hard-faced old bag — they'd stuck together, their love growing stronger by the day.

Her thoughts were interrupted by the whoops and squeals that drifted up on the light breeze as Jimby and the rest of the group could be heard chasing down the field.

'It'll end in disaster,' said Vi of her accident-prone boyfriend. 'It always does where Jimby's involved. He ended up in the pond again last week, chasing Reg, who'd taken exception to a delivery man.'

'Tell me about it,' said Kitty, giggling. 'He spent more time at Middleton Cottage Hospital than he did at home when we were ki...'

A shrill scream pierced through the lazy warmth of the early evening, halting Kitty's words and ceasing the birds' chatter from the trees. An uneasy silence followed as the women exchanged glances. Jack momentarily roused from his slumber with a loud snort, before settling back down again. In the yard, there was much squawking and wing-flapping from Delores and her friends.

'What the hell was that?' Molly's heart was racing as her

stomach lurched up to her throat. She went to stand up, looking over at Emmie, whose eyelashes fluttered again, but she remained firmly asleep.

'I'll put money on it being something to do with that brother of mine,' said Kitty.

Suddenly the air was filled with raucous laughter, and Lucas burst through the door to the garden, his young face rife with merriment. The dogs were in hot pursuit, their tails wagging vigorously, enjoying being in on the fun.

'Mum, you'll never guess what happened. Uncle Jimby...'

'Told you.' Kitty looked from her son to her friends. A giggle escaped Molly's lips, and Vi shook her head.

'Uncle Jimby chased me with a water-bomb, and I wriggled under the electric fence just in case it was on, but Uncle Jimby tried to jump over it, and it zapped him right in the nuggets.' Lucas's words tumbled out in a spurt of laughter.

Kitty clamped her hand over her mouth as she struggled not to laugh. 'Oh, no! Is he alright, Lukes?'

Lucas nodded, still giggling. 'He seems okay now, but he was jumping around like a looney before.'

'I bet he was,' Molly snorted.

At that Ollie and Pip rolled in, laughing heartily while Jimby limped theatrically behind.

'Jimby, what the hell did you do to yourself?' Violet rushed over to him, her green eyes wide with concern.

'Oh, my God, have you seen his hair? It's stuck up on end!' Molly spluttered, unable to keep control of her giggles.

'It's always like that, Moll,' said Vi.

'Well, thanks for the sympathy, you lot, that's all I can say. I gather you've heard what happened?' Jimby picked up his bottle of beer, and took a quick swig. 'There's me, chasing after that little bugger,' he pointed his thumb towards Lucas who was sniggering, 'who's thrown a water bomb at me – missed mind, but that's beside the point, he'll never beat the Master of Mischief. He then decides to play dirty and shimmies underneath the tape of an electric fence that I didn't even see until the last minute. Then I go to leap over it like a gazelle but miss and end up straddling it. And Jesus Christ, I nearly blew my bloody knackers off!'

If Jimby was hoping for sympathy, he was to be disappointed. Everyone collapsed into fits of laughter.

'I think poor old Jimbo needs a lie-down and a bottle of beer to fettle him, don't you, mate?' said Ollie.

Jimby leaned into him, a lopsided smile on his face. 'I was hoping to have them kissed better, actually,' he said under his breath, glancing across at Vi.

Ollie threw his head back and laughed before patting his best friend on the back. 'Good luck with that one, mate.'

'We don't want to know!' Vi rolled her eyes at the pair's private joke.

IT WAS LATE, and the sun had sloped off over the lofty rigg of Great Stangdale, leaving darkness to settle over the fields and moors. Despite the hour, the air was still warm, and the sun's heat was being radiated back from the large stones of the walled garden. Up above, the milky way was splashed boldly across the inky-black sky, its stars twinkling silently. Owls hooted to one another from the trees and the heady fragrance of the Night Scented Stock that Molly had scattered around the flower beds permeated the evening air. 'Right, time to tidy this lot up.' Molly heaved herself up and began clearing the table.

'Yep, time to head indoors and have a final snifter. I've got some rather fine damson gin from last year,' said Pip.

Molly and Kitty were alone in the kitchen, seeing to the detritus after the meal. The men had been waylaid in the yard where they were discussing Landies, the kids were in the living room playing on the games consoles and Vi had nipped to the loo.

'We're just off to bed now, Mum.' Ben popped his head around the door.

'Okay, love, goodnight, night Kristy.' She shot a look at Kitty.

'Night, Molly,' called Kristy.

'I only found out tonight that her mother doesn't know they're sharing a room,' whispered Molly.

'Oops.' Kitty pulled a sympathetic face. 'But like you said, they're eighteen, and you can't be responsible for her not telling her mum.'

'True.' Molly bent down to put a bowl into the dishwasher.

'It's been a lovely evening, Molly. I can't believe how things have panned out for all of us.' Kitty sighed.

'Same here, Kitts. And I'm so glad we've got you back, chick.' Molly put her arm around her cousin.

'Me, too.' Kitty gave her a peck on her cheek. 'I think the planets must've aligned for all of us.'

'I think you're right.' Molly sighed, looking out at the starry sky. She hoped it wouldn't be long before they aligned for Tom.

CHAPTER 12

A finger of early morning sunlight poked its way through the chink in the curtains, caressing Molly's cheek. She stirred and reached across the bed for Pip, anticipating the feel of his warm skin. Instead, her hand landed onto the empty space where he'd been. She opened her eyes to see a rumpled sheet and a dent in his pillow. Frowning, she turned back and picked up the alarm clock on her bedside table, brushing her hair out of her face and squinting at the numbers. Half-past seven. She sighed. She'd had a lie-in; he'd been long gone. She rubbed her eyes, and yawned, her thoughts slowly slotting into place.

She climbed out of bed, slid her feet into her slippers and padded along the landing to Emmie's room. The house was quiet apart from the odd creak of an old floorboard, grumbling at being walked on. She peeked into Emmie's room to see her still fast asleep, looking angelic and peaceful.

Molly headed downstairs and into the kitchen where Phoebe was curled up on the clippy mat. She wagged her tail at her mum. 'Morning, Phoebe.' Her words were stretched out by a yawn. 'Where is everyone?' she asked as she filled the kettle. Setting it down on the Aga hotplate, she headed over to the large window, sliding it open, allowing the cool, morning air to wash over. 'Mmm,' she sighed. Unusually for her, she'd been in a deep sleep and was finding it difficult to wake up.

Five minutes later, and with a few slurps of tea down her, Molly began to feel the fugginess in her head gradually receding. Sitting at the table, she pulled out the chair next to her and rested her feet on it. She sat quietly, listening to the sounds of the countryside pour through the open window, a cacophony that was easy on the ear. The familiar bay of the beast over at Tinkel Top Farm, the low thrum of a tractor, interspersed with shrill birdsong, the clucking of hens and the bleating of sheep. Farmyard sounds that Molly had known her whole life; they placed her firmly in her comfort zone. She wiggled her toes and sighed contentedly.

She was halfway through her mug of tea before she realised that it was Friday, the day that Pip was taking her for a romantic meal at the Sunne. Her heart leapt in happiness at the thought. She'd been shopping in York a few days earlier and had bought herself a pretty dress with matching shrug cardie. She'd even splurged on a pair of new shoes, too. Not usually a fan of clothes shopping, Molly had surprised herself with how much she'd enjoyed it, as well as having a few hours on her own to mooch around the shops at her leisure.

'Mamamama.' Emmie's cries from upstairs dispersed her thoughts, and she set her mug down on the table.

'Mummy's coming, Em.' Molly headed upstairs, pushing open Emmie's bedroom door. Her heart melted at the sight of her daughter standing up in her cot, all birds' nest hair, sleep-rosy cheeks and a patch of dried dribble by her mouth. 'Good morning, little pudding. How are you?' She scooped Emmie up and nuzzled into her, inhaling her delicious, warm scent. 'Mmmm. Mummy loves her special girl,' she said, delivering kisses to her cheek. Emmie chuckled and snuggled into her, triggering a warm flood of love right through Molly.

It was lunchtime and Molly had just finished buttering thick slices of wholemeal bread, in readiness for Pip and the boys coming home. As she carried the plate over to the table, adding it to the cold collation of chicken, ham and salad, her attention was drawn to the sound of the off-roader pulling into the yard, scattering the hens who objected vociferously. She headed to the window, peering out to see Pip in his usual camouflage print combat trousers and olive-green t-shirt. Her heart skipped a beat as a surge of love overwhelmed her. *Wow!* she thought to herself, wondering at just how incredibly sexy she still found him, especially with is hair ruffled like that. Hours of walking around on the moorland of the Danskelfe Castle Estate had kept him trim, while working on the farm had made him muscular. Her eyes roved appreciatively over his broad back as he bent down to pick something up.

Her deliciously wicked thoughts were interrupted by the arrival of the twins in the Landie. As they tumbled out, Ben called over to his father, 'We got them fence posts in Dad.'

'What, all of them?' Pip looped his thumbs through his trousers.

'Aye, all of them,' Tom called back. 'And we have the blisters to prove it. On top of the ones from all that fire-beating we did the other week.'

Pip shook his head. 'Hmm. Don't remind me about that. Anyroad, well done, lads. I thought you'd be on with that for another day at least.'

Molly stepped out of the kitchen and into the glare of the sunshine, shielding her eyes with her hand, a jug of homemade lemonade in the other. 'Are you lot coming in for your lunch, or what? Emmie's waiting for you, and she's starving.'

Pip sauntered over to her, smiling. Wrapping his arm around her shoulders he pulled her close, pressing a kiss onto her cheek. 'Ahh, and here's the woman I left home for all those years ago. The lovely Mrs Pennock.'

'Bleargh!' said Ben rolling his eyes at his brother.

'Get a room,' grinned Tom, before adding, 'Actually, don't. I'd rather not think about that.'

'Get on with you,' said Pip, as they headed into the house.

'Dadadada,' trilled Emmie from her highchair as she banged her hands excitedly on the table.

'Now then, little princess. Have you been a good lass for your mum?' He kissed her warm curls on his way to the sink to wash his hands.

'She's been as good as gold,' Molly smiled. 'Though, this heat has made her a bit drowsy.'

'She's not the only one,' said Tom.

'So, are you all organised for tonight then, missus?' Pip asked before splashing cold water over his face. 'Woah, that's better.' He grabbed the towel from the rail on the Aga and rubbed his cheeks dry.

'Just about and I'm really excited about it. I can't remember the last time we had a meal out, just the two of us.' Molly's face glowed as she poured lemonade into his glass, passing it down to him. 'Lemonade, Ben?'

'Yep, ta.' He slid his glass along the table to her. 'So, how long have you two been together exactly?'

Pip sat back in his seat, rubbing his chin with his hand. 'Ooh, about a hundred and fifty years, I'd say.'

'Yeah, but it feels like longer,' Molly shot back, a smile playing on her lips.

'Touché, missus.' Pip grinned at her affectionately.

WITH THE MEAL over and done with, Pip and the boys headed back to work, the twins with instructions to check over the sheep pens and then pop down to look over their grandfather's Cheviots.

'Right, I'm off to check some grouse-butts.' Pip climbed into the off-roader, setting the engine away.

'Okay, but please, Pip, don't be late. Try to get yourself back in plenty of time for a shower. The last thing I want is for us to be rushing around. I want us to enjoy tonight.'

'Look, stop fretting. I'll be back for six o'clock, which'll give me enough time to have a shower, wash my hair and get you to the pub in plenty of time for a drink before we have our meal, okay?' He shot her a heart-melting grin, happiness dancing in his slate-grey eyes.

'Okay.' Molly nodded, not totally convinced. Pip had a track-record for being late to everything. Once his game-keeper head was in action, he lost track of time and Molly had lost count of the times he'd rolled in late for parents' evenings at school or get-togethers at the pub. She hoped tonight would be different.

'WE'RE OFF, MUM,' Tom called from the hallway; he and Ben were heading to a party in Danskelfe and Molly was upstairs, getting Emmie's room ready for bedtime.

'One tick,' she called as she popped Emmie in her cot. 'Mummy won't be a minute, sweet pea,' she said softly as she headed towards the door and down the stairs.

'Well, don't you two look very dapper.' She smiled proudly at her sons whose smart appearance stood in stark contrast to their usual work one. 'And here was me thinking you were allergic to soap and water for all these years.' She sniffed the air. 'And you smell lovely; you've even managed to banish the smell of stinky socks and sweaty feet.'

'Haha, very funny, Mother.' Ben checked his watch. 'Half six, Dad's already late.'

'Good old Dad, he'll be late to his own funeral.' Tom joked.

Molly felt a pang of disappointment; after Pip had made such a big thing of promising her he wouldn't be late, the least he could do was be there on time. 'I reckon you're right. Anyway, you two get yourselves off and have a lovely time. You're staying over, right? So, no drinking and driving to worry about.'

'Stop fussing, Mum. We're all bunking down in the barn, and we'll be back tomorrow morning.' Tom bent to kiss his mum on the cheek.

'I can't guarantee there won't be any drinking, Mother, but we won't be doing any driving once we've parked up there.' Ben put his arm around Molly and gave her a squeeze. 'I hope you and Dad have an awesome night,' he said, planting a kiss on her cheek.

'Thanks, lads,' Molly followed them to the door, stopping while Tom grabbed the Landie key from the meat hook on one of the beams. 'Have fun,' she called after them as they loped off into the yard leaving a cloud of cologne in their wake. *Since when did they suddenly become young men?* she wondered as she watched the Landie bump through the gate.

Fifteen minutes later her parents arrived. 'Yoohoo!' Her mother popped her head through the kitchen door. 'We're here, lovie.'

Molly hurried along the landing and tiptoed down the stairs; in the short time she'd been saying goodbye to the twins, Emmie had fallen into a deep sleep. She knew her mum would be disappointed, she loved giving Em her bedtime story and watching her eyes succumb to sleep, but after a day in the fresh air, the tot was worn out, and Molly doubted anything would wake her now.

'Hiya, I was just in Emmie's bedroom. Sorry, Mum. I did my best to keep her awake after her bath, but she was getting crabby and was asleep in a flash.'

Annie smiled. 'Don't worry, I know exactly how she feels in this heat. And as for your poor old dad...' She bent to pat Phoebe's head, who'd trotted to greet them at the door. 'Hello there, Phoebe, you're a good girl, aren't you?' The Labrador wagged her tail, panting in the heat.

'Ey, less of the "old" if you don't mind,' her Dad said good-naturedly. Molly chuckled, pleased to see that he looked well. The sky blue short-sleeved shirt suited his colouring, he'd caught the sun on his cheeks, and even though the Parkinson's meant he could no longer form a smile, it hadn't taken away the glint of happiness in his bright blue eyes.

'Right, if it's okay, I'll just go and finish getting ready. Pip's not back yet — surprise, surprise — but I don't imagine he'll be long; our table's booked for half seven and he swore he'd be on time for it.'

'Okay, lovie, that's fine.' Annie turned to her husband. 'You get yourself in the living room, Jack, and I'll make us a nice pot of tea. Your programme will be starting soon, so go and get yourself comfy.' Molly smiled to herself as her mum bundled him into the living room, gently bossing him around as she'd done for the whole of their nearly forty years of marriage. Not that he ever objected.

'There's some of Dad's favourite biscuits in the tin by the cupboard with the mugs. It's the one with the daisies on,' she called after them. She'd made them specially for tonight; her mum's baking was no better than her cooking, and she knew her dad would be thankful for them. Phoebe's ears cocked at hearing the word "biscuit". 'Sorry, Phoebes, but they're not for you.'

AN HOUR LATER, Molly walked into the living room wearing her new clothes, a frown creasing her brow as she worried her bottom lip. Her levels of frustration were escalating by the minute. Several calls to Pip's mobile phone had proved fruitless, having gone straight to voicemail, and there was still no sign of him. Molly could feel her heart pounding as she let stress increase its grip on her.

'Try not to get yourself so worked up, lovie. There's bound to be some explanation.'

'Oh, Mum, this is so bloody typical of him. I was a fool to

even think for one minute that he could be on time for anything. Tom was bloody-well right, Pip would be late for his own funeral! I'm absolutely fuming with him. We're already late for the meal, and he still needs to get showered and changed.' She twisted her wedding ring round her finger in frustration. 'I'd better call Bea and Jonty, it's pointless us going out now. He's bloody-well ruined the night!'

'Calm your jets, lass,' her dad added in his soft moorland accent. 'You're doing yourself no good getting all het up like that. And I'm sure Bea and Jonty'll understand. Just give them a ring and have the table put back for a bit. Give Pip a chance to get home.'

Molly stormed over to the window, looking out over the fields. She didn't appear to hear his words, and she wished everyone would stop being so bloody reasonable and let her feel justified in being annoyed. Everyone made excuses for Pip because he was so easy-going, but she was fed up of making allowances all the time. 'I'll give him half an hour, and if he doesn't turn up, then that's it.'

'Why don't you try his phone one more time?' suggested her mum.

Molly picked up her mobile and found Pip's number. 'Voicemail.' She threw it down onto the coffee table with a clatter. 'There's a bloody shock.'

'Why don't you ring Jimby or Ollie? They might have seen him, or heard from him,' her dad suggested.

'Hmm. I'll try Kitty, see if she knows anything. If not, I'll try Vi. The girls seem to reply quicker than the lads.' She snatched up her phone and headed through to the kitchen, hearing her mother talking to her dad in a soft voice, still making excuses for Pip. Molly huffed impatiently.

The phone calls were a waste of time, but Molly had expected that. Neither party had heard from or seen Pip all

day. As far as they were aware, he was under strict instructions to be home for six, and he'd been determined to stick
to that. Apparently, he'd joked with Jimby and Ollie about
what a surprise it would be for Molly. 'Too bloody true,'
she'd muttered to herself.

While she had the phone in her hand, Molly rang the
Sunne and explained the situation. Jonty had sounded
surprised, he'd seen Pip the day before, and they'd
discussed how he was going to be home early. 'I'm sure he
won't be long m'dear, I know he has a lot on, and it really
isn't a problem for us to push your reservation back. It's
actually quite helpful as we've got a bit of a rush on, so you'll
be doing Bea and the kitchen a favour.'

'Thanks, Jonty. That's really good of you. We'll get there
as quickly as we can.' Why did everyone have to be so
flaming reasonable about Pip's lateness? Molly was grateful
for Jonty's understanding, but, ughh, Pip always seemed to
get away with being sodding late. That's why he never
changed. People were always so forgiving with him. Apart
from her; she was sick of his tardiness and his laid-back attitude. She was going to give him a right bollocking after this.

ANOTHER HOUR HAD PASSED, and Pip still hadn't returned.
On an average night, Pip could sometimes still be working
this late, juggling his jobs, but he would have popped in to
have something to eat by now, before heading back out
again. He was never good at keeping in touch, though, and
Molly was used to him landing whenever it suited him.

She'd hoped tonight would be different.

Phoebe was watching her mum intently, instinct telling
her that something wasn't right. Molly paced the floor, her

hands clenched into tight balls. She could feel her anger gradually being nudged to one side as a feeling of concern bloomed. It was making her breathing fast and shallow. 'I'm going to see if I can see him out in the fields.' She marched out of the living room, Phoebe following close behind.

'Ok, lovie,' said her mum as she glanced across at her dad who was rubbing his chin, a knowing look exchanged between them.

Out in the yard, Molly made her way across the worn York flagstones. Her feet feeling like they belonged to someone else as she walked in her new suede ballet pumps; she was used to wearing functional, chunky footwear, not this dainty, fashionable type. All was quiet, the chickens having gone to roost some time ago. She headed out onto the track that led down to the village. There was a good vantage point from there, and you could see a wide portion of the Danskelfe Estate. The moor was bathed in the mellow summer light that Molly usually loved, though it was beginning to slip away. She'd hoped to see the lights from Pip's off-roader weaving its way across the moor; he'd have put them on by now.

The air outside felt heavy, oppressive almost, as Molly, keen as a hawk, scanned the neat angles of the fields, her gaze moving slowly up onto the undulating swathes of heather that was in full bloom, before shifting to the charred patches from the recent fire, hoping that her eyes would alight on something. Something that would bring relief. But the land revealed nothing. Molly sighed as her heart sank. Phoebe, who'd been having a sniff around the yard trotted over to her, looking up, her own concern evident in her soft brown eyes. Molly rubbed her velvety head. 'Where is that dad of yours, Phoebes?' The Labrador responded with a wag of her tail.

Further along, the hum of Bill Campion's tractor as he finished off a round of silaging at Camplin Hall Farm was filling the dale. Her relations, the Welfords, were doing the same down at Tinkel Bottom Farm and the evening air was filled with the scent of freshly cut grass and heather, wafted on the breeze that had suddenly picked up. The weather had been hot and dry for weeks, with not a drop of rain. But the forecast had warned of change, with the threat of thunderstorms barging their way across the Atlantic, intent on wreaking havoc, and the farmers, though desperate for rain, were in a hurry to get their silage cut and bailed before it landed on their corner of the North Yorkshire Moors.

Molly headed over to the gate, disturbing a pheasant that was roosting in the low branches of a nearby rowan tree. It cackled its annoyance at her and flew off, gliding into the field below. Tucking her dress into the legs of her knickers, and too cross to care how many creases she'd put into it, she climbed onto the second bar of the wooden gate, hoping to gain a better vantage point. Frustration took a hold of her as she pushed her hair off her face and shouted for all she was worth, 'Pip!' Her voice was instantly scooped up by the breeze and carried off down the dale, scattering a handful of rabbits as it went. She didn't really expect him to hear her, but it felt better, felt like a release of the emotions that had begun to knot tightly in her stomach. But her cry fell on stony ground, bouncing off the fields and disappearing into nothing. Picking up on to her mum's mood, Phoebe whimpered and lay on the floor beside her.

'It's no use, Phoebes.' Feeling helpless, Molly climbed down and made her way back to the house, hoping there'd be some news. But then, she reasoned to herself, her mum would have come out and told her if there was.

The temperature had suddenly dropped, and the wind

had gained pace. As she brushed a handful of curls out of her eyes, she felt a large drop of rain land on her forehead and run into her eye. 'Bugger, that's all we need.'

In the living room, her stomach twisted as she was met by the worried expressions of her parents. 'No sign, lovie?' asked her mum.

'Nope, I'm afraid not.' Molly pressed her lips together. 'I was hoping you'd say that someone had been on the phone to tell me he was on his way and to get the shower running.'

'No, love, we've heard nothing.' Her dad's voice came out small.

Molly swallowed, pushing down a claggy lump of nerves that had worked their way up from her stomach and lodged in her throat. Feeling suddenly nauseous, she sat down on the sofa next to her dad. 'I don't know what to do. I'm beginning to feel a bit worried.' She looked from one parent to the other, knotting her fingers that lay in her lap. 'I don't want to bother the twins, and they'll know as much as me anyway, I'm sure of that. But this is late, even by Pip's standards.'

'What about ringing the Danskelfe Estate office?' asked her dad.

'There'll be no one there now, Dad. They clock off at five.'

'What about the...'

At that, the landline rang, making everyone jump. Molly froze. 'Do you want me to get it for you?' asked her mum, her hand pressed against her chest.

'No, it's fine. It's probably nothing.' Molly headed into the hallway, her stomach churning and her legs feeling like jelly.

'Hello.' She hoped the person on the other end couldn't hear the shake in her voice.

She returned to the living room and the expectant gazes

of her parents. 'That was Jimby. He said he'd checked his barn where Pip keeps some vehicles. Pip's off-roader is there but his new quad bike has gone.'

'Oh?' said her mum.

'What does that mean?' asked her dad.

'I'm not sure. I didn't even know he had a new quad bike.' Molly tapped her fingers against her mouth as her brow gathered together. Something from the back of her mind was reminding her of the conversation they'd had at the pub when she was questioning the others about a secret purchase of Pip's. She also recalled a conversation with him when he'd first told her about tonight's meal at the Sunne. Looks like she'd been right to doubt him after all.

'But why would he keep a quad bike there, when you've got plenty of storage space here?' Her mum looked puzzled.

Molly shook her head. 'You know what Pip's like, always keeping secrets about things like that. He knows we can't really afford one when we're spending so much on the glamping site. But he can never resist temptation.'

They sat in silence for a while, the three of them gazing towards the window, watching the gargantuan, pewter storm clouds inch ever closer, blooming like an angry bruise in the sky. The branches of the trees started to sway, creaking eerily in the increasing breeze. Molly spoke first. 'Look, why don't you two head home? It's pointless you being here. Pip's obviously got talking to some farmer and forgotten all about tonight; it wouldn't be the first bloody time, after all. It's too late to go to the pub – and I wouldn't want to now, anyway. I'm not in the mood for it.'

'We can't leave you on your own, lovie, can we Jack?' Her mother glanced at the window as large spots of rain started to splash against the glass.

'Er, no, love.' Jack jumped, he was beginning to doze off.

'Yes, you can. Dad's tired. And I'm just going to go and have a soak in the bath. I've got a throbbing headache, and that might clear it.'

'But I don't feel right leaving you.'

'Honestly, Mum. I'd put money on Pip coming home soon. He'll have got chatting to some like-minded loser, and got carried away with things, thinking it won't matter about our meal. That we can always do it another time. And, trust me, if that's the case, you won't want to be here for the bollocking I'm going to give him when he does get back.'

Her mild-mannered mother winced at Molly's threat. She regularly wondered where Molly had got her feistiness from.

'Please, Mum. You and Dad just get yourselves home, and if I need you, I can call you. It's not as if you've got far to come.'

Her parents hurried to their car, dodging the rain that was now pelting down. Molly closed the door behind them and leaned against it. Puffing out her cheeks, she released an angry sigh. A mild feeling of relief washed over her as she heard her parents' car drive down the track to their home at Withrin Hill Barn. Much as she loved them to bits, she'd she had enough of hearing about how wonderful and hardworking Pip was. They made excuses for him all the time, but tonight it had begun to grate. She needed time on her own to sort her head out, organise her thoughts.

The wind was flexing its muscles, angrily rattling the old Georgian sashes in their frames, howling, ghost-like down the chimney and hurling large spots of rain hard against the glass. At times like this, it was easy to see why the hill and the farm got their name; in such an exposed spot, the wind was definitely withering. Molly shivered, thankful that her dad had lit the fire earlier. She walked over to it and shov-

elled on some coal, throwing a log on top of that. It hissed
and spat, sending a plume of grey smoke whooshing up the
chimney.

Hugging her arms around herself, Molly headed over to
the window that looked out over the fields. Large rivulets of
rain now blocked the view out of the small squares of glass,
not that there was much to see now that darkness had
descended like a heavy shroud. 'Where are you, Pip?' she
murmured to herself, her eyes straining to seek out any tiny
speck of light that could signal her husband's return. 'Let
me know you're safe.'

But the moors were remaining tight-lipped, revealing
nothing, so she drew the heavy curtains, shutting
them out.

Unable to settle to anything, Molly went to check on
Emmie; looking at her chubby little angel always made the
world seem a brighter place. As she was heading upstairs, a
bright white bolt of lightning lit up the landing, creating
shadows that reached out in alarm; it was quickly followed
by a loud crack of thunder that shook the house. The storm
was beginning to bare its teeth. She hurried along to the
window and pulled the curtains closed, blocking further
intrusion from the inclement weather. She then turned
towards her daughter's bedroom, slipping noiselessly
between the gap in the door.

Molly peered over the side of the cot to see Emmie still
sleeping soundly, dimpled podgy hands up above her head,
blissfully unaware of her mother's worries or the storm that
was raging outside. She kissed her fingertips and pressed
them to the baby's damp curls. 'Sweet dreams, angel,' she
whispered, as Emmie stirred ever-so-slightly.

As she was making her way back downstairs, the landline began to trill. She quickened her pace and snatched the

phone up from its cradle. 'Hello,' she said, her words coming out in a snap, her heart pounding.

'Moll, it's just me.' It was Jimby's voice, serious for once.

'Jimby, have you heard anything?'

'Sorry, Moll, I haven't. I was hoping you had.'

'No.' Molly shook her head, her voice flat, starting as thunder crashed overhead.

'Look, it might be nothing, but it crossed my mind that Pip had mentioned something the other day about having trouble with poachers and that Lord Hammondely was keen for him to sort it out. Maybe he's got caught up dealing with that and has lost track of time? You know what he's like when he sets his mind on something. His Lordship, I mean.'

'Hmm. Pip mentioned the poachers to me, but he didn't seem that concerned about it for the minute. He's been more bothered about getting the estate ready for the shooting season, making sure the grouse butts are in good condition, and rubbish is picked up, you know, his usual gripes for this time of year.'

'Aye, right, well, I thought I'd best mention it in case it might remotely help somehow.'

'Thanks, Jimby.'

He paused for a moment, thinking. 'Look, Moll, I'll ring you back in five minutes, okay.' He hung up before she had chance to answer.

'Okay,' she said to herself.

Looking at the phone in her hand, she was torn between wanting to try the twins' mobiles and not wanting to worry them unnecessarily – she felt sure that if they'd known something they would have mentioned it before they'd left. She decided not to trouble them for now; there was no need to worry them just yet.

A flash of lightning lit up the kitchen, a crash of thunder

not far behind made her jump; it was getting closer. She could hear the rain bouncing off the ground like stair-rods. Tonight wasn't a good night to be out on the moors.

Molly's heart was racing, her pulse thrumming in her ears. She rubbed her hands across her face. *Christ I need a drink*, she thought setting her phone down onto the table before heading to the fridge, pulling out a half-finished bottle of Pinot Grigio. She poured herself a glass and took a generous slug, wincing at the bitterness of such a large quantity. 'Ughh.' It wasn't quite as palatable as usual.

She pulled out a dining chair and slumped into it, staring at the phone, willing it to ring with news of Pip. The rain had turned unseasonably to hail and now pummelled the windows relentlessly. Molly went over and pulled the curtains together, muffling the sound. She shivered; it was hard to believe they'd been broiling in a heatwave the day before.

Just as she was taking another sip of wine, the phone rang again. Jimby's number flashed in the caller display. 'Hi, Jimby.'

'Listen, Molly, Ollie and me have been ringing around, trying to find out who saw Pip last and as far as we can gather, he was seen by Tom Storr up on Danskelfe moor over by the Arkleby border stone at, he reckons, about half five. And Lucas thinks he saw him high-tailing it out of the village on a quad bike late this afternoon. No one seems to have seen him since then, so it all fits in.'

'Okay,' replied Molly. It was strange hearing Jimby's voice so serious. The last time it had a tone like this was when he was sharing his concerns about Kitty and that barrister git she used to be married to.

'Anyroad, Ollie and me have gathered some of the game-keepers together and we're going to go out looking for him.

They'll know the moors better than most, so we're bound to find him.'

'But, Jimby, it's wild out there, we don't even know that he's on the moor. You'll all get absolutely…'

'There's nowhere else he can be, Molly. He was so determined to get home on time for you tonight, the only reason for him not turning up is because he's stuck on the moor top somewhere. He's probably getting absolutely soaked walking back home. And it's pitch black out there now. I mean, I get that he knows the moors like the back of his hand, but when it's dark and chucking it down, he could quite easily have taken a wrong turn.'

'True.' Molly felt bolstered by her cousin's voice of reason. She grabbed his glimmer of hope gratefully. 'Knowing Pip, he'll be hiding from the storm in a sheep shelter or grouse butt, whichever's nearest.'

'Exactly. So, I don't want you to bother the twins just yet, give us chance to have a look for him — he'll probably be home before us.' Molly could hear the smile in his voice.

'I hope so. And thank you, Jimby.'

'Hey, Pip would do the same for anybody else.'

'He would.'

'Right, I'll get off. I need to go and pick Ollie and a few others up in my Landie. I'll ring as soon as I hear anything, Moll.'

Molly released a shaky breath. Jimby had hit the nail on the head, she was sure of it. Pip was on that bloody moor he loved so much. He'd have been engrossed in his work and lost track of time, or maybe the new quad bike had stopped working. Or maybe he'd fallen off it. That thought sent a new wave of worry coursing around her mind. She'd managed to talk herself in and out of Pip being okay in less than a minute. 'Oh, flaming hell, Pip. Please be alright.

Please be safe.' She felt tears prickle her eyes, spilling on to her cheeks before she had chance to think. 'I'm not bloody-well doing this!' She snatched them away with the tips of her fingers. 'Come on, Pip. Get yourself home.'

With that, she topped up her wine and took it into the living room.

CHAPTER 13

Just after five the following morning, Molly was awoken with a jolt by a loud thudding noise. Phoebe, who'd been curled up on the rug at her feet, barked and jumped up, trotting to the door. Molly sat up quickly and rubbed the crick in her neck. She looked around her, feeling confused; she must have fallen asleep on the sofa. She could remember checking the clock at just after four and had opened the curtains to see that the storm had all but burnt itself out. Sleep must have claimed her after that.

She rubbed her eyes, her thoughts slowly gathering, the heavy lump of dread returning to her stomach. *Pip.* There was the thudding noise again; it sounded like someone was hammering at the front door. *Who on earth would be making such a racket at this hour?* Whoever it was, they were persistent. *Jimby? Pip? Pip would have his key, surely?* Hope wrestled with anxiety as she heaved herself off the sofa, her half-asleep eyes landing on the undrunk glass of wine, the bluebottle floating in it making it look even less appetising than it had been the previous evening.

With trepidation, she opened the door to see PC Snaith

and a young-looking female police officer on the doorstep, their expressions sending a surge of panic through her. *Oh shit!* A wave of nausea swept across her stomach, making her legs feel weak. She stood looking at the officers, unable to form any words, wondering if they could hear her heart thumping in her chest.

'Molly, can we come in please?' asked PC Snaith. Molly noted that even his smattering of freckles had gone pale. 'This is my colleague, PC Chloe Dowson.' He nodded to the solemn-looking young police officer beside him. She offered a weak smile in return.

Molly glanced quickly over the tiny little thing in the police uniform. She was a slip of a girl, surely she should still be at school? She looked even younger than PC Snaith. Molly returned her attention to him. 'Is this something to do with Pip? Where is he? Where's Pip?' Her eyes darted from one to the other, as she tried to quell the panic that was rising like a tsunami inside.

'I think it's best if we come inside, Molly,' said PC Snaith gently.

'Is it Pip? Is he okay? Please, I need to know. Just tell me.' She felt rooted to the spot, her feet lumps of lead, her hands glued to the door.

'Molly, I'm really sorry, there's been...' He took his hat off, he looked distraught. 'Please can we come inside?' He took a step forward.

Molly turned and headed towards the kitchen, feeling as if somebody else's legs were carrying her along. She was aware of her breath, pushing its way out in short, impatient bursts and a shrill ringing in her ears. She stopped in the middle of the kitchen, bewildered.

'It's probably best if you sit down, Molly,' PC Snaith said softly as he pulled out a chair for her.

Molly paused for a moment, trying to read his expression. She didn't want to sit down, she couldn't. She felt stifled, couldn't breathe properly.

'Molly, there's no easy way to...'

She gasped as realisation hit. 'Don't. Don't say the words,' she said, shaking her head, pain in her eyes. 'Don't say the words. Don't say the words.' Her hands flew to her head, her fingers grabbing onto clumps of her hair. 'Don't say the words.'

PC Dowson tried to guide her to a seat, but Molly took a step back as tears spilled down her cheeks.

'I'm so sorry, Molly.' He looked down, shaking his head. 'Oh, God,' he whispered and looked back at her. 'I'm so sorry, Molly, there's been an accident. I'm afraid Pip's...Pip's,' he swallowed. 'I'm afraid Pip's dead.'

The agonising, primaeval howl that left Molly's lips was heard by her mother who dropped the cup of tea she was holding. Instinctively, she knew it was Molly. And that the pain in her cry could mean only one thing.

Molly's legs crumbled beneath her, as agonising grief tore its way out of her. 'No! No! No!' She started pummelling her head with her fists. 'No! No! No! Not Pip. Not my Pip! No! It's not true. You've got it wrong! It's somebody else! It's somebody else.'

The two police officers looked on, troubled and at a loss to know what to do. Consoling her was futile, she didn't want them near her; she'd made that clear enough.

At that moment Jimby and Ollie burst in to the room. 'Molly, Molly. Oh, shit, Molly. I'm so sorry. We tried. We found him, but it was too late. We were too late. We tried Moll. We really tried,' said Jimby, his voice cracking. He ran over to her, joining her on the floor, his clothes still saturated from searching through the night for Pip, wrapping his arms around her, stroking her hair as she sobbed into his shoulder and his own grief took hold.

Molly's parents arrived close behind. Hurrying into the kitchen. Annie looked from the crumpled figure on the floor being comforted by her nephew to Ollie. She clamped a hand over her mouth; the pain creasing his features said everything. 'Pip...is he...?'

Ollie, his breathing still rapid, nodded and cast his eyes to the floor as tears spilled from them.

'Oh, Molly, lovie. I'm so sorry.' Annie went over to her daughter, crouching on the floor beside her. Jimby pulled back and got to his feet, drawing a hand down his face, wiping the tears from his cheeks. He was suddenly aware of Emmie's cries from the bedroom. Awoken by Molly's screams, her own cries had been drowned out by her mother's.

'Emmie.' Jimby's voice wavered. He looked bewildered.

'S'okay, Jim, I'll go and get her. I've texted Kitty to come up. Anoushka's staying with Lily and Lucas. I've asked her not to say anything at the moment.'

'Thanks, Oll.' Jimby nodded and turned to his uncle; puffing out his cheeks, he let go a sigh. 'Oh, Jack. Poor Moll. Poor Pip. I'm so sorry we didn't get to him sooner.'

Jack rested a hand on Jimby's shoulder. 'You did everything you could, lad. Everyone knows that.'

'What am I going to tell the twins? Molly sobbed. 'How can I tell them? How can I say it?'

LIGHT WAS JUST BREAKING THROUGH, and birds were gradually coming off roost when Jimby and Ollie had found Pip. He'd been riding his new quad bike around the moor near to Swang Beck that threaded its way along the valley, like a glittering silvery ribbon. Until yesterday, it had been little more than a trickle thanks to the weeks without rain. But last night's storm had replenished the springs that fed it, and it was gushing along, crashing down the weir, creating a thick, creamy foam.

It was Ollie who spotted the bike first, down the bank side. 'Over here! There's something down by the beck. I think it's him,' he called, his heart racing. Jimby shot across to where Ollie had his vantage point and together they scrambled down the steep side of the bank, slipping and sliding in the mud and moss, grabbing the branches of trees to help them down, not feeling the gashes to their hands and legs where brambles and thorns tore at them.

'Oh, Christ, no!' cried Ollie when they reached the river.

'Shit.' Jimby dragged a hand down his face, tears in his eyes. 'What the hell are we going to tell Molly?'

Jimby stayed with Pip while Ollie ran back in search of signal on his mobile phone. He called the emergency services first, before contacting the other men who had joined their search. Once done, he returned to Jimby.

PC Snaith was the first official on the scene. The Air Ambulance arrived soon after him, declaring Pip dead, before scooping him up and transporting him over his beloved moors to hospital.

THAT EVENING, Molly's parents stayed with her and the family. Annie had called the local GP and filled her in with what had happened. She'd listened sympathetically and given Molly a tablet to help her sleep that night. Dr Beth then took Annie to one side and told her that Molly must make an appointment to see her, it would do her good to talk, and they had a grief counsellor who would be able to help. Annie had nodded, doubting that Molly would entertain the idea.

A POST-MORTEM REVEALED that Pip had received a blow to the head which had caused an acute subdural haematoma, probably as a result of him losing control of his quad-bike which had caused him to topple down the bank-side, stopping at the beck. His lungs had been full of water, so if the subdural haematoma hadn't killed him, the drowning would have. The one consoling feature was that bump to his head would have rendered him unconscious immediately, and he would have known nothing else after that point. And it would have been quick. Judging from the time of death, Pip was probably on his way home. He would have been on time, as he'd promised Molly he would be.

An examination of the quad bike had revealed that the brakes had failed. That news had sent a chill down Molly's spine.

CHAPTER 14

On the run up to Pip's funeral, grief had smothered Withrin Hill Farm house, quashing any tiny slivers of happiness that were brave enough to show. It pushed down any smiles that tugged at the family's lips, in the tiniest of moments when they managed to forget what had happened. And it sapped any glimmer of hope. A heavy silence loomed like a spectre in the tall rooms of the building; even the birds seemed to have stopped singing. And the only sound that could be heard was the sound of hearts gradually twisting and breaking with sorrow.

In the ten days since Pip had died, Molly had walked around in a daze, only functioning to look after Emmie, who constantly cried for her daddy. The twins moved around the house like shadows; they'd been inconsolable, blaming themselves for going out and having fun, when they should have been helping their father. They knew what he was like, always, "Just one more job, then I'll go home…" But they'd known nothing about the quad bike or where Pip had bought it from.

Molly had locked herself away, only answering the door

to her parents or her close friends. She hadn't thought it was possible for anyone to cry so much but any little thing seemed to set her off. She felt numb, as though her life was suddenly thrown into limbo.

On a rare venture out to the village, she'd run into Aoife Mellison. Sensing someone's eyes upon her, she'd turned to see the woman scowling at her from across the road. Dressed in her usual garb of Hi-Vis tabard and running gear, she was holding Rufus on a short lead, clearly on their way for a walk on the moors.

Feeling her hackles rise, Molly stormed across to her. 'What the bloody hell do you think you're staring at? I don't know who the hell you think you are, looking down your nose at everyone as if you're better than them,' she spat.

'For your information, I'm looking at nobody.' Speaking in her affected accent, Aoife's eyes bulged, and she jutted her jaw defiantly.

'Is that right? Well, let me tell you something. We all know it's your stupid bloody dog that's been worrying sheep round here. And we've got a pretty good idea of where to point the finger for that fire on the moor as well. And don't think you're going to get away with it.' Feeling her body shake with days of pent-up anger, Molly jabbed a finger at her.

'I'm not having that!' Aoife's face twisted. 'My dog is extremely well behaved, and he never runs off, and he never worries sheep. And as for the fire, it had nothing to do with my family.'

'Really? Well, why was Dave bragging to anyone who'd listen about his "extreme endurance" skills — as he called them — and saying he was taking the kids camping up on the moors then? And where's your tent? Your sleeping bags? Your camping equipment? If you're as innocent as you say you are, you'd have no problem with showing anyone them.'

'We, we gave them to er, charity, actually.' Aoife stumbled over her words. 'Not that I have to justify myself to you. And we're just in the process of replacing them for our camping trip to Northumberland in a couple of weeks. That's what Dave will have been talking about.'

'Rubbish! We all know you're a lying cow, don't we? Your bone-idle layabout of a husband put people's lives at risk when he decided to have a campfire in the middle of a heat wave, despite all the fire risk warnings dotted about. My husband and my sons were out there with the fire-brigade. Other people's husbands and sons were out there, doing all they could to stop the fire from spreading.'

'You don't know what you're talking about. He and the children were at home the night the fire broke out. I should know, I was with them! And it's not my fault your family were out there. We all know how that husband of yours liked to take risks, don't we?'

That was a low blow. Molly felt the knot in her stomach twist tighter. Tears threatened at the back of her eyes, and she clenched her jaw in an attempt to keep them from flowing. Aoife looked victorious. 'You're a toxic bitch aren't you? With an over-inflated opinion of yourself. You and your family just aren't cut out for village life. We live in a small community, and you can't seem to get on with anyone, can you?'

'That's not true, we get on with everyone except you and your family. And like I've already said, Dave and the children were with me the night of the fire; he didn't go anywhere near the moors.'

'Yeah, yeah! Aren't you just bound to say that? Well, you can tell him from me, he'd be better off spending his time where he usually does, propping up the bar at the Fox and Hounds in Danskelfe, or bumming around the village.'

'He does not do that! Dave is hard-working and dedicated to his business. He hardly ever visits that pub.' Aoife's mouth curled into a snarl. Molly had hit a nerve.

'Well, I'm afraid he does, Aoife. And if you asked around you'd find out that other people would tell you that Molly's right.' Jimby, over-hearing the altercation and recognising Molly's voice, had left his forge to see what was happening. He came to a halt beside the two women.

'Rubbish!' The chin was jutted again.

'And you'd better be keeping that dog on a lead once you get onto them moors, Aoife. We don't want to have to get more footage of it worrying sheep to pass on to PC Snaith, do we?' Molly was shaking.

'I don't have to stand around and listen to this. It's tantamount to bullying. Come on, Rufie.' She yanked the dog's lead and strode off.

Molly released a noisy breath as Jimby turned to her. 'You okay?'

She nodded. 'Sorry you had to witness that. She was scowling at me, and something just flipped, I saw red and couldn't stop myself. Before I knew it, I was walking over to her, and the words just came out.' Her voice wobbled, and tears began to flow as a weariness descended upon her.

Jimby put his arm around her. 'You probably needed to get it off your chest, Moll. And you couldn't have picked a more deserving target than that stuck up cow.'

'Hasn't made me feel any better, though,' she sniffed.

'Well, that's a shame, because she really deserved it.' He gave her a squeeze. 'That family can't keep on behaving irresponsibly. Once Snaithy's got things in order, he'll be doing something about it — the sheep worrying, at least. The arrogant Mellisons will get their comeuppance.' He pulled out a bundle of tissues from his jeans pocket and handed them to Molly. 'They're clean,' he added with a small smile.

'Hope so. I mean about the comeuppance, not about the hankies being clean, I couldn't give a bugger about that.' She offered a weak smile back as she dabbed her eyes.

At that moment, Kitty was passing, on her way to Violet's with a sketchbook of new drawings tucked under her arm. She looked from her cousin to her brother; the expression in Jimby's eye's spoke volumes. She hooked her arm through Molly's and gave it a squeeze. 'Right, my place, cuppa, no arguments.' Molly didn't argue, and by the time she left Oak Tree Farm she was feeling much brighter and had even managed to laugh about what she'd said to Aoife. 'Oh, I wish I'd been there,' said Kitty, cradling her mug of tea. 'It would've given me great pleasure to see her squirm, especially after what her family's done to mine. Witnessing her on the other end of a Molly-savaging would've been fab!'

But her altercation with Aoife had left Molly feeling unsettled, and she began to make more excuses to herself to avoid the village. Invitations to pop in for a drink at the pub, or to just call in for a coffee, were turned down. It wasn't like Molly to hide herself away, and her friends were beginning to regard her with concern.

It wasn't just socialising that Molly had lost interest in, it was life in general. Smudges of black sat like well-developed bruises beneath her swollen, red eyes. Her usually glossy curls hung matted and unruly. They hadn't seen a comb never mind shampoo since that fateful night, and weight had fallen off her at a rate of knots, leaving her looking gaunt. Grief had so efficiently sapped energy from her, it took every ounce of strength she had to simply put one foot in front of the other.

What she would give to just disappear, for the pain to go away.

'I THINK we need to make more of an effort to visit Molly or try to get her out of the house a bit.' Sitting in the studio of Romantique, Kitty was carefully stitching a crystal bead onto Lady Carolyn Hammondely's wedding dress. 'I haven't seen her since that do with the dreaded Mellison woman and I'm worried about her. It's like she's hiding away.'

'You're right,' said Vi, through a mouthful of pins, before taking them out one-by-one. 'Can't be easy for her, bless her. Shall we nip up there tomorrow?'

'Good idea. But it's probably best not to mention anything to her, then she can't make excuses for us not to go.'

'I agree, we don't want to give her chance to do that.' Vi nodded, and the pair made a pact to make sure at least one of them saw Molly every day.

MOLLY WAS SITTING at the kitchen table with Kitty and Violet, sharing a pot of tea, her fingers wrapped around her mug. Phoebe, confused by the lack of Pip's presence and never far away, was curled up by her feet. 'I just keep thinking Pip's going to walk through the door any minute and shout, "Sorry I'm late, but stick the kettle on, lass. I'm gaggin' for a cuppa," even though I know he's not. He's never coming back, I understand that. I've seen the horrible proof and my eyes can't un-see that it was definitely my Pip lying on that slab. My lovely Pip.' Molly's eyes filled with tears and she shuddered as she recalled having to formally identify her husband's body. Jimby had offered to go in her place, but she felt she had to do it for Pip.

Kitty and Vi exchanged concerned glances. 'Oh, Molly, chick.' Kitty gave her cousin's arm a sympathetic squeeze.

'So, when do you think that gorgeous goddaughter of ours is going to wake up so we can have a cuddle, Moll?' asked Vi, in a bid to lighten the tone.

Molly sniffed and rubbed her eyes with the heel of her hands. 'Oh, I wouldn't hold your breath, that one can sleep for hours — over three the other day. I think she's having a growing spurt.' Molly gave a watery smile, aware of her friend's thoughtful change of subject.

'Oh, I remember those days with my two. The amount I'd manage to get done in the time they were zonked was amazing. House hoovered, everywhere dusted, windows cleaned, you name it,' Kitty said with a laugh. 'Helped get rid of the baby weight, that's for sure.'

'You clean windows?' Vi asked, incredulous.

'Er, yeah. Why? Don't you?'

'Bloody sure I don't!'

'Kitts, this is Vi you're talking to. You might know she won't do anything that risks breaking a finger nail.' A faint smile hovered over Molly's mouth. 'She's such a princess.'

'Who's a princess?' Vi's tone was indignant.

'Who d'you think?' Molly looked across at Kitty who was smiling at the return of banter between her friends.

'Anyway, you two, all I'm saying is that I made the most of my time getting stuff done while my babies were asleep.'

'Yeah, Vi would use that time to paint her nails or get her hair done,' teased Molly.

'Get stuffed.' Vi laughed, giving Molly a nudge with her arm. 'I bet you do the same.'

'I don't think so. Have you seen the state of this?' She pulled at a handful of her hair.

'Er, now you mention it, you do have a point,' quipped Vi, scrunching up her face.

Molly nudged her back. 'Cheeky bugger, no need to agree so readily.'

HER FRIENDS GOING home had left a huge void in Molly's day. She felt a pit of sorrow developing in her stomach and a yearning to get out onto the moors. She needed to reconnect with Pip, needed to feel the moorland air in her lungs. She picked up the phone and dialled her mum's number. 'Hiya, Mum. Listen, would you be okay to have Emmie for a couple of hours. I wouldn't ask, only...' Her mum detected the crack in Molly's voice.

'Of course, lovie. Just drop her down to me, or I can bob up to you, whatever you prefer. Are you okay?'

Molly nodded, tears pouring down her face. 'I'm fine, Mum.'

Having dropped Emmie off, Molly strode out along the bridleway, walking in Pip's footsteps, Phoebe and Pip's dogs, Teal and Bert, running along beside her. She'd let them off the lead — Pip would be furious if he knew, but he'd trained them well, and she trusted them not to run off the track. She was glad to be in her own company for a while; she didn't want her sadness to rub off onto Emmie, but sometimes her grief just needed to be set free, or she felt as if she would burst. It had a habit of brimming over at unexpected moments and Emmie would look at her in puzzlement.

She continued the climb up the track, brushing her way

through the golden flowers of gorse and the lanky fronds of bracken, her breath getting shorter as she neared the top of the rigg. Once there, she whistled for the dogs, and they came tearing up to her, sitting at her feet obediently, tails wagging in expectation. 'Oh, Pip,' she sighed as her eyes swept over the wide expanse of Great Stangdale. An eclectic mix of moorland and farmland, it looked stunning, swathed in gentle shades of purple that contrasted with the verdant greens of the fields. It was easy to see why he'd loved it so much, wanted to be out there amongst it. It had been his first love, without a doubt, and Molly didn't mind one little bit.

Shielding her eyes from the sun's glare, her gaze landed on the large, blackened patch, scorched by the fire Pip and the twins had help put out. She felt a prickle of annoyance. 'Bloody Mellisons,' she muttered, quickly pushing thought of them away. She didn't want her moment with Pip's memory tainted by that family. The cry of a kestrel distracted her as it swooped by before stopping to hover overhead, its keen eyes trained on its prey. The moor was teaming with wildlife, the grouse and pheasants raised by Pip, calling out. But it wasn't grieving for him, it was carrying on as if nothing had happened.

In the distance, Molly heard a voice calling, followed by the bark of a dog. She looked in its direction, squinting to get a better view. Her heart sank, it looked like one of the Danskelfe Estate gamekeepers was out doing his job. Pip's job. Sorrow gripped her stomach, she swallowed, biting back tears. She wasn't ready to face that yet. She turned back and headed towards home.

≈

THE FOLLOWING DAY Kitty had called in on Molly whose mood seemed to have dipped again.

'I just can't get my head around it, Kitty,' Molly said, the circles below her eyes darker than ever. 'I can't believe he won't be coming back. I went up onto the moor yesterday, and it looked wrong without him. Empty, like there was something missing. He should be out there, walking all over it, with the smile on his face he always had just for that.' Tears brimmed in her eyes. 'Sorry I'm such a miserable cow,' she said, flicking them away.

'You're not a miserable cow and don't ever apologise for grieving, chick. You need to do it.' Kitty pulled her into a hug.

'He was the love of my life, Kitty; we were meant to grow old together. I just can't believe it.' Molly rested her head on Kitty's shoulder. 'Even after I'd seen him in Hopley's.'

She'd been to see him again, not wanting the last image in her mind to be of her husband looking as clinical as he had in the formal identification at the mortuary. Jimby had taken her to the funeral parlour in Middleton-le-Moors where she'd walked quietly over to the coffin, her eyes building the courage to look inside. 'Oh, Pip, what've they done to your hair?' Mustering a smile, she'd smoothed his short fringe, brushing it the way he liked it. Tentatively, she'd touched his hand, wishing he would wrap his fingers around hers, tell her it was all a joke. *Nightmare, more like*, she thought, as a solitary tear had broken free and trickled down her cheek.

Before she left, she'd kissed her fingers and pressed them against his cold lips. 'Goodnight, Pip. Sweet dreams. I'll never stop loving you,' she'd whispered, the words clogging in her throat.

'Why don't I make some tea? I've brought some of Lucy's

freshly-baked chocolate flapjack, and it looks extra delicious today, I think Luce must've slipped with the chocolate.' Kitty stood up to fill the kettle. 'I'm so lucky that my morning sickness only lasts for a few hours. And while I'm not quite as keen on tea as I would ordinarily be, it's not so bad if it's really strong. And I'm still definitely on chocolate.'

Molly glanced up at her, not hearing, her eyes full of pain. 'I feel like I'm trapped in some horrible nightmare, Kitts. One that I can't wake up from. And I keep wishing Pip would bowl in through that door, reeking of the moors, his usual smile plastered across his face. I still find myself looking out over the moor to see if I can see him like I did before...' She tried to steady the tremble in her bottom lip. 'That he'd wave back at me like he sometimes did.'

Kitty put her hand over Molly's, giving it a squeeze. 'I understand, Moll. And I know that it helps to talk, to just get your feelings out, without really wanting anyone to answer. So talk away, if it helps, and I'll listen for as long as you need.' It was only a few years since Kitty had lost both her parents in a car accident, and she could remember the feelings of disbelief, of hopelessness.

'It feels like this is happening to someone else. Like I'm an observer, looking in on someone else's life. On someone else's sadness, trying to make sense of it.' She stared at her fingers, picking at her nails. 'Everything feels just so numb, the world feels muffled, like my senses aren't feeling things properly. Even when I talk about it, it doesn't seem real. The only thing that does seem real is the pain, the awful bloody ache in my heart.'

'All I can say is that, in time, it does begin to feel better, gets easier to bear. That horrible pain will go, and then you'll be able to look back at all your wonderful memories with Pip and feel happiness again. It won't happen overnight, but it will, gradually. I promise. And, in the meantime, whenever you need to talk, or need to have some company, just call me, and I'll be there at the drop of a hat. I know I can speak for Vi, too, and Jimby and Ollie. We're all here for you and the boys.'

'Thank you, Kitty. I'm so lucky to have you; you're not just my cousin, you're my best friend.' Molly squeezed her hand.

'And you're mine, chick.'

MOLLY DIDN'T KNOW how she would have managed without her friends. Or her parents. Between them they'd taken control of her life, relieving her of the stress of having to deal with the everyday mundane tasks. And the not so mundane. Kitty had looked after Emmie, who, despite being confused as to the whereabouts of her daddy, had enjoyed the distraction of being spoilt by her older cousins at Oak Tree Farm. And when Kitty wasn't able to have her, Annie would take her little grand-daughter, keeping her young mind occupied.

Vi had cooked meals and helped with the washing — not Violet's favourite tasks, she'd be the first to agree, but her dislike of them had been over-ridden by the desire to help her friend.

'S'JUST ME, MOLL.' Vi walked in through the back door, kicking it shut with a designer shoe. 'Shepherd's pie for dinner tonight,' she said, heading into the kitchen. Molly was sitting at the table, her head in her hands, her eyes puffy and tear-stained.

'Oh, Moll.' Vi set the dish on the worktop and hurried over to her friend.

'It hurts. It actually physically hurts. Here,' Molly cried, thumping her chest, tears coursing down her face. 'It's an actual pain in my heart, and I can't get it to go. It even hurts when I breathe, Vi, and I can't bear it. I just can't bear it.' But Vi didn't need to hear her words; the agony in Molly's eyes said it all.

'How am I going to manage without him? He was my soulmate, and this wasn't part of the plan. Wasn't meant to happen; we have too much to do together. All our plans for the farm and the campsite; he was so excited about it all. We were meant to grow old together, Vi. He wasn't meant to leave me, and I wasn't meant to be a widow, the kids without their dad. Emmie won't even remember him at all.' She began to cry, great, wracking sobs.

Vi wrapped her arms around Molly's thin frame and let her sob into her shoulder. 'Of course she'll remember him, we'll make sure she does. No one could ever forget Pip. I, for one, feel a better person for knowing him, Moll. He was one of a kind,' said, Vi struggling to keep her own tears at bay.

'He was,' Molly sniffed.

'How are the twins coping?'

'They're being brilliant. Devastated — obviously — walking around in a bit of a daze, I suppose. I'm just glad they've got each other.'

The twins had done their best to cope by immersing themselves in work at the farm and preparing the campsite, seeking solace in one another, talking through their feelings and trying to make sense of what had happened. But it was a lot for them to take in. At times a sense of anger had overwhelmed them at the injustice of having their dad taken from them. Ben had even punched the kitchen door in an angry outburst, yelling at Pip for leaving them, then collapsing into floods of tears. Unable to concentrate on aligning the hinges on a gate, Tom had pushed it to the ground and stormed off, shouting and swearing as he went.

'I know it's a cliché, but things will feel better after the funeral, Moll.'

Molly wasn't so sure.

CHAPTER 15

The day of Pip's funeral arrived. Molly woke early, a heavy feeling in her heart, a fuggy feeling in her head. Her whole body ached, and her feet felt like they'd been encased in cumbersome lead boots, making it an effort to simply put one foot in front of the other. She didn't know how she was going to make it through the day when all she wanted to do was to go back to bed and sleep her heartache away. But Emmie's heart-melting smile kept her going. That, and the determination that she was going to give Pip the best send-off possible. His funeral wasn't going to be a gloomy affair, mourning his loss — he would hate that. It was to be a celebration of his life. She would do him proud.

Even though it wasn't far, the journey to the church felt like it went on forever, passing by the familiar sights of the village in slow motion. In the days since Pip had died, nothing seemed to have changed. And yet everything had. Molly's life had changed beyond all recognition. And it would never be the same again.

Drawing up outside St. Thomas's, Molly and the twins

watched as Pip's coffin was carried into the church by game-
keepers from the Danskelfe Estate and the neighbouring
ones of Arkleby and Middleton, all dressed in their game-
keeper tweeds as requested by Molly and the twins. As a
mark of respect for Pip, they'd lined the path to the great
oak doors, all wearing expressions of utter disbelief at their
reason for being there. Saying goodbye to their friend wasn't
something they'd considered having to do when he was so
young, a man so full of life and vitality, who never ailed
anything. And who was never without a smile on his face,
doing a job he loved. How bloody unfair, their eyes said,
moist with grief.

Molly walked in on legs that didn't feel like her own, her
boys beside her, heads hung down, eyes firmly fixed on the
floor in front of them. Her mum and dad followed close
behind, Annie with Emmie in her arms — with Pip being
such a well-loved member of the community, everyone had
wanted to attend his funeral, which left no one free to look
after the little girl. Molly was relieved when her mum
offered to have her on her knee in church.

The very church where the pair had exchanged their
wedding vows and their three children had been christened,
was packed, with the congregation spilling outside. The
service was wonderful — if ever a funeral could be
described in such a way. Rev Nev had done Pip proud and
even managed to bring a smile to the most grief-frozen
faces. Jimby, his voice cracking with emotion, spoke of his
friendship with Pip in a way that was heart-breaking and
heart-warming in equal measure. His voice had wavered
more than once, but he'd ploughed on. After him, Lord
Hammondely had done a reading, adding some personal
words.

Molly had managed to remain stoic until they got to the hymns, when grief had swamped her, making her legs buckle. The twins either side had slipped an arm through hers and supported her.

Leaving the church, Molly was touched to see that the gamekeepers who weren't carrying Pip's coffin had formed a guard of honour, making an arch with their guns so he could be carried beneath before being taken out into the churchyard and being laid to rest in a plot next to Kitty and Jimby's parents.

'That was a lovely service, lovie.' Annie smiled gently at her daughter, hoicking Emmie higher up her hip.'

'It was, Mum. It was perfect.'

'You okay to go to the Sunne, Molly?' Kitty asked, rubbing her cousin's arm.

Molly nodded. 'All these people have been good enough to turn up to pay their respects to Pip; it's the least I can do.'

'But everyone would understand if you didn't feel up to it,' added Mark, who'd travelled over from New Zealand. 'That was a pretty long service.' His Yorkshire accent was tinged with a hint of Kiwi.

'No, I'm going. I want to. I don't want to look back and regret that I didn't stay to the end of his send-off. But I just want to walk to the pub, I don't want to get back in the car; I fancy some fresh air and a minute with my thoughts, and it's only down the road.'

Everyone understood and respected Molly's need for a moment to herself. 'See you at the pub,' said Vi, giving her arm a squeeze before following the others.

'Molly, can I have a word?' Molly was walking along the trod, the twins in front of her, when a voice interrupted her thoughts. She turned to see the smarmy features of Trevor

Bottomley (or Arsely, as the twins referred to him), a property developer from Middleton-le-Moors. He'd grown a moustache since she'd last seen him, one that he'd troubled to curl up at the ends.

'Thought I'd catch you here.' He pressed his lips together into a lopsided smile and waggled his moustache.

'What, at my own husband's funeral?'

He ignored the comment, pulling up the smile that had momentarily dropped. 'I've tried calling the farm a couple of times, but there's been no answer, so I thought I'd, well...I just wanted to get in first, in case you were thinking of selling off any land, save you having to enlist the services of an estate agent and their extortionate fees. You know, if you thought the farm would be too big for you to manage without Pip.' He waggled his moustache again.

Molly listened, her face impassive, as he continued. 'I'd be very interested in those two large fields at the bottom, by the road — they're ripe for building, especially the one with the barn. I'm sure we could come to some mutually beneficial agreement.' There was that smile and 'tache waggle again.

'You did, did you?' Molly was struggling to fight the urge to rip his moustache right off. 'I'd heard from my parents that you'd been pestering them for the land.'

Bottomley laughed. 'I really wouldn't call it pestering. I think it was m...'

'That's what it felt like to them.' Molly cut him off. 'And that's exactly what it feels like to me. What kind of person uses a funeral to *pester* someone about a piece of land? A piece of land that's not even for sale? I'll tell you what sort: an inconsiderate, slimy creep.' She glared at him. 'And don't even think about waggling that bloody stupid rat you've got stuck to your top lip.'

'I don't think there's any need for that. I was just trying to make things easier for you.' He patted his moustache before reaching into the inside pocket of his jacket and pulling out a business card, pressing it into Molly's hand. 'Let me give you this; for when you change your mind.' He gave her a smile that bordered on smirk.

'I won't ever change my mind so you can just sod off.' She threw the card to the ground and stormed off to the pub.

With her hand poised, ready to open the door of the Sunne, Molly puffed out her cheeks and released a noisy sigh. She needed to calm the anger that was boiling in her gut before she went inside. 'Sod Bottomley,' she whispered to herself. Two seconds later, she was over the threshold, drawn in by warmth and familiarity. The place had been opened especially for Pip's wake, and Lord Hammondely had insisted on paying for the food that Bea and Jonty had put on, which was set out on a trestle table at the far end of the bar. He'd also instructed them that he wanted to pick up the tab for the drinks.

'You won't believe what I've just seen.' Jimby headed over to Vi who was chatting to Molly. He'd just returned to the pub after being informed by Bill Campion that Reg was giving someone grief outside, and had gone to investigate.

'What?' asked Molly. 'And it's okay to smile Jimby, I can see it's crippling you not to.' She noted the glint of mischief in his eyes.

'Where've you been? Have you been up to something?' Vi asked him.

'Not me, no. You know Bill told me Reg was bothering someone? Turns out it was that slimy prat, Bottomley.' He paused to control his laughter. 'Reg had only gone and perched himself on the bonnet of Bottomley's fancy car —

having crapped all over it — and when the slime-ball tried to get him off it, Reg flew at him and chased him off down the road.'

'Oh, I wish I'd seen that. Serves the creep right,' said Molly, smiling — something she didn't expect to be doing today.

'Well, it's good to know that Reg can come in handy sometimes,' giggled Vi.

'Too bloody right. Bottomley had collared me before I got here, asking me to sell those two fields at the bottom of the lane. Today of all days.'

'You're joking? What did you say?' asked Jimby, his smile disappearing.

'Can't you guess?' Molly cocked her eyebrows, and Jimby's smile returned.

'That's my girl.' He wrapped his arm around her and gave her a squeeze.

ONCE THE FOOD had been consumed, a screen was dropped at the opposite end of the pub, and a montage of Pip's life played out before them. Him singing at a twenty-first birthday party, dancing and grinning at a Young Farmers' event.

'Dadda! Dadda!' Emmie squealed, her face illuminated with joy. She wriggled down from Annie's knee and toddled over to the screen, steadying herself on a stool as she looked up at his image. 'Dadda!' She pointed up at the screen, looking back at everyone.

'Oh, bubba.' Molly pressed a hand to her mouth, as tears stung her eyes. She felt her mum take her hand and give it a squeeze. Molly swallowed; this was going to be tough.

The film continued with a picture of Pip with his arm slung around Molly's shoulders when they were in their teens, them both as young parents on the moors with the twins, running around, chased by a handful of excitable dogs. There was a collective "ahhh" at the final image, which just about finished Molly off. It was of Pip stretched out on the sofa, dozing, with Emmie on his chest, sleeping contentedly.

Hearing the sob that had escaped her cousin's lips, Kitty offered to take her back home.

'It's been a long morning, Moll, and you look drained. People will start heading off soon anyway, and no one will mind if you leave.'

'She's right, Moll,' agreed Mark.

Molly nodded, swallowing down the tears that threatened. 'I'll just check with Ben and Tom to see if they want to head back, too.'

'Okay.' Kitty smiled at her before going to look for Ollie.

Molly found Annie engrossed in conversation with Vi's mum, Mary, Emmie fast asleep in her arms, oblivious to the chatter going on around her. Not wanting to disturb the baby, they agreed that Kitty would give them a lift back up when they were ready.

LATER THAT EVENING, when Molly had gone to bed, Tom and Ben sat in the kitchen, drinking beers with their Uncle Mark. Tom paid particular attention to his stories of farming Corriedale sheep in New Zealand.

'Hey, son, if you ever fancy coming over for a break, then you'd be more than welcome. You too, Ben. Your Auntie Vicky and our girls would love it,' he said. 'When things have settled here, and not both at once, of course. I couldn't do that to your mum.'

The faraway look in Tom's eyes didn't go unnoticed.

CHAPTER 16

Pip's funeral signalled a change for the family. For the twins, it felt like a burden had been lifted from their young shoulders; they were no longer in limbo, their father had been laid to rest and was now at peace. For Molly, it offered some kind of closure, though she still found it hard to believe that Pip wasn't going to walk through the door. Even little Emmie had stopped asking after him which was as much a relief as it was heart-breaking.

Hard as it was, Molly was trying to pick up the pieces and carry on for the sake of her children. But it was a different Molly who faced the world. Her feistiness had returned, something Kitty and Vi had put down to self-preservation; putting on a hard veneer meant that nothing could hurt her.

She'd had a set-back the previous evening when she'd received a visit from PC Snaith. Her heart had lurched when she opened the door to him, memories of that horrible night flooding back in a rush. He'd seemed aware of it and had been keen to alleviate her worries.

'Hi, Molly, everything's fine. I'm just calling with an update about the sheep worrying.'

'Oh.' She stood looking at him, dazed for a moment.

'Can I come in?'

'Oh, yes, yes, of course,' she said, holding the door open wide. 'I was just in the kitchen.'

He nodded and headed down the hallway.

'Can I get you a cup of tea? There's some fresh in the pot.'

'That would be nice,' he said, removing his hat and placing it on the table. 'I'm really sorry, Molly, but we've just heard back from the CPS, and they say the footage you shot isn't clear enough for them to be certain what type of dog it is. Which would make it highly unlikely they'd be able to secure a conviction.' He gave an apologetic smile.

'So you're saying they're not going to prosecute?' She handed him a mug of tea and pulled out a chair.

'Thanks. I'm afraid not.' PC Snaith shook his head.

'Bugger. So the Mellisons get away with it again,' she said with a sigh. 'What about the fire? Have you made any progress with that?'

'Same problem; lack of evidence.'

Feeling deflated, Molly flopped back into her chair. 'This is just going to add to that family's bloody smugness and superior attitude.'

'I doubt that very much. I've just come from their house after having a word with them about it. I left them in no doubt that we know who's responsible for the sheep worrying and the fire and, trust me, nobody looked smug or superior then.'

'Well, that's something, I suppose.' Relief crept in. 'They'll have denied it, I'll bet?'

'Of course, but Aoife, in particular, looked very anxious.

She was shuffling about like a cat on hot bricks. Everyone knows how perfect she wants people to think her family is, and the thought of that being thrown into doubt by the police has her running scared. She was very het up when I left.'

'Good! She deserves to be.' Molly gave a satisfied smile. 'I only wish I'd been there to see it.'

'Mmm. She's one very highly-strung woman, that's for sure. And something tells me that there's going to be no further cases of sheep worrying for a while.'

'Well, that's a relief.'

MOLLY WAS GAZING out at the moors, her thoughts drifting away from the Mellisons as her eyes began their habitual sweep for Pip, hoping to catch a glimpse of him striding over the heather in the distance, checking the bird feeders, his dogs close behind him. 'Oh, Pip,' she sighed as realisation dawned. It was going to be a hard habit to break, but it didn't seem right that he wasn't in the thick of it all. Thriving on it. Especially now that the shooting season had started with the crack of the guns, the bark of the dogs and the voices, shouting out instructions, that carried across the heather.

AS THE DAYS WENT BY, Molly paid less attention to her appearance, not caring what she looked like now that Pip wasn't here to appreciate it. Never much of a one for make-up she no longer bothered with her habitual flick of mascara or hastily applied swipe of eye-liner. And — when

she got round to washing it — she left her hair to its own
devices. Blow drying it was too much of an effort, so she let
nature to take its course, which invariably resulted in a
frizzy mop. And since the day of Pip's death, a grey streak
had appeared in her fringe. It had spread wider over the
weeks, but she didn't care.

Molly's state of mind was also reflected in her clothes. To
her, the cheerful hues of summer didn't feel appropriate,
and she shunned her usual colourful outfits. Instead, she
dug out clothes in the drab tones of a muddy puddle; shades
that reflected the way she was feeling. Vi referred to them as
widow's weeds, but not within Molly's earshot.

Concerned, Kitty and Vi would do their best to cheer
her up. They'd called up one dank and rainy afternoon
armed with chocolate dipped flapjack and the intention of
adding a little bit of brightness to Molly's day. Vi caught
Kitty's eye. 'Hey, do you remember when our fellas dressed
up as a girl pop band for that Young Farmers charity event
in the nineties? Along with your Mark, Moll, and one of his
mates from school at Middleton.'

'Oh, don't remind us, Vi.' Kitty said with a giggle. 'Jimby
was not a pretty sight. Those fake boobs he'd stuffed down
his top that ended up somewhere round his ears. And as for
his chicken legs...'

'No, he definitely didn't have the legs to rock a skin-tight,
leopard-print body-suit,' snorted Violet.

'Oh, yeah, that body-suit. Who on earth round here
owned such a thing?' asked Molly mustering a watery
smile.

'Maneater. She even offered to take his inside leg
measurements to make sure it would fit him,' Kitty replied
with a wince.

'Bloody hell.' Molly pulled a face.

'And he was only, what? Seventeen? She hasn't changed, has she?' Vi said in disgust.

'No, she bloody hasn't, the mucky old bag,' said Molly.

'Anyway, from what I remember, true to form, old Jimbo took a tumble off the stage and landed right in her lap, didn't he?' Vi chipped in, giggling.

Molly's eyes brightened. 'Oh my God, that's right. She asked if he was giving her a lap-dance, didn't she?'

'I'd forgotten about that. She did, and I can honestly say I've never seen Jimby move so fast in my life. Which was impressive considering he was wearing platform trainers that were about five sizes too small.' Kitty's eyes twinkled at the memory.

'Oh, poor old Jimby,' Vi chuckled. 'And Ollie wasn't much better looking, was he? Lytell Stangdale really wasn't ready to see such scraggy, hairy legs in a mini-dress. But Mark thought he was hot to trot, do you remember? Pouting away and flicking that wig all over the place, he was.'

'Oh, don't.' Molly grinned. 'He flicked it so much it ended up flying off and landing in the face of the old vicar's wife. She just about jumped out of her skin. It was so funny.'

'Oh, yeah. I don't think I've ever heard anyone scream so loud. She told Mum later that she thought it was a rat landing on her!' Kitty said between giggles.

'And the old vicar had really bad eyesight, even with his specs on. He kept taking them off and wiping them, then trying to adjust them, because he didn't realise that it was a group of daft lads up there on the stage and not lasses.' Molly's shoulders were shaking with mirth.

'Oh, my God, yes.' Kitty wiped tears of laughter from her eyes.

'Urghh, don't remind me. I always thought he was secretly a bit of a perv.' Vi shuddered at the memory.

'The best was Pip, though. He excelled himself with those high kicks and cartwheels.' Kitty added. 'We all wondered where he'd got the energy from.'

'His performance wasn't exactly what you'd call smooth, though, was it? Especially when he accidentally kicked Jimby in the nuts and Mark's friend up the backside,' chipped in Vi. 'But it was hilarious.'

'Oh, it was. Their performance has become the stuff of Lytell Stangdale legend.' Molly sighed and smiled, looking across the table at her friends. Momentarily the room seemed brighter. The sadness that had slumped like a heavy, cloying fog had lifted. And, for once, Molly's throat didn't feel as tight as if holding back sobs. She took a deep breath. 'Thanks, lasses.'

'What for?' asked Vi

'For making me think happy thoughts for a few minutes. For chasing away the sadness.'

Kitty squeezed her cousin's hand. 'That's what friends and family are for, chick.'

Despite her friends' efforts, Molly continued to hide herself away, favouring supermarket home deliveries over popping down to the local shop or nipping over to Middleton. She'd been a stranger in the pub, too, declining offers of joining the others for a drink.

Though the family unit was healing and moving on in tiny steps, Molly made sure the boys knew that it was okay to talk about their father; she didn't want them to think that they had to tread on eggshells around her, never daring to mention his name. She was sensitive to their grief, too. Ben's girlfriend, Kristy, had been a godsend to him, offering support, listening when he needed to talk, comforting him and being a shoulder to cry on when he needed to cry. It was Tom that caused Molly the most concern. He was the quieter of her boys and, although she knew he talked to his brother, and he talked openly about Pip, she still couldn't shake the feeling that something else was bothering him. She'd talk to him, see if she could find out what was responsible for that troubled look. But not yet. It was still too soon.

CHAPTER 17

It was the second week in October and time had dragged painfully slowly since the day Molly had said goodbye to Pip. But that morning she'd woken early, feeling different. Brighter, almost. The heaviness in her heart had shifted a little, making it easier to breath. With a sigh, she pulled on her dressing gown, glancing over at Pip's side of the bed, as she did each morning, and headed over to the window. Pushing back the curtains, she smiled at the sight spread out before her: the moors were swathed in an ethereal mist and dew glittered on filigree spiders' webs as daylight peered over the rigg. Autumn — or back-end, as it was known in Yorkshire — had arrived, transforming the moors with its mellow sunlight and sumptuous shades of russets and golds. It was Molly's favourite season; she loved the idea of the nights drawing in, getting cosy in front of the fire, a casserole bubbling away gently in the Aga, a brace of pheasants hanging on the wall by the door. Well, that's how it had been when Pip was still there.

Her first autumn without Pip. *Another first*, she thought to herself. She felt her throat tighten and she quickly swallowed down the lump of sadness that had found its way there. 'Pull yourself together, Molly,' she whispered to herself. She wasn't going to wallow; Pip wouldn't want that. He'd want her to make the most of feeling a tiny glimmer of hope. She was a doer; she wasn't the sort of person who sat around feeling sorry for herself and today, she decided when she opened her eyes, she was going to get on with the work on the camp site in honour of his memory. She'd put it on hold since Pip had passed away; it had been too painful to face any decisions without him or tackle the projects he'd been so excited about.

Pushing her feet into her slippers, Molly tiptoed downstairs and padded into the kitchen where she was greeted by Phoebe. 'Morning, Phoebes.' She ruffled the Labrador's velvety ears, yawning as she made her way over to the door and let her out into the yard.

'Tea,' she said quietly to herself, picking up the kettle, and heading over to the Belfast sink to fill it before sitting it on the Aga hotplate.

As she waited for the kettle to boil, Pip's waxed jacket caught her eye from its peg in the porch. She'd have to go through his stuff soon, sort it, give it to charity. Would it seem like she was throwing him away? she wondered. No, it wasn't like that, every time she opened the wardrobe door, seeing his clothes hanging there, was a painful reminder that *he* wasn't, she reasoned. But she couldn't hang on to them forever, much as she'd like to. It wouldn't be an easy task. Maybe she should do it bit-by-bit, when she felt strong enough.

'Morning, Mum.' Her thoughts were interrupted by Ben. 'What's for breakfast?' He was up early to help with a few farm jobs before he went off to college.

'Whatever you fancy, love. Fry-up, scrambled eggs, porridge?'

'Fry-up would be great, thanks. It's getting chilly on a morning. I'll just go and check on grandad's Chevvies, then I'll have my breakfast, if that's okay?' He smiled at her. He was looking a little brighter, too, she thought. Just the previous evening, he'd been talking about Kristy, and she could tell by his expression he was very taken with her. In fact, the more Molly got to know the young girl, the more she liked her, too.

'Sounds like a good plan.' She smiled back at him. 'Any sign of your brother up there?'

'Aye, there were movements from his room. S'pect he'll be down any minute.' Ben shoved his feet into his wellies and pulled on a fleece. 'Won't be long.'

Molly blew her hair back from her face and eased herself up from the armchair. She'd make enough breakfast for both boys; once Tom got a whiff of a fry-up, there's no way he'd want anything else. It felt good to be cooking for them again; setting her family up for the day. It was a positive sign. She hadn't had that feeling since before Pip had died.

SHE'D JUST FINISHED SERVING up the bacon when Emmie's cries drifted downstairs, no doubt as a response to the smell of cooking wafting its way up to her; Emmie had developed a hearty appetite.

Molly set the frying pan onto a trivet by the Aga. 'Coming, bubba,' she called.

'Mamma! Mamma! Becksa!'

'We'd better get our grub down us before Emmie the Appetite sees it and wants it.' Ben laughed.

'Aye, she eats more than you. And you're a right skuttle-gob.' Tom grinned, giving his brother a nudge.

Back in the warmth of the kitchen, Molly sat Emmie in her highchair and pushed a beaker of milk into her outstretched hand. 'So, what are your plans for today, Tom?' she asked, whipping up some fresh eggs in a jug for scrambling for Emmie.

She didn't miss the exchanged glances between her boys. Ben coughed and looked down at his plate.

'Well, I was going to run it by you first,' Tom said, shifting uneasily in his seat, 'but I was thinking of having a look at that gipsy caravan, see if I could get cracking on it.' The tone of his voice told her he was testing the water.

Molly looked at her sons who were both observing her intently, expressions of hopefulness in their eyes. She put the jug on the work top. 'You know what, lads, I think that sounds like a great idea.' A smile inched its way across her face as she put her hands on her hips. 'I was thinking the very same thing myself when I woke up this morning. 'We need to pick things up again, your dad would want us to.' She smiled, a tentative feeling of optimism blooming in her chest.

'Really, Mum?' said Tom.

'Really, son.' She felt her smile grow wider. 'Why don't we get it up to the yard later this morning, so we can have a proper look around it? I'd quite like to have a hand in working on it myself. I can't keep wallowing; your dad would hate that; you know how busy he always was. We need to make the most of the good days when we have them. And it's time I made myself busy again.'

'Wow, that's great, Mum! We've been thinking of it for a

couple of weeks but didn't want to upset you or make you feel like we were pushing you into it.' Ben looked relieved that she'd taken his brother's suggestion so well. 'I just feel like I have to keep busy, keep my mind occupied.'

'Me, too.' Tom nodded.

'Mamma! Becksa!' shouted Emmie, indignantly, pointing at the jug and looking annoyed when everyone laughed.

'I'm on it, little one,' said Molly.

'Right,' said Tom, his chair scraping against the flag-stones as he pushed it back. 'No time like the present. I'm going to call Uncle Jimby and see if he and Ollie can give me a hand bringing the vardo up to the yard, so we can get stuck in to it, Mother.' He grinned, rubbing his hands together.

'Good for you, son,' she said giving the eggs another quick whisking.

Ben checked his watch. 'Bloomin' 'eck. And, I'd better get going, or I'll miss the bus to college.'

A shaft of sunlight reached in through the window and spread across the walls, making Molly's heart lift. She breathed in a lungful of air and smiled. To her mind, it was a sign from Pip, pleased that his family were gradually heal-ing, making plans and moving on.

MOLLY HAD JUST FINISHED POPPING things into a bag ready to drop Emmie off at her Mum's, when she heard the trundle of a Landie making its way up the farm track. She scooped Emmie up onto her hip and headed outside, where they watched, squinting in the bright autumn sunshine, as Jimby's Landie carefully nosed its way into the yard, the vardo on a trailer behind it, scattering Delores and her cronies, who clucked noisily.

Phoebe gave a bark and trotted over to it, tail wagging happily when the three men jumped out, sniffing round their legs with interest.

'Now then, Moll,' Jimby called over to her, one of his customary smiles lighting up his face.

'Hiya, Molly,' said Ollie.

'Hi, lads. Thanks for this, we really appreciate it,' she called back, smiling and brushing a handful of stray curls out of her eyes. 'Blimey, it's warm out here.'

'Aye, no probs. We're just happy to help. And you're right, it's bloomin' scorchio for October.' Jimby headed round to the trailer, unfastening the ropes that tethered the caravan to it.

'If you could just pop the vardo over there, in the shade, that'd be great. That way, the sun won't dry the paint-stripper out too quickly.'

'Yep, that's fine,' said Ollie. 'Then I'll get measured up so I can set about making a new wheel for her straight away. I can't wait to see what you're going to do with her, but if the train carriage is anything to go by, she'll be amazing. She's a real beauty, Moll.'

She headed over to them. 'Thanks, Oll. She is a beauty; I'd forgotten just how good she looks,' she replied softly, thinking how much Pip had been looking forward to restoring it. She felt the threat of tears and swallowed.

'Dat!' cried Emmie, pointing a pudgy finger at it, lightening the moment and giving Molly a chance to compose herself.

'Dat!' replied Jimby, ruffling her hair. 'You get cuter by the day little Emmie Pennock.'

'Aye, she does. And she'll soon have a little playmate,

won't you, Em?' Ollie chucked her under the chin, his blonde hair glinting in the sunshine. There was no hiding just how thrilled he was at the prospect of becoming a dad again.

'We're looking forward to it, aren't we, bubba?' Molly jigged Emmie on her hip.

'Same here, it'll give her someone else to boss around, instead of Ben and me,' Tom added good-naturedly as he wound the ropes up and put them to one side.

Jimby stood back, hands on hips and a mischievous glint in his eye. 'Can't think where she gets her bossiness from.'

'Watch it, buster.' Molly smiled, delivering a playful backhander to his arm. 'Right, I'm just going to pop Em down to my mum's; she said she'd have her for the day while I make a start on the vardo. But I promise to make a pot of tea when I get back.'

'I'll hold you to that.' Jimby grinned as he wiped the back of his hand across his forehead.

Back inside the house, Molly was glad to have a moment to herself, feeling slightly overwhelmed by the feelings that had resurfaced, an image of Pip's animated face the day he turned up with the caravan dominating her mind. A vardo was one of the first projects they'd talked about in the early days of planning their campsite. And she could tell by the way Jimby and Ollie looked at her that concern was never far from their thoughts. She wished it wasn't that way; she didn't want anyone to feel sorry for her or treat her differently, but she still couldn't make her face form a proper, full-on smile that reached her eyes. If she was honest, she couldn't ever imagine being able to do that again. Life was still going on, but the colours were muted, and happiness had had its edges knocked off.

WHEN MOLLY RETURNED to the yard, the three men were stood in deep discussion, admiring the vardo which was now off the trailer and positioned in the far corner, just as she'd asked. She noted they'd removed the damaged wheel and put a prop in its place. They didn't hang around. She was glad to be more in control of her feelings, having given herself a good talking to. There was no way she was going to back out of this, she'd told herself, reminding herself of the hopeful expressions of her boys earlier that morning. Yes, it was only a couple of months since that horrible day, but for her kids' sake she had to keep going; after all, that's exactly what they were doing.

As soon as she stepped out of her car, Jimby made a cup of tea gesture, making her chuckle. 'Two ticks,' she called across heading towards the house.

WITH CUPS of tea over and done with, and Ollie's promise of getting started on a new wheel pronto, Molly and Tom found themselves alone.

'If it's okay with you, I'm going to head into Middleton-le-Moors to pick up some woodworm treatment from Shackleton's; I noticed the vardo had a few woodworm holes and it looks like it might be active.'

'Oh, that's a shame,' she replied, stacking the mugs in the dishwasher and closing the door. 'Well, while you're doing that, I think I'll get started on stripping all the old paint off the exterior. That water-based stuff's great, and it doesn't burn your skin either. Though, I think I'm going to need loads of it, so maybe you could grab another tub from

Shackleton's while you're there.' She picked up her purse from the dresser, pulled out a couple of notes and handed them to Tom.

'Thanks, Mum.' He pushed the money into his wallet. 'You going to be okay while I'm gone?' The concern in his eyes was enough to break her heart.

'Course I am. Now you go and get to Middleton; the sooner you go, the sooner you get back and can get stuck into that caravan.' He was still looking at her, and she smiled at him. 'Really, Tom. I'm fine. Go!'

'Okay.' He smiled back and grabbed his car keys from the meat hook by the door. 'Won't be long.'

Molly watched him leave, wondering when he'd tell her what was going on in his mind. He was grieving, just like the rest of them, but she still couldn't shake that niggling feeling that something else was troubling him. And she had an inkling what it might be. After all, he didn't really need to pick up any woodworm treatment today, she'd need to strip the old paint off before he could use that – and that was going to take a good couple of days. There was clearly something else tempting him to Middleton. Hopefully, he'd tell her in his own time.

She changed into the old jeans and t-shirt she'd rooted out that would do for decorating and, taking the bobble she had round her wrist, she twisted her hair into a loose topknot, thinking that it hadn't taken long for it to get unruly. She then scooped up her paint-stripping tools and headed for the yard, Phoebe trotting behind her, never far away.

Before she started daubing paint-stripper everywhere, Molly couldn't resist the temptation to peer inside; she hadn't looked at it properly since the day Pip had arrived home with it. The door opened with a groan and a fusty smell hit her nose, making her sneeze. Carefully, she stepped into the tiny space, taking in the built-in bed with the cupboard below at the far end, the tiny window above it — its glass long-since gone — the seating area at the right and the little black stove to the left. Everything was constructed with such care and attention to detail that every inch was used to the maximum. It was utterly intriguing. 'Oh, Pip, I can see why you were so taken with this,' she said to herself as her eye landed on something that prodded at a long-forgotten memory. On the wall above the bed was an intricate wooden carving of two initials, an "M" and a "C", set against a background of curling tendrils. Molly went to look closer. The paint might have been worn and faded, but it was still clear to see that it had been painted with a delicate hand. And she'd definitely seen it, or something like it, before. She rooted round her mind to remember, but it remained, frustratingly, out of reach. With a sigh, she climbed out of the vardo and set to work, the initials niggling her all the while.

By the time Tom had returned home, Molly had covered the entire exterior of the vardo in paint-stripper and covered it in cling-film, as per the pot's instructions. She was just heading back to the house when he drove into the yard. It prompted the thought that she hadn't noticed any evidence of woodworm in the caravan. But seeing her son looking so upbeat, she decided against saying anything for the minute.

She thought she'd make life easier for him. 'I'm afraid there's not a lot you can do with the caravan today; the entire outside is absolutely covered in paint-stripper, and it needs to be left on overnight.'

'Oh, right.' He glanced across at it and laughed. 'I see what you mean.'

'It's already started to bubble, so I should be able to

scrape it tomorrow, then if you think it needs treating, you can get to work with the woodworm stuff.'

'Ahh, that.' He scratched his head, looking sheepish.

'Oh?'

'I forgot to pick some up.'

'Right,' Molly said slowly, trying to read her son's face. He looked torn, like he wanted to tell her something, but didn't know quite how. 'Look, why don't I stick the kettle on and we can have a cuppa?'

'Yep. Sounds like a plan.'

Inside, as Molly filled the kettle and set a couple of mugs on the table, she couldn't help but notice that Tom looked like his mind was wrestling with something. He was playing with his phone and sighing. When he eventually sat at the table, his legs bounced, and his fingers drummed on its surface.

'So, are you going to tell me what's bugging you?' Molly asked as she poured the tea, pushing a mug towards him, and changing her mind about not broaching the subject.

'What d'you mean?' He looked up, surprised.

'Well, you go to Middleton-le-Moors on the pretext of buying some woodworm treatment — that, incidentally, we don't need, there's not a trace of a woodworm infestation anywhere — then you come home without it, and when we get inside, you're fidgeting like you've got ants in your pants.'

She could see him struggling with what to say. He slumped into his chair and sighed. 'Oh, Mum.'

She placed her hand on his. 'What is it, Tom? Please tell me. I'm worried about you, I feel that you've had something on your mind for so long. Long before your dad...well, you know.'

He nodded. 'I know, and you're right, I have had something on my mind, and I didn't know how to tell you both. Didn't want you to be disappointed in me.'

'I could never be disappointed in you, son, no matter what it is you want to tell me. And I know your dad would feel the same.' She gave his hand a squeeze.

A frown gathered his brow together, and he swallowed, making his Adam's apple bob up and down.

'Is it the farm? Do you want to do something different? If it is, we can always think of ways around it. I don't want you to feel that you have to work here.'

He shook his head, knotting his fingers together. 'It's not the farm, Mum.'

Molly pressed her lips together and smiled. 'I didn't think it was, Tom. But, whatever it is, I'll be okay with it,' she said gently, watching as he took a deep breath.

'I'm in love,' he said, not looking at her.

'Well, that's wonderful news!' She felt her heart lift.

'Is it?'

'Well, of course it is! Being in love is...' She paused, taking in Tom's tortured expression. 'Being in love is the best thing in the wo...'

'I'm in love with another man, Mum. I'm gay. I'm sorry.' He looked at her with anguish in his large brown eyes.

'Oh, sweetheart. First things first, don't ever apologise for being you; being gay is most definitely nothing to be sorry about. And, actually, I already knew, son. I've known for quite a while.' She moved across and put her arm around him. 'And I'm over the moon that you've found someone.'

Relief washed over Tom's face. 'Really? How long have you known? Did Dad know? Did someone tell you?'

Molly laughed and rubbed his cheek. 'Your dad and I had a couple of conversations about it — and he was totally fine with it, by the way, and, like me, he wanted you to be happy, and not feel you had to bottle it up. We both hoped you'd soon be ready to share it with us, in the way that Ben could share his news about Kristy. And, nobody told us. To be honest, I'm not quite sure how we knew. Mother's intuition, I guess. But, once I'd mentioned it to your dad, he thought I was right.'

Tom rubbed his brow. 'Shit! I had no idea. And Dad was really okay with it?'

'Of course, why wouldn't he be? You, Ben and Emmie were his world, and all he ever wanted was for you to be happy. He was so proud of you, Tom, the way you stepped up to jobs on the farm, taking them in your stride. He was always singing your praises, ask Grandma and Grampy.' Molly smiled at the memory of the conversations with Pip, his eyes shining. 'And he'd be proud of you now, being open about your feelings.'

'Yep, I'm out of the closet now, Mum,' he said with a wry smile.

Molly laughed, feeling relief that her son had finally opened up. 'So, are you going to tell me about him then? And when are we going to get to meet the man in question?'

'Wow! Well, this conversation's a whole lot easier than I was expecting. Erm, he's eighteen, same as me, and his family farm over at Arkleby. Low Beck Farm, to be precise.' He glanced across at her.

Molly was aware of her brain slowly computing the information. 'What? Eighteen? Low Beck…that's Mortimer's farm, so it must be… Adam? Adam Mortimer?'

'Yep.' He nodded, a small smile tugging at the corners of his mouth.

'Oh, Tom. He's a lovely lad, always has been. And you two got on like a house on fire at playgroup. You were inseparable.'

'I know, I remember. I was gutted he had to go to Danskelfe Primary and couldn't come to school in the village here.'

'You were. Well, I couldn't be happier for you.' She gave his shoulder a squeeze, sitting up straight as a thought suddenly crossed her mind. 'Do his parents know?' Molly was familiar with them both, though they were a good ten years older than her and Pip. Sue, his mum, she thought would take it well, but his father, Garth, she wasn't so sure.

'No, not yet. He thinks his mum'll be okay, but he's worried about telling his dad.'

'Mmm. Garth can be a bit of a funny one, but you never know.' Garth, she recalled, could be a bit of a loose cannon with strong opinions, especially when he'd had a drink, but she kept it to herself. She didn't want to worry her son.

'Does Ben know?'

'Erm, I'm not sure. I haven't mentioned it to him directly but judging by some of the things he's said recently, I think he's guessed.' Tom nibbled at the corner of his mouth.

'Okay.' Molly nodded. 'Well, how about inviting Adam here for dinner one night? So I can get to meet him properly? After all, I haven't had a proper conversation with him since he was about four and a half and this high.' She held out her hand to demonstrate.

Tom laughed. 'He's a bit taller than that now, and it would be so cool if he could come over, if you're sure?'

'Of course, I'm sure. It would be just like Ben bringing Kristy home to meet us.'

Tom looked like he'd had the weight of the world lifted off his shoulders. He reached across and pulled Molly into a tight hug, kissing her noisily on the cheek. 'Did anyone ever tell you, you're the best mum in the world?'

'Not often enough,' she laughed.

'Well, you are. And thank you for making that so easy for me. I've been stressing for ages how to tell you. Then when Dad, well...I thought I couldn't say anything and it's been eating me away.' As he spoke a text pinged through on his phone. He picked it up and beamed. 'It's Adam.'

Seeing happiness light up her son's face made Molly's heart squeeze. 'Well, go on then, get him over here for some nosh. Oh, and before I forget to ask, are we not keeping this secret anymore? I mean, can we talk about it to Ben and the rest of the family?'

Tom thought for a moment, tapping his mobile against his mouth. 'I s'pose so, yeah. What do you think?'

'It's your call, but my honest opinion is that I don't think you should hide your feelings away, and I think you should feel okay to be you, son.' She smiled gently at him.

He looked at her intently for a moment. 'Hell, Mother, you're right. I'd better go and talk to Adam, see if he's okay with it.' With that, he shot off to his bedroom.

For the first time since Pip had passed away, Molly felt herself smile properly. Seeing their son look so happy and animated when he spoke about being in love warmed her heart. Her lovely, quiet, gentle boy had fallen in love, and she was overjoyed for him. It was just a shame Pip wasn't here to share it. He would have been glad that Tom felt he could talk to them.

Her mind moved on to Adam's parents, and a shadow crossed her face as she thought of Garth. Something told her he wasn't going to take things quite so well. Images from her memory began to play out, of Garth giving someone a beating at a Young Farmers' rally, of always mouthing off in the Fox and Hounds at Danskelfe after too much beer. If there was trouble, you could guarantee he was at the centre of it. He was a bombastic macho man who had an axe to grind with anyone whose face didn't fit. For a fleeting moment, Molly felt worried for Tom.

She finished her tea and looked at her watch, it was quarter-past one, she still had a good few hours before she needed to collect Emmie from her mum's. She'd rustle up a quick lunch then maybe make a start on sorting out some of Pip's things in his wardrobe – if she felt up to it when she got upstairs.

CHAPTER 18

With Tom out busy on the farm, Molly made her way to her bedroom. It was stuffy, and the sun was shining brightly, capturing the dust motes that hovered in its rays. She threw open the old sash windows, allowing fresh air and bird song to pour into the room. Taking a deep breath, she turned to face the wall of built-in wardrobes. She stood, frozen to the spot for a moment or two, her mind in conflict. Hanging on to Pip's clothes wasn't going to bring him back, she knew that. But was it too soon to get rid of them? Would it feel like she was throwing all trace of him out? Would people think she was cold and heartless, that she couldn't wait to get rid of him? She didn't know the answer to any of those questions. She'd asked her mum's opinion this morning and her advice had been that she'd know when the time was right. But that hadn't helped. The calendar told her that Pip had been gone for a mere two months but, to Molly, it had felt like a long, drawn-out forever. She couldn't see that changing any time soon. But what she did feel certain of was that putting off this day wasn't going to make the job any easier. And her gut was telling her that it was stopping her from moving on. It was one of the things that kept her awake at night, tormenting her that she'd have to face it sometime and she knew that the sooner she faced it, the better. She gave herself a shake; today was the day. She was feeling brighter and stronger. She was feeling ready. Kitty and Vi had offered to help her with it when the time came, but this was a job she wanted to do on her own. Alone, with her memories of her Pip.

She blew out her cheeks and pushed up her sleeves. 'Right, Pip, love, this isn't going to be easy,' she said to herself. 'But let's get started.' She reached in and unhooked his favourite checked shirt from the rail — the one she was always nagging him to get rid of. He'd had it for donkey's years and the moss green and purple fabric was threadbare in places, and missing a button from one of the cuffs, but he'd loved it. Slowly, she undid the buttons, eased it off the hanger and held the soft, brushed cotton fabric to her face. She breathed in deeply, inhaling the comforting, evocative essence of Pip. This was one item she wasn't ready to part with. She felt her throat constrict and tears burn her eyes. She sniffed. 'Stop it, Molly,' she snapped at herself, quickly swiping the tears away; she refused to give in to them today, especially when she'd been doing so well.

After giving herself a stern talking-to, Molly carried on, not stopping to think, lifting Pip's clothes out, folding them and putting them into bin bags ready to be taken to the Air Ambulance clothing bank. That's where Pip would want them to go. And that's what Molly wanted, too, after all they'd done for him. But she'd left his tweeds — his pride and joy — she wasn't ready to part with them yet, either. The sight of them had triggered a fresh wave of tears, but she'd swallowed them down, put the clothes back in the suit carrier and hung them back on the rail.

With all the clothing from the wardrobe sorted, Molly moved on to the drawers. Continuing with the same focus, she finished in no time. It was when she paused that the emotion of what she'd done caught up with her. She sat on the edge of the bed and before she knew it, tears were streaming down her cheeks and her body was wracked with sobs. Feeling absolutely drained, she lay down, resting her head on the pillow, fighting the urge to close her eyes. But she was exhausted and her eyelids were too heavy. In a matter of seconds, Molly had drifted into a deep sleep.

She was awoken by the sound of the landline ringing. She lay still, listening, slowly coming to, as the answer phone kicked in — it sounded like Kitty's friendly voice leaving a message. Molly rubbed sleep away from her eyes and looked at the alarm clock on the bedside table. 'Oh, bugger,' she groaned; she'd been asleep for a good hour, but it felt like she'd only had her eyes closed for a few minutes. Her head felt fuggy, too, almost like she'd got a hangover. Still feeling disorientated, Molly heaved herself up, pushed herself off the bed and made her way downstairs into the kitchen where she was greeted by an enthusiastic Phoebe who sprang from her bed, wagging her tail as if her life depended upon it. 'Hiya, Phoebes. Have you been sleeping, too?' Molly bent to rub the Labrador's head.

She trudged over to the kettle; cup of tea first, then she'd call Kitty back. Her mouth felt like the bottom of a bird cage, and she suspected she'd been doing a bout of the snoring that Pip used to accuse her of — which she always denied.

She'd just settled down with her tea when the phone rang again. 'Bloody hell, is there no peace?' Molly grumbled, padding across the kitchen.

'Hiya, Molly. I was just calling to see how you were

doing,' said Kitty. Though she sounded bright, Molly could still detect a trace of concern in her voice.

'I'm fine, thanks, Kitts. Just had a snooze.' Her voice still sounded raspy, Kitty would probably think she'd been drinking or shouting, both lent a gravelly tone to it.

'Oh, right. Well, would you like me to pop up and give you a hand with anything? Auntie Annie said you'd planned on, well, she told me what you were doing this afternoon, and I didn't want you to think you had to do it on your own, chick.'

Molly took a sip of her tea and cleared her throat. 'Thanks, Kitty, but I'm actually okay. I've got Pip's wardrobe sorted out, which wasn't as tough as I thought it was going to be, but I just came over feeling absolutely knackered and ended up falling asleep on the bed. I'm still not fully awake,' she said with a yawn.

'You must've needed it, I can remember when Mum and Dad, well, you know, it made Jimby and me feel absolutely jiggered, sorting everything out. And I just want you to know that you can shout up if you need some company. Mind you, I'm not so sure I'd be much use; I'd forgotten how tired being pregnant can make you feel. All I seem to want to do at the moment is nod off. Honestly, I can fall asleep anywhere.'

'Ah, yes, I can remember that with Em, well, that and stuffing my face with biscuits, d'you remember?'

'Oh, Moll, how could we forget that?' The warmth in her cousin's voice made Molly smile.

'I s'pose you do have a point. I was on four packets a day at the height of my cravings.'

'And the rest,' Kitty said with a giggle.

'Point taken.' Molly had actually lost track of how many packets she'd consumed in a day. 'Right, well, I've still got a while before my mum brings Em home, so I'm going to get back to it, Kitts. But thanks for ringing, I don't know what I'd do without you, hun.'

'Right back at you, Moll. It's not so long ago that you and Vi had my back and I won't ever forget how much that meant to me. Just holler if you need anything, petal.'

'Will do.'

'Right, Phoebes, time to get back to it.' Molly stood up and took her empty mug over to the sink, giving it a rinse out. She gave her habitual glance out of the kitchen window, looking for a glimpse of Pip on the moor top, sighing as she remembered. Despite the tragedy that had happened out there a couple of months ago, and though the heather had faded, the land was still looking beautiful, and the warm shades of autumn were doing a convincing job of hiding the cruel bleakness the moors were capable of.

Feeling her mood dip, she pulled herself away from the window. 'Stop it, Molly.' She checked her watch. There was still a good hour before she needed to go for Emmie. Her side of the wardrobe had looked like it could do with a good sort out, too. She pursed her lips together. 'Well, there's no time like the present,' she muttered to herself, unwinding a bin-bag.

WITH THE RAIL SORTED, it was now time to tackle the shoe boxes at the bottom. Why did she ever think she needed so many pairs?

At the back, behind the box containing her wedding shoes, was an old box she kept for mementos — she hadn't looked inside for a while, years in fact. The gift paper she'd wrapped it in when she was sixteen was torn at the corners and held together by years' worth of dried-out sticky-tape. Molly made herself comfortable on the floor, resting the box on her lap. She went to remove the elastic band that kept the lid in place, but it had perished and disintegrated as soon as she touched it. A mixture of emotions bubbled under the surface as she slid the lid off. Her heart lurched as she lifted out a folded piece of paper, dog-eared and slightly crumpled; it was the advert for the Young Farmers' Christmas Party where Pip had first asked her to dance. She smiled at the memory of him with his floppy, boy-band fringe, his self-conscious dancing. How her heart had somersaulted when he walked across to speak to her.

Next was a paper napkin, complete with food stains. One stain in particular was circled and the words "yummiest steak ever" was written beside it in Molly's girly hand, with the date written in Pip's. It was from a restaurant in the Lakes where they'd gone on honeymoon. Her parents had paid for them to have a long-weekend away after they were married, while they looked after the twins for them. They'd booked it as a surprise and given it to them as a wedding present. Molly smiled; they'd felt so grown-up, but so out of their depth at the same time.

Her hand fell onto a small teddy bear that Pip had won for her at the amusements in Whitby on a day out before the twins had come along. They'd mooched about the old cobbled streets of the Shambles, arm in arm, eating wisps of sugary candy-floss, admiring the goths in their spectacular outfits, as seagulls wheeled and cried overhead. Pip had talked her into going into a Dracula exhibition and had laughed at her when she'd squealed with fright at the "vampires" who'd silently stepped out of the shadows. Afterwards, they'd enjoyed takeaway fish and chips, devouring them on the pier, gazing out to sea. The memory was so vivid, Molly could almost taste the vinegar that had dripped off the chips.

Underneath the teddy was a strip of photos they'd had taken in the instant photo booth. In one, Pip was pulling a face while Molly was kissing his cheek. In another, she was striking a serious pose, while he was making rabbit ears with his fingers at the back of her head. But in all of them, there was no mistaking the pure happiness in their eyes. She ran her fingers over the image of his face. He was so handsome with his unusual almond-shaped eyes, he'd attracted plenty of admiring glances from other girls that day, but he only had eyes for her. With his arm flung posses- sively around her shoulders, pressing kisses onto the top of her head as they walked along, Molly had felt like she was the luckiest girl in the world.

She sighed and placed the photos back in the box. Next, her eyes landed on a small scrap of intricately worked silver that appeared to be broken in half. She picked it up, removing the fluff from it, and turned it over in her palm. It triggered a flashback to when she was fifteen, when she'd come to the rescue of a young gipsy boy who'd been on the receiving end of a vicious beating from a couple of thugs. He'd given her this, called it a talisman, if she remembered rightly. Her mind conjured up a hazy memory of his hand- some young face, the glossy, dark curls and inky black eyes that had twinkled at her. He hadn't crossed her mind for years. 'What was his name? It began with a "C". 'Connor? Callum? Chris? Nope.' She couldn't remember. 'I wonder what you're doing with your life now?' she murmured.

As Molly examined the talisman more closely, her heart began to pound. Was it just her imagination, or did it look familiar? She smoothed her fingers over it; she'd definitely seen this somewhere before, and recently, too. She closed her eyes trying to grasp hold of the wisps of an image that was taunting her mind. She pressed her hand to her mouth as realisation hit her with a bolt.

She ran downstairs, slipped on her wellies and hurried out into the yard, heading towards the vardo. Being careful to avoid any paint stripper, she eased the door open and climbed inside, making her way towards the far end. She held the talisman against the carving above the bed. 'Wow!' she gasped. It was a perfect match.

Her mind was racing; what did this mean? She was sure that the other half of the talisman contained the initial "M". This was too weird. Had the vardo belonged to the gipsy boy's family? She had a vague memory of him telling her that he was named after his grandfather and that the talisman had originally belonged to him. And he'd told her that his grandmother was called something beginning with "M". What was it now? She pressed her lips together as she tried to remember. But it was too far at the back of her mind to reach and get a hold of. What she could remember, though, was how her heart had beat fast that day, when the handsome gipsy boy had kissed her. As she remembered his parting words, that one day the talisman would bring him back to her, Molly shivered, this was way too spooky — and uncomfortably disloyal to Pip.

With thoughts bouncing around inside her head, she made her way back to the farmhouse, turning the talisman between her fingers as she went. Why did she have to find this now, of all times? She hadn't looked in that bloody box for years. It was weird — no doubt even more so, if she voiced the words aloud, which was something she wasn't going to do — but it almost felt like someone was trying to tell her something. And she didn't like it, not one little bit. It was too confusing, and she didn't believe in all of that psychic rubbish anyway. It was all good and well that Kitty's mum had sent her signs, but her cousin was open to that kind of thing, she was more spiritual than her. She, Molly, just didn't believe in all that bollocks. All of this initial, talisman business was just her grief's way of making her think things were okay. But it wasn't going to bring Pip back, was it? And that's what it would take to make her think things were going to be alright.

Inside the house, she made her way to her bedroom and dropped the talisman back into the memory box, before packing it away at the back of the wardrobe once more. Out of sight, out of mind, she reasoned as she scooped up the bulging bin bags and headed downstairs.

Molly sighed to herself as she placed the last of the bags in the utility room. It had been tough, but she'd done it. She'd crossed a painful hurdle and had sorted through her lovely Pip's stuff. 'Right, time to go for Em, then think about what to do for dinner,' she said to herself, resisting the pull of her aching heart to bring her spirits down. She grabbed her keys and left the house.

CHAPTER 19

'Food's up!' Molly called out into the farmyard where the twins were tinkering about with the Landie.

She headed back into the kitchen and took the large casserole dish out of the Aga. As she was setting it down on the table, the twins burst in through the back door, kicking off their wellies, engrossed in conversation.

'Whoar! That smells wicked.' Ben wandered into the kitchen, sniffing the air.

'Mmm. Dumplings as well.' Tom beamed and made his way over to the sink to wash his hands after Ben. He was still looking happier than Molly had seen him look for a long time.

'Tom-Tom! Bem! Dindin!' squealed Emmie to her brothers, pointing at the stew and smiling broadly. She was such an easy child to feed. Apart from cucumber, there wasn't anything she wouldn't eat.

'Yep, Em, it's din-din, alright. And I think I'm as hungry as you.' Tom ruffled his sister's curls.

'Ey up, Em, are you hungry again? You're worse than Tom-Tom, aren't you?'

'Tom-Tom,' she cooed, banging her spoon against the table of her high chair.

Molly laughed, as she lifted the plates out of the Aga's warming oven and started to set them out at the table. 'There's mashed potato, roast carrots and minted peas to go with it, and apple crumble and custard for afters.

'Awesome,' said Ben.

Tom placed a hand on his mum's shoulder, giving her a sympathetic smile and Molly watched as he took the extra plate away from the table; the one that she'd set at Pip's usual place. The place that now sat empty.

She rubbed her forehead with her fingertips and sighed. 'Sorry kids, force of habit.'

'No worries, Mum. You've been putting one there for a long time. Stopping it isn't going to happen overnight,' said Ben, rubbing her arm. 'Come on, let's tuck-in while it's hot.'

'Good idea.' She gave a watery smile. 'Then you can both tell me about your day.'

'And what a day, eh, Tom!' Ben waggled his eyebrows at his brother.

'Aye.' Tom smiled shyly as he spooned some mashed potato onto his plate.

Molly glanced between her two sons.

'Ben knows,' said Tom softly. 'I spoke to him about it. But he'd already guessed.'

'Ah, okay.' Molly nodded, looking at Ben as she ladled a portion of casserole onto his plate.

'I've known for ages. Well, had an idea, at least. And when I saw him and Adam together at that party in Danskelfe the night, well...you know, it was pretty obvious to me then,' he said with a shrug, shovelling food into his mouth. 'Aww, man. This is lush.'

Molly smiled as she chopped up the food in Emmie's

bowl. She was pleased that her son was so accepting of his brother, not that she expected anything else, they'd always been close and had each other's back.

'Yeah, but all the same, it was a massive relief to tell you.' Tom paused for a moment. 'Adam reckons he's going to tell his parents tonight — if the mood's right, that is. He thinks his mum'll be fine, but his dad can be a bit arsey.' He looked thoughtful, a shadow crossing his face.

'Mmm. Not sure his dad'll take it too well. He's a bit of a knob, especially when he's had a beer or two,' added Ben.

Molly thought the same, but not wanting to burst Tom's bubble, she kept it to herself.

Their discussion was interrupted by the ping of a text message arriving on Molly's phone.

She scooped up a spoonful of food from Emmie's bowl and popped it into her daughter's eager little mouth before half-rising to go and check.

'Hey, Mother, you know the rules: no technology at the dinner table.' Ben shot her a cheeky grin.

'Yep, you should lead by example, isn't that what you're always telling us?'

Molly smiled and sat back down. 'You know what, lads? You're absolutely right. Whoever it is can hang fire while I feed this little one. What d'you say, Em?'

'Dat!' She pointed at Ben's plate, her eyes wide. 'Bem! Dat!' she said, making them all laugh.

'Hey! This is my dinner, you little rascal,' he chuckled, and she laughed heartily with him.

THE TEXT TURNED out to be from Granny Aggie. She'd been

quiet on the texting front since Pip's death, but her latest one made up for lost time.

'Oh, Lord. Listen to this, you two,' Molly said, laughing as she sat down.

'This must be a Granny Aggie spesh.' Ben grinned, leaning back in his chair.

'Great stuff,' said Tom.

'You might change your mind when you hear what the old bugger's got to say,' added Molly.

'Budder,' said Emmie, with a serious expression.

'Where's that swear box, Mother?' Ben raised an eyebrow.

Molly pulled an "oops" face. 'Right, then, here goes; and don't say I didn't warn you.' She took a deep breath, '"Hey, Molly..."'

'Very current,' interrupted Tom making Ben snort.

'Shush! Let me finish.' Molly tried to keep a straight face. '"I need a plunger. The vicar says he will do it for me."'

'Why does that sound so very wrong?' asked Ben.

'You should see all the exclamation marks and smiley face emojis.' Molly struggled to keep her voice steady as she continued. 'And he says I need some lubrication.' Molly looked across at her sons who were silent. Ben looked like his dinner might reappear at any moment while Tom looked confused.

'I've got a feeling I'm going to regret asking this, but, why?'

'I dread to think,' said Molly.

'Can you imagine the headline "Local Vicar in Lubrication Plunging Old Lady Scandal"?' Ben snorted.

Tom laughed. 'Do you think she has any idea what she's saying?'

'I think she has every idea. Have you seen the books she

and Little Mary read? They're filthy. Trust me, she's no stranger to racy talk.'

'Right, I've heard enough. I'm off up to my room to do my homework.' Ben made towards the door.

'Ha! She must've scared you if you'd rather tackle that than stay and chat or watch the telly,' giggled Molly.

'He's not the only one; I'm going to fasten the hens up for the night,' added Tom.

'Little did I know that good old Granny Aggie's texts could be so useful for getting you two to do what I want.' Molly grinned as both boys disappeared. It felt good to see that the family were still capable of conjuring up a light-hearted moment now and again.

LATER THAT EVENING, Molly sat with a cup of tea, gazing out over the moor, watching the sun as it melted behind Great Stangdale rigg, her mind running over the events of the day. Today was the first day she'd woken up with a tiny sliver of optimism. It had given her the strength to face a tough moment and she'd got through it. It was still early days, and, in some respects, it felt like only yesterday that PC Snaith had delivered that horrible news. But sometimes it felt like they'd been the longest two months of her life, with time dragging on in a shroud of impermeable darkness. Molly had honestly thought she'd never be able to smile again. It made her thankful of today's lighter moments and the vague feeling of optimism they'd offered.

It was the same for the boys, too; she could sense it. Tom coming out probably couldn't have come at a better time, a welcome distraction from the heavy sorrow that had sat in her heart — and his. Instead of feeling shattered, it had quickly put itself back together, regrouped, and prepared itself to wrap its love around Tom, to make him feel safe and loved and supported. He needed her, and she needed to stop wallowing in self-pity. And it also assuaged her guilt for daring to smile only two short months after Pip had died.

Having a laugh and a joke with the boys had felt good; like old times...only without one very important person who would have sprinkled his dry wit over proceedings. But, nevertheless, the mood of the house had felt brighter for a moment.

As she cast her eyes in the direction of Arkleby, she wondered how things were going for Adam; if he'd told his parents yet. His father, definitely, would have something to say, and she doubted it would be anything good. A shiver ran up her spine, and the hairs on the back of her neck stood on end as she felt a fleeting shadow of worry pass over her.

CHAPTER 20

Molly was flicking through a magazine in the living room, the television burbling away gently in the background, when Tom loped in and flopped heavily onto the leather chair beside her.

'Everything okay?' Molly noted her son's miserable expression and the air of defeat that hung around him. Phoebe took a moment out of her snooze in front of the fire to glance up at him, before stretching with a mumble and settling back down on the rug.

Tom shook his head. 'No.'

'Want to talk about it?' Molly put the magazine onto the coffee table and flicked the television off. 'Is it Adam?'

'Yep.' He nodded, pausing for a moment. 'He told his mum about us.'

'Okay. Though, I'm guessing from your expression it didn't go down well.'

'That's an understatement. He dumped me. Decided he's not gay or bisexual after all. Said what happened between him and me was just a blip and he's going to ask Maxine Farrow if she'll get back together with him. Apparently, he wants to move on from the whole situation.' Tom's bottom lip quivered and Molly reached out to squeeze his hand.

'Oh, lovie, I'm so sorry.' Her heart twisted for her son as she watched him swipe away a tear from his cheek.

'From what he was saying, I kind of got the impression the real reason is because his mum's scared of his dad. She told him she was worried about the consequences of Garth hearing he has a son who's openly gay and "flaunting it with the pretty boy from the next village". But I reckon what finally got him to change his mind was because she told him that it would put a strain on their marriage and that she would be the one to suffer. So she managed to talk him out of being gay, and being with me.'

'Well, it's not right of her to guilt trip her son, but it doesn't surprise me, Garth can be a bit of a thug, especially when he's got beer inside him.' Molly recalled Garth's reputation of being handy with his fists.

'Yeah, she told Adam he'd beaten a lad half to death at secondary school when he'd heard a rumour that he was "that way" as she called it. The lad was apparently too scared to tell the teachers who did it, and his family ended up moving out of the area just to get away from Garth.'

Molly shook her head in disgust. 'That poor family, the man's no more than an animal. I don't know how Sue's put up with him for so long.'

'It's kind of like Auntie Kitty and Dan, though isn't it? It took her a long time to realise what he was like.'

'True,' Molly nodded. 'But at least your Auntie Kitty didn't absorb Dan's views.'

Tom nodded. 'Adam reckons he told his mum that you and Dad were okay about him and me, but it didn't make any difference.' He rubbed his forehead with his fingertips.

'And she actually let slip that she thought he was a disappointment.'

'She did what? That's horrible, he's her son and she should love him for who he is. It shouldn't make a jot of difference whether he's gay or straight and it certainly shouldn't be a disappointment.' Molly could feel her anger begin to simmer, but she pushed it down for Tom's sake. The last thing he needed was for her to lose her temper.

'Well, I'm afraid she doesn't think like you, Mum, and she's managed to talk Adam out of having anything more to do with me. He said we were a big mistake that he just wants to forget about and told me he didn't want me to mention it to anyone else.' Unable to hold back his tears any longer, Tom put his head in his hands and sobbed.

Molly rushed over to him, perching on the arm of the chair, she pulled him into a hug, pressing kisses onto the top of his head. 'Oh, Tom, don't cry. If that's what he said to you, then he's not worth it, lovie. And I know it hurts now, but one day you'll meet someone who's just as wonderful as you are; someone who'll appreciate your love and kindness. I promise.' She smoothed his close crop of curls, wishing she could take his pain away. *Hasn't my poor boy been through enough?* she thought, raising her eyes heavenwards.

CHAPTER 21

Molly eyed the stuffed black bin bags that were lined up in the utility room, her heart feeling heavy. Pip's clothes. She'd have to take them to the clothing bank over at Middleton this morning. The thought of having them in the house any longer than necessary, vying for her attention, forcing her to think about what she'd done, was making her stress and guilt levels climb. The feeling that she'd stuffed all evidence of Pip into bin bags ready to get rid of like it was just household rubbish was pushing its way into her conscience. And, in the cold light of a dank and miserable Wednesday morning, that's exactly what it felt like. Her optimism of yesterday seemed to have disappeared along with the sunshine, and she could feel her mood slipping into a pit of darkness.

With the twins out of the house and Emmie playing with her toys on the mat in the living room, Molly loaded the bin bags into her car before she could change her mind, before the guilt really kicked in and she felt compelled to put everything back into the wardrobe. She really didn't think she could face doing it all over again. She was moving on; she had to do this, for the sake of the kids, if nothing else. It wasn't fair on them having a miserable mother when they needed support with their grief.

Once she'd got the breakfast things washed up and tidied away, Molly got Emmie ready for playgroup. She'd drop her off there, at the local village hall, on the way to Middleton-le-Moors. Her mum had kindly offered to keep an eye on her and would call in after she'd changed her books in the mobile library bus that called at the village every Wednesday morning.

By the time they'd got to the village hall, Emmie had picked up on Molly's low mood, and cried hot, pleading tears when she tried to leave, clinging tightly on to Molly's clothes. Guilt made Molly's eyes sting and the knot of stress tighten in her chest. She was about to give up and take Emmie home when her mum arrived.

'Look what Grandma's got, Emmie,' said Annie, giving Molly a sympathetic smile while she distracted her grand-daughter, waving a toy at her.

'Seepy!' Emmie cried, her tears forgotten as she reached her arms out to the toy.

'Yes, sweet pea, you'd left Sheepy under Grampy's cushion. He was wondering why he couldn't get comfortable and then we found Sheepy hiding under there, the rascal.' She scooped Emmie from Molly's arms and planted a kiss on her chubby cheek, making the baby beam with delight.

Molly let out a sigh. 'Thanks, Mum. That was getting quite stressful.'

'I could see. But it's still early days. And it'll pass; Em's still feeling unsettled, and she'll sense your mood, too.'

Molly shoved her hands into the pocket of her jeans. 'I know, that's why I wanted to get it done today. You know... the clothes...'

'I know, lovie.' Annie sat Emmie down on one of the

play-mats and gave Molly's arm a squeeze. 'Look, it might be a good idea for you to make your escape while this little one's mind's on other things.' She nodded towards Emmie. 'I'll take her home with me, so you don't have to worry about rushing back. It's a pity you haven't got yourself an appointment booked in with Stefan while you're over there. You could've given yourself a bit of a treat and had your hair done. Maybe you could check to see if he's had any cancellations?' she said, looking at Molly's unkempt curls.

Molly bristled. 'It's really kind of you to have Emmie for me, Mum, but the last thing on my mind at the moment is my bloody hair or giving myself a treat.'

'Of course, I didn't mean anything...it was just a suggestion.'

'Yeah, well I don't need any suggestions like that.' Molly turned to leave. 'I'll call you when I get back,' she said snappily over her shoulder.

Outside, Molly stomped to the car, climbing in and slamming the door. Why the bloody hell did people think she should be thinking about having her hair done? At this very moment in time, it was the last thing she was bothered about. She flicked the engine on and drove off, not seeing Rosie waving at her on her way to the shop.

Molly drove along the winding country lanes to the market town of Middleton-le-Moors on autopilot, pulling up in front of the clothing bins, wondering how she'd got there.

The anxious feeling she'd woken up with had cranked itself up several notches, making her stomach churn and her breathing come in short bursts. As quickly as she could, before guilt could reign triumphant over her doubts, she hurled the bulging bin-bags into the clothes bank, then climbed into her car without a backwards glance and drove away.

Half a mile out of the town, she realised that she was shaking and fat, salty tears were pouring down her face and dripping off her chin. 'What have I just done? Oh, Pip, why did you have to leave me? No!' she yelled, hitting the steering wheel. 'Come back, Pip! I just want you back. You can be as late as you want, and I won't care. I promise. I just want you home, with me and the kids. I'm so sorry I was such a moody cow to live with at times. I didn't mean to be. But I love you. I just bloody love you,' she cried. She didn't care what the drivers coming in the opposite direction thought as she let her grief explode. She just needed to get home. Get home and hold Pip's favourite shirt.

BY THE TIME she arrived back at the farm, Molly's tears had dried, leaving her eyes red and swollen and a heavy feeling in her heart. Her head was throbbing, too. What she needed more than anything was some fresh air. She grabbed Phoebe's lead from the utility room. The Labrador read the cue and jumped up, running around in circles next to her. 'Sit still, daft arse.' Molly managed a feeble smile at Phoebe's enthusiasm as she clipped the lead to her collar. 'Come on then, miss. Let's go for a leg stretch on your dad's moor.'

Phoebe led the way, tail wagging and tugging on the lead as she followed a trail of delicious smells. A pheasant ran across the path before taking flight and cackling in annoyance at being disturbed. Molly watched it glide across the gentle folds of the burnished heather that was dying back. The sky had cleared in parts overhead, revealing an optimistic patch of blue, though, she noticed that a cluster of foreboding clouds were inching their way towards Danskelfe dale, bumping shoulders like a group of youths, bored and looking for trouble as they hung over the ramparts of Danskelfe castle. Hopefully, the gentle breeze would disperse them quickly.

As the pair made their way across the moor, Molly felt herself getting short of breath. Though Withrin Hill Farm sat high above the village, the track to the rigg that circumnavigated Great Stangdale was still quite a distance away, full of twists and turns, and steep in parts.

'Phew!' she said to herself as she paused to look over the dale and down on the thatched rooftops of Lytell Stangdale. A bright beam of sunshine reached down, picking out the lime-washed walls, making them glitter in the sunlight. It looked achingly pretty. Molly sighed as a feeling of peace washed over her. She'd lost Pip; he wasn't coming back, she accepted that — bloody hard as it was. But she wasn't alone. Quite the contrary. That quaint little village housed people who cared about her, people who loved her with a fierceness that could take your breath away. And she loved them back with equal ardour. Molly understood that her friends and family would be desperate to help, wanted to be there for her, but would be conscious of not wanting to say the wrong thing — like her mum had earlier today – of not wanting to push when their assistance or company wasn't wanted. Equally, she knew just how it felt when someone you cared about was feeling desperate and hurting. Kitty sprang to mind. She'd been trapped in an abusive marriage that had just about brought her to her knees. Thankfully, her family and friends — Molly included — had spotted the right moment to intervene. Very gently, they'd helped her see sense and gave her the support she'd needed to walk away. *And now look at her*, Molly thought to herself. She couldn't remember seeing her cousin look so happy. 'See,' said a little voice inside her head, 'given time, things can get better.'

Molly closed her eyes and inhaled a lungful of fresh earthy air, releasing it noisily through her mouth. Being outdoors, taking in this wonderful scenery certainly did a lot to brighten your perspective on life. Yes, dealing with Pip's clothes had been one of the hardest things she'd ever had to do, but she'd tackled the emotions it had generated head-on and was now on the right side of them. She knew the experience would make her stronger, though she couldn't appreciate it at the moment.

Molly was relieved when she reached the rigg road. She was out of breath and feeling decidedly unfit — she couldn't remember when she'd last tackled the climb, but judging by the ache in her calf muscles, it was quite some time ago. She couldn't use the excuse of being over-weight slowing her down; the baby-weight she'd had after Emmie had fallen off her since Pip's death and she could easily be described as scrawny right now. She'd have to do more walking; improve her fitness levels.

She carried on, heading in the direction of Danskelfe, when a cyclist appeared on the horizon. Molly squinted, even from this distance he appeared to be wobbly on his bike. As he drew closer, Molly recognised the jacket and helmet as those belonging to Dave Mellison. *Does that man ever do a day's work?* she wondered. If what everyone said was true, he'd probably be coming from the Fox over at Danskelfe and was returning this way to avoid being seen on the road. Whenever she was out in the village or on the moor, he always appeared on his bike. Since relations with the Mellisons and her family weren't good, she whistled for Phoebe who was busily snuffling around the edge of the heather, and the pair of them nipped down a smaller track that linked to the path back to the farm.

Back home, Molly splashed her face with cold water and assessed her reflection in the mirror. 'What a bloody sight,' she muttered, taking in the still-swollen eyes that were ringed with dark circles, the sunken cheeks with cheek bones protruding so dramatically they could justifiably be described as razor sharp. 'I've definitely looked better.' Taking in her matted birds' nest of hair with its flash of grey, she had to admit, her mum did have a point. Molly tried dragging a comb through it. 'Shit!' She winced. It was too painful. With a sigh of resignation, she gave up and raked it back into a ponytail.

Half an hour later, Molly scooped up the bunch of Michaelmas Daisies she'd picked from the walled garden — a peace offering for her mother. 'Won't be long, Phoebes. Be good,' she said as she closed the kitchen door behind her.

'Here you are, Mum. Sorry for being such a moody mare.' Molly handed her mum the flowers. 'And I take your point about my mop, it's wild, but I just can't face going to the hairdressers and making small-talk and having to tell Stefan about Pip. I'm just not strong enough for that yet.' Sally wandered across and nudged Molly's hand. 'Hiya, Sally.' She bent to ruffle the old Labrador's ears.

'I know, lovie. I could've bitten my tongue off after I'd said it. I'm sorry, it was insensitive of me.' She hugged her daughter close, pressing a kiss against her cheek. 'You go when you feel good and ready. And these are ever so pretty,' Annie said, looking at the flowers before making her way into the living room where a sleeping Emmie was being cuddled by her sleeping grandfather.

Molly smiled at the blissful image before her. 'Looks like they've both tired each other out.'

'They have, but they've both had a whale of a time. Emmie's such an easy-going little poppet. Having her here is like a tonic for your dad. Takes his mind off his Parkinson's, bless him.' Annie's smile momentarily dropped, and she turned to leave the room. 'Anyway, how did it go with the clothes?'

Molly blew a straggle of curls off her brow and followed her mother into the kitchen. 'It was hard, Mum. Bloody hard. But now it actually feels like I've had a massive weight lifted off my shoulders. I hadn't realised just how much the thought of doing it was bothering me, until now. And I'm so relieved I'll never have to face it again.' She pressed her mouth into a smile.

'I'm so proud of you, lovie. You're such a strong woman, and I know you'll get through this. But don't forget, you've got family and friends who are keen to support you. I know for a fact our Kitty and Vi would've dropped everything to help you with that.'

Molly sighed. 'I know, but it was something I just had to do myself. It wouldn't have felt right having anyone else go through Pip's things. I needed to do it on my own as part of the letting-go process. And in a weird way, it kind of helped with saying goodbye.' She swallowed down the wobble in her voice.

BACK AT WITHRIN HILL FARM, Molly was setting the table,

noticing that it was the first time she'd not set a place for Pip. She paused for a moment; it felt strange.

Her thoughts were interrupted by the ping of a text arriving on her mobile phone. It was from Ben, on the bus on his way home from college. She looked at the clock, he'd be home in ten minutes.

Hey Mum, what's for tea? X

Oh dear, she didn't know how she was going to break this to him.

Hi Ben, game stew and dumplings xxx

It was usually one of the twins' favourite meals.

Coooool!!! X

Grandma made it xxx

She winced as she pressed send.

Oh shit!!! Suddenly lost my appetite!!!

Molly laughed at the cheeky emojis that peppered her son's last text.

'What's that horrible pong?' Tom called from the hall where he was taking his wellies off. He padded into the kitchen, scrunching his nose as he sniffed the air.

Molly put her phone down. 'It's game stew and dumplings.'

'Doesn't usually smell like that.'

'Grandma made it specially.'

'Oh, Jesus!' Tom's expression made Molly laugh out loud.

'I'm sure it'll taste a lot nicer than it smells,' she offered, but Tom gave her a doubtful look and, if she was honest, even she wasn't convinced.

～

'There you go, Em,' said Tom as he finished fastening his little sister into her high-chair and ruffling her curls. 'Let's see what you make of tea.' He looked across at Ben who was washing his hands and pulled a face.

'That's enough, you two. This stew might be absolutely delicious, and it was kind of your grandma to make it for us.' Molly was ladling the casserole onto plates, having put some in a bowl earlier for Emmie, giving it time to cool down.

'Right, here goes,' said Ben holding a forkful in front of him. Everyone watched intently as he chewed on it. He swallowed slowly. 'Oh man, that is gross.'

Tom took a mouthful. 'Bloody hell! That's minging. It tastes like dog vomit.'

'Eurghh, man, the dumplings! It's like chewing on a massive snot, and if that wasn't bad enough, they taste like Tom's sweaty socks.' Ben chewed exaggeratedly.

'That bad, eh? Poor, mum, she does her best.' A reluctant smile hovered over Molly's mouth.

'Anyway, how d'you know what dog vomit tastes like, Tom-Tom?' Ben sniggered.

'S'what I imagine it would taste like. No wonder Grampy's as skinny as a rake. I bet he feeds most of his food to the dog. And how d'you know what my socks taste like?'

'Dindin,' shouted Emmie. Molly handed her a spoon,

sitting the bowl on the table in front of her. Emmie tucked in enthusiastically as the twins looked on.

'Let's see what Emmie the Appetite makes of Grandma's stew,' said Ben.

Emmie's chewing slowed down, and she began to gurn, pushing the food out of her mouth with her tongue. 'Bleargh!' Shaking her head, she pushed the bowl off her table and onto the floor. 'No!' she said, firmly.

Phoebe seized the opportunity for illicit food gains and trotted over. She sniffed the pile of food and snorted loudly before walking off, unimpressed.

Molly and the twins burst out laughing. 'See, even Phoebe won't eat it, and Labradors are supposed to eat everything.' Tom pushed his plate away.

'Yeah, Labradors and Emmie,' agreed Ben. 'Come on, Mother, you can't make us eat this crap.'

'Oh, you're right. Poor Mum. Not a word to her mind, you two.'

'We'll do whatever it takes,' said Ben, making a zipping motion across his mouth.

'Right, cheese on toast it is then, kids,' said Molly, peering into the fridge.

'Now you're talking,' said Tom as he went to clear the plates away. 'I'm gonna slather mine in brown sauce.'

Molly cast a fond glance across at her sons. Tom seemed momentarily brighter. Since his text from Adam a couple of weeks earlier, he'd withdrawn into himself, barely speaking to anyone, except for his uncle Mark who he'd chat to for ages over Skype. He'd carried out his duties at the farm with the usual diligence, but once they were done, he'd disappear into his bedroom, only venturing out to eat. It was good to see him smile again and it felt good to have laughter round the dinner table once more. She knew Pip would agree.

CHAPTER 22

'So, how's things, missus?' asked Kitty, pouring Molly a mug of tea. They were sitting in Kitty's kitchen at Oak Tree Farm and, judging by her cousin's expression, she was going through a bad patch again.

'Hello, ladies, sorry I'm late,' said Vi, pulling off her green suede driving gloves, while peeking in the pushchair at Emmie who was fast asleep.

'Hi, Vi,' Molly said before turning back to Kitty. 'Shit, actually.'

'Oh dear, that bad?' Kitty pulled a sympathetic face and set the teapot down.

'Anything we can do to help?' asked Vi, pulling out a chair and sitting down.

'Got a magic wand?'

'Sadly not. If I had, it would've had a lot of use, I can assure you.'

'How's Tom,' asked Kitty, pushing a plate of homemade biscuits towards her friends.

'Oh, don't ask, Kitts. He just looks so unhappy. It's bad enough for him that he lost his dad a few months ago but being dumped by Adam and told he was a "mistake", well, it's just heart-breaking for him. I don't know what I can do to help.'

'Surely he knows that was just Adam's mother talking. And I'd put money on it that it was just to stop Garth from finding out. We all know what an animal he can be.' Vi helped herself to a chocolate chip cookie.

'I know you're right, but it still doesn't change things. Ben, bless him, is trying his best to get his brother out socialising again, but Tom just doesn't want to know.' She felt exhausted; drained of every last drop of energy, and it showed.

'And in the middle of this you're all still grieving for Pip,' Kitty added, pouring a mug of tea for Violet.

'I know,' Molly whispered. If she was honest, since she'd got rid of Pip's clothes her mood had been slowly dipping again. It was taking every ounce of strength she had to get out of bed in the morning.

'Right, here's a plan.' Vi sat up straight in her seat. She'd been watching Molly, wondering how long it was since she'd had her hair cut, how long since she'd actually set some time aside for herself. It was clear she was shouldering too much, trying to make life as smooth as possible for everyone else. But, judging by the exhaustion in her friend's eyes and the smattering of grey hairs that had appeared alongside the streak in her fringe, Molly needed some support.

'Woah, lookout world, Vi means business,' said Kitty, running a hand over her growing bump.

'I so do,' she agreed, looking serious. 'Molly, you've said that Tom's been spending ages on Skype talking to Mark about farming and showing an interest in what's happening over in New Zealand, am I right?'

'Yes,' she nodded.

'So — and hear me out.' She held a hand up. 'Why don't you suggest that he goes over there for a couple of months; put some time and space between him and everything that's happened with Adam?' She sent Kitty a look that said, "back me up on this".

Molly didn't look too sure and was about to speak when her cousin interjected.

'That might not actually be such a bad idea, you know, Moll.'

Molly looked between her two friends, the cogs of her mind whirring. 'Do you think?'

'Yes!' they both said together.

Molly slipped her shoes off and rubbed her feet across Ethel's stomach. The Labrador stretched and sighed in delight. 'Actually, the more I think about it, the more it makes sense, especially when I remember some of the conversations Tom and Mark have had.'

'There you are.' Vi smiled, pleased that her suggestion was being well-received.

'So, why don't you have a word with Mark? See if they'd be happy for Tom to stay for a while; I mean, he'd have to run it by Vicky and the kids before you mention anything to Tom,' said Kitty.

'Of course, though neither of Mark's girls have shown any interest in the farm, and I think he'd be chuffed to bits if our Tom went over there. It could do the pair of them the world of good. There's only one problem.'

'What's that?' asked Vi.

'We're going to be a man down on the farm; we were going to have a big push on getting the campsite ready for next summer. I've already got my hands full with little Emmie until she starts school.'

'I'm sure Ollie and Jimby would be more than happy to help out.'

'True,' agreed Vi. 'And if you need any help paying for a flight, then just let us know, and we can all chip in.'

'No.' Molly splayed her palms. 'We're not a charity case. And Pip's insurance policy left us well looked after. But don't either of you dare feel sorry for me,' she said fiercely.

'Message understood, sassy pants,' said Vi, rolling her eyes at Kitty.

CHAPTER 23

A heart to heart with Tom confirmed in Molly's mind that Vi's idea was a good one, and it was agreed that they'd ask Mark if he could go over and work on the farm for six months. Molly got on to this the following day, emailing her brother, explaining the situation and testing the water. Mark replied quickly, saying he and the family would love to have him, and arrangements were made for Tom to fly out in the New Year.

'I can't tell you how happy I am to have him come to work on the farm with me, Moll. It means the world.' Mark couldn't hide his enthusiasm. 'And, you do know you're all welcome, any time you want. We'd all love to have you.' They were talking over Skype, while the twins were out.

'That's really kind, Mark. And I know it'll do Tom the world of good to get away from here for a while, put some distance between him and Adam.' She smiled across the miles at her big brother. 'He's a different lad since we looked into organising a working visa and checked out flights.'

'Well, I'm pleased. And, as I say, I'm really looking

forward to him landing here and hearing his suggestions for the farm — fresh ideas and all that.'

'Yes,' she said with a sigh. 'He's always got plenty of ideas, has Tom. Just like his dad.'

'And are you okay, sis? You look knackered.' Mark took in his sister's unruly curls and drab clothes. She looked like she'd aged a good ten years.

'Oh, you know me, Mark. I'm fine.' But both of them knew she wasn't telling the truth.

The following evening, Vi and Kitty arrived unannounced at the farm. Molly was just stacking the dishwasher when she heard a car pull up in the yard, making Phoebe bark. Moments later there was a knock at the door, and Vi's voice called along the hallway. 'Hiya, Moll. S'just us.'

'Hi, Vi, hi, Kitty.' Molly was surprised to see her friends. 'If we'd arranged to do something, I've clean forgotten about it,' she said, bemused.

'No, Moll, you haven't forgotten anything. We've got a surprise for you.' Kitty beamed at her.

'Yep. Put those dishes down and get your shoes on. We're carting you off down to Rosie's for a pamper session. She's got her beauty rooms finished, and you're going to be her first client. Everything's set up for you to have an aromatherapy massage, a luxurious facial, manicure, pedi-cure and anything else you fancy,' added Vi.

'And I can stay and look after Emmie, see to her supper and give her a bath, if that's okay. Get me back into practice for this one.' Kitty patted her bump.

Molly looked from one to the other, frozen to the spot, anger bubbling up inside her as she absorbed their words.

Who the hell did they think they were, organising her life like this, without checking to see if it was okay? She just wanted to get the dishwasher filled, get Emmie to bed and lie on the sofa watching mindless telly.

'What makes you think I want to do any of that? Which incidentally, I don't.' She shot Violet an icy glare.

'Well, you might not think you want it now, but you'll change your mind the second you get to Rosie's — or Manor House Sanctuary as she's called it. Honestly, hun, it's gorgeous there,' Vi continued.

'We just thought you might like a little treat, a bit of "me time", Moll. You look jiggered, and you never seem to stop,' Kitty said softly.

'Well, I bloody well don't. And, yes, I am absolutely knackered, but a sodding pamper session with someone fussing over me is the last thing I need, actually.' Molly's breathing was shallow, her lips pinched in anger.

'Molly, we just...' Kitty could see her cousin's distress.

'Don't.' Molly held her hands up. 'Please, Kitty...'

'Come on, Molly. You'll enjoy it when you're there,' said Vi.

'I'll tell you what I would like right now, and it's not some stupid pamper session — which is something I've never, ever gone in for, as well you both know. What I would like, is my husband back. That's all. Nothing fancy. I just want my Pip back. Here with me and the kids.' She struggled to fight the tears that were stinging her eyes. Kitty and Vi ran over to her, wrapping their arms around her.

'Oh, Molly, please don't cry. We're so sorry. We didn't mean to upset you.' Kitty fought back tears of her own.

'Moll, chick. We didn't mean...we've just been so worried about you,' said Vi.

Molly shrugged the pair off. 'Well you should've bloody-well thought before you organised it, shouldn't you?' Tears were now pouring down her cheeks. I don't want a sodding pamper session. I hate sodding pamper sessions. In fact, I hate sodding everything right now, and I want you both to leave.' She flashed her eyes angrily at her friends.

'Molly, you don't mean that. We're sorry.' Kitty reached out to her cousin who took a step back. Vi swallowed, her face ashen.

'I do bloody well mean it. Both of you, just go. Now.' She pointed to the door, tears dripping from her chin onto the flagstone floor. Phoebe ran over to her, nudging against her leg, whimpering.

Vi stepped forward, but Kitty pulled her back. 'No, Vi. Come on, let's go. See you later, Molly. Call us when you're ready. And we're really sorry.' Kitty spoke softly as she guided Vi to the door.

'Bye, Molly.' Vi looked chastened. 'I'm really sorry.'

Molly watched them leave. Her thoughts were in turmoil, but anger still jostled for supremacy and quashed any feelings of guilt, remorse or anything else that was vying for her attention.

The sound of Emmie crying pierced her thoughts. 'That's all I need.' Molly threw her head back and sighed noisily.

'Mamma. Mamma. Mamma.' Emmie's cries were getting louder.

'Shit,' Molly muttered, dragging a hand down her face, suddenly feeling very weary. She just wanted to have a bath, go to bed and get this horrible day over with.

CHAPTER 24

The following morning, Molly woke to the sound of rain drumming against the window. There was no sign of any sunshine trying to squeeze its way through the gap in the curtains today. Slowly, the events of the previous evening filtered into her thoughts. 'Oh, shit!' She clamped a hand to her forehead. She'd have to speak to Kitty and Vi, put things straight. The last thing she wanted to do was to push her dearest friends away. She threw the duvet back, Kitty's hurt features appearing in her mind as she did so. Grief and anger had erased some of what had happened the previous evening, and Molly couldn't remember exactly what she'd said — apart from telling her friends to leave. She winced at that memory. Kitty was more sensitive than Vi, and Molly hoped she wasn't hurting too much. She'd call in at Romantique later this morning. Hopefully, they'd still be speaking to her.

AFTER RUSTLING up a batch of biscuits, Molly got herself and

Emmie ready to head down into the village, a feeling of trepidation giving her butterflies in her stomach. 'Come on, bubba. Let's take these biscuits as a peace offering to Auntie Kitty and Auntie Vi.' She held Emmie's hand as she toddled to the back door.

'Bikkit,' said Emmie, her big brown eyes looking up at Molly.

'Yes, you can have one when you get there, sweet pea.'

'Knock, knock!' Molly pushed the door of Romantique's workshop open to see Kitty and Vi sitting having a cuppa with Rosie. All three looked surprised to see her.

'Akiki. Wyett.' Emmie beamed at her godmothers.

'Hello, you two. It's lovely to see you both.' Kitty rushed over to the pair, scooping Emmie up. 'Hello, little pudding.' She peppered her cheeks with kisses. 'You okay, Moll,' she asked, her dark eyes searching Molly's face.

'I'm fine, chick. Peace offering?' She held the biscuit tin out in front of her. 'I just wanted to apologise for last night.'

'It's us who should be apologising, hun. But we'll be happy to take your biscuits.' Vi rushed over to Molly, enveloping her in a fragrant squeeze before taking the tin off her and lifting the lid. 'Ooh, yum. Ginger and chocolate chip. My absolute faves. You can shout at me as much as you like, if you're going to supply us with these little beauties!' Vi grinned.

'Language, Vi. Little ears and all that.' Kitty nodded to Emmie.

'Oops. Sorry.'

'I owe you an apology, too, Rosie.' Molly turned to the young woman who was sitting quietly sipping her tea. 'I'd had a rotten day yesterday, and these two caught the brunt of it.'

'No apology necessary. I completely understand.' Rosie gave her a warm smile.

'Phew! Well, I'm glad we've got that over with. Time for a cuppa?' Vi raised a questioning eyebrow.

'Definitely.' Molly smiled, a huge sense of relief washing over her. 'Someone's looking snuggly and tired.' She looked at Emmie who had cuddled into Kitty, sucking her thumb, her eyelids getting heavy as she fought sleep.

'I think it's because I'm all squishy. This baby's got my boobs so enormous, I don't know what to do with them.' Kitty prodded at them.

'I'll bet Ollie knows what to do with them,' quipped Vi with a giggle.

'Must you, Vi? Anyway, it's usually our Moll here who lowers the tone.'

'Ah, well, I'm just standing in for her until she's up to it again. Isn't that right, Moll?'

'Yep, sure is.' Molly smiled; it was good to be having banter with her friends. 'And Rosie, I'd really love to have a pamper session at your new rooms; it sounds lovely. It's not the sort of thing I've done before, but I know I look a wreck at the moment, so it'd probably do me good.'

'That's fine, Molly. Just shout up, whenever you're ready.'

'Oh, you should see the rooms, Moll. They're sumptu-ous. You'll honestly be a convert.' Vi passed her a mug of tea. 'There you go, chick.'

'Thanks. I'm so ready for this. And I just want to say that at the moment every day is different. Some days I wake up and there's a glimmer of hope, and I feel like I'm making progress. Then others, I feel so low I can barely drag myself out of bed. And the prospect of another long-drawn out evening on my own...ughh.' Molly shook her head. 'Unfortunately, yesterday was one of the bad days.' She smiled apologetically.

'We understand, petal,' said Kitty, rubbing her cousin's arm. 'But, from where we're standing, you're making amazing progress. You just need to think about yourself for a change.'

'Yeah, it's been a bit tricky recently, what with Pip and now Tom and his broken heart. Honestly, you think when your kids get to a certain age, you won't have to worry about them, but, I swear, their worries get bigger as they get older. And if I have any spare time, I'd rather spend it with you lot, not using it to treat myself or get my hair done. No offence, Rosie.'

'None taken.' Rosie smiled at her.

'We understand, it's been a bugger of a year for you. But I've got a feeling that things will get better,' said Vi.

'Hey, ladies, I've got an idea,' said Rosie. 'How about you have a joint pamper session? That way, Molly can have a treat while she's spending time with you two? I could do it at mine, or bring my stuff up to the farm if you'd prefer, Molly?'

'Ooh,' said Vi and Kitty simultaneously, their eyes lighting up as they looked across at Molly.

'You know what, Rosie? That sounds like a great idea. But, from what Vi's said about your place being so fab, I think I'd like it there, have a change of scenery. If that's okay with everyone else?'

'Sounds perfect to me,' enthused Vi.

'Me, too,' said Kitty.

'Great. And I've got some oils, specially for pregnant ladies, Kitty. Is this Friday any good? I don't mind what time.

Morning, afternoon, evening?' She looked around at the three friends.

'Ooh, if it's evening we can bring Prosecco,' Vi said with a grin.

'Evening it is,' said Rosie.

THE THOUGHT of Friday night and their pamper treat had gone a good way to lightening Molly's mood, and she was surprised at how much she was looking forward to it. The twins had agreed to stay in and look after Emmie, and Kristy was coming over to stay the night. So, for once, Molly could rest easy about her brood.

CHAPTER 25

'Have fun, Mother. And don't forget to relax,' said Tom, grinning at Molly as he dropped her off outside the Manor House, in readiness for her pamper session. 'And just text when you want me to come and get you.'

'Thanks, lovie. Will do.' She grinned back at him. 'I'm not really sure what to expect, but it'll be nice to spend the evening with the lasses and have a catch-up. I feel like I've been out of the loop for a bit.'

'That's because you have but, hopefully, you'll come out floating on air.'

'Or crawling in the gutter after too many glasses of this.' They both laughed as she waved the bottle of Prosecco she was holding.

'Well, whichever it is, just make sure you enjoy yourself.'

'I'll do my best.'

Molly rang the doorbell of the large, timber-framed building and the ex-home of Kitty's in-laws, George and Gwyneth — they'd sold up and moved away after their son, Dan's, misdemeanours became too much for social-climbing Gwyneth to bear.

Rosie answered wearing a white tabard, ready for business, a welcoming smile on her face. 'Come in, Molly, I'm so glad you're here.'

Molly kicked off her shoes and was unbuttoning her coat just as Rosie's husband, Robbie, poked his head around the door to the living room.

'Hello there, Molly, it's good to see you.' He gave her a friendly smile. 'Here, let me take that,' he said as their chocolate Labrador, Truffle, joined them, her tail wagging.

'Oh, hi, Robbie, thanks. You, too,' she replied just as Violet's throaty laugh drifted down the hallway. 'I hope you weren't planning on having a peaceful evening.' She smiled as she handed him her coat.

'Don't you worry about me. I've got a nice bottle of claret, and an action film lined up for company. You ladies aren't the only ones having a treat.'

'Quite right, too,' she said. 'Hi there, Truffle.' Molly ruffled the dog's ears then followed Rosie down the hallway to a room where Kitty and Violet were already reclining on a large, squishy sofa, dressed in fluffy, white robes. The room smelt heavenly as the aroma of essential oils permeated the air, while soothing music was playing softly in the background. Releasing a deep sigh, Molly felt her troubles melt away.

'Now then, missus.' Vi beamed at her, a glass of something bubbly and alcoholic in her hand.

'Hiya, Moll.' Kitty set her glass of fizzy water down on the table in front of her, before jumping up and wrapping her cousin in a hug, planting a kiss on her cheek.

'Hi, girls. I see you've got the party started. There you go, Rosie,' she said handing over the bottle of Prosecco. 'You've got it lovely in here.' Molly gazed around at the décor of sumptuous purples and golds, the thick curtains puddling in folds of rich silk, the deep pile of the plum carpet soft beneath her feet.

'Thank you. Robbie and I have had a great time redecorating but doing these treatment rooms was my favourite project.' She smiled at Molly.

'It's so tasteful, a far cry from Gwyneth's stuffy style.'

'Er, yes, it was a bit old fashioned — no offence, Kitty.'

'None taken; it was very dated. And, don't worry, you couldn't offend me with anything you say about that old bat.'

'Evil old witch,' Vi snarled, making everyone laugh.

'Anyway, here you go, Molly just nip in there and pop these on.' Rosie handed her a folded-up robe and nodded to a doorway to the left.

Molly looked at her aghast. 'What the? You seriously want me to put my arse in this?' She held up the tiny paper G-string that had been placed on top of the dressing gown. 'I've seen eye patches with more fabric in them.'

Kitty and Vi dissolved into fits of giggles. 'We've put ours on. What makes your arse so special, Moll?' quipped Violet.

'You don't have to wear them if you don't want to, Molly. You can keep your own knickers on. I only really ask clients to use them to stop the essential oils from staining their own underwear, or for waxing purposes, but you don't have to have that done tonight,' said Rosie, trying to keep her face straight.

'Well, if I'm honest, waxing isn't exactly top of my list of pamper treatments, so if it's all the same, I'll keep my trusty belly-whackers on and continue to rock the seventies vibe down there.'

'Oh, lord. TMI, Molly, as per,' cackled Vi, before taking a sip of her Prosecco, her expression suddenly changing to one of disgust. 'Actually, talking of rocking a seventies vibe.

On my way here, I had the unfortunate experience of catching a glimpse of Gerald's, er, lady garden, and he's most definitely rocking one, and it's dyed the same colour as his beard.'

'How on earth did you see that?' Kitty looked horrified.

'It was when I was walking by on the opposite side of the road to his cottage, my eyes were drawn to a light on in one of the upstairs windows where Gerald was stood completely knack-naked, in what I assume was the bath, soaping himself down in all his glory, his fuchsia pink bits on display for all the world to see. Of course, he was totally oblivious to it, just stood there whistling away.'

'Oh, please.' Kitty pressed a hand to her mouth.

'Fuchsia pink bits?' Rosie's brow was troubled by a deep frown.

'Well, not his "bits" exactly, but his, er, lady garden or whatever you call it,' said Vi.

'Vi, blokes don't have *lady* gardens,' said Molly.

'Well, his equivalent, whatever you call it.' Vi gave a shrug.

Molly snorted. 'I've no idea, but it's definitely not *lady garden*, you nutter. Well, at least we know his collar and cuffs match,' she said, earning herself a look of disgust from Violet.

'And, in case you're wondering, Rosie, yes, we always have high-brow conversations like this,' Kitty chuckled.

'Especially, when Molly's involved,' said Vi.

'Hey, you were the one who brought up nether regions tonight, so don't go pointing the finger of blame at me.'

'Er, it wasn't actually, but never mind, Moll, petal, just go and get changed, while I pour you some of this.' Vi jumped up and guided her friend through the open doorway before grabbing a bottle of Prosecco and an extra glass.

'Actually, talking of lady gardens, have any of you told Rosie about Ollie's stag night?' asked Molly as she returned to the room, all robed up. 'Ta, Vi.' She took the glass of fizz from her friend.

'Now I'm really scared.' Rosie said with a giggle.

'It may come as a surprise to you, Moll, but we haven't had the opportunity to just casually throw that into the conversation,' answered Vi.

'It was hilarious, Rosie. Talk about crossed wires,' Kitty said. 'The men had gone to York to celebrate Ollie's stag night and they rang us the next morning when we were up at Moll's farm.'

'Well, it was Pip who started the confusion — typical.' Molly smiled, as they took it in turns to tell Rosie the story.

THE THREE FRIENDS were sharing their habitual pot of tea at the kitchen table of Withrin Hill Farm, waiting to hear from the men, when Molly's mobile started to ring. She leaned across the table and scooped it up. 'It's Pip. This should be good,' she said with a grin as she pressed the "answer" icon. 'Morning, Philip. How are we?' Molly's face dropped. 'What? All of you? I don't believe it!'

'Moll, what's happened?' Vi cast a concerned look Kitty's way.

'Why do you always have to do something stupid when you've had too much to drink?'

'Is everyone okay?' asked Kitty.

Molly shook her head, a furious expression clouding her features. 'Just a minute, let me put you on speaker phone, save me having to repeat this crap.' She placed the phone on the table, chuntering as she did so. 'Right, tell Kitty and Vi what you've just told me.' She sat back in her chair, her arms folded across her chest.

'Now then, lasses.' Pip's bright and cheery voice bounced around the kitchen, a post-drinking ropey tone to it. 'I haven't a clue what's up with Moll. All I said was that we had a great time last night. We had a few beers and then went for a Brazilian — which was awesome; honestly, we all agreed that we'd never experienced anything like it before.'

'Tell Vi I'm going to take her for one; she'd love it.' Jimby's voice piped up in the background.

The women looked at Vi, whose eyes were like saucers. Kitty struggled to stifle a giggle.

'Jesus.' Molly's expression changed to disgust. 'We don't need to know that thank you very much, James.'

'You had what exactly, Pip?' Vi asked, puzzled.

'We had a Brazilian.' His voice tailed off as he obviously turned to his accomplices. 'Looks like we're in bother, lads, they all sound brassed off. Bloody women.'

'Listen, daft arse, put Ollie on; he talks more sense than you and Jimby put together,' snapped Molly.

'Well, let's hope so,' said Kitty.

'Hiya, ladies. What's the problem?' Ollie's voice sounded rough around the edges, too.

'Hi, Ollie,' Kitty couldn't hide the smile in her voice. 'Did you have a good time last night?'

'Hiya, gorgeous. Yeah, it was brilliant. Missed you, though.'

'Missed you, too.' She giggled as she looked across at Molly who was rolling her eyes and pretending to stick a finger down her throat. 'Okay, well, there seems to be a bit of confusion over what you lot did last night. Something about a Brazilian?' She pulled a worried face at her friends as the words left her mouth.

'Well, there's nothing to be confused about. We just went to two or three pubs for a few beers — or several — then went for a Brazilian. Simple as that.' He sounded like it was a perfectly reasonable thing to do.

'What, all of you?' Vi called across the table.

'Er, yeah. Why wouldn't we all go?' Ollie sounded puzzled. 'Beats going for a pint and a kebab. It was very reasonably priced and absolutely spotless. One of the under-gamekeepers who works with Pip had one recently, told him how good it was. Honestly, you girls would love it, too.'

'Christ all-bloody-mighty! They're all as daft as each other. You can bloody-well tell Pip he needn't bother coming home until it's grown back. It's not as if his balls aren't ugly enough.'

Vi and Kitty exchanged amused looks, both knowing that to laugh would be to invite Molly's wrath.

'I think I'd better put Pip back on.' Ollie sounded scared. 'Speak to you later, Kitts.'

'Moll?' It was Pip's voice. 'Look, love, I'm not exactly sure what we've done wrong, but my head feels like it's been hit with a sledge-hammer and…'

'Well, it's just as well you're on the other end of a phone, because I'd be very tempted to take a swing at your nuts with a sledge-hammer, never mind that bloody thick head of yours.'

'Ouch! Don't say stuff like that, love.' They didn't need to see him to know that he'd winced at her words.

'Listen, Pip. I really don't know what gets into you when you get pissed, but it isn't big and it isn't clever — and I'm not just referring to that pathetic excuse of a manhood of yours.' She flashed an angry look across at Kitty and Violet who, despite themselves, had dissolved into fits of giggles.

'I think the question we should really be asking is, which poor beautician had the unfortunate luck to actually give you lot Brazilians?' Kitty pulled herself together enough to ask.

'Beautician? Why would a beautician work at a restaurant?' asked Pip.

Vi clamped a hand to her forehead and burst out laughing. 'Oh, my God, Pip. I've just realised what you mean! You haven't had your nuts waxed.'

'I'm bloody sure I haven't!'

Vi was finding it difficult to speak, she was laughing so hard. 'You had a meal at that new Brazilian restaurant around the corner from the Shambles, the one that just opened up a couple of weeks ago.'

'Er, yeah, we had a Brazilian. What did you think I meant?'

The women fell into fits of laughter, tears pouring down their cheeks.

'You three have lost the plot,' said Pip, confused.

'Oh, Pip, in women's speak, having a Brazilian means having your lady garden waxed.' Vi spluttered.

'Your lady what?'

'He won't have a clue what you're on about, Vi,' sniggered Molly, which triggered more laughter from the women.

'Oh, you lot thought we'd had that thing Vi has done,' Jimby called from the background again, his ensuing laugh echoing around the kitchen.

'Thanks, for sharing that, Jimby.' Vi rolled her eyes.

'Right, you crazy lot, we're off for a walk along the river. See you some time this afternoon. Hopefully, we'll get some sense out of you by then.' Pip hung up.

THE BEAUTY ROOM was filled with the sound of the friends' laughter. 'Oh, that's so funny,' said Rosie, wiping tears from her eyes when they'd finished telling her. 'There's never a dull moment in this village, that's for sure.'

'Too right,' said Molly

THE EVENING FLEW BY, and Molly couldn't remember when she'd last felt so relaxed or enjoyed herself so much; definitely not since Pip had passed away.

'Thank you, ladies.' She was sitting beside Kitty on the sofa, her feet tucked underneath her.

'What for?' asked Vi.

'For taking me in hand and helping me not feel guilty about having a lovely time.'

'Ahh, come here, chick. You so deserve to have a lovely time.' Kitty leaned across and wrapped an arm around her cousin. 'We love you and we've been worried about you. And, if you remember, not so very long ago, you were doing the same for me, dragging me out to the pub when I really didn't want to go. If it wasn't for you lot, well...'

'Which, incidentally, is our next plan for you, Moll. Jonty and Bea have been asking about you, and it's time you showed your fizzog in there,' Vi added, draining her glass.

'Vi's right,' agreed Kitty. 'We should try to do something every week — if you're feeling up to it.'

'I like the sound of that. And, now I've had a taste of it, a regular pamper session like this would be something fab to look forward to — if you think you can put up with us again.' Molly looked across at Rosie.

'Of course. I've had a really great time, too. I already know Kitty pretty well, but it's been nice to get to know you and Violet better.' Rosie beamed at them.

'Ditto!' said Vi, unfurling her legs from beneath her and leaning forwards. 'I think we should toast to that. To friends; old and new.'

'To friends,' they chorused, clinking glasses.

CHAPTER 26

The year inched by at a sluggish pace. It seemed like a life-time since Pip had been taken from her, yet at other times it felt like only yesterday. And Molly's moods continued to yo-yo.

She found the dingy days of October a struggle to get through. The dense, stifling mists that hung heavy and lethargic in the dale had the power to smother any glimmer of happiness. Some days, it was so difficult to get motivated, Molly felt like she was wading through mud. Though, thanks to Kitty and Violet, she was making more of an effort to socialise, which always succeeded in making her heart feel a little lighter.

The twins seemed to be coping. Ben was all loved-up with Kristy, who was a regular visitor at the farm, and Tom was looking forward to heading out to New Zealand — he only occasionally mentioned Adam. As for little Emmie, the faster she was growing, the more distant a memory her dad was becoming, which saddened Molly. And, though, the family were moving on, an air of loss still had the knack of settling over the house at times but, for Emmie's sake, Molly did her best to be cheerful in front of her oblivious little daughter.

The gloomy clouds of October were soon replaced by the crisp, bright days of November. Molly felt a flicker of optimism on the mornings that broke with a thick hoar frost; they invariably led to bright sunny days with clear blue skies and her spirits were lifted by the low, winter sun.

The one month Molly had really dreaded was December and the family's first Christmas without Pip. Thankfully, Carolyn Hammondely's wedding to sound engineer, Sim, on Christmas Eve was a welcome distraction and kept Molly back from disappearing over the brink of despair. It was held at St. Thomas's church which had been decorated in a festive theme of sumptuous reds, vibrant greens and a splash of shining berries. Caro looked stunning in the crystal-embellished dress Kitty and Vi had designed and made for her. It drew gasps as she made her way up the aisle, twinkling on the arm of her father, Lord Hammondely. Pretty much the whole village had been invited, their outfits standing in stark contrast to Sim's musician friends, in their designer gear and sunglasses, and Molly's eyes had been drawn to more than a couple of surgically enhanced trout-pouts on the women. Gabe Dublin — who'd played at the castle's first music venture of Music in the Woods and Kitty and Ollie's wedding — was there along with the York band, Tykes!, who'd played support to him. In the middle of it all, Caro's mother, Lady Davinia, was bustling around, bossing everyone about. Dressed in her usual garish colours, her coiffed, bird's nest of hair looked so set, Molly thought it would take a hurricane before a single hair would move out of place. She wasn't a particularly likeable woman, Molly mused as Davinia's shrill voice echoed around the church, bouncing off the walls and clawing its way to the rafters. But Molly couldn't help but admire her. Yes, Molly had lost a husband, but Davinia had suffered the worst loss a woman could ever have to bear: she'd lost a child. Her son, Jolyon, had died of a drugs overdose whilst at boarding school. How did you ever get over that, Molly wondered? Yes, to onlookers she seemed brittle and cold, but it was her way of coping and, somehow, she'd still managed to keep going, still managed to drag herself out of bed, to breathe in and out, put one foot in front of the other and face one day after another. All without her child. Molly gave a shudder, being in that position herself didn't bear thinking about. But, if Lady Davinia could keep going, then she could, too.

Christmas day was the day that gave Molly the biggest lump of dread in her stomach. And she was grateful for Kitty and Ollie's invitation to join them, along with Jimby and Vi and her own parents. Which at least meant she and the kids didn't have to suffer her mother's bloody awful cooking — though the twins had joked that they'd be losing out on a game of "Spit the Sprout" which was something they did every year, when her mother wasn't looking. With so many children around, the day had been upbeat and lively, and Molly had saved her tears for when she was alone.

That night she'd gone to bed and curled up with Pip's favourite shirt. 'Another first,' she'd whispered to herself as tears rolled down her cheeks and soaked into the fabric. 'Oh, Pip, the pain's still there, and I miss you more than I can say, but it doesn't hurt quite as bad. I know you're looking down on us and I hope we're doing you proud. I'll love you forever, Pip.' She cried herself to sleep.

∼

In mid-January, Tom had flown across to New Zealand on a working holiday visa, which had proved bittersweet for Molly. She knew she'd miss her son terribly, but his excitement at leaving was clear for all to see. He needed to put the Adam situation behind him and she couldn't help but be happy for him. As Molly had kissed him goodbye at the airport, she knew in her heart that he would never call Lytell Stangdale his home again and she'd squeezed him extra tightly, reluctant to let him go. She was pleased she had Ben and Emmie to keep her mind occupied, not to mention Kristy, to whom she was growing close, and was proving to be like a daughter to her.

January had also brought a visit from Trevor Bottomley. As usual, he'd caught her off guard, creeping up behind her as she was sweeping the yard. She'd turned to see him standing there, the usual smarmy expression plastered across his face. 'Shit! What the bloody hell are you doing here?'

Phoebe jumped up from her spot on the doormat, her hackles raised; she crept towards him, growling.

Bottomley eyed the Labrador warily before turning back to Molly with a waggle of his moustache which made her blood boil. 'Sorry, did I startle you, Molly?'

'What do you want?' she asked, gripping firmly onto the sweeping brush, struggling to resist the temptation to hit him with it.

'I hear your son's hopped over to New Zealand,' he said, surveying the yard. 'Hmm. I've just come to see if you've had time to reconsider my offer of buying up the two fields we were talking about last year?'

'There was nothing to consider, and like I told you before, they're not for sale.' She felt her jaw clench as she took in his swaggering body-language.

'Come on now, Molly. Surely you can see the sense in selling them?' he said with a supercilious laugh.

She glared at him. 'Just leave.'

'I don't know why you're being so unfriendly, I'm only trying to help.'

'You're not my friend. The fields aren't for sale. Nothing is for sale. You're trespassing on my farm, and you need to leave. So clear off!' she spat as Phoebe moved towards him, snarling.

He held his hands up. 'Okay, okay. I'm going. It's obviously too soon. I'll give you some time and ask again.' He backed off towards his Lexus which was parked on the lane. 'But you won't get an offer in the same league as mine,' he called as he disappeared around the corner.

'My answer will still be the same, Arsely,' she yelled after him, her whole body shaking as she listened to the purr of his car heading down the track. 'Pffftt. I need a sit down after that, Phoebes. Come on.' Molly propped the broom against the wall and headed into the house.

THE NEXT "FIRST" Molly had been dreading was Valentine's Day. Neither she nor Pip had ever made much of it, but in recent years he'd bought her some gifts that had made her smile. The last one had been a caricature of the pair of them — him in his tweeds and her in her district nurse's uniform. It had pride of place in the downstairs loo and proved to be quite a talking point; the previous year's gift — a couple of pigs — even more so.

This year, on Valentine's Day, a heavily pregnant Kitty had taken a tumble. Unable to get hold of Ollie, Molly had rushed her to hospital in York to have the baby checked out.

The pair were there for hours, with Kitty hooked up to a variety of beeping monitors.

'Honestly, Kitts, you didn't have to go to such drastic measures to keep my mind occupied today,' Molly said, giving her cousin's hand a squeeze.

'Oh, Moll, I just wish this baby would hurry up. I'm the size of a house. That's why I fell; my bump's so big, I didn't see Ethel and ended up tripping over her and landed in a heap on the kitchen floor. I was like a sheep in a riggwelter, lying on my back, unable to get up.' Kitty waved her arms around in demonstration.

'What you need is a ride in Pip's Landie, Derek. Worked a treat for me.' The pair laughed at the memory of Molly going into labour at the music festival in Danskelfe Wood.

'Not sure Vi would agree with that.' Kitty grinned.

'No. I don't think she's ever forgiven me for ruining her shoes.'

Kitty was kept in overnight and Molly was relieved of her duties when Ollie arrived at the hospital, his wan face etched with worry, peering out from behind a large bouquet of flowers. She'd rubbed his arm and assured him that both mum and baby were fine. He was a good man, and it warmed Molly's heart to see her cousin so happily settled at last.

Once home, she'd gathered up the Cartwright kids, bundled them into her four-wheel drive and taken them home where she fed them on pizza and garlic bread. Once again, Withrin Hill Farm was brimming with laughter and chatter, which was the perfect distraction for Molly on her first Valentine's Day without her beloved Pip.

A week later saw the arrival of baby Cartwright, which brought with it a jumble of emotions for Molly. Though she was thrilled for Kitty and Ollie, Molly was suddenly swamped by a feeling of loneliness. There was no Pip to share the news with, or to visit Kitty in hospital, armed with cuddly toys, baby clothes and excitement. Instead, Molly went with Vi and Jimby, whose togetherness only highlighted her loss. As did the happiness that radiated from Kitty and Ollie. Tough as it was, she did her best to hide it and hoped she'd done a good job for Kitty's sake.

Tackling all of these firsts told Molly one thing: life went on, and she was coping. Days like these proved that, one step at a time, grief was slowly releasing its grip on her, allowing a little bit of hope to bloom in its place.

CHAPTER 27

MAY

'That was somebody else booking the train carriage,' said Molly, feeling pleased. 'All of the slots have been filled in July and August, and there's just a couple free in June.' She set the diary on the dresser and headed back to the Aga to check the casserole that was bubbling on the hotplate, filling the kitchen with a mouth-watering aroma.

'That's great. Dad would be chuffed,' said Ben, looking up from his revision books at the table. 'There's still a lot to do, but the campsite's really taking off. I'm going to get cracking on that old horse-box he brought back. There's not much left to do on it, but it's a bit of a struggle fitting it in what with my exams and everything.'

'I appreciate all you do, Ben. And I know Tom leaving for New Zealand has put extra pressure on you, which I don't feel good about.' Molly looked at her son as she gathered up cutlery from the drawer and started to set the table.

'Don't worry about it. Tom needed to go. And he's dead happy now, so...' He shrugged his shoulders.

'And you would tell me if you wanted to do something

else with your life. I mean, I wouldn't want you to think that you had to stay here on the farm for me. If there's anything else you'd rather do, well, it's important that you follow your dreams, too.'

Ben looked up at her. 'There's nothing else I'd rather do, Mum. I love it here on the farm. It's in my blood. And, actually...' He paused for a moment, his face flushing. '...me and Kristy have been talking.' He coughed. 'It's what she wants, too.'

'Oh?' Things were getting serious then.

'Er, yeah. Well, I know we're young — like you and Dad were — but she's definitely "The One."' With an awkward laugh, he put finger quotes around the expression. 'Her brother'll take over the running of their farm when their dad retires — like I will here when you eventually retire. And Kristy, well, er, we've talked about her moving in here in a couple of years' time when we've finished at college.'

'Into the farmhouse?' Molly wasn't sure what to think of that.

'Er, no, er, we've talked about converting the stable block across the yard.' His face was beetroot now.

Nibbling on her bottom lip, Molly glanced across the yard to the stables he was referring to. They'd been empty for years; Pip had been using them as a bit of a dumping ground. Seeing the space put to good use was suddenly growing on her. With a smile, she said, 'You really have been giving it some thought, haven't you?'

'You don't hate the idea?'

'No, Ben, I absolutely love it.'

'Cool.' A look of relief washed over his face.

'Though, I'd just like to add that, yes, your dad and me were young when we got together, but things were definitely rushed and brought forward because I was expecting you and Tom. And, while we absolutely loved you to bits, it would've been nice for us to have a little bit of time together, just the two of us, before we became parents. What I'm trying to say is that I really think you and Kristy should both get your studying out of the way before you commit to working full-time on the farm. I had to put mine back until you and Tom were a bit older and even though Grandma helped out with looking after you both, it wasn't the easiest or the best way to go about it.'

'Don't worry, Mother, we've got it all planned.' He grinned at her.

'Sounds like you have.' She smiled back at him. 'And, in the meantime, you need to focus on your exams. So, why don't you let me carry on with the horse box? Grandma and Grampy are always happy to have Em, and the forecast's good for the next few days; I'll be able to get a couple of coats done.'

'If it's alright with you, Mum, I'd actually like to finish it. In memory of Dad. If that's okay? I've done everything else on it and, well, you know.' He pressed his lips together in a smile.

Molly rested her hand on Ben's shoulder. 'Of course, lovie. And your dad would be so proud.' A rush of love filled her chest. She didn't know when her son had transformed from being a stroppy teenager into a thoughtful young man, but that's definitely what he was now. Tom, too. Pip and she must have been doing something right.

Ben pushed back his chair, stood up, enveloping her in a warm hug as Phoebe trotted across, not wanting to miss out. 'Thanks, Mum, you're the best.'

'Well, this is a treat. Thought you'd be too old for this sort of thing.' Molly squeezed him tight, rubbing his back.

'Hey, you're never too old for a cuddle from your mum.'

'Well, that's good to hear.' Her heart squeezed, and she couldn't hide the smile in her voice.

'Actually,' Ben swallowed and sat back down, 'I've been meaning to have a word with you about something else.'

'Oh?' Molly pulled out a chair and sat down, too. 'Sounds serious.'

'It's nothing bad, it's just that what with the campsite getting busy and work on the farm and my college work... and I know Uncle Jimby and Ollie help all they can, as well as you...it's just that there's so much to do, I never seem to get on top of it and the campsite's taken a big step back. And since we've been talking about my studies, I'd really like to stay on at college and do a degree in agriculture. I've learnt so much while I've been there; I think it can only be good for the farm. If you don't mind, that is?'

'Ben, lovie, I'm chuffed to bits you're enjoying your studies. And if you want to do a degree, then go for it, I was worried you were going to back out what with, well the situation we're in, but I'm so pleased you want to stay on. It's what your dad would've wanted, too.' Molly gave her son another hug. 'And you're right, there is a lot to do. I should've done something before now, but my mind's been all over the place with, with... well. Look, why don't we advertise for some help? We can both do the interviews, what do you think?'

'Actually, Mum. I think I know someone who would be really good and he's looking for work. He's been working for Kristy's dad while her brother recovered from his broken leg, but it's mended now so they don't need him anymore.'

'Oh, right, well, bloomin' heck, Ben, you don't mess around, do you?'

'Chip off the old block, me, Mother.' He grinned at her.

'Why don't I ask him to call round tomorrow, seeing as though it's Friday — my placement day here, and I'm not at college?'

'Sounds like a plan.' She grinned back.

CHAPTER 28

Molly awoke early the following morning, thanks to the squawking of Reg who had obviously invited himself over for the night yet again — no doubt with the intention of ravishing Bernard's ladies. He must have arrived after the hens had gone to roost in the coop and she'd locked them away. He was persistent, she'd give him that. The bedroom was in darkness all but for the faint outline of daylight around the curtains that were doing a good job of keeping daybreak at bay. Reg crowed again and Molly reached for the alarm clock. 'Ugh,' she groaned; it was way too early for this.

She flopped back on her pillow, her mind suddenly crowding with thoughts of her conversation with Ben the previous day and the prospect of hiring someone to help on the farm. Her stomach lurched at the implications; the family dynamic had changed again. Tom had moved to the other side of the world and she didn't know when he was coming back — if ever. And Pip...well, Pip was never coming back. Her stomach clenched, forcing a wave of nausea to rise up inside her, settling in an acidic lump in her throat.

She sat up and took a sip from the glass of water on the bedside cabinet, washing it away. Would Tom have gone to New Zealand if Pip was still here she wondered? *Yes*, she answered herself, he'd been mooning about it since he was sixteen, so they would still have had to find someone else to help on the farm anyway. Working full-time as a game-keeper meant that Pip didn't do that much on the farm, she reasoned, so it wasn't as if he was being replaced. What a horrible thought. Pip being replaced. Molly shook her head; Pip was irreplaceable. She reached under her pillow and pulled out his shirt, pressing it to her face, inhaling the soothing, reassuring scent of him that still lingered.

And what about Ben? Poor old Ben had shouldered the bulk of the work, granted with help from Jimby and Ollie, but still...he'd managed for a long time. How they'd got through lambing time was beyond her, but it wasn't fair on him to carry the full weight. Withrin Hill Farm wasn't the biggest farm in the county — not by any stretch — but now the campsite was a reality, there were no two ways about it, they needed extra help if it was to continue in the way they hoped and provide the family with a decent income.

Molly's thoughts were pierced by an enthusiastic bout of cock-a-doodle-do-ing from Reg. 'Obnoxious little shit,' she muttered under her breath as she climbed out of bed and padded over to the window. She peered out to see the cock-erel perched on a drystone wall, strutting about, head thrown back, crowing like there was no tomorrow. Behind him, the landscape was shaking off its slumber, as the light mist was slowly clearing, being gently nudged to one side by the sun as it began to trickle into the valley. It had all the hallmarks of being a beautiful early summer's day. Well, it would have, if it wasn't for Reg. She'd have to ring Jimby and get him to come and retrieve him before he got too comfortable here, letting rip with his voice as if he owned the place. He was in danger of waking Emmie, and Molly needed a little more time alone with her thoughts this morning.

She slipped her dressing gown on and headed downstairs where she was met by Phoebe, all waggy tail and wiggly bottom. 'Morning, Phoebes. Did that annoying little plonker wake you up, too?' Phoebe's otter tail-wagging increased in speed. 'I'll take that as a "yes" then shall I? Don't worry, I'm just going to put the kettle on, then I'll put my cunning plan into action.'

Out in the yard, Molly reached for the hosepipe, fixed it to the outside tap and adjusted it to the full-force jet spray setting. Reg was becoming increasingly vocal, his strutting more Gestapo-like, and it was causing a kerfuffle inside the hen house. He was undeterred by Molly as she marched across to him. Giving her a defiant look, he threw his head back and was mid-crow when she aimed the hosepipe, and released a powerful jet of water which knocked him off the wall in a flurry of feathers and strangled squawks. 'That'll fettle you, you obnoxious little git,' Molly hissed after him. Phoebe, never a fan of the hosepipe, looked on with interest from a safe vantage point.

In the next second, the cockerel was over the wall and heading towards her, water dripping from his brandished spurs. 'Oh, no you don't,' said Molly as she aimed the hosepipe at him again. He squawked in consternation before running off down the field in a soggy flap of feathers, with Molly in hot pursuit as far as the hosepipe would allow. 'And don't come back, you little strutting git,' she called after him as he raced towards Lytell Stangdale. She returned to the yard feeling victorious, a grin tugging at her lips.

'You've got a real evil streak, Mother.' Molly looked up to

see Ben leaning out of his bedroom window, wearing a face-splitting smile.

'Evil, but necessary.' She smirked back at him.

'I'LL JUST GO and check on the sheep, then I'll come back and give you a hand moving the hen house,' said Ben as he pulled on his wellies. 'That should give us time for a cuppa before the bloke comes for a chat about the job.'

'Okay.' Molly felt a knot of anxiety twist in her stomach.

'You sure you're alright, with this, Mum?' Ben stopped, his eyes searching her face.

'Course. It just feels a bit funny, you know?'

'I do, and it feels funny for me, too. Replacing Tom and...'

'Yeah.' Molly sighed. 'But we shouldn't look at is as replacing; just moving on, being positive and keeping things going.'

'You're absolutely right and that's exactly what it is.' Ben walked over to Molly and gave her a peck on the cheek.

'What's this? Yesterday you surprised me with a hug, today I get a kiss on the cheek. Are you after something, Ben Pennock?' Molly smiled.

'No reason. Other than you're a great mum and I love you.'

'Now I know you're definitely after something. Clear off and get those Chevvie's sorted.' She flicked a tea towel at him and he leapt out of the way with a laugh.

'I hope you're not going to be as fierce as that when the bloke comes round, Mother. You'll frighten him off.'

'Get away with you.' She laughed, flicking the towel again. 'Does he have a name, by the way?'

'Er, yeah, it's a funny name. Camm, I think he said it was.'

'Oh, right,' said Molly, feeling a small flicker of recognition.

THAT MORNING, Emmie had awoken in a grizzly mood. Molly scooped her out of her cot and pressed the back of her hand to the toddler's brow. 'Mmm. You're a bit clammy, sweet pea. Looks like you might be coming down with something. I think we'll give you some medicine and keep an eye on you.'

As the morning progressed, Emmie had become increasingly clingy and niggly. And, despite another dose of paracetamol, her temperature was escalating. 'Right, bubba, I think we need to get you to a doctor,' Molly said, pressing a damp flannel to Emmie's forehead.

Molly had managed to squeeze in an appointment with Dr Beth Gillespie over at Danskelfe surgery for later that morning. It coincided with the time Ben had mentioned the chap was calling about the job, but Emmie was her priority. She'd tried to call her son to explain, but his mobile was out of signal. She'd probably catch him as she passed the lane end to her parents' house but she'd leave him a note, just in case. She was happy to go with his decision; if he liked Camm and Camm liked the farm, she was fine for Ben to seal the deal. And if he could start straight away, then all the better; the prospect of having to look for someone else and for Ben to have to struggle on just wasn't appealing. She loitered on her thoughts for a moment, wondering why that name triggered a thin wisp of a memory.

As MOLLY PULLED up in the yard, straight from visiting the doctors, Ben came out to greet them, a look of concern etched on his brow. 'How's Em?' he asked as she climbed out of the car.

'Ear infection,' Molly answered with a wry expression. 'Poor little soul didn't know where to put herself, it was that painful.'

'Oh, poor Em, earache's rotten. Come and have a cuddle off your big brother.' He reached into the vehicle and lifted a poorly-looking Emmie out. 'Bloomin' heck, you don't look well.'

'Bem,' she whimpered and rested her head on his shoulder. 'Poorly.'

'You are poorly, but the medicine will make you better soon, little love,' said Molly, smoothing her daughter's damp curls.

'Mamam,' Emmie whined, reaching for Molly.

'So how did it go, the chat with the bloke for the job? Camm, was it?' She took Emmie from Ben, gently patting her back. 'Sorry I had to leave you to it, by the way.'

'No worries. And he was great. Said he could start right away if we wanted him to.'

'And?'

'He's starting tomorrow morning.' Ben grinned at her. 'Then he'll be back on Monday so I can show him the ropes for the rest of the week while college is closed for the holidays.'

'You really don't mess around, do you?' She smiled back at her son, shaking her head affectionately as she followed him into the house.

'Nope. But, honestly, Mum, he's a really nice bloke.

Quiet; has a nice sort of air about him and a kind face —
reminds me a bit of Ollie, except he has darker hair. Similar
age, too. Knows his stuff, farming-wise. I didn't have time to
show him the camping fields, but he came up with some
really cool suggestions for the campsite.' Ben opened the
fridge door and reached for the milk.

Molly looked thoughtful for a moment. 'Well, that's a
relief. Though, do you think he sounds a bit too good to be
true? Here, can you take Em while I sort her a drink? And
don't forget about your studies,' she added.

'You're such a cynic. But, nope, he seemed genuine
enough. Already done it, Mother.' Ben produced a beaker
for his little sister. 'And I won't — forget about my studies,
that is.'

'I may be a cynic, but you're an angel,' she said with a
sigh as she sat back in a chair. 'I'll let Em have a drink, get
the first dose of antibiotics down her, then make a bed up
for her on the sofa. Poor little thing looks like she could do
with a good sleep. Mind you, couldn't we all, thanks to that
bloody cockerel of Jimby's waking us up at some ridiculous
hour?'

'After what you did to him, I don't think he'll be back in a
hurry,' Ben said, making them both laugh.

EMMIE HAD HAD A RESTLESS NIGHT, with Molly being up to
see to her several times, eventually bringing the little tot
into her bed at about two in the morning. She didn't want
Ben to be disturbed; he needed to be up early in the
morning to see to the farm.

After a restless few hours, mother and daughter had
drifted into a deep sleep at around five — as Ben had

predicted, Reg hadn't returned — the pair not surfacing until just before ten when Molly was awoken by Emmie asking for a drink. 'Poor Ben, he'll have had to get his own breakfast,' she said. 'I'll see if he wants something now. And how about you, little one? Are you hungry?'

Emmie replied with a shake of her head.

ALL WAS QUIET DOWNSTAIRS, apart from Phoebe snoring in her basket. She jumped up and trotted over to Molly as she walked into the kitchen. 'Morning, Phoebes,' she said. With Emmie on her hip, Molly went to go out into the yard in search of Ben. She wanted to make him a hearty brunch to compensate for him missing out on a decent breakfast. From the sound of things, he was working in the top field nearest the house, fixing the rotten fence posts, no doubt. Molly turned out of the yard and stood, stock still, mouth agape. A brazen bolt of lust seared through her arid body, taking her breath away. Before her, oblivious to her presence, a tall man was hammering wooden posts into the ground. He appeared to have thrown off his shirt, which was now hanging over the gate, revealing a broad, muscular back, his golden skin glistening with perspiration.

Molly swallowed, her eyes drinking in every inch of him. Oh. My. Days. He was hot to trot.

As if aware of the weight of Molly's gaze on him, he turned, brushing his long dark curls out of his eyes with the back of his hand. 'Hi.' He smiled revealing white teeth, set in a handsome, sun-kissed face, his dark eyes crinkling at the corners.

'Oh, er, hi, I, er I was just...' Her stomach leapt and she could feel her cheeks flush crimson. Her words had suddenly become large, dry lumps in her mouth and she struggled to marshal them into a coherent sentence. Molly hoped he hadn't noticed. She'd been caught red-handed having a blatant perv at a half-naked, hunk of a man. The man her son had hired to help out on the farm. Oh Lord, this didn't bode well. She cleared her throat and tried again. 'Er, have you seen Ben?'

'He's just checking on his grandaddy's sheep. Said he wouldn't be long.' He smiled again and bent down to fuss Phoebe who'd run over to him. 'Hello there, girl. How're you doing?'

Molly's heart flipped once more and she cursed inwardly. 'Oh, okay. Well, if you see him, will you tell him I was looking for him?'

'Sure.' He nodded, the smile never leaving his mouth. The mouth that Molly couldn't take her eyes off.

For fear of making herself look even more stupid, she about-turned and hurried back to the house, aware that the handsome stranger was watching her. She tripped over Delores on the way, sending the hen scattering and complaining profusely. 'Sodding chickens!' she said through gritted teeth.

Once back in the kitchen, she settled Emmie in her high-chair, plonked a beaker of milk in front of her and started pacing around the room. Her heart was all of a flutter and her stomach was churning with a confusing mixture of guilt and unexpected sexual attraction. And something in her gut told her that today wasn't the first time their eyes had locked, but the memory was annoyingly elusive. 'What the hell just happened out there?' Molly muttered to herself. 'I shouldn't be feeling this way. Not one tiny, little bit. Pip hasn't been gone five minutes. And here I am lusting after the first strange bloke I set eyes on. Admittedly, he is out of the way good-looking, but that's beside the bloody point. You're nothing more than an old slapper, Molly Pennock!' She threw herself down on the armchair and started nibbling on a finger nail as guilt began tormenting her.

The back door flew open and Molly jumped to her feet. 'S'just us.' Ben's voice carried down the hallway as he kicked off his wellies.

Us? Molly found herself smoothing her hair, suddenly wishing she'd had an appointment with Stefan before now. *Behave yourself!*

'Bem,' said Emmie in a small voice.

'Hiya, Em. You look a bit better today.' Ben strode into the kitchen, smiling at his sister. 'Time for a cuppa and a bite to eat, methinks. I gather you and Camm have already met?' he said as he made his way over to the sink to wash his hands.

'Oh, er, yes, we, er, just met. I, er, was just looking for you and I, er.' Molly cursed inwardly. Why the bloody hell was she talking like a love-struck school girl? *And Camm? Why did that name set something swirling in her mind?*

'You okay, Mother? You don't seem yourself.' Ben cast a concerned look her way, as he dried his hands and hung the towel back over the rail of the Aga.

'I'm fine.' She flicked her hair out of her face, trying to sound casual. 'Just lack of sleep.'

'Ah, I'd heard the little one was poorly. Ear infection is it?' Camm looked at her, once more triggering the bolt of lust which did something deliciously wicked in her knickers and made her knees turn to jelly.

Traitorous buggers, she thought as she attempted to regain composure. Molly turned her attention to Emmie.

'Yep, she's got a nasty one, haven't you, little love? She had a cold and it seemed to follow on from that.'

'Oh, dear.' His voice sounded rich and chocolatey, almost like a caress. Molly's stomach responded by unleashing a host of butterflies. 'Well, I hope she gets on the mend soon.'

Molly swallowed, the last thing she wanted was to make a fool of herself in front of her teenage son. 'So how's about some late breakfast for you both?' she asked as she unhooked a large skillet from above the Aga, deliberately avoiding eye-contact with Camm.

'Sounds great, I've only had a couple of slices of toast and I'm starving,' said Ben. 'How about you, Camm?'

'If that's alright with you, Molly?' She could feel his eyes on her.

Oh shit. She felt her heart rate up its pace. Just the way he said her name, made it sound so personal, intimate almost. She cleared her throat. 'Of course.'

MOLLY HAD no idea how she managed to get through break-fast with her nerves jittering around. But get through it, she did. And before long, Ben and Camm had left the kitchen and gone back to their work outside. She breathed a sigh of relief. It had been exhausting; she didn't know how she was going to face Camm every day without turning into a complete gibbering wreck. There was nothing for it, she'd just have to avoid him.

Later that evening, with Emmie tucked up for an early night, Molly and Ben were sitting round the dinner table, enjoying a homemade chicken curry. Molly was conscious of her son's eyes on her. 'You okay, Mum?' he asked, reaching for a piece of naan bread.

'I'm fine — well except for feeling absolutely jiggered, but that's nothing a good night's kip wouldn't fix. Why?'

'You would tell me if you didn't like Camm, wouldn't you? If you didn't feel comfortable having him around? We could always find somebody else.' He was looking at her intently.

'What do you mean?'

'Well, you just seemed a bit...I dunno...a bit like you weren't very keen on him. Like you were uncomfortable when we came into the kitchen.'

Oh, bugger! she thought, *If only you knew, son*. She swallowed. 'Oh, love, it's not that I don't like him, it's just, you know, it feels a bit weird having a different man working on the farm. It's been in our family for generations and, after all these years, I'm just so used to it being family working on it. That's all.' This was partially true, and she hoped she sounded convincing.

'So you're happy for Camm to stay?' Ben shovelled a forkful of curry into his mouth.

'Yes, of course — as long as he does his job well.' Ben didn't seem to notice her shuffling uncomfortably in her chair as the thought that Camm looked like he was doing it extremely well earlier crossed her mind.

Ben beamed and tucked into his food with renewed enthusiasm. 'That's good. I really like him, and I think you will, too, when you get to know him. And Phoebe certainly seemed keen on him, she never left his side when he was here, did you, Phoebes?' Phoebe, who was curled up in her basket, answered with a vigorous wag of her tail.

Molly smiled, she'd noticed that Phoebe had been stuck to him like a limpet while he was having breakfast and whined to be out with him after he'd gone outside. 'Where's he staying? Locally?'

Ben shook his head, swallowing his mouthful. 'Nope, says he's in digs over at Middleton-Le-Moors. Got here on his bike.'

'Motorbike?' Molly scrunched up her nose; she didn't think she'd heard the sound of an engine when he left.

'Bicycle.'

'Really? But Middleton's miles away.'

Ben shrugged. 'He seems okay with it. He'll probably move to somewhere closer, especially when the bad weather comes.'

'Mmm, maybe,' answered Molly. *Or maybe he'll move on.* But she kept that thought to herself.

CHAPTER 29

The morning had arrived in a blaze of golden sunshine, a tantalising whiff of summer hovering in the air. Molly gazed out of the kitchen window across the moor which had well and truly shaken off its winter cloak; it was now a vibrant green and teeming with wildlife. Up above, the sky was a cheerful splash of cornflower blue, the occasional wisp of a cloud sauntering along on a mere whisper of a breeze. And, was it just her imagination, or were the birds singing with extra gusto? The buzzing of a honey bee caught her attention and she watched as it landed on the flowers she'd planted in the window box a few weeks earlier. It moved from bloom to bloom, industriously gathering nectar from the cheery faces that were offered up to the warm rays of the sun.

A ripple of something — Molly didn't know quite what — took her by surprise, making her shiver. There was a feeling of not-quite-anxiety in the pit of her stomach, tinged with a very definite hint of excitement. Camm ventured into her thoughts. She hadn't seen him so far this morning; by all accounts he'd got straight to work on the fencing and some dry-stone walling. But she was determined not to make a fool of herself in front of him and her son when they came in for something to eat.

'Mamma.' Emmie's little voice pulled her away from the window. 'Dat.'

'What, little love?' Molly turned to her daughter, who'd now fully recovered from her ear infection and her appetite had returned with a vengeance.

'Weeties.' Emmie pointed at a bag of chocolate buttons that were on the kitchen work top.

'You want some sweeties?' she asked. Emmie nodded enthusiastically. 'And what do you say?'

'Pease.' She beamed at her mum.

'Good girl.' Molly returned her daughter's smile and tipped the chocolate buttons into a bowl.

EMMIE HAD CONTINUED HAVING an afternoon nap on the living room sofa after she'd recovered from her ear infection; she seemed to settle better there than her bed, which she now associated with bedtime. Each day, Molly would line the floor next to where Emmie slept with cushions — a soft landing in case the toddler rolled off in her sleep.

She'd settled her daughter down one afternoon, and started on her list of jobs. Molly was just in the middle of answering queries about the glamping-site on the laptop at the kitchen table when the phone rang. It was a Mrs Barker wanting to book the train carriage for a week in August when it was already fully booked. She had a snotty attitude, and demanded that Molly contact the couple who'd already booked it and cancel it.

'I think my situation should take priority,' she said. 'It's my son and daughter-in-law's wedding anniversary and a week staying in the train carriage was going to be my gift to them, so I'd very much appreciate it if you'd do what I ask.'

Mrs Barker went on to say that she'd just seen the farm's advertisement for the glamping-site in a magazine and had visited the "very poor" website.

'I'm very sorry, Mrs Barker, I can't do that, but if you'd like to leave a number in case we get a cancellation...' Her words were cut off by the phone being slammed down at the other end. 'Obnoxious old bag,' Molly shouted. Though, Mrs Barker did have a point about the website, it was very basic. She'd take Kristy up on her offer of setting up a new one and all of the other social media platforms she'd told her about.

'Right, after that I think I need a brew,' she said to herself, running her fingers through her knotted curls.

As she was filling the kettle, gazing out of the window, Camm strode into view. His shirt was off again, revealing a smattering of dark curls on his chest and a set of well-defined abs. There was no getting away from it, he was absolutely bloody gorgeous. An image of her fingertips touching his skin, running her hands down his muscular arms and pressing herself against his firm body barged into her mind, making her gasp. *Stop that right now, Molly Pennock*, she remonstrated with herself just as he glanced up and caught her staring. He raised a hand and waved. 'Bugger!' she whispered as she felt her face flame. She gave a quick wave back before pulling herself away from the window and hurrying over to the Aga, setting the kettle down with a clatter. *You're nothing more than a mucky tart; stop this behaviour now!*

Molly puffed out her cheeks and sighed. 'Right, back to reality,' she muttered as she sat herself in front of the laptop screen.

An hour later, Molly checked the clock. 'How the hell's it got to that time?' she asked herself, thinking that Emmie must be having a deep sleep.

In the hallway she sensed a light draft on her bare arm and turned to see the door to the yard swinging idly in the breeze, and a parcel left abandoned on the doorstep. As she approached the living room a sense that something wasn't right caused a flutter in her stomach. 'Emmie!' she gasped as her eyes alighted on the empty sofa, the cover thrown back. Her heart plummeted and fear prickled over her face. *Surely, she can't have been gone long? Can't have gone far?*

'Emmie. Emmie, where are you?' she called, running back into the hallway. She stopped in her tracks, her thoughts barging into one another. Could Emmie have opened the door herself and sneaked out? No, she wasn't tall enough. It must have been the delivery man. She'd obviously been so engrossed in her work she hadn't heard his van.

As she ran out into the yard, calling her daughter's name, the fingers of panic began to squeeze the air from her lungs, making her heart rate surge. 'Emmie, no more hiding, sweet pea. Come out now.' She ran across to the stables, flinging the doors open, one after the other, but there was no sign of her.

Tears began to burn her eyes and nausea raged in her gut. 'Oh, shit, shit, shit. Where are you, Emmie?'

She peered into her car. Empty. Then she ran across the yard, out over the path and climbed on the gate to the top field — the very gate she'd looked out for Pip on that fateful night. 'Emmie!' she shouted for all she was worth. And again, 'Emmie.'

The thrum of a tractor over at Tinkel Top Farm caught her attention. She shielded her eyes from the sun, squinting as she scanned the area. The sudden thought that farms could be dangerous places pushed its way into her mind. Just a couple of years ago, the Sampson family over at Middleton were devastated when their thirteen-year-old son, Tommy, was killed by his own father accidentally reversing a tractor over him, crushing the very life out of him. Molly's heart lurched as an image of Emmie's broken body flashed into her mind. 'Emmie.' She gave a blood-curdling scream as she waved her arms to get the driver's attention. 'Stop!' But they didn't seem to notice her.

Panic had a tight grip of her now, and she was beginning to cry hysterically, running to the other side of the farmhouse. 'Emmie, where are you,' she sobbed as she barrelled straight into Camm.

'Woah! What's the matter, Molly? What's got you so upset?' Two strong hands held on to her shoulders, steadying her.

'It's Emmie,' she wept. 'She's gone.'

'Gone where?' His dark eyes, full of compassion, looked at her intently.

'I don't know. I don't know.' She dragged a hand through her hair. 'I was on the phone, working on my laptop in the kitchen. I don't know what happened. I thought Emmie was asleep in the living room, but when I went to check on her she wasn't there. She was gone.' She snatched away the tears that were streaming down her cheeks.

Camm bent to look directly into her eyes. 'Molly, stop worrying. Emmie won't be far, we'll find her. Safe. I promise.' He squeezed her arms. 'But first of all, I need to ask, did you check everywhere in the house?'

His calm voice had a soothing effect on her. 'Er, no. I just checked the living room then saw the back door hanging open and feared the worst.' She sniffed, wiping her nose with the back of her hand.

'Okay, well, I think you should go and check thoroughly around the house – upstairs, everywhere. Then ring your mother, see if Emmie's made her way down there. I'll look all around here, and in the fields. Trust me, little Emmie will be fine. I've got a good feeling about this.'

The way Camm said her daughter's name, with such tenderness, almost broke her heart. 'Okay,' she nodded.

Molly checked her watch, it had been fifteen minutes since she'd first noticed Emmie was missing. The longest moments of her life – like the night Pip didn't come home, but worse. Emmie was her baby.

She called her parents' house; her father answered saying her mum was out at one of her meetings. He hadn't seen Emmie and they'd agreed that he should search around their garden and sheds and if there was no sign of her, he'd stay put in case the toddler turned up there. 'Don't go worrying, Molly, love, she'll turn up, I can feel it in my waters.'

'I hope so, Dad,' she said as a sob caught in her throat.

Molly was searching behind the walls of the fields that lined the track on the way down to the road when she heard someone calling her name. 'Molly. Molly. There's someone here wants to see you.' Camm's voice wafted across the field, a lilt of happiness in it. She turned to see him striding across the long grass, Emmie safe in his arms.

'Emmie,' she cried, and though her legs felt like they would buckle with relief, Molly raced towards the pair, leaping over the tall blades of grass.

'Mamma.' Seeing her mum, Emmie started to cry, reaching out her arms towards her.

'Oh, bubba, you're safe.' She scooped Emmie out of

Camm's arms, showering kisses over the toddler's face as tears of relief streamed down her cheeks. 'Oh, Emmie, Emmie, Emmie. I'd lost you. Don't ever do that again.'

'I found her heading towards the camping field. She was crying, but fine, weren't you, little lady?' He said, smiling gently, stroking Emmie's curls.

'Camm,' she replied, wiping her tears away.

'You gave your mummy quite a shock there, Emmie.'

Molly glanced up to see him looking down at her daughter with tenderness in his eyes.

'Thank you, Camm. Thank you.' The awkwardness she usually felt had been chased away by relief at having Emmie in her arms.

'I DON'T KNOW how we'd manage without him now, Mum.' Ben was sipping a mug of tea, leaning against the Aga.

I'm not so sure, either. Molly almost gasped as the thought jumped into her head.

'He's made such a difference to the farm, tidied things up, gets things done before I even get chance to ask him to do it. It's like a huge weight off my shoulders.'

'I'm pleased to hear it, Ben. I was getting a bit worried about whether we'd be able to manage the farm, to be honest. And there have been moments when I've seriously considered Bottomley's offer.'

'Shit, don't even think about troubling that loser, Mum.' Ben grimaced. 'Actually, I'm a great believer in the saying that everything happens for a reason.'

'Oh?' It wasn't like her son to be philosophical.

'Yeah, I think Camm was sent to us via Kristy's farm at exactly the right time.' He nodded. 'Just imagine how far Em could've got if Camm hadn't found her that day? Doesn't bear thinking about, does it?'

'No, it doesn't.' Molly shuddered.

'So, does that mean you like him better now?' He was looking at her hopefully.

'Ben, I've never not liked him. It just felt weird, that's all.' *Oh bugger,* she could feel herself blushing. 'What with losing your dad, your grandad being poorly, Tom going to New Zealand; the family's been through a lot.'

Ben pushed himself away from the Aga and went across to his mum, putting his arm around her. 'I know, Mum, but we've tackled it and come out the other side. We've done really well.'

'Let's just get the anniversary of your dad's...well, you know, over and done with, then I'll really feel we've come out the other side.' She sighed and rested her head against his shoulder.

'Well, be fine, Mum. I promise.' He gave her a squeeze 'Now, I really must go and ring Kristy; we're planning how to spend our one-year anniversary and she'll be wondering where I've got to.'

Molly watched her son leave the kitchen, her heart full of pride. How had she, Mrs Grouchy-Pants, managed to churn out such a wonderful lad, she wondered? *He had Pip's easy-going temperament, that was how.*

CHAPTER 30

'Camm this, Camm that, am I the only one who thinks we seem to be hearing an awful lot about Camm?' asked Vi. The three friends were relaxing at their monthly pamper session at Rosie's house. Vi was enjoying a hot stone massage while Kitty and Molly were curled up on the sofa, nibbling on chocolates.

'Oh, bugger off, you with your over-active imagination.' Molly picked up a magazine from the table and started flicking through it.

'I'm only saying. We've got a proven track record of reading *the signs*. Like with this one, here.' She flicked her eyes in Kitty's direction. 'We'd guessed her and Ollie were going to get together before they even did.'

Kitty looked across at her cousin and gave her a wry smile. Molly rolled her eyes and threw the magazine down. 'Listen, you two, before you start your super-sleuthing and getting your over-active imaginations together, there's absolutely nothing between Camm and me and there never will be. I don't really have anything to do with him. I barely see him.' She felt her face burn as her memory rather inconveniently hauled out an image of him shirtless, lugging huge bits of stone around as he fixed a drystone wall earlier that day. She quickly elbowed it out of the way before it could take root.

Vi raised her head and squinted across at her. 'Why, Molly Pennock, I do believe you're blushing.'

'Oh, shut your cakehole, Vi. I'm flushed because it's warm in here.'

Rosie glanced across at Kitty; both struggled to suppress giggles.

'And, if I'm completely honest, I'm not that keen on him — not that I'd say anything to Ben,' she continued, giving an unconvincing shrug. 'It's just we needed someone to work on the farm to relieve the pressure on Ben so he could concentrate on his studies. And Camm, well, he just keeps himself to himself.'

'Keeps out of your way more like. Before you pounce on him with all that pent-up sexual tension bubbling away.' Vi giggled as Rosie slid the hot stones up and down her back.

'If you take the piss one more time, Vi, I swear I'm going to come over there and stick one of those hot stones up your bloody ar...'

'How's Emmie doing, Moll?' Kitty cut in before things got too personal.

'Fine, thanks.' Molly glared across at Vi whose shoulders were shaking with mirth.

'I really don't know how you two are cousins,' said Violet. 'There's Kitty, who's all dainty and lady-like and there's Moll, who's about as feminine as a carthorse and has a mouth like a cess pit. They really couldn't be more different, could they, Rosie?'

'Hey, don't drag me into this,' Rosie answered, continuing to smooth the stones over Violet's skin. 'I think you're all great, and I just love the way you bounce off each other. I know you take the mickey, but it's so obvious you all love each other to bits and would do anything for one another.'

Molly sighed. 'Yep, that's true. You may be a right pain in the arse, Violet Smith, but I'd kill anyone who hurt you.'

'Ahh, Moll, right back at you, chick.' She reached out for Molly's hand. 'And you know I'm only teasing about Camm.'

'Hey, no worries, I give as good as I get,' she said, taking Vi's hand and giving it a squeeze.

CHAPTER 31

On Ben's weekly placement day at the farm, Camm joined him and Molly for lunch at the kitchen table. Always quiet and polite, he never spoke about himself. His background remained a mystery; his only choice of conversation was usually farming or wildlife related. Molly didn't know what he did about lunch on the days Ben was at college, but he never seemed to assume it was okay to join her without him. She was secretly relieved about this.

Today, over a ploughman's lunch, he and Tom were discussing ideas for the conversion of the stables, which they'd decided to start over the winter, when things were a little quieter on the farm. Molly liked his suggestions, and Ben seemed to appreciate his input, nodding enthusiastically in response. The pair appeared to get on like a house on fire, bouncing ideas off one another, Ben chatting away animatedly.

As Molly served up some apple pie, she suddenly became aware of a warm feeling spreading up her chest. *If he's talking about working here in winter, then he must be staying.* She found herself quite liking that thought.

'Mmmhmmm. Now that's what I'd call tasty,' said Vi, arching an eyebrow.

'Mmm, he is very handsome,' Kitty agreed with a grin.

The pair had called in for a catch-up with Molly and were both peering out of the kitchen window at Withrin Hill Farm, admiring a shirtless Camm as he dug out an area of ground for a new apple tree. Phoebe, as ever, was by his side.

'There's definitely something rather delicious about him. I'm afraid handsome doesn't cover it, Kitts. Shaggable, more like. Just look at those abs, those arms...don't tell me you haven't been tempted, Moll, because I won't believe you.' Vi pinned Molly with a knowing look.

'Bugger off, Violet, and put your tongue away; you're drooling.'

'Hah, she so has! See how she's blushing, Kitts.'

'Oh, Molly, there's nothing wrong with that. It's perfectly natural; he is very attractive.' Kitty came and sat next to her cousin. 'Phoebe seems very taken with him, too, so he's obviously a nice person.'

Molly squirmed and she could feel the colour flame in her cheeks. 'Well, I'm sorry to disappoint you both, but that part of me has well and truly shut down and shrivelled up. I don't think of him in that way at all,' she said with a sniff, before taking refuge behind her mug of tea.

'Well, I do.' Vi gave a dirty laugh as she joined her friends at the table. 'And I think it would do you the world of good if you did, too, Moll.'

'Shut your face, Vi, or I'll tell our Jimby that you've been perving over another bloke. And I'll ban you from calling up here ever again.'

Vi giggled into her mug. 'Soz, hun. Promise I won't do it anymore. Cross my heart.'

AS THE WEEKS INCHED BY, with a rainy July morphing into a sunny August, the day that Molly was dreading drew closer: the anniversary of Pip's death. And as hard as she'd tried to push it away, Saturday the sixth of August arrived, just like any other day. But at Withrin Hill Farm it brought with it a heavy cloak of gloom that draped itself over the house, snuffing out any sparks of happiness. The night before, Molly had dreamed of Pip, of how he'd returned, apologising for being late. She'd rushed to him, flinging her arms around him, squeezing him tight and pressing hard kisses to his lips. Her heart, pounding with excitement and full of hope had woken her and she lay still as reality hit and the images crashed to the ground. She'd reached under her pillow and pulled out Pip's shirt. She hadn't washed it since he'd died — she never would — and if she inhaled deeply enough, her senses could still reach down and grasp the scent of him.

As memories drifted in and out of her mind, she suddenly remembered that today would have been their wedding anniversary, too. 'Oh, Pip,' she said, her voice wavering.

Biting back tears, Molly dragged herself out of bed, her heart feeling like a lead weight filled with sorrow. The glow behind the curtains gave a hint at the bright summer's day that lay behind them, but Molly wasn't interested and they remained firmly shut. She wasn't ready to face the day's inconsiderate happiness or listen to the birds that were singing as if everything was wonderful when it wasn't.

She was the first downstairs, Phoebe, oblivious to the significance of the date, trotted across the floor to Molly as she usually did, wagging her tail enthusiastically. The kitchen, whose curtains she'd neglected to draw the previous evening, was bathed in the bright summer light Molly had been reluctant to face upstairs. And, as she knew they would be, her eyes were drawn to the open window, pulled towards Pip's beloved moorland. He would have been in his element, striding out across it, breathing in the fresh air. She sighed and a plump tear rolled down her cheek. The moor looked stunning. The thick swathes of purple heather were draped in a gossamer-light film of dew, making them shimmer with an ethereal glow, oblivious to what had happened out there a year ago; nothing had stopped, life was still going on. The Danks's cows were moseying their way back to the fields from the milking parlour. The sheep were still chomping away on the grass, the birds still flitted about playfully. It seemed like Pip's beloved moors had forgotten about him. Molly sighed; it felt like she was in a cocoon and nothing around her seemed to notice that it was a year since that God-awful day. Nothing. She snatched her tears away and reached for the scissors, shoving them into her dressing-gown pocket; she'd need them for later.

Phoebe, sensing Molly's sadness, came and sat beside her. Pressing a paw against her mum's leg, she let out a whimper. 'S'alright, girl.' Molly rubbed the Labrador's head earning a thudding tail wag. 'Come on, let's face this day.'

Unlocking the back door, Molly stood aside and slipped her feet into her wellies, while Phoebe barged out with unbridled enthusiasm. 'Steady on, miss,' Molly said in a loud whisper. The Labrador charged on, regardless. Molly followed her to the top of the field where the hen house was situated. Thankfully, Reg hadn't been back since the day she'd given him the soaking. She raised the door and watched as the hens made their way out, one after the other, clucking busily behind Bernard. She noted there was no sign of Delores; she must be feeling broody again. She'd check on her later.

Molly made her way along the path that led to the track down to the village, stopping when she came to a clump of vibrant purple heather. Taking out the scissors, she cut a large bunch, disturbing its sweet, honey scent that wafted into the air.

Back at the house, Ben was busying himself in the kitchen making a pot of tea. He gave a weak smile. 'Morning, Mum. You okay?'

She nodded. 'Yep, you?' Her voice came out in a whisper as she swallowed down a lump of grief that had wedged in her throat. She walked over to her son and hugged him tightly. 'Oh, Ben.'

'I know.' He sniffed and Molly knew he was fighting back tears, too.

'We just need to get through this day and we'll be fine.' She was struggling to speak and felt him nod into her shoulder.

Ben pulled away and wiped his eyes. 'I think we should make today a day about celebrating Dad. I know it's hard, but I don't want to feel sad when I think about him — and I know he wouldn't want that, either.'

'Yep, I like that idea, and you're right, your dad would, too.' Molly dabbed her eyes with the sleeve of her dressing-gown. 'I'm going to go and lay this heather on his grave later today – he loved it when it was in full bloom. I can't guarantee I'll be singing and dancing when I'm doing that, though.'

'Fair enough. Would you like me to come with you?'

His voice told Molly he wasn't really keen. 'Only if you want to, but I'm okay to do it on my own.'

'Cool. Don't forget Tom's skyping later this morning; feels like ages since we've spoken to him.'

'I couldn't forget about that. I won't set off until afterwards.' A bright spot in a dark day, there was no way Molly was going to miss that.

THOUGHTFUL AS EVER, Kitty and Vi had offered to do whatever she wanted to keep her mind occupied, but Molly had declined, feeling that she needed to be up at the farm with Ben and Emmie, and where she felt close to Pip. She'd spoken to them both over the phone and reassured them that she'd be fine. Rosie had called, too, which Molly found touching. There'd also been an invitation to go to her parents' for lunch, but seeing Ben's face drop when she'd told him, meant she'd invited her parents up to them instead; today wasn't a day for tackling her mother's cooking. She made the excuse that she was going to cook Pip's favourite dinner: roast beef and Yorkshire puds, with all the trimmings.

TEN O'CLOCK ARRIVED WITH MOLLY, Ben and Emmie sitting around the laptop at the kitchen table, awaiting Tom's call. They didn't have long to wait. Molly's stomach leapt with excitement at seeing her son's face on the screen. 'Tom-Tom,' squealed Emmie, making them all laugh. He was in the living room at the farm, his uncle beside him on the sofa, each with a bottle of beer in their hand, it being nine o'clock in the evening there.

'You look well, Tom. New Zealand is obviously good for you,' Molly chipped in before things had a chance to get maudlin.

'Yeah, it's awesome out here, Mum,' he replied. Molly smiled at the slight New Zealand twang to his Yorkshire accent. 'It was definitely the right thing to do.'

'Couldn't manage without him now, Moll,' said Mark, giving him a hug. 'He's a great lad.'

'How much did he have to pay you to say that, Uncle Mark?' grinned Ben.

'Very funny.' Tom smiled back at his brother. 'Your warped sense of humour is definitely something I don't miss.'

'You know you don't mean that,' Ben laughed.

The banter continued for a while, before the conversation turned to Pip. And, though it took every ounce of strength she had, Molly was determined not to cry.

THE SKYPE CALL had left Molly feeling brighter, seeing Tom looking so settled was like a weight off her shoulders; she only wished he could have found happiness a little closer to home, like his brother.

'Right, I'd best get back to it. Camm will be wondering where I've got to.' Ben got to his feet, pushing the chair back with a loud scrape.

'Camm's here? I thought he didn't work weekends.'

'He doesn't, he just thought I might need a hand today, what with it being...you know?'

'That was considerate of him.'

'Yep, I keep telling you what a decent bloke he is, but you either don't look at him, or you give him one of your death stares.'

'I do not!'

'I'm afraid you do, Mother. I think that's why he doesn't come in for something to eat when I'm at college. I think he knows you don't really want him around.'

'That's not true.' Molly felt a flush creeping into her cheeks.

'Anyway, today's not the day to discuss that sort of thing. And he won't be joining us for lunch, because, well...you know.' He bent and gave her a peck on the cheek. 'I'll see you later.'

LATER THAT AFTERNOON, with dishes washed and put away and her parents taking Emmie with them for a couple of hours, Molly grabbed the bunch of heather and whistled for Phoebe. 'Come on, girl, let's go and see your dad, and walk off some of those Yorkshires.'

Phoebe jumped to attention and the two of them headed out of the yard and along the bridleway, down Fower Yatts Lane and across the moor to Lytell Stangdale.

Molly still struggled to understand how the sun could shine so brightly on a day when there was such a solid lump of sorrow in the pit of her stomach. It didn't seem right. Especially when exactly a year ago, the heavens had opened and deposited over a month's worth of rain in one night. The British summer was more than a little capricious.

As she made her way along the track, the sun's rays beat down with an unforgiving intensity. Soon, beads of perspiration began to prickle her brow and a trickle of sweat ran down her back. It was hard work walking in wellies and she was beginning to regret not putting her walking shoes on. Pausing for a moment, she took her shirt off, tying it around her waist, thankful that she'd put a vest top on underneath. 'Phew, Phoebes, it's a hot one!' Phoebe looked up at her, panting heavily.

With Phoebe on the lead, Molly was making her way along the road, just two minutes from the village, when Lycra Len whizzed by on his bike. 'Now then, Molly,' he called. She responded with a nod.

She passed Hugh Heifer walking Daisy; his awkward gait seemed more pronounced since she'd last seen him. 'Afternoon, Hugh,' she said with a smile. 'How're you doing?'

'Now then, young 'un. Me and Daisy here are in fine fettle, aren't we, lass?' He gave the cow a sound thwack on the rear.

Molly continued along the trod, past the thatched cottages that lined the road, their gardens brimming with cheerful, blowsy flowers. Across the road, Gerald was taking a break from mowing his postage-stamp of a lawn, wearing a pair of voluminous shorts, while Big Mary was gathering in the washing from the line.

'Hiya, Molly, pet,' he called across in his lilting Geordie accent.

'Oh, hi there, pet-lamb.' Big Mary turned and waved enthusiastically, setting her bingo wings flapping. 'Nice to see you.'

'Hi.' Molly smiled and walked on; she wasn't strong enough for small-talk today.

'See, Phoebes, life goes on as if nothing's changed,' she said, as the ear-splitting squawks of Reg cut through the peace and quiet.

MOLLY ARRANGED the heather in the vase and gave Pip's grave a quick tidy. She found she didn't want to hang around there for long. It wasn't a place she felt close to him; that was up on the farm, looking out over the moor. Pip's moor.

She decided to go the road way back, which at least offered some shade from the overhanging trees and hedgerow that lined it. She was just about to take the turn up to the farm track when Dave Mellison suddenly appeared, riding his bike unsteadily down the middle of the road at considerable speed, forcing a delivery van to swerve to avoid a head-on collision. Before Molly had a chance to think, the van driver beeped his horn, and she leapt out of the way, dragging Phoebe with her and landing awkwardly in a ditch. 'Warghh!' she gasped, her heart pounding. He'd missed them by inches.

Dave, who was clearly on his way back from the Fox at Danskelfe and on the wrong side of a few beers, cycled past Molly, blanking her. 'Arsehole,' she muttered under her breath, but she was relieved he hadn't stopped; the last thing she wanted was for him to ask if she was okay.

Taking a deep breath, she went to stand up. 'Arghh!' she cried out as a searing pain shot through her ankle. 'Shit, shit, shit.' She could feel it swelling up inside her wellie. 'Of all the bloody days.'

With tears brimming in her eyes, she checked her back pocket for her mobile, knowing straightaway that she hadn't remembered to pick it up before she left the house. 'Bugger.' She rubbed her chin, wondering what to do. Heading back into the village and explaining what had happened wasn't tempting, nor was the ensuing fuss it would generate; she'd just have to hobble home as best she could.

'Come on, Phoebes. Let's just take it steady,' she said, resignedly.

It was much more painful than she'd anticipated and Molly found herself crying angry tears as she limped her way up the track to the farm. She hadn't got far when another cyclist caught her attention on the way down and she hastily swiped her tears away. If she wasn't mistaken, it looked like Camm. Phoebe, who she'd let off the lead, barked and trotted towards him. In a second he was beside her, throwing the bike down on the grass verge, taking in her tear-stained face. 'Molly, what the hell's happened?' Before she had chance to answer, he'd taken hold of her, supporting her with his arm, which was suddenly wrapped around her.

Relief at seeing a friendly face and the kindness in his voice was too much and her tears flowed once more, her words coming out in sobs. 'I...I...fell...over...a van...Dave...Mell...'

'It's okay, we need to get you home.' With that, he scooped her up off her feet and turned towards the farm. 'Come on, Phoebe.'

Molly gasped, the shock of being swept up had brought an abrupt halt to her tears. She didn't know where to look, her face being so close to Camm's. She swallowed, the sudden intimacy making her feel awkward. 'You can't carry me the whole way, I'll cripple you.'

'Yes I can, and no you won't.' Camm strode on.

'Look, why don't I try to walk, you could support me?'

'Nope, this way's best, you'll only end up being in more pain if you try to walk on that foot. And you could make it worse.'

This was uncomfortable on so many levels. For one thing, she had her arms around him, and for another his face was so close to hers she could hear him breathing. And, if she wasn't mistaken, she could feel his heart beating against her side. What would anyone think if they saw them? She stole a quick glance at him, taking in the small scar just above his full top lip, the smattering of freckles across his nose that spread across his cheeks. Dark stubble peppered his strong, square jaw. His black hair, just a little too long, curled over his eyebrows. A faint glimmer of a memory or something at the back of her mind flickered for a moment but was quickly chased away when he turned his gaze to her and her eyes darted away. 'You okay?' His breathing was heavier.

'Yes, thanks, but I'm worried about you. Your back must be killing you.'

'I'm fine, you're light as a feather.'

His comment made her chuckle. 'No one's ever said that before.'

He looked at her and smiled, making her stomach do an unexpected somersault. She looked away, feeling uncomfortable that her emotions were being disloyal to the memory of Pip.

They were about three-quarters of the way up the bank when the sound of a Landie made them turn to look behind them. It was Ben, concern etched across his young face. He pulled up beside them, yanked the handbrake on and jumped out. 'Mum, what the bloody hell's happened? Are you okay?'

'I'm fine, I just fell, landed badly and sprained my ankle. Camm was heading down the track on his bike and insisted he carried me back home.'

Before she knew it, Molly was bundled into the Landie and, after they'd retrieved Camm's abandoned bike, the three of them were pulling up in the yard. Camm insisted on carrying her into the house where he set her down gently on the armchair by the Aga.

'I'm afraid I'm going to have to cut that boot off; it'll be too painful to remove any other way.' Camm was kneeling down in front of her.

'Really? They were expensive.' She winced as he took her foot in his hand.

'Yes, really, your foot's more important.'

'Here you go.' Ben handed him some heavy-duty scissors and in no time the boot was off, revealing a badly bruised and swollen foot.

Molly sighed with relief as she wiggled her toes. 'It's just a sprain, no broken bones, thankfully. But it'll be a bloody nuisance for a few days, and I won't be able to drive.'

'At least you didn't have Emmie with you, Mum,' said Ben after she'd filled him in on what had happened. 'There you go.' He passed her a freshly-made mug of tea.

'Thanks,' she said taking it from him. 'Ughh. That doesn't bear thinking about. That bloody Mellison family have been nothing but trouble since the day they moved here.'

'That's an understatement — I've told Camm all about the fire on the moor and the sheep worrying. Lucky for you, Camm turned up when he did.'

'Yes, thank you, Camm,' she said quietly.

'No problem, just glad I could help.' Their eyes met for a second and something undefinable passed between them.

'Hey, why don't you stay for tea, Camm? It's alright if he does, isn't it, Mum?'

Oh, Lord, Molly thought to herself. She went to speak, but Camm got there first.

'It's okay, I'd better get myself home. But thank you, Ben.'

Something tugged deep at the core of Molly. There was

an air of sadness to Camm that made her heart ache a little for him. He seemed resigned to rejection, as if it was part of his everyday life, an acceptance of not quite fitting in, not quite being welcome.

Yes, today was the anniversary of Pip's death, and she would have preferred to spend it alone with her family. But this man had helped her and had helped Ben and the farm more than she'd ever expected. She would feel unkind, cruel almost, if she didn't extend the invitation to dine with them. The fact that Ben's words of earlier still rang in her ears had more than a little to do with it, too.

'You're very welcome to stay, Camm. We're just having left-over beef and whatever I can throw together.'

'Looking at that trotter, Mother, I don't think you'll be doing much throwing of anything together, but I'm happy to help. And it would be great if you could stay, Camm.'

Hope brightened Camm's eyes. 'If you're sure? But you must let me help with the food.'

'Hey, I'm not gonna argue with that. That's awesome, isn't it, Mum?'

'It is.' Molly laughed as her stomach began to churn with mixed feelings.

While Ben went to collect Emmie from his grandparents', Camm made a start on preparing dinner, after propping up Molly's injured foot on a stool and insisting that she stay where she was. Conversation focused mainly on Molly telling him where he could find utensils and ingredients and she was relieved to find that the time passed surprisingly quickly until Ben returned. Molly noted how Phoebe gazed adoringly at Camm the whole time.

'This is lush, Camm. I've never had a salad that tasted as good as this before – no offence, Mum,' Ben enthused, tucking into a large portion of potato salad he'd slathered in coleslaw. 'Mmm. Mmm.'

'None taken,' she laughed. 'I'm loving what you've done with the feta cheese and beetroot, Camm.' She helped herself to more from the bowl. 'Mmm, it's got walnuts in, too.'

'Nice, dat.' Emmie beamed, chewing on some sweet red pepper.

'I'm glad you all like it.' Camm smiled at them. 'Especially you, little miss.' He chucked Emmie under the chin, making her giggle. Molly found herself returning his smile.

'I think someone's in love,' Ben joked.

Molly's cheeks flamed in an instant and she went to flash him a warning glare. She felt a tsunami of relief wash over her when she saw her son was looking at Phoebe. 'Oh, er, yes. She had her eyes on him the whole time you were out.'

'Ah, I think it's the food, rather than me that Phoebe's in love with, isn't it, girl?'

Phoebe's tail wagged furiously and she trotted over to Camm, only to be shooed away by Molly. 'No scrounging from the table, Phoebes. You know the rules.'

'How on earth did it get to that time?' They'd migrated to the living room where Ben had lit the fire and tall flames crackled and leapt in the grate. Molly checked the clock on the mantelpiece; it was nearly half-past eight.

Camm sat up straight. 'Right, well, I'd better get going.'

'You can't cycle home now, Camm, it's late. Can he, Mum? You'll have to stay here for the night. We've got a spare room, you can kip in that, can't he, Mum?'

Before Molly had a chance to answer, there was a ping

from her mobile phone on the sideboard. 'Ooh, I'd best check that.' She seized on the distraction and went to stand up. 'Arghh! Ouch!' She'd forgotten about her sprained ankle and the knife-sharp pain took her breath away.

Camm rushed over to her. 'You okay?'

'Mmhm.' She nodded as he helped her back down.

'Careful, Mum. You stay put, I'll get your phone,' said Ben reaching for it. 'Oh, Jesus! It's from Granny Aggie.'

'Oh bugger,' said Molly, her eyebrows shooting up as she read the opening line of the message.

Camm looked from one to the other, confused.

'Go on, Mother, you can't leave Camm in the dark, you'll have to share it.'

'Really?'

'Yep.'

'I'm intrigued now,' said Camm, smiling.

'Don't worry, your intrigue will soon change to horror,' assured Ben.

'Too right. Anyway, here goes,' said Molly, taking a deep breath. '"Dear Mollusc" — that's me — "I'm going pole-dancing in the village hall with Little Mary and Rev Nev. We need outfits. I said you'd get them".' Molly took a moment to absorb the message. 'Pole-dancing?' Realisation dawned and she clapped a hand to her forehead. 'The bloody old minx. She knows exactly what she's doing.' Molly glanced up at Ben and Camm who were both spluttering with laughter. 'Honestly, that woman!'

'So how do you work out what she means?' asked Camm. 'Presumably there's no pole-dancing in the village hall?'

'There's everything but,' said Ben. 'Belly-dancing, Vi's burlesque classes, Gerald's art classes — remember when he took Big Mary along as a life model?'

'Oh, Lord, how could I forget? He'd told his class to take along an item with deep sentimental value for them to draw. His item was his wife — completely starkers!'

'Wow. And here's me thinking Lytell Stangdale was a quaint little country village; it's anything but,' said Camm.

'Nothing's quiet here, Camm, I can assure you. Especially Granny Flaming Aggie and her texts. But this time, she's got pole-dancing confused with line-dancing.' Molly glanced across at Ben who'd suddenly doubled over with laughter.

'Ah. Big difference,' said Camm.

'Just a bit.' Molly grinned.

'Hey, Mum, do you remember the one about the pens?'

'Uggh! Don't remind me. It took me ages to smooth that one over.' She turned to Camm. 'Granny Aggie typed penis instead of pens. Caused all sorts of trouble.'

'I can imagine.' His eyes danced with amusement.

'She blames her arthritic fingers and predictive text, but that's a load of old tripe; she just likes making mischief. I'm going to have to square her up and threaten to confiscate her phone again.'

'Did you know she's on Twitter, Mum?' asked Ben, as if the thought had suddenly struck him.

'No.' Molly's stomach sank and she put her head in her hands. 'How did you find out — and please tell me it's nothing to do with her putting out — or whatever you call it — tweets like she texts?'

'She just came up in recommendations for me the other day. I checked her page and she's just posting selfies of herself and Little Mary at the moment. They were quite sweet, actually. Though one of them did have her holding a copy of raunchy-looking book in it.'

Molly rolled her eyes. 'Well, I've never heard the word

"sweet" used in the same sentence as Granny Aggie before. Just keep an eye on it for me, will you? It's one thing having to apologise for her mess locally, but globally doesn't bear thinking about. Pip's got a lot to answer for, leaving me to deal with her on my own.' Though Molly made a joke of it, a sudden shadow crossed her face and she felt her mood plummet as she thought of her husband.

Camm picked up on it. 'Look, I'd really better go. I've got some things to sort out back at my digs that really can't wait.' He stood up to leave and, despite Ben's protestations, he retrieved his bike from the back of the Landie and cycled off down the track into the dusky summer evening.

IN BED THAT NIGHT, snuggling in to Pip's shirt, Molly's mind was crammed with thoughts, all jostling for her attention. Her heart twisted as she relived what had happened a year ago — it was still hard to believe it was only that long ago. Laying heather on Pip's grave this afternoon didn't seem real, almost like she was acting out a scene. She knew she was still coming to terms with the fact that she'd never see him again. Dave Mellison pushed his way in, taking her from sadness to anger. That family seemed hell-bent on causing trouble for hers — the bullying poor Kitty and Lily had endured at their hands. Thoughts of Tom nudged them out of the way. Her boy had looked happy and carefree over Skype; the frown that had taken up residence on his young forehead had been smoothed away and there was happiness in his eyes again. She found herself smiling at the thought. Ben next, he was coping better than she could have hoped — she had Kristy to thank for a lot of that, she was a lovely girl and Molly couldn't think of a nicer girlfriend for him.

Emmie. Little Emmie, the daughter Pip had longed for, she'd never remember how she was the apple of her daddy's eye. But she'd been a little ray of sunshine in a dark and unhappy world since he'd gone. She may have been a surprise, but she was a very welcome one.

Before she knew it, Molly's mind had pushed Camm to the forefront. She tried to skirt around the image of his handsome face, the pain in his eyes, not really wanting to confront the turmoil of feelings he triggered inside her. No! She wasn't going to tackle them now, they could go away for another day and not the day a year from when her soulmate and the love of her life had died. With that she pulled the duvet over her head and pressed Pip's shirt to her cheek. Before long, slumber had taken her and she'd succumbed to a deep sleep.

CHAPTER 32

It was the last Wednesday in August, and Molly was taking advantage of an afternoon of Emmie playing with her cousins down at her parents' house by getting some outside jobs done. She was busily sanding down the front door of the farmhouse, lost in her own thoughts — facing out over the dale, the door bore the brunt of the weather and needed a new lick of paint. It was another job she was keen to tick off her list before the weather changed.

'Hello, Molly,' came a voice from behind her, making her jump out of her skin. Phoebe growled. Without having to turn around, Molly knew who the owner of the smarmy tone was: Trevor Bottomley. With Camm tackling gorse with the brush cutter in the next field, she hadn't heard the tell-tale sound of the car as it made its way up the track and come to a halt in the yard.

Feeling her hackles rise, she turned around, hands on hips. 'Trevor. To what do we owe the pleasure?' The note in her voice told him he wasn't welcome, while Phoebe's growl deepened.

'I've just come to see if you've reached a decision. I've

kept my word and given you plenty of time.' He dusted an imaginary speck of dust off the jacket of his pinstripe suit. 'And can you shut that dog up.'

'My decision is the same as it was the last time we spoke. And this is Phoebe's territory; she gets protective when she senses a threatening presence.' They both glared at him.

He pursed his lips together and waggled his moustache. 'I think you're being very foolish. Those fields at the bottom are standing empty. It's a complete waste, when I could be putting them to good use.'

'Well, it just goes to show how much you know about farming. Those fields had sheep in them a couple of weeks ago; you've obviously never heard of rotational grazing.'

Trevor snorted. 'Do you really expect me to believe that? You're sitting on prime building land, but you're just too stupid to sell it...'

'Everything alright, boss?' Molly turned to see an ape of a man swagger around the corner, a tattoo covering one side of his face, reaching up onto his shaved head. She felt herself shiver involuntarily. He'd obviously been snooping. Phoebe started snarling — Molly had never seen her like this before.

'Not really, Ste. Molly here doesn't know a good deal when she hears one,' he said, one eye on Phoebe as he inched away.

'That right?' Ste looked at Molly, a vein throbbing in his temple.

Molly swallowed. 'Look, I'm not selling, and I want you both off my land now. You're trespassing.' Her heart was pounding like the clappers, but there was no way she was going to show that she was scared.

Trevor narrowed his eyes. 'You need to see sense, Molly.'

'I don't think so.' Camm appeared behind Bottomley,

standing tall, holding the brush-cutter in his hand. 'I've just heard Molly ask you to leave and I think it's what you should do. The police are on their way; they'll be here any minute.'

Bottomley's face paled and his mouth fell open as he took in Camm and the glinting blades of the brush-cutter. He cleared his throat, attempting to recover his composure. Molly watched as his face slowly morphed from shock to a sneer. 'Well, well, well. What have we here then? I didn't know you had the gipsy to protect you. How the mighty have fallen, eh? Still sleeping rough, are we, or are you keeping the widow's bed warm at night?'

Molly looked across at Camm, his face remained impassive. 'You seem to have a problem with your hearing, Mr Bottomley.' Camm stepped forwards as Bottomley stepped back, just missing Phoebe.

'That's just what I was thinking. Now bugger off back under your stone, you slime-ball and don't come back,' Molly snarled as the sound of a police siren could be heard heading towards the village, it's slow whine wending its way up the bank.

Bottomley's face dropped. He turned to his ape, 'Come on, Ste, I'm done here,' he said, quickly heading back to the yard.

Camm and Phoebe followed the pair out, watching them until they climbed into the car and drove off. Molly joined them, still feeling shaken. Camm turned to her. 'You okay, Molly?'

She nodded. 'I am now. He gave me the shock of my life, creeping up behind me like that.' She shuddered. 'Thank you for getting rid of them. Seems you're good at coming to my rescue. I don't know what I'd do without you.' The words were out before she had chance to stop them. Realising how it must have sounded, she bit her lip, feeling her face burn. Molly chanced a look at Camm from beneath her eyelashes. He was looking back at her, the familiar expression of she knew-not-what in his eyes. Feeling awkward, she rubbed imaginary goosebumps on her arms. 'Well at least Arsely took the hint,' she said in attempt to carry on as if nothing had happened.

'The man's a worm.'

'You're not wrong. Actually, what's happened to the police siren? It's stopped?'

'That was a complete coincidence, I reckon it'll be PC Snaith late home for his lunch, he'll have set the siren going to let his mum know he's on his way.' Camm smiled. 'I gather it's not the first time he's done it.'

Molly scrutinised his face to see if he was joking. His expression told her he wasn't. 'Come to think of it, I have heard it a few times recently. I had no idea Snaithy was still a mummy's boy.'

They stood in silence for a moment. Molly was still struck by embarrassment, but something compelled her not to turn away. 'I was just about to stick the kettle on. Do you fancy a cuppa?'

'Sounds good,' he said, his eyes searching hers for a moment.

'Tell you what, I'm glad I had this locked, or that creep would've been having a poke around, I'm sure of it,' she said as they reached the back door.

'I don't doubt that for a second.'

THE PAIR WERE SITTING at the kitchen table, mugs of tea in hand as they negotiated a stilted conversation. Curiosity soon got the better of Molly, and she decided to tackle the elephant in the room. 'Is it true what he said about you?'

Camm sighed and dragged a hand down his face. 'About being a gipsy, or about sleeping rough?'

'Both.' Molly sipped her tea, peering over her mug at him. She doubted he slept rough; he certainly didn't look like he did.

'Yes, Molly, it's true.' He looked at her directly, his eyes containing the shadows of pain she'd seen before. 'I'm a gipsy and I sleep rough. I have no home.' He paused for a moment before pushing the chair out behind him. 'Look, I'll go. I understand, no one wants a gipsy hanging around their home.'

'No!' Molly reached out and grabbed his hand. 'I mean, I don't want you to go. Please sit back down.' Her heart suddenly ached for him. She wanted to snatch away his pain and make things better. And she had an overwhelming urge to go and kick Trevor bloody Bottomley in the bollocks.

Camm looked at her, the traces of sorrow damping the brightness of his eyes. He sat back down, and Molly released his hand. 'But I thought you were in digs in Middleton. Why on earth didn't you say you had nowhere to stay?'

'I was in digs at Middleton, had a really nice landlady — Mrs Ovington — but Mr Bottomley told her I was a "thieving gipsy" so she asked me to pack my bags,' he said with a shrug. 'It's okay, I'm used to it.'

Her usual reluctance to make eye contact with him had evaporated and she met his gaze as realisation slowly dawned on her. 'We've met before haven't we?' Her heart began to race as her mind pieced together fragments of the day when she was fifteen and first saw Camm.

He nodded slowly, his eyes searching hers to see if they would betray her innermost feelings. 'We have, Molly.'

'You're the gipsy boy who was getting the shit kicked out of him down on the road to the village.'

'I am — and I've got the scars to prove it,' he said touching the one on his top lip. 'And you're the fearless girl who came to my rescue.' He chanced a smile.

'Shit a brick!' Molly clamped her hand over her mouth. 'I can't believe this. Did you know who I was when you came here? Is that why you came?'

'No, I had no idea. Obviously, I knew your name was Molly like the girl who helped me — I could never forget her. It wasn't until just before Emmie went missing I started to get an inkling, but I didn't know what to say, and there never seemed to be a right time to bring it up.'

'This is unbelievable,' she said, her eyes still searching his. 'I've still got it you know — the talisman.'

'Really? You kept it?'

'Yes, in fact, I came across it not that long ago. It's in my box of treasures.'

'You kept the talisman in your box of treasures?'

'Yes, to keep it safe.'

The look he gave her reached into her very core, sending shivers of she knew not what deep inside her.

'For all these years?'

There was that expression again; she couldn't decide if it was heartbreak or happiness. 'I'll got and fetch it. Two ticks.' With that, she went to her bedroom as fast as the twinge in her ankle would allow.

While she was gone, Camm reached into the small pocket of his jeans and pulled out the tiny piece of intricately worked silver he'd been carrying with him for over twenty years.

'There you go.' Back in the kitchen, Molly placed the half talisman on the table in front of him. He picked it up, smiling as his eyes roved over it, smoothing it with his finger.

'And here's the other half.' He placed both pieces in the palm of his hand and held it out to Molly. 'Together again.'

'Together again,' she whispered.

'I told you I'd come back for you, Molly Harrison.'

She looked up at him, seeing a glimpse of the boy that had morphed into a man reflected in his eyes.

CHAPTER 33

A few beats fell before Molly spoke. 'Have you seen the vardo in the glamping field?' She hoped Camm couldn't hear the shake in her voice betraying the butterflies that were fluttering about in her stomach.

'Yes, it's a beauty.'

'Have you seen inside it?'

'I've never had any reason to; it wasn't my place to go nosying. Why?'

'Come with me.'

Camm followed her down to the glamping field, stopping in front of the vardo. Molly unlocked the door. 'It's empty until the weekend,' she said as she stood back. 'Go on, take a look.'

Camm gave her a quizzical look as he climbed inside. A moment later she heard his breath catch in his throat. She climbed in after him to see him smoothing his hand over the carved initials that matched the talisman. He brushed a tear away. 'Where did you find it?'

'It had been abandoned in one of the fields at Pip's

parents' farm over at Middleton — just after the fair last year. Why?'

'It belonged to my grandparents. These are their initials. I'd heard it had been stolen. I haven't seen it for years.' His voice was barely a whisper.

Molly's heart twisted, a lump of sorrow wedged in her throat. She swallowed it down. 'Oh, Camm. I'm so sorry; we didn't know. We just thought whoever it had belonged to, they didn't want it anymore.' Resisting the urge to wrap her arms around him, she placed her hand on his arm.

'It's not your family's fault, Molly.'

'If we'd known, we would've given it back to your grand-parents.'

'How could you have known?'

A thought suddenly crossed her mind. 'You can have it back, Camm. It's rightfully yours. And you can have the money from the people who've camped in it.'

Camm shook his head and turned to look at her. 'No, Molly. I don't want it, and I don't want your money, it's yours now. And you've done such a beautiful job of restoring it – it looks even better than I remember. I wouldn't take it from you.'

'But it's yours by rights.'

'No, Molly, it's not.' They stopped for a moment, their eyes locked as electricity crackled between them. Camm was turning the pieces of the talisman over in his hand, his eyes growing darker as his pupils dilated. Before she knew it, he'd clasped his free hand around the back of her head and pulled her towards him, pressing his lips against hers with a burning passion she hadn't felt for a long time. Molly groaned, and ran her fingers through his unruly curls, returning his kisses with equal ardour.

Just as desire was scorching its way up inside her, Camm

pulled away. 'I'm so sorry, Molly. I shouldn't have done that. Please forgive me,' he said, shaking his head. In the next moment, he'd left the vardo, leaving Molly gasping for breath and her heart thumping.

She pressed her fingers against her lips; they felt bruised and swollen. Her mind raced with thoughts that were skittering about, all colliding into one another. Before she knew what was happening, her legs were carrying her down the steps of the caravan. 'Camm!' she cried. 'Come back! Camm!' But there was no sign of him.

She ran up the path, past the other glamping pods where a middle-aged couple, sitting in fold-out chairs watched her with interest. She continued around the hedge into the next field, the twinge in her ankle reminding of her recent injury, but he was nowhere to be seen. 'Camm!' she called again, stopping to get her breath back.

Back at the farm yard, there was no sign of him. Molly noticed his bike had gone and she felt her heart sink. He'd left. She headed back into the house, her mind in turmoil. The day had taken an unexpected turn, knocking her off-kilter and her heart wasn't in getting back to sanding the door.

The day hadn't panned out quite as she'd hoped. She stood, gazing out of the window, trying to make sense of what had just happened, wondering which part of it had made Camm run away. But it was no use; her mind was too jumbled with emotions. The urge to get away from the farm for a while found her grabbing her bag and her keys and making for her car. 'See you later, Phoebes,' she called to the Labrador who was watching her intently.

CHAPTER 34

'Hiya, Moll, it's good to see you.' Kitty looked up from her work at the sewing machine and beamed at her cousin. 'You okay?' Her smile dropped when she took in her cousin's expression.

'Hi. Yep,' Molly answered, giving an unconvincing smile.

'Hi, Moll. I'll stick the kettle on.' Vi gave Kitty a knowing look.

'What's up, chick? You don't look yourself. Has something happened?' Kitty asked.

Molly wandered over to the kitchen area and flopped down at the table. 'I've just been having a real bugger of a day and needed to get out.' She puffed out her cheeks and looked up, 'I'm not interrupting you am I?'

'No,' they answered together.

'We were just about to have a break, weren't we, Kitts?'

'Yep, so it's good timing,' said Kitty, heading over to Molly.

'Come on then. Spill.' Violet placed a mug of tea and a plate of biscuits on the table. 'What's up?'

'Nothing,' Molly replied, dunking a biscuit.

'You sure, Moll?' asked Kitty.

'Listen, petal, we know you too well, you can't expect us to believe you've got a face like a slapped backside for nothing.'

Molly put her head in her hands and groaned. 'It's everything. Everything's the bloody matter, and I don't know where to start.'

'Oh, Moll,' said Kitty, rubbing her cousin's arm.

'Has it got anything to do with Mr Hot-To-Trot?' asked Vi, earning herself a stern look from Kitty.

'Mr Hot-To — I mean Camm — Trevor sodding Arsely, me making a complete tit of myself. The list goes on.' She counted them off on her fingers. 'Sorry, I didn't mean to just come here and moan at you.'

'You did, and it's fine. We want to help, Moll. So come on then, we're all sitting comfortably, tell us everything,' said Violet.

Molly told them what had happened with Bottomley, but when she got to Camm, she found her feelings harder to put into words and felt her cheeks flame.

She was relieved when Kitty came to her rescue. 'Listen, Moll, you've coped amazingly well since Pip passed away — all of you have — but you can't just stop living your life. Tom hasn't, and Ben hasn't; they're both doing a brilliant job of moving on and facing life without their dad — and that's got a lot to do with you being a fantastic mum to them. But you've got to think about yourself in all of this. You're a young woman with your whole life in front of you. Isn't that right, Vi?'

'Kitty's absolutely right, Moll. You do need to start thinking about yourself.' Vi nodded. 'First things first, if you want my opinion, I'd get a restraining order or cease and desist letter to keep that reptile Arsely away from you – from what I've heard, if he thinks he's genuinely wasting his time, he moves on. And then, and I'm going to be completely honest, chick, I'd take stock of your feelings for Camm. We've seen the way he looks at you, haven't we, Kitts?' Kitty nodded, giving Molly's arm a squeeze. 'And if you feel the same way, then why shouldn't you go for it? You already know that Ben thinks he's the best thing since sliced bread, so that shouldn't hold you back.'

'Phoebes, too, she makes moon-eyes at him all the time he's there, and dogs are very good judges of character. Humph never liked Dan,' added Kitty of her elderly Labrador who had passed away.

'Humph and everyone else,' muttered Vi, bringing a smile to Molly's lips.

'Oh, I don't know.' Molly rubbed her hands across her face. 'It all feels too...I mean...it's only just over a year since Pip...well, you know. And I didn't expect to be having feelings like this. People will think I'm a cold-hearted cow and that I didn't love Pip.'

'Nobody in their right mind could ever think that. But, Molly, the universe is talking to you. Camm said he'd come back to you when you were both just teenagers, and he's done just that, without even realising. It's fate. And you can't ignore it.' Kitty's enthusiasm made Molly smile.

'Yep, and if it doesn't work out and all you get out of it is a bloody good rogering, then that's fine, too. Look at the good it did Kitty when her and Ollie first got it together — you must remember that cheeky little twinkle in her eyes.'

'Thanks for that, Vi. It's usually Moll who lowers the tone with smutty talk.'

'It's true, though, Kitts,' agreed Molly, giggling. 'You were so radiant, you dazzled us.'

'Haha.' Kitty giggled, too. 'See, at least we've made you smile,' she said.

Molly sighed. 'Thanks for helping me see straight, ladies. I don't know what I'd do without you.'

AN HOUR LATER, Molly's world didn't seem such a complicated place. 'Right, I'd better go and rescue Emmie from Mum's cooking,' she said, looking at her watch. 'She's threatened to make lasagne for tea, which Ben compared to dog poo last time he had it.'

'No wonder your dad's as skinny as a rake,' said Vi.

'That's what Ben says,' replied Molly.

'Poor Auntie Annie, she means well,' added Kitty. 'Lucas and Lils made me tell her that they're having tea at home — which is true, I've got a casserole cooking slowly in the Aga. Please don't say anything, Moll. I wouldn't want to hurt her feelings, and it's so kind of her to have my three.'

'Wouldn't dream of it, she loves having your kids and Em loves playing with them.'

'Think about what we said, Moll,' said Vi, giving her a hug.

'Promise?' Kitty planted a kiss on her cheek.

'Promise.' Molly smiled.

THE HOUSE WAS SLUMBERING under a blanket of quietness, the only sound the occasional hooting of an owl and the rhythmic ticking of the grandfather clock from the hallway. Molly lay in bed, alone with her thoughts. Pip's shirt remained firmly under her pillow; it didn't feel appropriate to snuggle into it when thoughts of another man featured so heavily in her mind. She revisited the events of the day. She'd take Vi's advice and speak to her solicitor about Bottomley; he needed to stop making a nuisance of himself, and she couldn't be bothered to deal with him anymore. With that box very neatly ticked, she moved on to Camm. What did she feel for him? She'd never admitted anything to herself up to now. But that kiss! Wow! That kiss had changed everything. She pressed her finger tips to her lips as a warm glow radiated through her body. It felt too nice to push it away, so Molly let it linger.

But what if he didn't come back? He'd taken both halves of the talisman with him. What did that mean? The warm glow was replaced by a feeling of panic pushing its way around her veins. Did she want him to come back? Yes, more than she'd care to admit. Ben would, too. Ben would definitely want him back. Oh, God, Ben. She'd made up some excuse about Camm having to leave suddenly. Ben had looked surprised, but he'd accepted it. She didn't know what she'd say if he didn't come back tomorrow. 'What a bloody mess,' she said with a sigh as she turned over and plumped up her pillow.

CHAPTER 35

Over a week had passed since Camm had left. Molly struggled to know what to say to Ben, who'd taken it hard. He clearly missed more than just Camm's help. With Ben about to start his new course at college, Jimby and Ollie had stepped into the breach, generously offering their services and helping out whenever they could. But it wasn't the same. And she felt bad about pulling them away from their own livelihoods.

Emotionally, Molly felt like she'd taken a huge backwards step. Gone was the feeling of optimism that had crept its way into her psyche without her noticing, making the world look a brighter place. Gone too, was the smile that had started to revisit her features; instead a frown furrowed her brow.

She was pushing Emmie on the swing in the garden, her thoughts miles away, when her daughter's face suddenly lit up. 'Camm! Camm!' she squealed. 'Mamma! Camm!' She pointed a little podgy finger, and Molly turned to see Camm standing at the gate, his raven curls blowing gently in the breeze.

'Hello, Molly. Hello, Emmie,' he said with a small smile, his eyes uncertain.

Molly felt her spirits soar as a huge grin spread across her face. 'Camm!'

'See Camm,' shrieked Emmie, trying to climb out of the swing. Molly brought it to a halt and lifted her out. As soon as she was set down on the grass, Emmie ran towards him, her chubby arms outstretched.

'Hello there, little lady,' he said scooping her up, undoubted pleasure in his eyes when she rested her head on his shoulder and patted him.

'Someone's pleased to see you,' said Molly, brushing her hair out of her face.

'I'm pleased to see her, too. I've missed her.' He paused, his eyes searching Molly's face. 'I've missed you, too.'

'And I've missed you. We all have.' She still couldn't stop smiling. 'Are you...? How long are you staying?'

Before he had chance to reply, Emmie wriggled to be put down. 'Camm, puss,' she said, pointing to the swing. She took hold of his hand and dragged him towards it.

'She knows what she wants,' he laughed as he lifted her into the swing and started pushing her gently. 'Can't think where she gets it from.'

Molly stood beside him feeling like a tongue-tied schoolgirl. Her heart was thudding wildly in her chest, and her stomach was doing somersaults. She eventually managed to marshal her thoughts. 'Where did you go?'

'Back to Middleton. I just needed to sort my head out.'

A couple of beats passed before Molly spoke. 'I was worried about you; Ben was, too.'

'I felt ashamed for what I'd done. Didn't want you to think I'd taken advantage.'

'You've nothing to be ashamed of. You didn't do anything I didn't want you to do.'

He turned to her, a glimmer of optimism in his eyes. 'You're sure?'

'I'm sure. I hardly fought you off; surely you felt me kiss you back.' She reached up, touching his cheek with her hand. He covered it with his own hand, pressing it to his face.

'Molly,' he said softly.

It had taken until now for her to realise just how gentle his eyes were, how the rich, dark brown was flecked with flashes of gold. And now he was looking at her with such tenderness, she thought her pounding heart would explode.

Before she knew it, he'd cupped her face in his hands, and brushed his lips against hers. Molly felt herself melt as their kiss deepened and passion began to burn its way up inside her.

'Camm! Puss!' cried Emmie, when the swing had slowed down, her voice crashing into their moment, forcing the pair to reluctantly pull apart.

'Oh,' gasped Molly, suddenly dizzy with desire.

BEN WAS THRILLED to see Camm when he returned home from college that evening, quizzing him and making him promise not to leave again and, after hearing that he'd lost his digs, making him agree to stay in the spare room. The look on Camm's face told Molly he was genuinely surprised to have been so missed by the family.

Later that night, Ben disappeared up to his room to Facetime Kristy, leaving Molly and Camm alone in the living room. Molly looked across at him. 'Do you still have the talisman?'

'Of course.' He reached into his jeans pocket and spread it out in the palm of his hand. ' Would you like your half back?'

'Yes please.' The pair smiled at one another, the implications understood. She left her chair and went to sit beside him on the sofa.

'Look, Molly, I just need to explain something, if that's okay?' He looked serious and Molly felt her heart fall like a lead weight taking her smile with it.

'Okay.'

'All of this,' he spread his hands out, 'the kindness your family has shown me, being made to feel welcome, being trusted, well, it's all new to me, and it's taking a while for it to sink in.'

'Oh, Camm, it's...'

'I don't want you to feel sorry for me,' he said fervently. 'It's just how it is. What I'm trying to say is, well, that I've got feelings for you that I haven't had for a while, that I'd locked away and I didn't expect to see again. I didn't *want* to see them again if I'm honest. Ever.'

'Oh.' Molly swallowed.

Camm looked down, fiddling with his fingers. 'You see, Molly, like you, I know the pain of losing someone you love; I understand your grief.' He took a deep breath. 'I was married — a long time ago now — to a beautiful, vibrant girl called Kosella — she was a gipsy, like me.' A shadow of sadness crossed his face, and for a moment, he fell silent.

'What happened?' asked Molly softly.

'She, er. She died.'

'Oh, Camm. I'm so sorry.' Molly lay her hand on his arm.

'Like I said, it was a long time ago. But she died giving

birth to our baby girl. The baby...I called her Kezia...she didn't make it either.' His bottom lip trembled as he wiped his eyes. 'The pain was unbearable, and ever since then, I swore I'd never love anyone else; never let anyone get close. There was no way I wanted to risk going through that again.'

'I can totally understand that.' Molly looked down at the floor, feeling her own sorrow rising.

'Until I saw you again, Molly. And then everything changed.'

She raised her eyes to his; the hope that a second ago she thought was quashed, suddenly resurrected. She took his hand, giving it a squeeze and he wrapped his fingers around hers. 'I get where you're coming from, Camm. The pain of losing someone you love *is* unbearable. It's an actual, physical pain, and you never, ever think you'll get over it. And then, one day, you suddenly feel a tiny ray of hope, and get a glimpse of the person you used to be before. The pain's still there, but it's not quite so raw. You realise that life goes on, and that you are, very slowly, beginning to heal.'

He looked at her and smiled. 'Yes.'

'I've had the support of my family and friends who've been totally amazing, and I don't know what I would've done without them. And having little Emmie has given me a reason to get out of bed on a morning when I'd much rather hide under the duvet and tell the world to bugger off. But I get the feeling you didn't have that.'

'No, but that was through choice. I cut myself off. I didn't want to talk about it to anyone, especially not my parents who weren't particularly understanding. I went off on my own, travelling all over the country, getting work where I could, sleeping rough.'

'That sounds awful.'

'It wasn't so bad. In fact, some good came out of it; it

brought me back to you.' He turned to her with a heart-melting smile, his dark eyes shining brighter than she'd ever seen them.

In a moment, his lips were upon hers, kissing her with such tenderness it almost made her weep.

At the sound of Ben heading downstairs, Molly jumped up like a scalded cat and hurried back to her seat. He popped his head round the door. 'I'm off to bed now, so I've just come to say goodnight.'

'Night, son. Sleep tight.'

'Night, Ben.'

'It's good to have you back, Camm.' Ben beamed.

'It's good to be back, Ben.' Camm returned his smile.

With Ben safely ensconced in his bedroom, Molly moved back to the sofa. Sitting close to Camm, she rested her head on his arm. 'We're going to have to be very careful how we handle this one. The last thing I want to do is to alienate Ben from you; he thinks the world of you and I wouldn't want that to change.'

'I think a lot of him, too. He's like the son I never had — I realised that while I was away. Little Emmie, too, she's got right inside my heart.'

'And I think we both know she feels the same about you.'

His face wreathed in smiles, Camm sat back and wrapped his arm around her. 'I think we'll just have to take things slowly — for all our sakes.'

'You're right. Maybe it's best if we keep things to ourselves for now, let Ben get used to you living here first — staying in the spare room.' She curled her feet up on the sofa and snuggled into him.

'Yes, I'm happy with that for now. Though he's not daft, and I wouldn't want him to think I was betraying him or trying to step into his father's shoes.'

'I doubt he'd think that. But for now, can we just enjoy this moment because it feels so lovely?'

'Molly, there's nothing I'd like more than to enjoy this moment here, having you in my arms. I feel like the happiest man in the world.' He squeezed her tight, pressing a kiss onto her head.

THE FOLLOWING DAY, with Ben at college, Molly was in the kitchen preparing lunch when Camm appeared in the doorway. 'Is this okay?' he asked. 'Coming in for lunch when Ben's not here?'

'Of course it is,' she said, pulling him in. 'Please don't ask anymore. I'm sorry I was such a witch about it before.'

'Camm!' Emmie squealed with delight and ran over to him. 'Tactar.' She held up a toy tractor to him.

'Now, that's a smart tractor you've got there, little miss,' he said, picking her up. She put her arms around his neck and delivered a sloppy kiss to his cheek. 'Well, wasn't that just lovely?' He chucked her under the chin.

'Roast beef sandwiches okay?' Molly asked, smiling at the heart-warming sight of her little daughter in Camm's muscular arms.

'Great. And you weren't a witch, by the way.' He set Emmie down while he went to wash his hands at the sink. 'I didn't come in before, because it didn't feel right at the time.'

'But it does now?'

'Yes. It does now,' he said with a smile that lit up his face.

They chatted away over the meal, with Camm sharing some suggestions for the campsite and Ben's plans for converting the stables that they'd be starting on soon.

Emmie chipped in, babbling away at ten to the dozen, while Phoebe gazed lovingly at Camm from her basket.

'RIGHT, this little one's ready for her afternoon nap,' Molly said, lifting a sleepy-looking Emmie out of her high-chair. 'I'll just settle her down upstairs. Don't go anywhere.'

'Okay,' Camm replied. 'Wouldn't dream of it,' he added when he saw the suggestive way Molly raised an eyebrow at him.

Since the day she'd disappeared, Emmie had gone back to having her afternoon nap in her bedroom, safely on the other side of a baby-gate.

'Bless her, she was flat out by the time I'd tucked the blanket around her,' said Molly, coming back into the kitchen. She stopped in front of Camm, who was leaning against the Aga. 'Shame the weather's changed and you have to keep this on all the time,' she said, rubbing the fabric of his shirt between her fingers, a flirty smile playing at her lips.'

He looked down at her, amusement dancing in his eyes. 'Is that right?'

'Mmhmm.' She nodded.

'Well, we'll have to do something about that, won't we?' He undid a handful of the buttons before pulling it over his head. 'That better?'

'Oh, much,' she smiled, taking in his smooth, tanned skin, the smattering of dark hairs on his chest. 'And I've wanted to do this since the moment I saw you working on those fence posts.' She ran her fingers down his biceps, then back up again, across his muscular shoulders and along his pecs. She inhaled his intoxicating scent of amber and sandalwood, mingled in with fresh air and a hint of sweat. A flash of desire burned through her core, causing her heart rate to race so fast, she could feel it pulsing in her lips.

'And I've wanted to do this to you since that day, too.' Effortlessly, Camm picked her up and carried her across to the worktop, sitting her on it as she wrapped her legs around him. Fumbling, she unbuckled his belt as he pressed burning kisses all the way down her neck. He pushed her skirt back and tore at the fabric of her knickers, throwing them to the ground. Molly gasped, pushing her fingers into his curls. 'Camm,' she moaned as she lost herself in the moment.

'Wowzers! Any more secrets you're keeping there, Camm Ackleton?' Molly picked the remains of her knickers off the floor. 'Not sure these are much use anymore,' she giggled.

'Secrets?' he asked, tucking his shirt back into his jeans.

'How to make a woman feel like *that*?'

He laughed, leaning across to kiss her. 'It's been a while.'

'Too bloody right.'

CHAPTER 36

'Moll, can I have a word?' Camm popped his head around the kitchen door.

Molly looked up from her laptop. 'Course. What's up?' she asked, taking in his concerned expression.

'It's Ben,' he said hesitantly, rubbing his forehead with his fingertips.

'Ah, you've noticed, too?' she said, closing the laptop and pushing it away from her.

'Yeah, he's been a little bit cool, stand-offish almost,' he said. 'Do you think he knows?'

'About us?'

Camm nodded. 'It's the only reason I can think of for him being less friendly. Everything else is fine, we work well together — I don't want you to think I'm telling tales, by the way, my concern is for him, I don't want to upset him or make him feel uncomfortable.'

Molly puffed out her cheeks and released a noisy sigh. 'I know, and I don't think you're telling tales, he's been off with me as well. Tom's been a bit frosty over Skype recently, too.'

'Right. What do you think we should do?'

Before Molly had a chance to answer, the door flew open and Ben burst in. 'Thought I'd find you here,' he said, barely looking at Camm. 'I need a hand with the sheep in the top field. If my mother can spare you, that is.' He stormed out before Camm could answer.

Molly felt herself prickle with annoyance at her son's bad manners. 'Sorry about that,' she said, glancing at Camm who winced as the back door was closed with a slam.'

'Don't be, it's perfectly understandable. He's a good kid, and if he's got an inkling about us, it'll be a lot for him to take on board.' He turned to leave. 'I'd better go and help him.'

'Okay, but it's probably best not to say anything to him about it at the moment. We need to think hard about how we play this,' Molly said, her mind in turmoil.

'I understand,' said Camm, giving her a small smile.

'WHERE TOM-TOM?' asked Emmie as she climbed onto a chair at the kitchen table and peered into the laptop screen.

'He'll be there soon, bubba,' said Molly, checking the kitchen clock. 'Just five more minutes.

'Fife mimits, Bem.' Emmie gave her brother a toothy smile as he ambled into the room with Kristy. 'Kissty, sit dere.' She pointed to the seat next to her.

Kristy obeyed with an easy-going smile. 'Does that mean I get to sneak a little cuddle with you, Em?' She wrapped her arm around Emmie and planted nibbly kisses on her cheek, making the toddler squeal with delight.

'Stop that, Kris,' Ben said huffily as Tom's call was coming through.

'Okay, keep your knickers on, Mr Huffy,' Kristy hit back, rolling her eyes.

'S'alright for you to say. And, anyway, where am I supposed to sit?'

'Here,' said Kristy, pulling Emmie onto her knee and freeing up a chair. 'That do you?'

Ben replied with a grunt as he flopped onto the seat.

Oh dear, that's not good, Molly thought to herself. *He's obviously taking his mood out on Kristy, too.*

The Skype call was the most stilted so far, with Tom replying to his mother with one-word answers and not volunteering any conversation himself.

'Christ, this is like pulling teeth.' Molly's patience was wearing thin.

'Well what do you expect, Mother? I don't know what to say to you.' Tom's icy glare didn't lose its impact across the miles.

'He has a point, Mum,' added Ben.

Molly paused, pressing her lips together as she thought for a moment. 'Right, we might as well get this out in the open. I think you both need to tell me what's on your mind.' She sat back, bracing herself for the onslaught.

Ten minutes later, with both boys having aired their feelings and the atmosphere thick with recriminations, Molly was struggling to marshal her thoughts. She'd been bombarded by her sons' words, the worst being accusations of her not loving Pip. Feeling battered and bruised, she was struggling to fight the tears that were burning at the back of her eyes.

'I'll tell you what I think. I think the pair of you are absolutely disgusting,' Kristy piped up, her eyes blazing. 'I've sat here and listened to you both having a go at your mum and I think the pair of you ought to be ashamed of yourselves.'

Both boys wore expressions of shock as Kristy got stuck into them. 'Don't you think your mum has a right to be happy? The pair of you are moving on and getting on with your lives, and you're doing it with love and shedloads of support from her. She doesn't think twice about doing her absolute bloody best — sorry for swearing in front of Em — so you can fulfil your dreams. Anything you ask for, she makes sure you get. Tom, have you forgotten how she did everything for you so you could go to New Zealand? Looked into the visa, booked the flights, paid for it. You didn't have to lift a finger, it was all organised so you didn't have to have any stress about it. All your mum wanted was for you to be happy after your heartbreak over Adam.'

Tom hung his head.

'And don't think you're getting off lightly, buster.' Kristy turned her attention to Ben, two spots of pink, burning brightly on her cheeks. 'You, you spoilt little shit — sorry for swearing again, but my blood's boiling with this one — you just have to click your fingers and you get everything you ask for.'

'Like what?' Ben asked, rattled.

'Well, how about the stables across the yard, for example? It's not that long since you told me how all you had to do was suggest converting them into a house for us, and Molly agreed to it, there and then.'

'Alright, you've made your point,' Ben replied, his eyes cast down.

'Oh, not nearly well enough, matey.' Kristy prodded him in the arm. 'Let's not forget, just how generous your mum's being here. By her letting us convert the stables, she's actually letting us have a home — designed the way we want it — for free. How many people of our age do you know are lucky enough to have that, eh?' She didn't give him chance to answer. 'I'll tell you exactly how many, none! And you might not be grateful for it, but I am. So I suggest you and Tom get over yourselves pretty sharpish, and realise that your mum has a right to be happy without you judging her and without you thinking that she didn't care for your dad.'

For several long seconds, silence hung in the air, everyone absorbing Kristy's words. Molly's mind was racing, did she really give the boys everything they asked for? She'd never thought about it. Maybe she did, but it was never a conscious thing, she just wanted them to be happy and would do anything she could to help them — just as her parents had done for her and Mark. And Kristy, wowzers, what a girl! Where did that feistiness come from?

'Bem and Tom-Tom naughty boys,' said Emmie, interrupting Molly's thoughts.

'You're right, Em, they are,' agreed Kristy. 'Very naughty boys.'

'Sorry, Mum,' said Tom, sheepishly.

'Yeah, sorry, Mum,' added Ben.

'It's okay, boys, I understand why you would feel upset.' She reached along and squeezed Ben's hand. 'That's why I didn't want to say anything just yet. Camm and I weren't being secretive or sly, we were just trying to protect your feelings.'

'I get that now, Mum,' Ben said quietly.

'Me, too, Mum,' agreed Tom.

'And I can assure you that my relationship with him doesn't, for one second, mean that I love your dad any less. I'll always love him with all my heart — he was my first love and I adored him, I still do.' Molly took a fortifying breath and continued. 'In all honesty, my feelings for Camm took me by surprise and I tried really hard to ignore them, but the truth is, he makes me happy and makes the days not seem not so dark and lonely anymore.'

'Oh, Mum, I'm so sorry.' Ben sniffed and snatched away the tear that had spilt onto his cheek. He pushed his chair back and went over to Molly, wrapping his arms around her.

'Please don't be sorry, Ben, lovie.' Molly rubbed his hand. 'Just get your friendship with Camm back on track. And thank you, Kristy.' She turned to the young woman. 'I had no idea you thought that, but your words mean a lot.'

'Aww, you're welcome. I think you're totally awesome to cope with everything the way you have and still make sure your kids are okay.'

'Well, I'm not sure I've ever been called awesome before.' Molly turned to Kristy and grinned. 'But I'll tell you what, I like your sass.'

'I'm not so sure I do,' said Ben pulling a face and making everyone laugh.

'Well, there's plenty more where that came from,' Kristy quipped, giving him a nudge with her shoulder.

'Good for you, Kristy,' said Molly, realising she could see a bit of her younger self in Ben's girlfriend.

'Time to move forward, Mum,' said Tom. 'I'm sending a massive virtual hug over to you.'

'Yep, time to move forward, son, and I'm sending one right back.'

'I'M SO RELIEVED we've got it out in the open,' said Molly later that evening when she was curled up on the sofa in the living room with Camm. 'It's a massive weight off my shoulders.'

'Same here, I'm just happy it went well. I'd hate to come between you and the boys.'

'Well, we've got young Kristy to thank for it. You should've seen her, she was taking no prisoners.' Molly smiled as she pictured Kristy's face.

'Can't think who she reminds me of.' Camm looked at Molly, quirking an eyebrow.

Molly giggled. 'Oh don't worry, it's already crossed my mind, too. I'm just glad everyone's happy.' With a contented sigh, she rested her head on Camm's shoulder.

'Me, too,' said Camm, pulling her close.

CHAPTER 37

Molly was battling with the wind, trying to hang washing on the line when Vi's little purple car rolled up into the yard. Molly watched, across the garden, giggling as Vi climbed out of the car, trying to stop the full skirt of her dress from blowing above her head. In the next moment, Kitty jumped out, followed by Lucas and Lily from the back where Kitty reached in and lifted Lottie out of her car-seat.

'Hiya, lasses, over here,' Molly called.

Emmie, who'd been helping by handing pegs to her, squealed with excitement when she saw her young cousins and abandoned the peg bag on the floor as she ran over to them.

Kitty waved, while Vi shouted, 'This flaming wind's playing havoc with my hair. I'll go straight in.'

Molly smiled, if Pip was here, he would have called Vi a princess. 'Okay, I'll just be two ticks. Stick the kettle on, will you? You take Lottie in, too, Kitts.'

'Okay.' Kitty's voice was whipped out of her mouth and carried off down Withrin Hill.

'Phew! It's wild out there, I hope I won't be chasing my

washing all over the moors,' Molly said, once inside. She hung the washing basket back on its hook in the utility room. 'And, to what do I owe this pleasure — not that it's not good to see you?'

'No reason, other than coming to see how our lovely friend's doing,' said Violet, walking in from straightening her hair in the hall mirror.

'Yep, the kids asked if they could come up as they haven't seen you and Emmie for a while,' added Kitty. 'And Sunday morning's the only time when we're usually all together.'

'That right?' Molly sensed there was an ulterior motive. 'Then how come the two of you have got an air of plotting about you?' she asked as she disappeared to the living room with a tray of drinks and biscuits for the kids, where they'd gathered to play on the games consoles.

Back in the kitchen, with the three women sitting round the table Molly gave her friends a look. 'So, come on then, what's the real reason you're here? And don't go giving me any more rubbish about Lucas and Lily wanting to come and see us. I know when you two are up to something.'

'Well, we just wondered,' said Vi.

'Because you haven't done it for ages...'

'Woah, where the bloody hell are you going with this, Kitts? We don't want to rub her nose in the fact that she hasn't done *it* for ages.' Vi giggled. 'Sorry, Moll, she's going off track here, this isn't what we'd discussed.'

'Ha-bloody-ha,' said Molly.

'Vi!' admonished Kitty, giving her a mock stern look. 'What I was trying to say was, do you fancy joining us for the music night at the Sunne next Thursday? That's what I meant you hadn't done for ages.' She stuck her tongue out at Vi.

'Actually, now you come to mention it, Kitts.' Vi gave her

friend a nudge. 'Just take a look at your cousin. If I'm not mistaken, she has a certain look about her. A certain sparkle. Wouldn't you agree?'

'Bugger off.' Molly snatched her mug up and held it in front of her face.

Kitty giggled. 'Oh, Vi, she has. And look how much she's blushing. Beetroot doesn't even come into it.'

'Come on, tell all.' Vi grinned.

'And again, bugger off.'

'Moll, you so can't grumble about this. I can remember what you were like when you were interrogating me about Ollie. And you were far worse than Vi.'

'True.' Vi nodded.

At that, Camm walked in from the yard. 'Hello, ladies.' He smiled at them. 'Molly, Ben and I are just going over to Arkleby to have a look at those sheep of Titch Ventress's at Ellerby Farm. We shouldn't be long.'

'Okay, see you later.' Molly could feel her face flaming.

Kitty and Vi watched as he grabbed the Landie keys and headed out. 'Nice to see you, Kitty, Vi.'

'You've had a little sample, haven't you?' Vi grinned, eyeing Molly. 'You can't deny it. The way Heathcliff was looking at you just then, told us all we need to know.'

'Well, as we're on the subject, it wasn't a little sample, I can tell you! Just about blew my socks off,' Molly said, with a dirty laugh.

'Molly! TMI,' said Kitty sticking her fingers in her ears and making her friends laugh.

'Go, Molly,' said Vi, raising her hand for Molly to high five.

Giggling over, Molly went on to share her conversation with Camm and about how they were going to take things slowly, and keep their relationship under-wraps with everyone except family; there was no way she wanted to be the subject of village gossip. 'I just wish there could've been a bigger gap between Pip and Camm. I don't want people to think I'm being insensitive, or I didn't love Pip properly. Or that I can't manage without having a man in my life; it's none of those things. It just happened.' She sat back in her chair, trying to read her friends' expressions.

'Look, Moll, like we said before, anyone who thinks like that doesn't know what they're talking about and isn't worth knowing anyway,' said Vi.

'And anyone who knows you, will know that none of that is the case,' added Kitty. 'Lord knows, you fought it for long enough. And, anyway, who says there's an acceptable time-scale on things?'

Vi nodded. 'And no one can control timing, specially you, Moll. Look at what happened with the twins. Falling pregnant at sixteen wasn't part of your plan but look how that worked out. And I bet you wouldn't change it for the world.'

Molly shook her head. 'You're right. And you know, I always thought Pip was my soulmate — and he was, he is — and when he died, I thought I'd never be able to love anyone again — a man, I mean — but I have. I've fallen in love with Camm, but it's a totally different type of love to the one I had — have — for Pip. That one was a cosy, steady kind of love — Pip was like a comfy old pair of slippers, reliable, did the job, safe and I absolutely adored him. But the love I have for Camm is so intense and passionate and burns really hot in here.' Molly patted her chest. 'We have a real connection, but it doesn't mean that it's any better or worse than the one I had for Pip; it's just different.'

'Well, we're just so glad that you're smiling again, Moll.

And don't feel you have to explain yourself to us; we just want you to be happy,' said Kitty.

'True, we were really worried about you at one point,' added Vi.

Molly reached across and took hold of her friends' hands. 'Lasses, I really don't know what I'd do without you. I love you both so bloody much,' she said, her eyes brimming with tears.

'And we love you, too, Moll,' replied Kitty, her eyes doing the same.

'For crying out loud, no bloody tears, please or you'll have me looking like a panda,' said Vi with a sniff, and blinking quickly. 'I haven't got my waterproof eyeliner on, and you've no idea how long it takes to perfect these cat-flicks.' The three looked at each other and laughed.

Molly gave a sigh. 'It's been a roller-coaster of a few years for the three of us, hasn't it?'

'It has, especially for you and Kitty,' agreed Vi.

'Mmm.' Kitty nodded.

'Well, let's hope stays quiet for you, Vi,' said Molly.

'Bloody hell, I hope so.' Her friends didn't notice the frown that momentarily troubled Vi's features.

CHAPTER 38

'It's nearly ten o'clock, Ben,' Molly called upstairs. It was Sunday morning, and they were due to Skype Tom any minute.

'Coming,' he called from his bedroom, where he was with Kristy.

Molly headed back into the kitchen and sat in front of the laptop at the table, pulling Emmie on her knee.

'Where Tom-Tom?' asked Emmie.

'He'll be on there soon, sweet pea.' Molly pressed a kiss onto her daughter's head, inhaling her gorgeous girl's delicious scent and giving her a squeeze.

Just as the ringing tone started, Ben came into the room, pulling his chair out and sitting down. 'Kristy's just nipped for a shower.'

'Hi, everyone.' Tom's smiling face appeared, his North Yorkshire accent more heavily tinged with a New Zealand twang since the last time they spoke.

Molly's heart lifted with happiness at seeing her son. 'Oh, Tom, you're looking really well.' She reached out to touch the screen.

'Tom-Tom,' shouted Emmie. 'Hi dere.'

'Hi dere, Emmie,' Tom said, laughing.

After exchanging news, Tom took a deep breath. 'Right, Mum. There's someone here, who'd like to say hi.'

'Oh, now I'm intrigued,' she said.

At that, Adam Mortimer appeared in view beside Tom. 'Hi there, Mrs Pennock,' he said, grinning broadly.

'Adam!'

'Yep.' He and Tom exchanged happy glances and laughed.

'What? Why? How come?' You're in New Zealand?' Molly looked at Ben in disbelief, noting he didn't look so surprised.

'Hiya, Molly,' Mark called from the background.

'Hi, Mark,' she called back. 'You've suddenly got a houseful.'

'Just the way I like it, little sis. Bill, the farmhand, has moved on, and we needed someone to take his place. Adam sounded perfect, so here he is.'

'Wow. And I gather you've been in on this?' She turned to Ben, who grinned back at her, his eyes twinkling.

'Adam got a working holiday visa, like me, and we're going to see how it goes.' Tom looked the happiest she'd seen him in a long time; her heart could have burst with joy for him.

'Well, that's great, you two. How long have you been there, Adam? And it's Molly, not Mrs Pennock.'

'Just a couple of days, Mrs Pen, I mean, Molly. My dad's not very happy about it, but my mum's really chuffed for me.' His smile matched Tom's in wattage.

'Well, I'm really pleased for the pair of you.'

'Thanks, Mum,' said Tom. 'Anyway, how's things with Camm?'

'Oh, er, Camm's doing a really good job, isn't he, Ben?' Once again, Molly felt her cheeks burning.

'Too right he is. He seems to be having the same effect on Mum as Adam's having on you, Tom.' He flashed her an impish smile.

As Molly struggled to calm her blushes, she heard Camm come in from the yard, ease his wellies off and pad to the kitchen.

'Camm here!' Emmie cried.

'I'm not interrupting anything, am I?' Camm asked as he started to wash his hands.

'Er, no,' said Molly.

'Camm!' Emmie reached her arms out to him for a cuddle; he dried his hands and obliged by picking her up.

'Hi there, little lady,' he said.

'Camm, I was just telling Tom here how you've been making Mum smile.' He shot him a cheeky grin, while Tom could be heard chuckling in the background.

'You have?' Camm asked.

'And we both think it's great that you make each other really happy, don't we, bro?'

'You do?' asked Molly, her stomach in the throes of a butterfly rebellion. This was so different from the last time her relationship with Camm was discussed over Skype.

'Yep, you deserve it, Mum, and from what Ben's said, Camm's a great bloke.'

Molly looked from Ben to Camm.

'Couldn't agree more, Tom,' said Ben putting his arm around Molly and giving her a squeeze.

'WAS THAT A SET-UP?' Molly asked Ben when the call had

finished and Camm had taken Emmie outside to see a flock of geese flying by.

'Not strictly speaking, no. I knew that Adam had flown out with a view to working there. Tom mentioned it a while ago, but I didn't want to say anything in case it fell through.'

'And what you said about Camm?'

Ben stopped what he was doing. 'Look, Mum, I'm not blind. I saw how miserable you were when Camm went away. And then how glad you were when he came back. You've got as much right to be happy as me and Tom. It felt strange when I first realised, but after what Kristy said, Tom and me talked it over and we think it's cool that you've found someone like Camm.' He looked at her and smiled. 'Oh, and by the way, Mother, when you're sitting next to him on the sofa, there's no need to scuttle off back to your chair just because you hear me coming downstairs. I don't have a problem with you being close.' He waggled his eyebrows at her as he headed through the door.

Nonplussed for a second, Molly was lost for words. 'The little sod,' she said to herself as she shook her head and laughed.

'And don't forget I liked him before you did,' Ben called down the stairs.

CHAPTER 39

Thursday arrived, and after talking herself in and out of it, Molly decided to join her friends for the music night at the Sunne that evening. She'd only ventured to the pub once since Pip's funeral, and by early afternoon, her stomach had started to twist itself into knots at the thought of going, especially since Camm would be accompanying her.

Stefan had very kindly squeezed her in at the salon the day before and had touched-up the roots where her grey streak was pushing through. She'd been pleased she went; his entertaining banter had made her giggle. She looked in the mirror and assessed herself, something she'd been reluctant to do since the last time it told her she looked a good ten years older than she actually was. Today, she was pleasantly surprised; her dark curls were a rich, glossy chestnut with a smattering of golden highlights, her complexion had lost its sallow tinge — she could almost swear it was glowing (in no small way that was thanks to Rosie and her wonderful facials) — and her eyes had allowed themselves a little sparkle. The Molly of before she lost Pip might no longer be there — that one would never return — but she'd been replaced by a new Molly, a Molly who realised she had to start living her life again.

'WILL I DO?' Camm came into the kitchen wearing a light blue grandad shirt over a white t-shirt and blue jeans. His dark curls had been combed, and he was clean shaven. Molly inhaled the exotic scent of his cologne that wafted in with him, the hints of sandalwood and amber triggering a memory of their love-making the night before. 'Mmm. You smell delicious. And you look very handsome.'

He laughed, walking over to her. 'And you look good enough to eat,' he said slipping his hands around her waist and taking in the conker coloured sweater dress that clung gently to her curves. He pressed his face into her hair. 'Do we have to go out? I'd much rather take you back upstairs.'

'Down boy!' she said, laughing. 'Ben'll be here with Kristy any second and I don't want to embarrass them, or us.'

Though Molly and Camm still kept separate bedrooms — having agreed to take their relationship very slowly, especially for Ben's sake; they didn't want to rub his nose in it — Molly would sometimes tiptoe across to Camm's room in the dark of night and slip between the sheets beside him. She'd feel herself tingle with the illicit deliciousness of it.

CAMM PULLED on the handle of the large oak door of the Sunne, holding it open for Molly to walk through, triggering a rush of nerves that played havoc in Molly's stomach. 'You go first,' she said, hanging back.

'You'll be fine, Molly. People will be pleased to see you, and you aren't doing anything wrong,' he said softly.

She puffed out her cheeks and exhaled noisily. 'You're right. Let's get ourselves in there.' She gave him her biggest grin and stepped into the pub.

The place was already heaving with regulars, and the hum of their friendly banter hung in the air. Molly inhaled the smell of wood-smoke from the open fire and mouth-watering aromas from the kitchen, scanning the room, happy to see the same old familiar faces dotted about. She spotted Jimby waving, trying to attract their attention, from their usual table in the corner by the fire, his habitual smile lighting up his face. Molly felt herself relax as the feeling of anxiety fell away.

As she made her way across the room, Jonty stopped her, patting her arm affectionately. 'Molly, it's good to see you, m'dear. Bea will be thrilled when I tell her.'

'Thank you, Jonty, it's good to be here.'

'Hiya there, Molly, pet.' Molly turned to see Gerald standing behind her. 'It'th about time you got yourthelf out and about.'

'Gerry, man, get your gnashers in,' said Big Mary. 'Hello, there, chicken.' She smiled at Molly. 'I keep telling him he'll never get used to those teeth if he doesn't keep wearing them.'

'Thorry, folkth.' Gerald gave a gummy smile before rummaging around in his trouser pocket for his teeth.

'Anyroad, it's good to see you, pet-lamb,' added Big Mary.

'Aye, it is that,' agreed Gerald, pushing his teeth into his mouth.

'No worries, Gerald, and it's good to see you both, too.' Molly stifled a giggle and wove her way across to the table.

Kitty got up from her seat on the banquette next to Ollie

and came across to her. 'I'm so glad you came.' She planted a kiss on her cousin's cheek, giving her a squeeze. She glanced behind her at Camm. 'Hi, Camm, it's great that you could come, too. We've saved a seat for you both over here,' she said, leading Molly by the hand.

'Ey up, Moll,' said Jimby, grinning broadly. 'Come and park your arse down here.' He pointed to a seat. 'Now then, Camm, me aud mucker, how're you diddlin'?' he asked, patting Camm soundly on the back, before moving his guitar aside, allowing the pair to get in.

'I'm fine thanks and thank you all for inviting me.'

'Hey, no probs, you're part of the gang now,' said Ollie, standing up. 'Right then, it's my round. Pinot, Moll? How about you, Camm, pint?'

Camm nodded. 'Yep, a pint of the local stuff would be great, thanks.'

'I'll give you a hand, Oll,' said Jimby.

'God help us,' giggled Vi. 'Good luck with that, Ollie. He's already tipped a packet of crisps over Nomad and Scruff and knocked Little Mary's sherry into Lycra Len's crotch, and we haven't even been here for half an hour.

'What can I say, it's a skill.' James shrugged and flashed her a cheeky grin. 'Nomad and Scruff didn't complain, and neither did Len for that matter. Looked like it was the high-light of his week when Bea came out and started to mop up the spillage on his Lycra with a tea towel.'

'Ahh, nothing's changed then?' laughed Molly. Vi shook her head and rolled her eyes heavenwards.

'Molly, darling. Jonty said you were here,' enthused Bea who'd come over to see her specially. She pushed her glasses up on to her sleek blonde bob and bent down to kiss Molly's cheek. 'I'm so pleased you came. It's lovely to see you. And you look fantastic.'

'Thank you, Bea. It's good to be here.' Molly's heart swelled with happiness at being made to feel so welcome.

They were soon joined by Rosie and Robbie, who pulled up a couple of chairs and sat beside them. The pair slotted into the group nicely, Molly thought to herself.

As the evening progressed, the new, slightly awkward feeling of being out with Camm began to slip away. She looked across at him, smiling, taking in his handsome face, his dark eyes glittering in the soft light. Memories of last night and his tender love-making crept into her mind, making her heart flutter. He caught her watching him and gave her a smile, loaded with meaning only they would understand. She sent one back, catching Kitty and Vi exchanging a happy glance out of the corner of her eye.

'There you go, Moll,' said Ollie, passing her a glass of wine.

'Ooh, thanks, Oll.' She took a sip, savouring the lemony tang.

'Looks like the singing's starting up.' Jimby turned to where Jonty was introducing proceedings.

First to sing was Lianne whose stunning vocals were greeted with enthusiastic applause.

Next up was Anita Matheson with her Songs at the Sunne debut. As usual, she was dressed like a teenager in a plunging sparkly mini-dress which showed an eyeful of crepey bosom and a pair of scrawny legs.

Jimby turned to the group. 'If Maneater's dress was any lower you'd be able to see her fan...'

'Thank you, Jimby.' His words were cut off by Vi. 'We don't need to know.' She pulled a face, and the friends all spluttered with laughter.

Jonty's face fell when Anita started to belt out an out-of-tune version of something unrecognisable. This was just the sort of thing he and Bea were trying to discourage. She slinked her way across the room to Camm, where she proceeded to run her fingers through his hair and thrust her chest into his face. He sat, frozen to the spot, his eyes wide with fear, as everyone looked on in morbid fascination. Anita finally finished her performance, straddling his lap with a cry of, 'Tada!'

Molly snorted with laughter — rather than feeling threatened by the display, she couldn't hide her amusement as Camm's eyes darted from side to side, his face wearing an expression of "help me".

'Thanks, handsome,' said Anita as she grabbed his face in both hands and kissed him full on the mouth before jumping off and smoothing her dress down. 'Ooh, me knickers have wedged themselves right up me bum-crack,' she cackled as she wiggled her way back to her seat, doing a thorough job of fishing them out.

Dumbstruck, Camm looked around at the group in disbelief, while Kitty and Violet laughed into their drinks.

'Classy lady,' said Jimby, turning to Camm. 'You look traumatised, mate.'

'Don't worry, buddy, we've all been on the receiving end of her advances,' said Ollie, his shoulders shaking with laughter. 'And it can be bloody-well scary when it happens.'

'Bloody terrifying, more like,' added Camm, suddenly finding his voice. 'Thanks for the warning, Moll.'

Molly was still struggling to keep her giggles under control. 'Well, I didn't know she was going to pounce, did I? Not so sure I would've stopped it anyway, it was so hilarious to watch.'

Their attention was diverted by Jonty calling Jimby up to sing. 'How're you going to follow that then, mate?' asked Ollie with a grin.

'I'm going to fail miserably.' Jimby smiled and grabbed his guitar.

Perched on a bar stool, Jimby cleared his throat, his expression serious for once, before giving a mesmerising performance. You could have heard a pin drop, as the whole place listened in awe.

'Right, Violet. Your turn,' he said when he'd finished and she made her way over to him. Jimby strummed on his guitar as Vi did justice to a sultry number, her voice soft and smoky.

Jimby had barely climbed off his seat when Dave Mellison appeared, saxophone in hand.

'Oh, look out.' Molly leaned into Camm. 'This will be fabulous for all the wrong reasons.'

'Oh?'

'Oh, yes. And I dare you to keep a straight face.'

Dave made a big display of fiddling around with his saxophone and performing a series of bizarre mouth exercises.

'He is such a knob,' muttered Molly.

'King of the knobs,' added Vi. 'Just look at that arrogant expression.'

'Actually, the more I look at him, the more I think he's got the face of a bloke who looks like he needs a bloody good kick in the nuts,' observed Molly.

'Ouch,' said Camm.

'Does a man ever wear an expression that says that?' asked Ollie, looking worried.

'Well, in case you're ever wondering about any of my expressions, none of them will *ever* say that,' said Jimby. 'Just putting that out there.'

'Hmm. I'm not so sure about that,' said Vi, an eyebrow

raised. 'I could've sworn I've seen you wearing an expression very like that a couple of times.'

'You can be one very scary woman, Violet Smith.' Jimby waggled his eyebrows at her and flashed a cheeky smile.

'You'd better believe it,' she quipped back.

A long, tuneless note brought their focus back to Dave Mellison. He was perched on the stool, his eyes closed as he slowly began to crucify a vaguely familiar tune, oblivious to the sniggers and snorts going on around him. Once he'd finished, he took a self-satisfied bow and sat back down.

'Shit a bloody brick with your name on it,' said Molly, wiping tears of laugher from her eyes, earning herself a scowl from Aoife who had plonked herself next to Rosie. 'What the chuffing hell was that?' She looked around at her friends who were laughing so hard, they weren't fit to speak.

'Did I ever tell you my Dave was in a band, Robbie?' Aoife's affected accent drifted across to them. 'He's a very talented musician.' She seemed to be ignoring Rosie, leaning across her to get Robbie's attention, flirting clumsily.

Dave was about to launch into another song — when Jonty jumped in and, using the excuse of lack of time and other performers needing a turn, managed to put a stop to it.

For the next half hour the pub was treated to a medley of upbeat folk music, rounded off by an enthusiastic perfor-mance by Gerald and Big Mary, which went down a storm, especially when Big Mary decided to throw in a couple of moves she'd learnt at Violet's burlesque classes.

When they'd finished, the well-loved pair were met with huge applause. Molly put her fingers between her lips and let rip an ear-splitting whistle.

'Ooh, you're ever so ladylike, Moll,' said Vi with a nudge.

Molly laughed. 'They were great. Better than the crap

that Me...' Vi, seeing Aoife looking their way, gave her another nudge. 'Oops!'

'I see some people seem to have moved on very quickly,' Aoife said, her voice deliberately loud. 'Seems a short space of time to replace someone, don't you think, Rosie?' Aoife was looking daggers at Molly.

Vi squared herself, ready to give the woman a mouthful, but Rosie beat her to it. 'Actually, Aoife, I've just about had enough of your sniping. You can't say a nice word about anyone, especially Molly and Kitty — who happen to be my *friends*. So, if you don't mind, I'd appreciate it if you would go and take your spiteful, manipulative arse and find somewhere else to sit.'

Aoife's mouth was pinched tighter than a cat's bum, and her eyes bulged. 'I don't know how you put up with that, Robbie. I pity you.'

'Well I happen to agree with everything my wife has said,' he replied calmly. 'Just go and sit somewhere else, Aoife, we've come out to have a nice time with our friends.'

Aoife snatched up her bag and stormed out of the pub, collaring Dave on the way out.

'Well, I think that's a cheeky little cheers to Rosie and Robbie,' said Vi, raising her gin and tonic.

'Cheers,' said everyone, clinking glasses.

'That should shut that toxic woman up for a while.' Kitty smiled.

'It's been good, seeing you out, enjoying yourself, Moll.' Jimby smiled before taking a sip of his beer.

'It's been good to be out, Jimbo.'

'And how have you enjoyed things, Camm?' asked Ollie. 'D'you think you can put up with us lot?'

'It's been great. I've loved every minute of it — apart from the Maneater bit. Molly's very lucky to have such amazing family and friends.' He looked at Molly with unmistakable affection in his eyes.

'Well, you're part of that, too, now, Camm.' Kitty smiled.

'A toast!' said Vi.

'Vi and her toasts,' chuckled Jimby.

'To friendship,' she said.

'To friendship,' they chorused.

CHAPTER 40

'Penny for them.' Camm walked towards Molly, an easy smile on his face. She was standing in the top field looking out over the dale, a mug of tea in her hand, her curls blowing out behind her in the breeze.

'Oh, I was just thinking about things, you know?' She smiled back at him. 'Cuppa?'

'In a minute.' He put his arm around her, and she rested her head on his shoulder.

'I just can't believe how lucky I am.'

'Lucky?'

'Yes, lucky that I've got Tom and Ben and Emmie, my parents, my wonderful friends.' She paused. 'And you.'

He stood silent for a moment. 'I'm the lucky one, Molly.'

'We're both lucky.' She looked up at him and smiled. 'Who'd have believed, all those years ago when we first met, that we'd end up together, like this.'

He cupped her face in his hands, his eyes gentle with affection. 'I'd have believed, Molly. I've always believed in fate. We've both suffered the indescribable pain of losing someone we love. We've both been brought so low, it seemed like there was only darkness ahead. But somehow, we got through all of that sadness and suffering and pulled ourselves up.'

'We did.' Molly nodded, her thoughts falling back to earlier that day.

She'd been tidying her bedroom, changing her bedding. She'd looked for Pip's shirt, not wanting that to go into the wash, but it was nowhere to be found. With a feeling of panic taking hold, Molly had hunted around for it. She didn't find it until later that afternoon when she went to hang a dress up in the wardrobe. There on a hanger, next to the suit cover containing Pip's tweeds, was his shirt, hanging neatly with the buttons done up. Molly gasped, pressing a hand to her chest. Who would have done such a thing? Suddenly, without warning, the shirt began to sway on the hanger, slowly, back and forth. Molly felt a shiver prickle up her spine as goose-bumps peppered her skin. 'Pip!' She took a step back, recalibrating her thoughts, before sitting on the bed. Was this a sign? If so, what was it telling her? Suddenly, a wave of peace washed over her. Her beloved Pip was telling her it was time for her to move on, and he was okay with it.

Camm's voice brought her back to the present. 'We're on the other side of it now. Yes, we'll have days when a shadow might return, a memory will catch us unawares, but we've got through it.' He looked down at her. 'And, in the process, I've fallen in love with you, Molly. Hook, line and sinker.'

'And I've fallen in love with you, Camm.' A smile spread across her face.

Camm bent and gently kissed the tip of her nose. 'I didn't think it was possible to ever feel this happy again.'

Molly gazed into his eyes. The shadows of pain had gone, they'd been banished with the sadness that had tortured him for years. In their place, warmth and happiness shone brightly. 'Me neither.' She turned to look out over the moor as a feeling of tranquillity descended, slowly seeping through her veins.

It was time to start living again.

The End

AFTERWORD

Thank you for reading The Talisman — Molly's Story, I hope you enjoyed it. If you did, I'd be really grateful if you could pop over to Amazon and leave a review right here:

The Talisman - Molly's Story - UK

The Talisman - Molly's Story - US

It doesn't have to be long — just a few words would do — but for us new authors it makes a huge difference. Thank you so much.

If you'd like to find out more about what I get up to in my little corner of the North Yorkshire Moors, or if you'd like to get in touch — I'd love to hear from you! — you can find me in the following places:

Blog: Eliza J Scott
Twitter: @ElizaJScott1
Facebook: @elizajscottauthor
Instagram: @elizajscott
BookBub: @elizajscott

ALSO BY ELIZA J SCOTT

Book 1

The Letter - Kitty's Story

UK: www.amazon.co.uk

US: www.amazon.com

Book 3

The Secret - Violet's Story

UK: My Book

US: My Book

Book 4

A Christmas Kiss

UK: My Book

US: My Book

YORKSHIRE GLOSSARY

The Yorkshire dialect, with its wonderful elongated, flat vowels, can trace its roots back to Old English and Old Norse, the influence of which can still be found in some of the quirky words that are still in regular use today. As I've used a few of them in The Talisman (and The Letter), I thought it might be a good idea to compile a list of them for you, just in case you're wondering what the bloomin' 'eck I'm going on about. I do hope it helps!

Aud — old

Aud mucker — old friend. Used in greeting i.e. 'Now then, me aud mucker.'

Aye — yes

Back-end — autumn

By 'eck — heck

Champion — excellent

Diddlin' — doing

Ey up — hello/watch out

Fair capt — very pleased

Famished — hungry

Fettle — fix/put right

Fower — four

Hacky — dirty

Jiggered — tired

Lug/lug 'ole — ear/ear hole

Mash — brew, as in a pot of tea

Mucker — friend

Nithered — very cold

Now then — hello

Nowt — nothing

Owt — anything

Raw — cold, in reference to the weather

Reckon — think

Rigg — ridge

Rigwelted — word used to refer to an animal that has fallen over and got stuck on its back

Snicket — an an alleyway

Summat — something

Yat/Yatt —gate

ACKNOWLEDGMENTS

I've really enjoyed getting better acquainted with Molly in this, her story. She's a wonderful mix of feistiness and straight-talking, and is fiercely protective of those she loves — quite a scary combination if you get on the wrong side of her! I'd say she definitely makes a better friend than enemy! And, although her sassy personality is the polar opposite of her cousin, Kitty's, they, together with Violet, are a great combination and bounce off each other beautifully. In fact, I feel that their individual differences are what makes their friendship so strong, and it's been fun to see how their dynamics play out in their individual stories.

For me to get to this point in my book, there are several people I need to thank. First up has to be my husband and my daughters for providing me with a plentiful supply of Yorkshire Tea, ginger biscuits and words of support when I was wavering — and for putting up with the dining table still being hidden beneath my piles of writing mess!

Special thanks must also go to Berni Stevens for designing another beautiful cover. I don't know how you do it, Berni, but you always manage to gather the chaotic images I have in my mind, and magically transform them into the perfect book cover! I can't wait to see what you come up with for Violet's Story.

Huge thanks also to Alison Williams for her amazing editing skills, guidance and kind words of support for my manuscript — you've no idea just what a boost they are.

Many thanks must also go to Rachel Gilbey at Rachel's Random Resources who banishes the stress of pre-publication day madness with her swift organisational skills and wonderfully calm manner.

It's been such a rewarding experience working with these wonderful women and my book certainly couldn't have arrived at publication day without their skills. Thank you once again, ladies.

I'd like to give an enormous thank you to all of the book bloggers who have been involved in the Cover Reveal and Blog Tour for The Talisman, and for giving my book a space on their gorgeous blogs. Thanks must also go to the wonderful book community who have offered so much support over social media. I've absolutely loved hearing from you, and it's been awesome getting to know you all. Once again, your generosity of spirit has blown me away.

ABOUT THE AUTHOR

Eliza has wanted to be a writer as far back as she can remember. She lives in a village in the North Yorkshire Moors with her husband, two daughters and two mischievous black Labradors. When she's not writing, she can usually be found with her nose in a book/glued to her Kindle, or working in her garden, battling against the weeds that seem to grow in abundance there. Eliza also enjoys bracing walks in the countryside, rounded off by a visit to a teashop where she can indulge in another two of her favourite things: tea and cake.

Printed in Great Britain
by Amazon

37516356R00199